A SOFT PLACE
TO FALL

BARBARA BRETTON

BERKLEY BOOKS, NEW YORK

A SOFT PLACE TO FALL

A Berkley Book / published by arrangement with
the author

PRINTING HISTORY
Berkley edition / November 2001

All rights reserved.
Copyright © 2001 by Barbara Bretton.
Cover art by Arthur Gager.
Cover design by George Long.

This book, or parts thereof, may not be reproduced in
any form without permission.
For information address: The Berkley Publishing Group,
a division of Penguin Putnam Inc.,
375 Hudson Street, New York, New York 10014.

Visit our website at
www.penguinputnam.com

ISBN: 0-425-18216-9

BERKLEY®
Berkley Books are published by The Berkley Publishing Group,
a division of Penguin Putnam Inc.,
375 Hudson Street, New York, New York 10014.
BERKLEY and the "B" design
are trademarks belonging to Penguin Putnam Inc.

PRINTED IN THE UNITED STATES OF AMERICA

10 9 8 7 6 5 4 3 2 1

For my mother,
Vi Fuller (1924–2001),
who gave me the gift of life and the gift of words.
Thank you for making my childhood the stuff of dreams.
I am so proud to be your daughter.

Acknowledgments

A very special thanks to the very special women at Penguin Putnam Inc. who make the business side of writing such a pleasure: Leslie Gelbman, Judith Palais, Hillary Schupf, Amy Longhouse, and Sharon Gamboa.

Much love, as always, to Inez Perry and Beth Beckett, two of the finest nurses on the face of this earth. They actually make chemotherapy fun. You know Melvin and I love you both.

Love also to my beloved Mary Preisinger, who was kind enough to write me my very first reader fan letter way back in 1983 and who ended up being a dear friend. Every book's for you, Mary.

And here's to the bright and vibrant memory of Joyce Bradsher (March 10, 1955–May 28, 2000), who fought the good fight with dignity, courage, and a sense of humor. I hope you found your ruby slippers, JB. I miss you every single day.

How It All Began

Late summer—Shelter Rock Cove, Maine

"No good." Warren Bancroft pushed the sheaf of papers back across his desk. "The price is too high."

His attorney, a pig-headed Yankee named Stoney, allowed himself to register his shock. "Too high?" He glanced down at the number Warren had written across the top of the appraisal. "That's absurd! It isn't high enough."

"Not a penny more." Warren capped his fountain pen, then leaned back in his leather chair. "It would be highway robbery."

Stoney punched the appraisal with the tip of his forefinger. "The property alone appraised for more than this."

"The house is the size of a broom closet," Warren said, enjoying the confrontation. "That's as high as I'm going to go."

"You drive a hard bargain."

"Damn right," Warren said. "That's why I'm rich."

Stoney took another look at the number scrawled on

the top line. "You won't stay rich long if you keep this up."

"Call her, Stoney, and tell her I'm rejecting her offer. If she balks, go down another ten percent."

"I suppose you want to renovate the place while you're at it."

Warren's laughter filled the spacious office. "I've already taken care of that. I sent a crew over this morning to paint and spruce things up a bit."

"You'd be better off giving her the house. At least then we could take a tax deduction."

"You're a damn fine attorney," Warren said, "and I'm grateful for your advice. Now go do what I told you."

That was the trouble with Ivy League types, he thought as Stoney left the room. They thought too much. They paid too much attention to the way things were and not enough to the way things ought to be. Hell, if he had done that all those years ago, he'd be another in a long line of fishermen claimed by the sea.

Not that he hadn't made his share of mistakes. His book was full of them, all laid out there in black and white. Of course, he hadn't let Annie see the good stuff yet but he would one of these days. She was only a kid of thirty-eight after all, and she needed some more seasoning.

He could tell her a thing or two about loneliness. He could tell her that there was nothing wrong with spreading her wings and seeing if she still remembered how to fly. He could tell her a lot of things, but he wasn't sure she was ready to listen. She had been loyal and true to the people she loved, and that loyalty had cost her dearly. He'd watched her grow from a fun-loving young girl with big dreams to a quiet, tired-looking woman with no dreams at all.

Lately he'd noticed a change in her, a restlessness that

he understood in his bones. The time was right for new beginnings.

He reached for the dark-blue folder marked "Sam." Who would have thought the wise-talking fifteen-year-old he'd met at the marina near the site of the World's Fair twenty years ago would one day be Warren's hero? He'd never told Sam Butler that, because it would embarrass him, but it was true. Warren was more than twice Sam's age, but he knew he was only half the man. Life had dealt Sam a losing hand, but somehow he'd managed to turn a pair of deuces into a full house. Nineteen years old and left with the care of five younger brothers and sisters— not too many men would have put their own lives on hold to see it through, but Sam had done exactly that.

When Sam called last week and asked if he could rent Ellie's old house for a while, Warren knew that fate was knocking on the door with both fists. Sam Butler would never take charity, but he understood a good business deal when he heard one, and the deal Warren was offering was damn close to irresistible. Sam would have free use of a house on the water, and all Warren asked for in return was that he work on finishing the boat.

Sam had taken the bait.

He was pretty sure Annie would, too.

The whole thing was a long shot, and he knew it. But if ever two people deserved happiness, it was these two children of his heart. Life hadn't seen fit to bless him with children of his own, but he loved Annie and Sam as if his blood flowed in their veins. They were two halves of the same whole, and it was up to him to bring them to- gether.

What was the point of being rich if you didn't use the money to take care of your own?

ONE

❧

They saved the bed for last.

Annie Lacy Galloway stood at the bottom of the stairs and watched as the two impossibly skinny young men maneuvered the huge sleigh bed through the narrow upstairs hallway. She winced at the sound of wood scraping against wallpaper. She knew it would be a tight fit, but she hadn't let herself consider that it might be impossible.

The moving boys paused at the top of the stairs and considered their options.

"How'd you ever get this up here anyway, Mrs. G?" Michael, the one whose voice still hadn't made up its mind between soprano and tenor, called down to her. "This is like shoving an elephant through a keyhole."

She'd found it at a yard sale six months after Kevin died, a wreckage of wood that looked much the way she'd felt inside. "I feel bad taking your money for this," the man had said as they loaded the pieces into the back of her Jeep. She had spent weeks sanding the elegant curves and flat planes, stripping away years of neglect and damage, not even sure if the pieces could ever be put back together again into a recognizable whole. It still wasn't finished yet. Come spring she intended to stain the sanded wood a deep cherry, then coat the whole thing with a satiny finish that would grow more lustrous with the years.

"Turn it toward the window," she said. "Once you clear the top of the railing, you'll have it made."

Danny, her nephew by marriage, crouched down near the foot of the bed. "It comes apart," he said, fingering the supports. "Maybe we could—"

"No!" Annie forced her voice down to a more acceptable volume. The poor boys looked downright scared. "I mean, feel free to remove the stair rails, if you have to, but please don't touch the bed."

"You're the boss, Mrs. G," Michael said.

She turned in time to see a third moving boy grab for the cardboard box near the front door. The box marked "Fragile."

"Not that one." Annie raced back downstairs. "I'm taking that one in the car with me."

"You sure?" Scotty had been Kevin's top student, the one who was on his way toward bigger and better things. He was smart and funny and built like a two-by-four, all straight edges and long lines. *Scotty nailed the Bancroft Scholarship, Kevin. You would've been so proud of him.* Years ago, she had been the one with the Bancroft and the big dreams of studying art one day in New York. It seemed so long ago, almost as if those dreams had belonged to somebody else. The sight of the young man in her foyer awoke so many memories of Christmas parties and summer barbecues when they had opened up the house to students and their parents. Kevin had loved those parties, loved being at the center of all the activity, laughing and joking and—

"There's plenty of room in the truck, Mrs. G."

"That's okay, Scotty," she said, wondering when he had started shaving. Wasn't it just yesterday that he was raking their lawn for two bucks an hour? "I'll take it over in my car." Her life was tucked away in that box: old love letters, wedding photos, newspaper clippings, and sympathy notes. The sum total of her thirty-eight years on the planet with room left over for her best wineglasses and her journals.

He pointed toward a box resting near the piano. "How about that one?"

Annie grinned. "Be my guest."

He hoisted it onto his shoulder with a theatrical grunt. "See you at the new house."

"The new house," Claudia Galloway said as she appeared in the doorway to the living room. She dabbed at her eyes with a linen handkerchief, one of those flimsy bits with the hand-crocheted edging that were her trademark. "It's not too late to change your mind, Anne."

Annie thrust her clenched fists deep into the pockets of her bright red sweater. "Claudia, we've gone over this before. I—"

"This is your home," her former mother-in-law broke in. "This is where you spent your entire married life. My God, you've even sold most of your furniture. How can you turn your back on everything Kevin meant to you?"

"I don't need this house to remind me of all that Kevin meant to me."

"Is she at it again?" Susan, Claudia's oldest daughter, poked her head in the front door. "Ma, you already built a shrine to Kevin. Annie doesn't need to build one, too."

Annie shot her best friend a look of pure gratitude. *I owe you big time, Susie. Godiva, if I could afford it, or Dom Perignon.* "Are they finished in the garage?"

"The place is stripped bare as chicken bones after a barbecue."

"Really, Susan." Claudia frowned at her daughter. "A bit less colorful language, if you please."

"Mother, I sell real estate for a living. I am a master of the colorful metaphor."

"I could do with a tad less sarcasm as well."

"Coming through!" Michael and Danny had found a way to maneuver Annie's sleigh bed downstairs without major architectural damage and had it aimed at the front door.

"That ridiculous bed," Claudia murmured as she stepped aside. "Really, Annie. I don't know what you were thinking."

I wasn't thinking, Claudia. You've been there. Don't you remember how it was? I hurt too much that first year to think of anything at all.

"Mother," said Susan, "why don't you go have lunch with Jack and the boys? I know you love the chicken sandwich at Wendy's. We'll see you later at the new house."

Claudia looked from Annie to her daughter, and in that instant Annie regretted all the sharp words she had bitten back. She was family to Claudia, same as any of the children of her body, and that gave her the right to annoy the daylights out of Annie. Suddenly her redoubtable mother-in-law looked small and old and vulnerable, and Annie's heart twisted in sympathy. She loved Claudia dearly, even if sometimes she wished for a bit more breathing room.

"I have a better idea," Annie said, putting an arm around Claudia's fragile shoulders. "Why don't both of you have lunch with Jack and the boys, and we'll meet up at the house."

"We can't leave you alone," Claudia said, and for once Susan agreed with her mother.

"Sure you can." Annie started moving them toward the door. "I'll be fine. I promise."

"Are you sure?" Susan asked. Her eyes were wide and dark brown, and she looked so much like Kevin that there were times when Annie had to turn away.

"Positive." She waved goodbye to them from the top step, then closed and locked the door. The movers were gone. The only thing she had left to do was sweep the floors, coerce the cats into their carrying cases, then load the last boxes into her ancient four-wheel-drive. She grabbed the broom and began to move living room dust into one central pile. The Flemings were due to arrive at three o'clock, and by nightfall this quiet old house would be bursting with laughter and children, the way it was always meant to.

"We're crazy," Annie had said the night they moved in. They were lying on afghans in front of the fireplace in the living room, watching the flames flicker and dance. "You know we can't afford a house like this." They were only a handful of years out of college. Neither one of them was established in a career. He had only just started teaching, and she had yet to sell one of her paintings, much less study in Rome. It would be a long time before they could even think about putting down roots.

"We can't afford not to buy it," Kevin had said, filling her wineglass from the jug of Chianti they'd purchased at the discount liquor store near the state line. "Face it, Annie. This house has family written all over it. We're going to grow old here." They clicked glasses for the third—or was it the fourth?—time. "One day our grandchildren will play in that backyard."

"Grandchildren?" she'd said with a laugh. "First things first, Mr. Galloway."

"Five kids," he said, pulling her over onto his lap. "Three girls, two boys."

"Five?"

He grinned at her. "It's my lucky number."

"We only have four bedrooms."

"We'll add as many as we need."

"Kids or bedrooms?" She loved the way he was stroking her hair, her shoulder, the warmth of his lips against the side of her neck.

"Both," he said, sliding his hand under the hem of her sweater. She gasped when he cupped her breast. He murmured words of praise, wonderful, honey-drenched words against her skin, the kind of words that melted a woman's bones. He could talk a statue to life with those words, turn cold marble into warm flesh. He had been doing it to Annie from the very first.

"We should wait another year or two," she whispered, struggling to stay reasonable against the sensual onslaught of his hands and mouth. "We don't even have furniture yet."

"I love you, Annie Rose Lacy Galloway. I love the family we're going to have together. Life is short. We're young and strong and healthy and we love each other. Let's make a baby, Annie Rose. Let's start tonight."

Annie turned away from the empty living room. The ghosts were everywhere. There wasn't a corner of the house that wasn't filled with them. They had made love that first night with a sense of sacred abandon, and Annie had been sure they had made a baby. A son with Kevin's dark brown eyes and ready laugh . . . or maybe a daughter with his strength and kindness. They were so young then, so innocent. Believing in miracles came as naturally to her back then as breathing. Why else would she have stayed with Kevin until the very end?

"There's nothing to worry about," her doctor had said to her as the months passed and there was still no baby. "The test results are all unremarkable. You're healthy.

Kevin's healthy. Give it time, Anne. You'll have your baby."

But it took two to have a baby. A man and a woman who loved each other and shared the same vision of their future. A man and a woman who shared a bed and made love with tenderness if not passion, not two strangers who lived alone in the same house. He refused to listen when she suggested they look more deeply into their infertility problem. He turned a deaf ear when she spoke about adoption. Months turned to years, and after a time she began to believe that it was for the best. You didn't bring a child into uncertainty and chaos. Not if you had a choice in the matter. There was so much she hadn't known about her husband until it was too late.

Nobody ever told her that you could fall in love with a boy only to wake up one day and discover you were living with a man you didn't really know at all. A man whose problems ran deeper than your solutions, to a place not even love could reach.

But then she probably wouldn't have believed it. Kevin had taught her to believe in happy endings, and right up until the moment he drew his last breath she had thought they still had a chance for happily-ever-after.

She knew better now. They'd never really had a chance for happily-ever-after. Kevin had seen to that the day he placed his first bet.

George and Gracie's plaintive yowls sounded from somewhere upstairs and reminded Annie that she still had a lot to do before the Flemings arrived to take possession of the house.

She swept out the living room, the foyer, the kitchen. She wiped down the counters, cleaned the sink, dried the faucets carefully until they gleamed. She wiped a hand-print off the door of the fridge, then stood back and scanned the kitchen with a critical eye she had rarely brought to housework before. The house was over forty years old, and unfortunately so were most of the appliances. At first the ancient heating system and outdated refrigerator had been a source of amusement for Kevin and Annie, two of the many things they would take care of some day in the far-off future when their bankbook recovered from the shock of home ownership.

The only thing was, it never did. She put aside her dream of pursuing a career in art and opened a flower shop instead. Annie's Flowers took a while to get on its feet, and for some reason Kevin's salary didn't increase the way they had hoped. Every month it seemed to Annie that the number of unexpected bills went up and their checking account balance went down, and no matter how hard they tried to keep up with the house's demands, their income couldn't keep pace with the required outgo.

"You're lucky it's a seller's market," Susan had told her when she first mentioned putting the house up for sale. "No offense, Annie, but your place is falling down around your ears. You'll have to replace the windows and put on a new roof if you expect to even come close to getting top dollar."

It took three months for the house to sell, and then, as Susan had predicted, the price was well below the going rate for big old houses on large lots of land.

"We could have done better," Susan lamented after the Flemings went to contract. "You should've listened to me about those windows, Annie. You would've earned back the cost three times over."

Annie nodded and tried to look suitably disappointed, but the truth was she was grateful the sale had gone through before she ran out of options and ended up with nothing at all. Of course she wouldn't tell Susan that. She wouldn't tell anybody. Kevin's secrets were safe with her, same as they had been right from the start.

• • •

"I think Anne's making a terrible mistake," Claudia said as Susan backed her minivan down the driveway.

Susan, never one to consider her mother's feelings, rolled her eyes and groaned. "And why do you think that, Ma? Because she's moving out of that white elephant of a house or because she didn't want you to stay for lunch?"

"I don't appreciate your sarcasm," Claudia said with a slight lift of her chin. She chose to ignore the lunch remark, even though there was more than a touch of truth to it. "Anne loves that house. It's where she and Kevin were happiest. Why on earth would she want to sell it and move into that—that shack out by the water?"

"Don't let Annie hear you call her new home a shack."

"Of course not! I would never hurt her." Claudia was stung that her daughter thought she was capable of such thoughtless behavior. "I blame it all on Warren Bancroft for taking advantage of Anne this way." She glanced over at her eldest child. "You must know she's lowered her standards with this move."

"Ma, there are times I wish I were adopted."

Susan screeched to a halt at the corner stop sign, barely missing the rear end of another minivan. Claudia gripped the edges of her purse and forced herself to keep her remarks on visual acuity and reflexes to herself. Her daughter was forty-two years old, and her eyesight wasn't what it used to be, but Claudia knew better than to comment on her daughter's driving, weight, or marriage. Not if she wanted to keep peace in the family.

"Annie doesn't need three bathrooms," Susan went on as if they hadn't come this close to calamity, "and she definitely doesn't need all those memories. I just wish she'd done this sooner."

"There's nothing wrong with memories," Claudia said, fixing her daughter with a sharp look. "There will come a time when a woman is very glad she has them."

"Annie isn't you, Ma."

"Watch the road." Claudia refused to acknowledge the statement. "We don't need an accident."

"You know what I'm saying."

"I don't pressure Anne to do anything. She makes her own decisions." Selling the house was certainly proof of that. Claudia would never sell the house where she and John had spent their married life. Selling it would be like losing him all over again. His spirit still filled their house the way it had when he was alive. Her children didn't know it, but she talked to him sometimes. She didn't expect an answer; it was more like a running conversation that was part monologue, part prayer.

If the kids knew she did that, they would think she was crazy. Claudia had seen the looks Susan and Eileen exchanged when they thought she wasn't looking, one of those Mother-is-losing-her-marbles looks that Claudia hated. They would make an appointment with that fancy therapist John Jr. was seeing, and she would have to waste fifty dollars of her late husband's hard-earned money to find out what she already knew: She was lonely and she was old.

Why was it nobody seemed to understand that without being told? She didn't *have* to work four days a week with Annie at the flower shop. John had been very careful with their money, and, while she wasn't rich, she was certainly comfortable by anyone's standards. She tried to keep up with the financial news by listening to the experts on the radio and following their advice when it felt right to her. So far, thank the good Lord, the market had been kind to her. If her children stopped racing through their lives for just one second and thought about it, they would realize she worked at the flower shop because sometimes she needed a reason to get up in the morning, someone to smile at her when she walked through the door. They laughed at all of the seminars she took on topics as diverse as money management and *ikebana* and never once considered that maybe she just needed the pleasure of being among people.

It was the same with the house. She and John had moved in on their wedding day. Every significant event of their married life had happened within its four walls. Living in the house where she and John had raised their family made her feel connected to him even though he was gone. Love filled her heart each time she walked through those dear and familiar rooms. Oh, there were too many rooms by half. She would be the first to admit that. She couldn't keep to her old standards of housekeeping any longer. Dust lingered a little longer. The floors weren't as shiny as she might like. She told herself it was all part of getting old, the letting go, the giving up, turning a blind eye to the same things that drove you mad when you were young and strong.

Last Christmas her children and their spouses had converged at the old house to celebrate the holiday, same as they did every year, but with one small difference. This year they were determined to convince her it was time to move on.

"It's time to simplify things, Mom," Eileen, her youngest, had said to her as she served the eggnog. "This house is way too big for one person. You'd have so much more free time if you didn't have this barn to take care of."

"And where would the lot of you stay if I didn't have this barn?" she had tossed back. "You'd be sleeping in tents in the front yard."

Of course, Eileen's was only the opening salvo in an assault designed to open her aging eyes to what they considered to be reality. Terri commented on how difficult it must be to keep four bedrooms and two baths clean and sparkling, which made Claudia smile into her eggnog. It was certainly easier now than it had been years ago when the house was bursting at the seams with toddlers and teenagers and John's hobbies. The boys talked about taxes and upkeep and how the plumbing was going to need repairs before next Christmas rolled around and why hang onto a money sink, as if she didn't have the right to make up her own mind. Finally she had to stand her ground.

"This is where I lived with your father, it's where you grew up, and it's where I'm going to die," she had said in a tone of voice that brooked no argument. "Now, who'd like another piece of pie?"

Annie was the only one who understood what Claudia was talking about. In an unfair twist of fate, Kevin's death had united the two women in a way not even Claudia's flesh-and-blood daughters could understand. Annie knew how it felt to lose the man you loved, how it felt to sleep on his side of the bed because it made you feel less alone. Annie knew without being told that time didn't heal a broken heart; it only helped you learn how to live with it.

You can't run away from your memories, Anne, she thought as Susan barreled into the parking lot at full speed. The world wasn't big enough. Better to stay in the house where they had been happy and comfort herself with the dear and familiar. Didn't Annie know that she would still see him in every shadow, hear his voice when the room was still, feel his touch where no one had touched her in a very long time?

It was enough for Claudia. Sooner or later, it would be enough for Annie, too.

Annie was wiping down the sink in the master bathroom when she heard the Flemings pull into the driveway. They drove one of those minivans that sounded like a thousand hamsters spinning one gigantic wheel. The neighbors would hear them coming three blocks away. She glanced down at her watch, visible above the worn cuff of Kevin's old denim work shirt. It was only ten minutes to three.

"You're early," she muttered as she pushed her hair away from her face with the back of her hand. What kind of people were they? Didn't they know that being early was every bit as rude as being late? She still had to vacuum the bedroom, coax George and Gracie into their cat carriers, and then make sure the felines hadn't left any personal messages behind for the new owners to discover. She would need every single moment of the nine minutes and thirty-seven seconds she had left.

She tossed the paper towel into the garbage bag she'd been dragging from room to room, then moved to the bedroom window that overlooked the driveway. The Fleming children were already in the backyard. She could hear their shrieks of excitement over the groan of the tree swing that had been Kevin's last project the summer before he died.

Joe and Pam Fleming were leaning against the passenger door of their minivan. Her head rested against his chest, and he stroked her hair while they talked. Soft whispers of conversation floated up toward the second-floor window where Annie watched them from behind the pale green curtains. It hurt to look at them, but she couldn't seem to turn away. She wanted to tell them to hang on tightly to each other, that life wasn't always fair or kind, but they would probably think she was crazy. They were young and in love, with their whole lives stretched out before them like a summer garden on a sunny day.

Down in the driveway the Flemings stole a kiss. The sweetness of that gesture made Annie turn away from the window. She missed the touches, the whispers, the laughter that smoothed the bumpy patches every marriage encountered. She missed the lovemaking, that sweet escape from reality. She missed being the other half of someone's heart, and the temptation to barricade herself behind a wall of memories was hard to resist. Staying, however, was a luxury she couldn't afford and, in a way, she was grateful. She might never have gathered the courage to leave if she had a plump bank account and endless prospects.

It was time to go. She had known it for months now. One morning she woke up, and the house no longer felt like home. Suddenly the old ways, the old routines, didn't fit, and she found herself dreaming about starting all over again in a place that was hers alone. She had had that dream before, but this time was different. This time she was free to do something about it, and so, against everyone's advice, she put the house up for sale and began the painful process of finally letting go of the past. She paid off the last of Kevin's debts and bought the tiny Bancroft cottage with the cash that remained. Warren tried to lower the price three times, but she stood firm when it came to accepting charity, and they negotiated a figure that satisfied both his kind heart and her need to stand on her own two feet. The four-room cottage near the water was a far cry from her sprawling Victorian on an acre of land, but it represented a triumph of sorts to Annie.

Her dreams of a family of her own had died with Kevin, but she still had a future, and for the first time in years, that prospect made her happy.

How long had it been since she had felt deeply happy? She couldn't even begin to guess. For a long time she had known happiness only in fleeting bursts: a beautiful sunset, a well-told joke, a good hair day. She missed that deeper sense of joy that had been as much a part of her as the rhythm of her heartbeat and she wanted it back. This move was a step in the right direction.

Sometimes she wondered how Claudia did it, living all these years in that big old house without John by her side. As it was she saw Kevin everywhere, in every room, around every corner. She heard his car in the driveway, his footfall on the steps, the wail of the ambulance on that last night when nothing, not even love, could save him. He had died in their bed, the big brass one they had fallen in love with and couldn't afford, died before the emergency crew could slap the paddles on his chest.

He died before she had a chance to say goodbye.

Before she had a chance to say, "I still love you."

She couldn't remember the last time she had said those words to him. She had been angry with him for so long that love was more a memory than the living, breathing sacrament it had been at the start. There were times when she had thought about leaving him—throwing her clothes into a suitcase, grabbing the cats, and starting new someplace else, someplace where the phone didn't ring in the middle of the night and strange men didn't wait on the porch in the darkness for her husband. He had taken everything they had worked so hard to achieve and thrown it away on horses and cards and the spin of a roulette wheel—and in the process, he had thrown away her love as well.

"Give me time, Annie," he had said not long before he died. "I know I can make it all up to you."

Why hadn't she told him that she still loved him, that she wanted to believe in him, that if he met her halfway maybe they could find their way back to the life they'd dreamed about when they were high school sweethearts and the world was theirs for the asking? Instead, she had simply turned away from him, and after a few moments, the front door closed softly behind him and the distance between them grew a little wider until three weeks later he was dead, and there was no turning back.

Susan and Eileen found her on the morning after the funeral, alone in the bedroom, slamming an old wooden baseball bat against the tarnished brass. "I hate you!" she'd screamed with each slam of the bat. "Why did you do this to us?" They'd tried to grab her arms, to hold her still, but she was wild with rage and anger, stronger than she had ever been in her life, and she broke free. She smashed mirrors and lamps, pulled his clothes from his side of the closet and threw his running shoes against the wall.

Her sisters-in-law tried to reason with her, but Annie was beyond their reach. It wasn't until they helped her drag the mattress, box spring, and dented frame down the stairs and outside with the rest of the trash that her adrenaline-fueled rage ebbed and she sank to the curb, buried her face in her arms, and sobbed as if her heart would break.

There had been times when she hated him, times when she wondered why she stayed, but through it all she had never once stopped loving him. She knew that now, two years too late, when it no longer mattered to anyone but herself. Maybe if she had loved him a little less and helped him a little more, she wouldn't be a thirty-eight-year-old widow with two cats, bad credit, and the feeling that after today nothing would ever be the same again.

TWO

If somebody had told Sam Butler last summer that the following Labor Day weekend would find him sharing the front seat of a used Trooper with an aging yellow Labrador retriever, a stack of banker's boxes, and the remnants of a Big Mac with fries, he would have settled back on the deck of his shorefront rental and laughed.

Twelve months ago he was still the top guy in the Personal Investment division at Mason, Marx, and Daniel on Wall Street. He had the fat salary, the fancy car, and the great apartment that went with it. He was the one they called "the natural," the kid who had started in a boiler room making cold calls, then worked his way up to a corner office with a window and a list of accounts that was almost legendary. "If we could bottle what Butler's got, we'd rule the universe," Franklin Bennett Mason had said to the assembled troops at the last Christmas party. Nobody had Sam Butler's drive, his determination, his sheer ability to persuade strangers to hand over their life savings to a man they'd met only fifteen minutes ago.

He was the best of the best, Sam Butler was, and everyone in that tightly knit world in which he operated knew it. He was the one you wanted on your team. He kept his emotions out of the workplace. He was everybody's pal but nobody's friend, and that touch of mystery only served to burnish his glow. The truth was, he hadn't had time for friends. He'd been too busy raising five brothers and sisters.

Sam never lied to his clients. He never encouraged them to take risks he wouldn't take himself, but if a client was looking for a walk on the wild side of investing, Sam would clear a path and serve as bodyguard. He understood responsibility in a way few people his age could, and he took his clients' plans for the future as seriously as he took his own. People responded to Sam. They always had. And in the narrow universe called finance, he was a rising star. One of the cable money channels had given him a ninety-second spot one Tuesday night a few years ago, and that minute and a half had turned into a daily three-minute closing-bell gig that polished his reputation to the same high gloss as the one on his leased BMW.

When he first began to suspect something was wrong, he told nobody. He was pulling in the same amount of business, but his cumulative numbers were going down. The market was bullish, bonds were soaring, and neither recession nor inflation were anywhere on the horizon. His closing-bell reports were sunny and bright. Visibility unlimited. The economy was about as good as it could get, and the fact that his clients weren't raking in the bucks disturbed him, but he did nothing about it. One more year, he told himself. That was all he needed. One more year and the last of his siblings would be finished with college and ready to tackle the world on her own. Maybe then he'd have time for niceties like ethics.

He spent a few long weekends at the office going through his files, and an unsettling trend began to appear through the endless streams of data. His clients were actually beginning to lose money. Nothing significant—at least not yet—and nothing that couldn't be explained away with terms like *profit taking* and *seasonal adjustments*, but Sam could easily see the pattern being established. Someone was quietly shifting small quantities of blue chips into high-risk ventures that in Sam's eyes had FRAUD written all over them in capital letters and signed in his name.

He told himself that it didn't matter. His clients were only names and Social Security numbers attached to a dollar figure. Hell, he wouldn't know most of them if he bumped into them on the street. He had learned a long time ago that personal attachments had no place in his business. He didn't want to know about hospital bills or new grandchildren. He didn't want to see family photos or share any of his own. He had made that mistake early on in his career, and it was a dangerous one. They were accounts, not friends, but sometimes it was hard to remember that.

Ten more months, that was all he needed. Forty weeks longer, and he'd be able to walk into Mason's office and say goodbye.

And he almost made it. Nine weeks before the day he planned to hand in his resignation, he came home to find two guys in black suits waiting for him inside his apartment. He didn't ask how they got in, and they didn't volunteer. He didn't need to ask why.

It seemed he wasn't the only one who had caught onto what was happening at Mason, Marx, and Daniel, and, thanks to some clever planning, so far all roads led straight to Sam. The scope of what they were telling him almost made his knees buckle. While he had been busy looking the other way, someone had managed to erase one set of fingerprints from the scheme and replace them with another set: Sam's. The men in the black suits had a prop-osition for him, one he could refuse if he didn't mind going directly to jail without passing Go. They needed information culled from the inside and they pointed out to Sam that it was in his best interest to become their number one source.

He began to keep a detailed log of names, dates, and percentages, and when that log became too hot to store on his computer, he started snapping photos of the data onscreen with a tiny camera he kept hidden in his shirt pocket. He filled notebook after notebook with contem-poraneous data, suspicions, and thoughts, then locked them away in a safe-deposit box back in his old Queens neighborhood, along with the files and the photos and everything else he'd been able to lay his hands on. A second key to the box had been mailed to an address in Arlington, Virginia.

He probably would have been able to pull it off if it hadn't been for Mrs. Ruggiero. Mrs. R was his first client, a widow from the old neighborhood where he'd grown up. Mrs. R was the one who'd made sure they were fed and watched out for during those first few weeks after their mother's death and then again after their father died. Years later, she had come to him with the insurance money from her late husband's policy and asked him to invest it for her "so I should be comfortable one day." Something came over him when he saw what was hap-pening to her bottom line. It hit him in a way nothing else had. He thought of the box of homemade cookies that arrived at the office every Christmas, the invitations to Easter Sunday dinner that he always refused because the old neighborhood sometimes seemed light-years away. He thought about his mother and how she and Mrs. R used to head out to All Souls Church on Francis Lewis Boul-evard for the Friday night bingo games.

Mrs. R deserved a hell of a lot better. And that was
how he came up with the bright idea to move her monies
back into the safer holdings they both preferred, a painstakingly laborious process made more so by the fact that
he wanted to stay off the radar screen. So it began with
Mrs. R, and when that seemed to work, he remembered
the old guy in Brooklyn, Ben Ashkenazy, who had fought
in World War II with their next-door neighbor, then
worked his butt off at AT&T for thirty years. He deserved
better than a year of diminishing returns, didn't he? It
worked for Ashkenazy, too, which got Sam thinking about
Lila Connelly, who took a buyout from IBM and now her
entire retirement fund was in Sam's hands and disappear-
ing. These clients were small fish in a big sea, the for-
gettable ones, the ones you practiced on before you
moved up to the whales. Why in hell were they the ones
who reminded him he had a heart?

Lila used to get her hair done at the place where his
mother worked, and when his mother died, Lila was there
at the funeral with a fifty-dollar bill for the Butler kids
and a promise of more. Now he was letting them screw
her to the wall, take all her dreams and run them through
a giant shredder called business.

The hell he was.

So he began moving Lila's funds, too—slowly, so
slowly—and that was when the clock finally ran out.

On a sunny Friday morning in early August, Franklin
Bennett Mason, senior partner and occasional racquetball
opponent, called Sam into his office and told him he was
through. Mason gave him the company line about new
directions and how much they appreciated everything Sam
had done for them over the years, but they both knew
what was really happening. The stone-cold look in Mason's eyes gave it away. They'd noticed that Sam was
quietly shifting monies away from the questionable ven-

tures and back into the blue chips and they were smart enough to know exactly what that meant.

Lucky for Sam they didn't know everything.

They cut him a nice goodbye check, and he was out the door thirty minutes later. Sam knew the talk would start as soon as he stepped out onto the street. *Another head case,* they would say. *A burnout. You can't keep the heat turned up that high for so long and not pay a price.* They would wonder over lunch where he would turn up next. Maybe Morgan Stanley. Maybe Salomon. Maybe he'd even pull a Jimmy Buffett and live on a sailboat moored down in the Keys. But nobody would call to see how he was doing. The pace was too fast, the competition too intense. His desk would be claimed by the next morning, and his television spot would be given to someone else before the closing bell rang that afternoon. He would be forgotten before the end of the quarter.

Within the hour his friends in the expensive black suits showed up at his door to relieve him of his key to the safe-deposit box and to warn him that things were going to get a lot worse before they got better.

If they got better at all.

They advised him to make himself scarce for a while. Pick a spot, they'd vet it, then disappear. They gave him a cell phone equipped with all sorts of fancy blocking devices and a number to call every day to check in. He was to stay in the country, keep the phone with him at all times, and be ready to be brought back on a moment's notice to testify against his former employer. They made no promises. With luck, the information he'd gathered would clear his name. Without it, he was looking at serious jail time.

He thought about renting a room in the Hamptons, but that was still too close to ground zero. The Jersey shore was a possibility, but it would be too easy to bump into someone he knew. He hated Florida and California and couldn't afford Hawaii. He had, however, always liked Maine with its three thousand miles of coastline. Warren owned at least a half-dozen houses in Shelter Rock Cove. Maybe he would rent one of them to Sam on a monthly basis until he found out if his next address came with a number embroidered on the back of his shirt.

Warren said yes before Sam had time to finish his question.

Shelter Rock Cove was vetted and okayed. He told his brothers and sisters that he was taking off into the wilds of Maine on a sabbatical. He told them that he wanted to get in touch with nature, clear his head, whatever excuse he thought they would believe. What he didn't tell them was the truth.

"I give you six months up there, Nature Boy," Courtney had said as they loaded his sound system and television into her U-Haul van. "You'll be knocking on my door, asking for your stuff back."

He grinned and ruffled her short red hair, the same way he used to do when she was six years old and afraid of the monsters under the bed. She was two weeks shy of her twentieth birthday now, just one year away from graduating from Columbia University and diving headfirst into life. Her tuition fees and living expenses for her senior year were paid in full. He'd sold off everything he could to see to it. Too bad he hadn't been able to make sure his clients had been able to do the same.

"Don't worry, kid," he said in his best *film noir* impression. "Nobody's going to ask for your stereo."

Courtney thought he was coming off a bad love affair and heading north to lick his wounds. Their brother Tony said it was a midlife crisis ten years too early. Instead of hair plugs and a phallic sports car, he was chucking it all for life as a loner up in Nowhere, Maine. Kerry, Dave, and Marie just thought he'd gone nuts. He didn't argue with any of them. How did you tell the people you loved, the brothers and sisters who looked up to you, that you'd done some things along the way that you weren't proud of, that some of the decisions you'd made to keep the family together had hurt innocent people?

He hadn't planned it that way. Hell, he hadn't planned any of it. He went to bed one night as your average party-hearty college kid, only to wake up the next morning to discover he was the unemployed, uneducated, scared-shitless head of a family of six who ranged in age from nineteen down to three. Somehow he managed to survive and pull the rest of the Butler family along behind him. After a few rough patches they'd managed to stay on the right road, and their bright futures made his own short-comings easier to bear. When the waiting was over and the stories were told, he hoped they would understand.

And so there he was in his secondhand car, with his secondhand dog, and his secondhand life, wondering if the dreams he'd put aside when he was nineteen would play half as well now that he was thirty-five. For a man with so much family, he had never felt more alone.

By seven o'clock, Annie had retreated to the back porch with a cup of coffee to revive her spirits and a bottle of aspirin for the world-class headache pounding away at her temples. It wasn't that she didn't appreciate the help and the company, but after a full day of packing, sweeping, cleaning up, making conversation, and trying to stay one step ahead of her memories, she had just plain had enough. She loved every single one of the people who had come to help her out, but right now she found herself wishing they would disappear.

Or maybe that she could.

Nothing was quite the way she'd thought it would be.

The house that had seemed cozy and affordable last month now looked more like an overstuffed pup tent. Cardboard boxes filled with books, pots and pans, clothes, bath towels, and bed linens littered every available surface, yet her only real piece of furniture was the refinished sleigh bed that filled up most of the bedroom. She wasn't a stupid woman. Why hadn't she realized a king-sized bed required a king-sized room to accommodate it? She'd have to somersault across the mattress in order to get to the closet, because the foot of the bed was almost welded to the wall.

To make matters worse, the cats were taking swipes at anyone who dared venture into their territory, which, to the dismay of all, included the only bathroom. Susan's husband, Jack, dug out her tool kit from one of the many cardboard boxes and set to work installing a new lock on her front door while Eileen and Claudia began unpacking her glasses and dishes, and the boys continued lugging in boxes of books from the U-Haul. They all worked with such good cheer and high spirits that Annie felt ashamed of herself for wishing she could be alone with her disappointment, instead of being surrounded by assorted friends and Galloways, who were trying very hard to pretend they loved her new house at least a little.

The fact that they were also whispering among themselves about her sanity wasn't lost on her. *Somebody should have stopped her . . . Why would she leave that beautiful house for this place . . . She still isn't thinking clearly, is she . . . so sad . . . so terribly sad.*

How much easier it would have been if she had sat down with them after he died and simply told the truth. If she had told them that their beloved Kevin, the man she had vowed to spend her life with, had gambled away everything long before he died and left her alone to clean up after him. The Galloways would have rallied around her, the same way they had rallied around her when she was sixteen years old and her world went up in flames. They welcomed her as family years before she became Kevin's wife. They gave her a home and love and security, priceless gifts for a teenage girl with nothing of her own. Kevin was the shining star of the family, the poet and dreamer, the one they believed would have made his mark on the world if only he hadn't been struck down so terribly young.

She loved them all, Kevin and his family, too much to destroy those memories.

"You're out of soda," Susan said from the kitchen doorway.

She swallowed two more Bayers. "Let them drink beer."

"You're just about out of that, too."

"Do you think anyone would notice if I sneaked out to replenish supplies?"

"They will if you don't come back." Susan joined her at the railing. "It's written all over your face."

"I'm tired," Annie said. "That's all you see on my face. All I need is some curtains, a few rugs—it'll feel like home here in no time."

"There aren't enough curtains in three Wal-Marts to make this place feel like home, and you know it." Susan rested her elbows on the porch rail. An unlit cigarette dangled from her right hand, her latest attempt at kicking the habit. "Fran at the office told me that Bancroft decided to rent out the other house on your block."

There were only two houses on Annie's block, and both belonged to Warren Bancroft, Shelter Rock Cove's greatest success story. He had parlayed one small fishing boat into a major operation worth millions, yet he had never turned his back on the town where he was born. He had grown up in the tiny cottage that now belonged to

Annie. The place on the water had belonged to his sister Ellie, who died the same year as Kevin.

"Anyone we know?" she asked Susan.

"A retiree from New York. Fran said she heard the guy is an old fishing friend of Warren's."

One of the best things about Annie's new house was the fact that it was within a few hundred yards of a private beach that had gone ignored for the last few years. She had spent considerable time daydreaming about long morning walks on a deserted stretch of sand. Now some bigmouth from New York was going to move in and claim it all for himself.

"What kind of loser would move to this godforsaken town?" she asked, feeling uncharacteristically peevish. She should be grateful that she had a roof over her head and that it was all paid for. "Doesn't he know every retiree worth his salt lives up Bar Harbor way?"

"Bar Harbor's overrated," Susan said. "Too many tourists—" She stopped and tilted her head toward the door at the sound of high-heeled footsteps. "Oh, great," she muttered, "here comes Bigfoot." The Galloway clan was merciless on their tiny mother's love of excessively noisy high heels, even though that early-warning system had come in handy many times when they were teens and sneaking dates into the house after hours.

"I should have known I'd find you two girls hiding out here." Claudia stepped out onto the porch, still looking perfectly groomed and coiffed. You would never guess she had spent the last few hours cleaning the stove and refrigerator and performing other odd jobs. "Where are your manners, Anne? You have company inside."

"Annie's thirty-eight years old, Ma," Susan tossed over her shoulder. "This is her home. She can stay out here all night if she wants to."

Claudia picked her way carefully across the uneven

porch, avoiding bent nails, warped boards, and Susan's sharp tongue. "Did I hear you say someone's moving to Bar Harbor?" Claudia was the only woman on earth who could make the famous resort town sound slightly downscale. "Anne, I hope you aren't—" Her words trailed off, and she looked so suddenly vulnerable and worried that Annie's heart twisted. In all the ways that mattered, this woman had been her mother for the last twenty-two years, and she deserved better than Annie's bad mood.

"Don't worry." She landed a quick kiss on her mother-in-law's forehead. "The only place I'm going is to the store for more soda."

"You look so tired." Claudia's voice softened, and she reached up to smooth a lock of Annie's hair from her forehead. The touch brought back a thousand memories, some of them too painful for Annie to bear. She was relieved when Claudia turned toward her oldest daughter, who was slouched over the porch rail, dangling the still unlit cigarette between her fingers. "Susan, why don't you go to the market so Anne can relax?"

"Susan's done enough," Annie said before Susan had a chance to respond. She wished she didn't sound quite so edgy and irritable. Claudia was only trying to help. They all were. She took a deep breath and regrouped. "You've all done enough for me today. The least I can do is keep you in beer and soda."

It wasn't their fault she suddenly hated everything and everybody. The town. Her new house. The way her life was playing out. When she went to bed last night she had been reasonably sure she was doing the right thing. Now, less than twenty-four hours later, she felt like grabbing George and Gracie and running away from home.

Wherever home was these days.

• • •

Hall Talbot was running late. The Preston baby had decided to surprise everyone, her obstetrician most of all,
with her early arrival, and it was nearly seven o'clock by
the time he finished his office appointments and made his
rounds.

"Don't forget you have an eight A.M. cesarean," his
partner Ellen called out to him as he headed for the exit.

"The Noonan baby," he said, stopping in the doorway
of her office, "unless we lose the room." Saturdays were
always dicey.

Ellen stifled a yawn and leaned back in her chair. She
was a tall, lanky redhead with strong features and a soft
heart. "Feel like stopping at Cappy's for some chowder
and blueberry pie? My treat."

"Sounds great," he said, "but—"

"Hey, no problem." She straightened up, all angles and
sharp lines. "Another time."

"Any other night," he said, feeling off-center and
slightly defensive. "Annie Galloway's moving into her
new place and—"

Ellen pushed back her chair and stood up. Her serious
expression gave way momentarily to a smile. "You don't
have to explain anything to me."

"It's no big deal," he said, thereby making it a much
bigger deal than it had any right to be. "Susan mentioned
they were getting together at the new place and—"

"Really," she said. "We're business partners, Hall, not
life partners. If you want to spend your life sitting on
Annie Galloway's front porch waiting for her to give you
the time of day, that's your business. Me? I keep out of
other people's lives."

"Damn New Yorker," he said, softening his words with
a smile of his own. "I should've found myself a Mainer
for a partner. At least New Englanders know when to keep
their mouths shut."

At that Ellen threw back her head and laughed. "I might have believed that malarkey about taciturn New Englanders before I moved up here, but not anymore. When it comes to gossip, Shelter Rock Cove is ground zero."

Ellen was right, as usual, about both the town and his feelings. You couldn't hide much from your partner when you ran a small practice in an even smaller town. Ellen had been in Shelter Rock Cove for less than a year, but already she had a better grasp on the town's history, both social and cultural, than most of the born-and-bred townies. She had an instinctive understanding for family dynamics and she could sniff out a budding romance from six blocks away.

She pitied him. Didn't that beat all? He was a highly respected member of the community, a doctor who loved his patients and dedicated himself to their care. Hell, he gave out his home phone number to nervous expectant parents, so when the big moment came, they knew they would be able to find him. Even his two ex-wives sent him Christmas and birthday cards every year. He had a great car, a big house, a fat bank account, two healthy and happy college-age daughters and two more barely out of preschool. Not exactly the kind of guy most people would pity, but, damn it, that didn't stop Ellen Markowitz, M.D., from doing exactly that. He saw it every time she leveled those big gray eyes in his direction or wrinkled her brow at the mention of Annie Galloway's name.

You're right, Markowitz, he thought as he climbed behind the wheel of his Land Rover and started the engine. *I've been in love with Annie Lacy Galloway since high school, and she doesn't know I'm alive, not the way I want her to.*

She was the standard by which he judged all women and found them wanting. He'd loved her when he was a senior in high school and she was a painfully young freshman with eyes for only Kevin Galloway. He and Kevin's sister Susan ran with the same crowd, and most nights they all ended up on the front porch of the Galloway house, laughing and talking while the The Knack and Blondie provided the soundtrack to their lives. He remembered the day Annie moved in with the Galloways. She was a junior by then, more lovely than ever before and even more out of his reach.

He was the Kindly Family Friend, comfortable and dependable as an old pair of Birks and about as exciting.

Not exactly the way a man wanted the woman of his dreams to think of him.

Susan had been on his back for months now, urging him to step out of the shadows and into Annie's life, but after twenty-five years of playing background music, he wasn't sure he knew how to solo.

"What are you waiting for?" she demanded. "You're alone, and so is she. You've known each other since forever. Don't you think it's time you made your move?"

He stopped for a red light where the hospital parking lot fed into Harbor Road, the town's main thoroughfare. He watched, mesmerized, as the young couple in the lime-green VW behind him fell into a tangled embrace the second their car rolled to a stop. Over the years he had imagined Annie Lacy Galloway in just about every situation a man could invent, but he couldn't imagine her going at it at a stoplight. Annie was too self-assured, too dignified for that. He had no doubt she was a warm and passionate woman, but she was the kind of woman who kept those passions private.

The couple behind him untangled themselves. The driver beeped his horn twice and gestured toward the green light swinging overhead. Red-faced, Hall gunned the engine and sped away, feeling like a middle-aged pervert.

"What are you dragging your feet for, Talbot?" Susan had asked him. "An engraved invitation from Annie?"

What was wrong with picking up a stack of pizzas and running them by her new house? He'd grab a couple of six-packs, a few sodas, maybe a half-gallon of ice cream and a dozen roses, and take his chances. He wasn't entirely sure he was doing the right thing, but so far doing the right thing hadn't helped him win the fair lady's heart. Maybe it was time to step out on a limb and take a chance.

It wasn't as if he had anything to worry about. Annie's manners were impeccable. She would never embarrass him. If she thought he'd gone too far, she would never say so. She would greet him warmly, hand him something cold to drink, then drift away into the crowd, leaving the family friend to fend for himself.

Ceil had been packing groceries at the Yankee Shopper for as long as Annie could remember. Each morning she took her place at register one and watched the people of Shelter Rock Cove come and go. If you wanted to know what was happening in town, all you had to do was ask Ceil. She had been the first one to know that the Liccardis had broken up. Ceil claimed if Angie hadn't wanted the world to know her business, she shouldn't have bought the single lamb chop and one sorry little baking potato, then waited five minutes for Ceil's line to move when Dave at register three was standing there twiddling his thumbs.

It wasn't Ceil's fault that she was a natural-born detective who had every episode of *Murder, She Wrote* on tape. Besides, what woman worth her salt wouldn't have noticed that Frankie Carll was drowning his sorrows in Oreos and Heavenly Hash and growing jowls like a basset hound? When a middle-aged man buzzed through the express lane twice a day, you knew things weren't going well at home.

So it was no surprise to Annie when Ceil glanced at the bags of potato chips and pretzels, the popcorn, and the four dozen cans of soda on the conveyor belt and said, "Moving day, honey?"

Annie smiled at the older woman and nodded. "Afraid I misjudged my helpers' appetites. I'm always amazed at how much food teenagers can consume." Not to mention their parents and friends.

Ceil slid a bag of chips across the scanner with a world-weary sigh. "You wouldn't say that if you had a tribe of your own. When my boys were young, I swore they were going to eat us out of house and home. Why, my milk bill alone would have set a grown man to weeping." She peered at Annie with curious dark eyes. "Not meaning any offense, honey. No, you have it easy, all things considered. At least you're not a single mother, struggling to make ends meet without a husband."

Years ago Ceil's innocent words about her childless state would have cut Annie to the quick, but she had long ago learned how to deflect these little unintentional hand grenades. All you had to do was smile, nod, and keep your mouth shut. It was easy, really, once you got the knack of it, especially if you had bigger secrets to keep.

"So how did your daughter-in-law's blueberry jam turn out?" she asked, and Ceil, bless her chatty heart, shifted conversational gears and launched into a detailed critique of Emily's canning technique that made Annie shudder inwardly. Poor Emily used too much sugar, didn't clean up after herself, and wouldn't know a ripe blueberry if it jumped up and bit her on the ankle. Annie whispered a prayer of thanks that she had never had those problems with Claudia. If anything, Claudia loved her so much that her own daughters sometimes grew irritated. "Don't forget

I'm the one who inherited your thighs," Susan had been known to say to her mother upon occasion—a gentle, daughterly reminder that never failed to infuriate Claudia, who didn't think her thighs were jokeworthy, and made Annie (who wouldn't have minded inheriting Claudia's thighs) laugh.

"You take care now, honey," Ceil said as Annie pocketed her change, "and don't eat too many of those potato chips. We both know where all that grease ends up once a girl hits that certain age." She eyed Annie's midsection and ran a plump hand over her own size-eighteen hips in warning, then turned to the next customer before she had a chance to see Annie's jaw drop open in utter astonishment.

Okay, so maybe her jeans were a bit tighter than they had been six months ago, but since when did an extra ten pounds merit a lecture from the nosiest woman in town? If she was really blimping up the way Ceil suggested, you would think Susan or Eileen or surely Claudia would have dropped a subtle hint or three. They had all been quick enough to tell her she was skin and bones after Kevin died. Shyness, after all, was not a Galloway family trait.

Still, she was thirty-eight now, the age when all of those nice friendly hormones begin to shift and move around in preparation for some major redecorating. And it wasn't as though she spent a lot of time gazing at her body in the mirror or anything. She couldn't remember the last time she had paid any attention to herself at all except to take care of basic grooming.

She glanced at her reflection in the plate-glass window as she headed for the Yankee Shopper exit. Her denim shirt was easily three sizes too large for her. Who knew what horrors were going on under there. And what was the deal with her hair anyway? She touched the top of her head and winced. She looked like she'd been in a fight with a Weedwacker and lost the battle.

To hear Ceil tell it, bad hair was the least of her worries. She was wondering whether she'd be able to maneuver her hips through the exit door this time next week when she noticed the dog sitting behind the wheel of her car.

It wasn't so much that there was a dog in the driver's seat that brought her up short; it was more the size of the dog. The Labrador retriever filled the seat so completely, like a big yellow bear, that Annie couldn't imagine how he had been able to squeeze through the partially opened window to climb inside in the first place.

Annie wasn't a dog person. She could pill a cat without breaking into a sweat, trim razor-sharp feline claws, even bathe a reluctant tabby who had had an unfortunate encounter with a neighborhood skunk, but when it came to dogs, she was clueless. The dog behind the wheel of her SUV was so big he could probably swallow a pot roast whole and consider it an appetizer.

"Nice doggie," she said, wheeling her cart a few feet closer. "Don't you have someplace to go?"

The yellow Lab ignored her and kept looking straight ahead.

She angled the cart to a stop near her right front tire, then approached the door. "Out!" She patted the side of her leg and made a clicking sound. "Come on, pooch. It's too far for me to walk home, and I doubt if you know how to drive."

She reached for the door handle, then jumped back when the dog's upper lip lifted just enough to reveal an impressive set of teeth.

She didn't need to be told twice that it was time to regroup. She leaned against the shopping cart and considered her options. She wasn't a risk taker by nature. She had never jumped out of an airplane, kayaked the rapids, or tried to smuggle homemade popcorn into the Shelter Rock Cove Cinema. She could always call home and ask Susan to come rescue her. Susan had a houseful of dogs. She would know what to do. Dog people always struck Annie as being very practical and down-to-earth.

She glanced around the parking lot. A white Chevy Malibu was double-parked in front of Kate's Laundromat next to the Yankee Shopper. The driver was a middle-aged woman named Marcy who Annie knew from the Annual Three Towns Firemen's Fair Bake Sale. Marcy was one of those skinny, nervous types who baked with applesauce instead of butter then swore she couldn't tell the difference. Marcy caught sight of Annie and waved a well-manicured hand in her direction.

Annie considered cupping her hands around her mouth and bellowing, "Did you lose a yellow Lab?" but thought better of it. Marcy wasn't the kind of woman who ever lost anything, including (or so her ex-husband said) her virginity. She waved instead. The two Coleman girls ran barefoot along the sidewalk, shrieking as they burst through the Laundromat door, which meant Sarah's washing machine was still out of service.

Near the pizza parlor, Fred Custis of Custis Hardware and Marvin Applegarth of Computer Solutions were engaged in conversation with Dave Small, owner of the diner up the road. They were the ones who had supported her successful bid for president of the Shelter Rock Cove Small Business Association. Their matching minivans were all parked facing north. She was sure they'd be glad to help her out of her current predicament.

"Hey, guys," she called out. "Anybody lose a yellow Lab?"

They glanced her way, laughed when they saw the dog behind the wheel, then shook their heads and kept on yakking. *That's it, guys? Nobody's going to come over here and take a closer look?* Whatever happened to chivalry? When it came to things like spiders, stinging insects, and strange noises after midnight, Kevin had been her knight in shining armor. She would have liked to believe his chivalrous nature belonged to her alone, but the truth was that Kevin had loved to ride in on his metaphorical white charger and make things right for everybody. He was the one you turned to if you ran out of gas on the back road or your car wouldn't start on one of those famously frigid Maine mornings. He was always happy to shovel your walk for you or help you dry-dock your boat in the fall.

It was only when it came to the bigger things, like keeping a roof over their heads or trouble away from their door, that her knight in shining armor revealed his tragic flaw: real life.

The dog leaned his big face out the window and looked straight at Annie.

Annie leaned against her shopping cart and looked straight back at the dog. "I can outwait you, pooch."

The dog, obviously unimpressed, yawned.

Annie didn't.

She considered it a moral victory and settled down to wait.

The cashier, a pillowy white-haired woman with curious brown eyes, slid the container of milk across the scanner then pointed toward the fifty-pound bag of dog chow. "Read me the numbers under the bar code," she told him in a no-nonsense tone of voice. "No reason for me to get myself a hernia for Yankee Shopper, is there?"

"None that I can think of," Sam said, wondering when New York attitude had made it up to Maine. He recited the string of numbers, then waited for her to punch them in before he swung the bag to the end of the counter.

She scrutinized the two dozen eggs, pound of bacon, bag of blueberry muffins, and can of coffee as if his order were the Rosetta Stone. "You're the one who's moving into the Bancroft place, aren't you?"

"Lucky guess," he asked, "or do you have a mug shot of me back there?"

"I know everyone in town," she said in a matter-of-fact tone, "and I don't know you. If you were passing through on your way to Bar Harbor, you wouldn't be here buying fifty pounds of dog chow and two dozen eggs. It's too late for the summer season and the only place up for rent was Bancroft's place and I heard it was going to a man from New York and with that accent where else could you be from?" She said it all without taking a breath.

"You're good." He was impressed, if a bit taken aback by this introduction to the intimacy of small-town New England life.

He paid the bill, then tucked the bag of dog chow under his right arm and gathered up his grocery bag in his left.

"We have a special tomorrow on ground beef," she called out as he headed for the exit. "You might want to stock up."

She probably kept a mental list of the dietary peculiarities of everyone in town. Buy an extra quart of milk, and she'd suspect you of harboring a fugitive.

He stopped on the narrow strip of sidewalk outside the store and stared at the handful of vehicles in the parking lot. Where the hell was his BMW? All he saw were aging Chevys, a cluster of minivans, and two beat-up SUVs. No sign of his BMW anywhere. His blood ran cold for a second as he thought about his beloved car being stripped and sold for parts, and then he remembered that it wasn't his beloved car any longer. He had quit the lease early, paid off the penalty, then turned around and bought this junker.

Thirty-five, and he was losing it already. One of those beat-up black SUVs belonged to him, the one with the big yellow Lab sitting behind the wheel. But wait a second. The truck with the dog had Maine plates while the dogless truck boasted tags from the Empire State.

Near the trucks a girl was leaning over a shopping cart piled high with potato chips, pretzels, and cases of soda. She wore a pair of faded and patched jeans, high-top sneakers, and a denim shirt big enough to cover the cast of *Friends,* both male and female, but not so big that he couldn't see the dip of her waist or the sweet curve of her hips. Her hair, soft and curly and chestnut brown, was pulled back into a ponytail that danced between her shoulder blades. Sexy, artless, and off-limits because she couldn't be more than seventeen.

"Your truck?" he asked.

She nodded her head, then turned slightly and looked up at him. "Your dog?"

She wasn't seventeen after all, and the realization brought him up short. Her dark blue eyes crinkled a bit at the outer corners, and there were faint worry lines between her brows. She wore no makeup. Her skin was fair, and the slightest shadow of freckles dusted her straight nose. She looked exhausted and more than a little bemused, and he found himself imagining a husband and horde of hungry kids waiting for her at home.

Definitely off-limits.

"I didn't know Max could pick locks," he said for lack of anything better.

"He didn't have to," she said, gesturing toward his vehicle. "He used the window."

"Impossible," he said, looking back at Max, who seemed to be having the time of his life. "Max only moves when there's food involved."

She groaned. "Oh, no! I have three pizzas in there."

"Not anymore you don't." He reached into his back pocket and pulled out two twenties. "It's the least I can do," he said, handing them to her.

"That's not necessary."

"My dog ate your pizzas."

"I should've kept my windows closed."

"I should've kept a closer eye on Max."

Her serious expression softened, and he felt something shift slightly deep inside his chest. A small shift, but significant, as if time had stopped for an instant, then started again when she smiled at him. Her mouth was full, and he saw the faintest memory of smile lines at either side. He had never been the kind of man who read deeper meanings into every gesture a woman made, but somehow he knew she hadn't been smiling a lot lately.

Not your problem, Butler. Don't you have enough of your own these days? Married women had married problems, and it was the wise single man who kept his distance. Especially if the single man found himself wondering how the married woman would look with that beautiful hair cascading over her bare shoulders . . .

She pushed away his money with a firm but friendly gesture. "I don't know how such a big dog managed to get through such a small opening."

"I have newfound respect for him."

Her gaze drifted discreetly to the watch on her left wrist. "I tried to lure him out but I haven't had much luck." She gave him another one of those sideways looks that exerted an almost gravitational pull on his erotic imagination. "I think he showed his teeth."

"All six of them?" *Who's waiting at home for you? Do they know how lucky they are?*

"I don't know how many there were, but the ones I saw were pretty big."

"Max wouldn't bite you."

"You don't sound very sure." The frown lines between her brows deepened. "He *is* your dog, isn't he?"

"As of two weeks ago. We're still getting to know each other."

Another quick glance at her watch. "I don't mean to be rude, but do you think you could continue the process in your truck? If I don't get home soon, they'll come out looking for me."

Her family. The ones who were waiting for the sound of her truck in the driveway. Funny how those words acted like a metaphorical cold shower. He knew without being told that she had three freckle-faced kids and a husband who wore plaid flannel shirts and a gold wedding band that matched the one on her left hand.

He dumped his packages on the ground and swung open the driver's door. "C'mon, Max," he said. "You've had enough fun for one day. Let's go."

Max rested his noble head on the steering wheel and closed his eyes. Pizza sauce was clearly visible on his graying muzzle. It was clear the dog wasn't going anywhere in a hurry.

They didn't call them man's best friend for nothing.

The moment the man turned his back, Annie frantically tried to smooth her hair, her work shirt, and her hormones back into place. Unfortunately she failed on all fronts. Her hair was determined to spring free of any and all attempts to tame it. Her work shirt refused to morph into her favorite red sweater, the one with the sexy zipper up the front. And her hormones? They were careening through her veins like bumper cars gone amok.

The fates had themselves one strange sense of humor. Why else would they send a woman out looking like an unmade bed when that poor unsuspecting woman was on a collision course with a man so hot he could boil water just by looking at it? It wasn't simply unfair, it was down-right sadistic. She never went out of the house looking like this. She always wore a little lipstick, a pair of ear-rings, a dab of perfume. Even on her worst days she managed to be presentable.

But not today. Today she had to go out looking like an unemployed lumberjack who ate like one. Even the contents of her shopping cart embarrassed her. He must think she was a sexless, middle-aged woman whose hobby was drinking beer and eating nachos in front of the television.

Which, all things considered, wasn't that far off the mark.

No wonder he had turned his full attention to his dog.

Annie almost felt sorry for him as he struggled to lure his sleepy, pizza-sated Lab out of her truck. He was trying so hard it made her smile. He coaxed. He prodded. He demanded. He even opened up the sack of dog chow and offered the dog a bribe. Max merely opened one eye, surveyed the situation, then went back to sleep.

What a wonderful dog!

Good boy. I'll buy you another pizza if you'll nap just a little bit longer. What a pleasure it was to lean against a shopping cart in the Yankee Shopper parking lot and ogle a gorgeous man who didn't know or care that you were ogling. She might look like a hausfrau but inside she was still sixteen.

Clay, she thought. It had been years since she'd last brought an image to life with clay, but the sense memory was sharp and clear. Slick hot clay between her fingers, clinging to her skin as she molded it slowly into the torso of a man. She could feel the deltoids taking shape, the swell of bicep, the clean power of shoulder and chest. Naked he would be a god. If he had any fat on his frame, it was well concealed. What Annie saw was sinewy muscle and coiled strength beneath a wrinkled work shirt and seen-better-days jeans. All he would have to do was walk into an art class at Bowdoin and offer to model and he would have work well into his golden years.

Enjoy him while you can, Galloway. He's probably married with five kids and a minivan in the driveway.

She tried to picture him in a small Colonial with a smiling wife and kids who brushed after every meal, but the image wouldn't stay in focus.

"Open the other door," he said over his shoulder. "Maybe if we double-team him . . ."

She crossed in front of the truck and opened the door on the passenger side. The smell of pizza and dog breath hit her right between the eyes. "Whoa!" she said, waving a hand in front of her face.

Max sat up and looked at her, then his gaze fixed on a point just beyond her head. A dog person might have recognized that look, but Annie was owned by cats, and that was all it took.

The yellow Lab exploded out of the truck. He slammed into Annie, sending her spinning into the door, where her shoulder clipped the frame. The collision apparently surprised the dog as much as it surprised Annie, because he sat down quite abruptly and took stock of the situation.

Max's owner was by her side in a flash. He gripped her shoulders to steady her and the rest of the universe dropped away. He smelled like soap and cinnamon and freshly cut grass. She wanted to bury her nose against his neck and just breathe for a year or two.

"Are you okay?" The warmth of his hand came right through her shirt. "You hit your shoulder on the door."

"I did?" Right now her shoulders were the blissful center of her universe. How long had it been since she had been touched with tenderness and concern by a man? Longer than she could remember, years, maybe eons. His hands were large and strong, his touch wonderfully gentle.

Something inside her chest went a little bit haywire.

"Are you hurt?"

She shook her head. "Max," she said. "You should—"

Their gazes locked. His eyes were green with golden flecks, like sunlight splashing through a forest, and they came alive when he smiled.

"Max," she said again. "He was here a second ago—"

Max's owner seemed to go from zero to sixty in a split second, his lean body taking flight like a racecar at the starting flag. Annie, who had never believed in walking when she could drive, watched in a combination of awe and admiration as he took off after Max, who was about to disappear into the woods. Whoever said the male body wasn't beautiful obviously hadn't watched Max's owner run.

She leaned against her truck and absently rubbed her shoulder. Any second now Max and his owner would stride out of the woods, and she wanted to make sure she didn't miss the sight. The staff at Annie's Flowers liked to tease her about her lack of interest in male pulchritude, but the truth was they simply hadn't a clue. She wasn't likely to sit through three showings of the latest Mel Gibson movie just so she could gaze into his blue eyes but she had more than a passing interest in the male form. A lobsterman's forearms, the mail carrier's broad back, Max's owner's beautiful hands.

Ceil waved to her from the other side of the parking lot, and Annie waved back in return. Yankee Shopper was closing early so their employees could enjoy the start of the Labor Day weekend, and moments later Annie was alone. She was debating whether she should head for the woods to lend a hand in the search for the dog when she heard the sound of a vehicle approaching. Her heart sank. The odds were she would be either related to, friends with, or an old schoolmate of whoever was behind the wheel.

"Annie! Great luck!" Hall Talbot brought his Rover to a stop next to her. "I was on my way to the new house."

"How nice of you," she said, meaning it. "Susan's been asking about you all afternoon."

"Three deliveries today," he said, shaking his head. "Must be the full moon."

"You must be exhausted," she said.

"Don't let the new mothers hear you say that. They're the ones who did the work."

Statements like that weren't lip service from Hall. He really meant them. No wonder he was the most popular OB-GYN in three counties.

"If you're ready, I'll follow you back to your place." He pointed to a stack of boxes on the seat next to him. "Hope it isn't too late for pizza."

"You're a sprinter, Max," Sam said as he picked up the exhausted yellow Lab. "Squirrels are long-distance runners. Remember that."

Max's poor old heart was beating fast and hard. He rested his head on Sam's arm and pretended he wasn't listening.

"Getting old's a bitch," Sam said as he carried the dog out of the woods. That wind sprint across the parking lot hadn't been his shining moment either. Might not be a bad idea if he stopped for a second to catch his breath before he strode back toward the woman with the sad eyes and the beautiful smile.

Then again maybe it didn't matter.

She wasn't alone. A man with thinning blond hair towered over her. Their two SUVs were nose-to-nose. He looked annoyed. She looked amused. She was probably telling him all about her run-in with some New York dumbass and his pizza-eating dog, and he was getting all hot under the collar. He stepped back into the cover of trees and shadows.

Married, he thought, as he watched them climb into their respective vehicles and drive away. No doubt about it.

They would go home, feed their kids pizza, then climb into bed and make love by the light of David Letterman.

Boring.

Dull.

Routine.

Every cliché ever invented to describe the life of a married couple who'd been together for a very long time.

And for a moment Sam Butler would have sold his soul to trade places with the guy.

THREE

❧

"What's the matter with Hall?" Susan whispered to Annie later as they nuked a few more slices of pizza for the waiting throng. "He's awfully quiet tonight. Did you two have a fight or something?"

"A fight?" Annie threw a stack of plastic cups into the waiting garbage bin. "I've barely had a chance to speak with him."

"Well, something's got his goat. He's been walking around like he has the weight of the world on his shoulders ever since the two of you pulled into the driveway together."

Annie sighed and leaned back against the sink. "I laughed at him."

"Why would you laugh at Hall? That man has carried a torch for you since high school."

Annie had been hearing about that imaginary torch for years, and she still didn't believe it. "I didn't really laugh at him," she said, "but he thinks I did. He pulled up with those pizzas and—well, I lost it."

Susan's eyes flashed with outrage. Hall had guided her

through three high-risk pregnancies, and he was now on a par with God and Moses in her estimation. "You mean the poor man showed up with a half-dozen pepperoni pies, and all you could do was laugh in his face?"

"It wasn't Hall I was laughing at," she explained, "it was the situation." She tried to tell Susan about the truck and the man and the yellow dog behind the steering wheel and the massacred pizzas and the squirrel, but the words were almost lost amid huge gales of laughter she couldn't control.

Susan looked at her as if she'd lost her mind. "You're telling me a squirrel ate the pizzas?"

"No, no!" She wiped her eyes with the back of her hand, struggling not to start laughing again. "The dog ate the pizzas. The squirrel just ran by."

"And where does the man come in?"

"It's his dog."

"The dog behind the wheel of your truck?"

"Yes."

"And the man took the pizzas?"

"Haven't you heard a word I said, Susan? The dog ate the pizzas. The man wanted to pay for them."

"But you wouldn't let him."

"He ran off into the woods before I could change my mind." Not that she would have, but she was enjoying the look of confusion on her best friend's face.

"And then Hall happened to drive by with a six-pack of pizza."

"Exactly. I took one look and—" She started laughing again, and this time Susan joined her.

"It's good to hear you laugh again," Susan said as she slid slices of warm pizza from the microwave, then divided them among four paper plates. "You used to be a world-class laugher. I've missed it."

Annie slid four more slices into the microwave. "There

hasn't been all that much to laugh about lately." She pressed the ON button. "Losing Kevin hit us all very hard."

Susan shook her head. "No," she said, "you changed long before Kev died. Maybe around the time you two quit trying for a baby." She stopped short. "Sorry. I never know when to shut up."

"Let's turn over a new leaf," Annie said. "From now on we laugh a lot, say what's on our minds, and quit apologizing for it." She grinned at her best friend and sister-in-law. She felt downright rebellious. "How does that sound to you?"

Annie was still smiling when she bumped into Hall near the entrance to her postage-stamp-sized living room.

"I hope I thanked you properly for the pizzas," she said as she offered him a freshly nuked slice dripping with cheese and heavy with pepperoni. "You were sweet to think of us."

The guarded expression in his eyes lifted a little, and for the first time she wondered if Susan just might be right about Hall's feelings for her. He had been part of her life for almost as long as she could remember, one of Susan's many friends who had floated in and out of the Galloway house at all hours of the day and night while she was dating Kevin. Later on he was a frequent guest at family celebrations as well as her doctor, until she began seeing fertility specialists and her life turned upside-down.

Hall Talbot was a lovely man, a gentleman in the truest sense, and if he had even the slightest interest in her as a woman he had done one fine job of concealing it all these years.

You're wrong, Susie, she thought as he helped himself to a slice of pepperoni. *You're mistaking kindness for chemistry.* She'd seen the kind of woman Hall Talbot

dated and married and she wasn't anything like them.
Both of his wives had been small-boned, well-dressed,
and perfectly groomed. Annie, at best, managed charm-
ingly rumpled two or three times a year. Not that it mattered, because she didn't feel that way about Hall. She
wasn't blind to the fact that he was a very handsome man,
but her heart didn't do backflips when she looked at him,
and it never would.

There were people who said that sort of thing didn't
matter, and sometimes she wondered if maybe they were
right. Her heart had done backflips and cartwheels when
she looked at Kevin, and see how that had ended up. Still,
what was the point to love if it didn't make you feel like
you could fly? You might as well live alone.

Her brief interlude with Max's owner had been a powerful reminder of how wonderful it could be.

"How bad's your car?" Hall asked between mouthfuls
of pizza.

"Remember how Susie's house looked after her big
Y2K party?" He nodded. "Add dog spit and you're close."

"He's paying for the cleanup, isn't he?"

"He offered to pay for the pizza."

"He should've offered to pay for the wreck his dog left
behind."

"I'm sure he would have," she said, "but, if you recall,
we left before he came back to his truck." *I should have
helped him look for his dog. Why didn't I tell you to go
on without me?*

Hall looked unconvinced. "He was probably hiding in
the woods, waiting for you to leave."

Her eyes widened in surprise. "A bit harsh, aren't you?
You don't even know the man."

"I know the type."

"Really, Hall," she said, astonished by his over-the-top

response. "You sound like his dog smeared pizza all over your upholstery instead of mine."

"My mistake," he said, his manners reasserting themselves. "You're right. It's not as if you'll run into him again, is it?"

No, she thought as she headed back into the kitchen for more pizza. *Not very likely at all.*

Sam drove out to Warren Bancroft's house at the far side of town. Warren had been called down to New York on business, but he left the keys to Sam's temporary digs with Pete and Nancy, the couple who had been taking care of Warren's place for the last twenty years. Unfortunately Pete and Nancy had decided to drive into town for some ice cream, and it was nearly nine o'clock by the time they returned to find Sam and Max asleep on the front step.

"Well, look who's here!" Nancy said, dragging a drowsy Sam into her embrace. She hugged him then pushed him slightly away so she could peer into his face. "Too skinny and too tired. We'll take care of that while you're in town."

"You never change," Sam said, hugging her back. "You're the same shy woman I met almost twenty years ago." He had been fifteen at the time, filled with ambition and ready to see the world. He had signed on as part of Warren's crew for the summer and had spent two weeks right there at Shelter Rock Cove before sailing down to Key West.

Pete, never one for small talk, shook Sam's hand and then dug out the keys. "Watch out for the plumbing," he warned. "Ellie never was good at keeping up with repairs." He patted Max, then went inside.

"Annie Galloway moved into the house down the road from you today," Nancy said when the door swung shut behind her husband. "She's a widow, real nice gal. If you need any names or phone numbers, she's the one to go to."

He imagined a weathered New Englander, much like Nancy herself, who could probably cope with just about anything life threw her way. "I'll keep that in mind."

"You might want to introduce yourself. Just two houses on that road. Might settle her down some, knowing there's a man she can turn to."

A sinking feeling settled itself in the pit of his stomach. The last thing he needed right now was to have anyone depending on him for anything.

"So how's the boat coming along?" he asked, changing the subject. "Has he made any progress?" Warren Bancroft's dream had been to build a museum as a memorial to Shelter Rock Cove fishermen who had lost their lives to the sea, and that dream was scheduled to come true next spring.

"He works too hard down there," Nancy said with a shake of her head. "Do him good if he spent more time working on his boat and less on his payrolls."

They walked around back to the old barn that Warren had turned into a boat builder's paradise. Long planks of unblemished wood. Buckets of nails. Hammers in all sizes and shapes hung from hooks on the wall next to saws, hasps, clamps. Two table saws were pushed up against the back wall next to a special steamer used to shape straight planks into graceful curves designed to glide through the water.

And there in the middle of it all was the *Sally B*, the lobster boat his father had used right up until the day he died. She was in sorry shape right now: half of her hull was in the process of being restored by Warren and had been for almost as long as Sam could remember. Warren's sister Ellie had remarked that the restoration reminded her of Penelope at her loom, a reference Warren and Sam had to look up in the *Britannica*.

"He hasn't touched it since I was up here at Easter," Sam said, running his hand along the sharp edge of the keel. The third Mrs. Bancroft might have been right. "He'll never get it finished if he doesn't put in the time."

Nancy shot him a look that was sharper than a bandsaw. "You don't think you're up here to watch the snow fall, do you? He'll put you to work proper."

"There's a good four months of eight-hour days left on this baby," he said. "I think that works out to sixteen blueberry pies."

Nancy's narrow face broke apart with her smile. If the way to a man's heart was his stomach, the way to a cook's heart was through her blueberry pies.

"I have half a pie on the counter right now," she said, bending down to scratch Max behind the ear. "You look like you could use a little sustenance."

"I'd better push on to the cottage, Nance. I've been on the road since the crack of dawn and I'm ready to crash."

The old woman linked her arm through his and walked him to the truck. "You're sure you can find the place on your own now? It gets wicked dark around here at night."

"I remember how dark it gets." The difference between Shelter Rock Cove and Bayside, Queens, could have been measured in light-years instead of miles. The teenage Sam had been pretty sure he'd landed on another planet. "I have the map Warren faxed me," he said, and they both laughed.

"A map won't do you much good in the dark. Maybe I should drive you down there. Wouldn't want you rolling into the water now, would we?"

It took another five minutes to convince her that he was capable of finding his way to his new home. She wanted him to call her when he got in, and only the fact that his phone service wasn't turned on yet made her back down. His mother had been the same way, watching over each member of her brood as if nobody else on earth mattered. He had the feeling she would have been every bit as zealous today over her adult children.

"Been one hell of a day, Max," he said as they made their way along the twisting road that led to the beach. "Too bad you had to take off after that squirrel."

He had wanted to square things with the woman with the sad blue eyes and, if he was being completely honest, square things with himself as well. It seemed to him that he had been leaving nothing but loose ends behind these last few months. Something about her had reached deep into his soul, far deeper than a casual encounter in a parking lot would justify. He had felt a connection, a sense of rightness, that he'd never known before.

Who are you kidding, Butler? She's married. You saw the guy. You saw the married way they talked to each other.

That still didn't change the way he'd felt when she turned around and looked up at him. There was something in her eyes, something in the sound of her voice, that seemed familiar. As if he'd waited his whole life to meet her.

"I take it all back, Max," he said as he rounded a tight curve. "You did me a favor back there." Max's squirrel-chasing stunt had broken the spell long enough for Sam to regain some perspective. He was pretty sure he would see her again. Shelter Rock Cove was a small town, and sooner or later their paths were bound to cross. Maybe then he could undo some of the damage Max caused and prove to himself that the churned-up feeling inside his chest was nothing more than a blip on his radar screen.

A thick, hubcap-level fog was rolling right across the narrow, twisting road, and he focused his concentration on keeping the Trooper from a close encounter with the run-off ditch that ran parallel. Winter driving must be a bitch. Good thing he was free to head south when the new year rolled around.

Next to him Max whimpered twice and nudged Sam's arm, the dog's signal that a quick stop might not be a bad idea.

"Not here, buddy," Sam said as he switched on his high beams. "Just wait. We'll be home before you know it."

By eight o'clock the last of Annie's helpers had left, and she was alone in her new home for the first time. "Make sure you eat something," Claudia cautioned her. "You haven't had a bite since breakfast."

Annie promised her mother-in-law she would heat up a slice or two of leftover pizza before she went to bed, then locked the door behind her. She had been starving a few hours ago but now she was too tired to think much beyond a warm bath and sleep.

The boxes were all unpacked and neatly broken down and stacked out back for recycling. Her dishes and glassware were washed, dried, and put away in the cupboards. Her books lined the living room shelves, and her television was hooked up and working. Most of her clothes were still draped across the sleigh bed, mainly because nobody wanted to walk across her mattress to reach the closet by the window, but that was okay. She wasn't in any rush.

"I think I love it," she said to George and Gracie, who were crouched in the bedroom doorway. They looked up at her as if she'd lost her mind. "I think we're going to be very happy here."

Gracie chose that moment to hack up a hairball the size of a wonton.

"Tell me how you really feel," Annie muttered as she cleaned up after the feline.

Unlike Gracie, it had been hard for Annie to know how she felt with the place crammed with people and noise and more opinions than you could shake a stick at. But now that she was alone, she knew she had made the right decision. This was her home. This was where she belonged. She loved the bleached wood floors, the white-washed walls, the tiny stone fireplace, the double-hung windows, the old-fashioned clawfoot tub so deep you could almost float in it. Sure, it would take a while to buy things like chairs and a sofa and a kitchen table, but those were small considerations. She had paid off all of Kevin's gambling debts, she owned the roof over her own head, and, knowing Warren Bancroft, that roof probably came with a lifetime guarantee. She couldn't prove it, but she was reasonably sure Warren had made a few improvements on the place since she had last seen it. The kitchen seemed brighter, and that pedestal sink in the bathroom didn't look like original equipment. She would have to take him to task on Tuesday when she dropped off the latest batch of freshly typed memoir pages. The extra income she earned transcribing his handwritten notes had been a big help to her.

"I'd be happy to hold a mortgage for you, Annie," he had said a few days before closing. "No need for you to be cash-poor just because you bought a house."

Annie had been adamant in her refusal and the deal had gone down in cash. No mortgage. No bank. No strangers at the door or phone calls in the middle of the night. Nobody could take it away from her. If that wasn't cause for celebration, she didn't know what was.

Maybe a celebration was just what she needed. A housewarming party for one. She'd splurged on a bottle of domestic champagne the day the Flemings closed on

her old house with the intention of popping the cork when
she moved into her new place. Well, she'd moved into
her new place, and the cork was still in the bottle, which
struck her as a terrible waste of occasion, not to mention
champagne.

Ten minutes later she stripped off her clothes and sank
into the warm, fragrant clawfoot tub. Chunky white candles scented with freesia glowed from the windowsill, the
counter, and along the baseboard. Good thing candles
didn't come with an expiration date, or she would have
passed it five years ago. The door was closed against an
onslaught of cats, but the gentle sounds of Mozart found
her just the same. A stack of new towels, a housewarming
gift from Susan, were piled high on the shelf next to the
window, and her favorite silky green robe was tossed over
the towel rod by the door. The belt, a beautiful braid of
green and gold cord, swayed gently to the music a few
inches above the floor like a charmed snake. She'd indulged in a glass of champagne while the bathtub was
filling and she felt relaxed in a lovely boneless way that
was unfamiliar to her. She reached for the beautiful crystal
flute of golden liquid balanced on the edge of the sink,
then sank back down into the warm and welcoming water.

"To me!" she said, lifting the glass high. She took a
sip. "To the future!"

For the first time since Kevin's death she actually believed she had one. She decided that deserved another sip
of bubbly.

Champagne? She could hear Claudia's voice clear as a
bell. *Champagne will give you a terrible headache, honey,
especially on an empty stomach.*

"Shut up, Claudia," she said out loud. "Champagne is
the elixir of the gods."

*You really should eat something, Anne. A slice of pizza
or a nice sandwich. Pour yourself a glass of milk.*

"I don't want milk, Claudia. I want champagne. And if you don't keep your thoughts out of my head, I just might drink the entire bottle."

The house was at the end of the road, as far east as Sam could drive without plunging into the Atlantic. It was larger than he had expected and a hell of a lot older.

He pulled into the driveway, turned off the engine, then opened the door. Max, eager to respond to nature's call, was the first one out.

"Stay close," he warned the dog. "You might be a Lab, but I'm not convinced you know how to swim."

Max, giddy with freedom, took off down the road at a surprising clip.

"We're getting you a leash tomorrow," Sam grumbled as he headed after the dog.

He didn't have far to go. Max came to a screeching halt in front of the only other house on the block, a small shingled cottage half-hidden in the trees. Max barked once, then twice more at increasing volume.

This wasn't the right way to meet the neighbors. Sam made to grab the dog by the collar, but Max ran closer to the house. He barked again. Nancy said a widow had just moved into the house. He could imagine the poor old woman cowering behind the door while a strange man and his crazed dog lurked outside. For all he knew she was dialing 911 right now.

He grabbed for Max again and managed to make contact, but the dog ran straight up the porch steps and began scratching at the door.

What the hell was going on? The dog bounded off the porch, then ran to the side of the house, where his frantic barks brought Sam running. The dog's full attention was directed to the single small window where a faint yellow and red light flickered crazily behind the shade.

• • •

Annie was floating naked on a raft in the middle of a turquoise lagoon while tropical sun kissed every part of her body. Her right hand clutched a piña colada while her left hand trailed lazily through the balmy waters. Somewhere on shore a campfire burned merrily. If only the crazy man would stop yelling in her ear—

"Fire!"

She opened her eyes and saw the man from the Yankee Shopper parking lot advancing toward her, brandishing a flaming bathrobe.

She sighed deeply and closed her eyes again. Empty stomach. Lots of champagne. Terrible combination. She was quite happily drunk, and he was a figment of her grape-sodden imagination.

"Out of the tub, now!"

Since when did gorgeous figments of the imagination yell at you? They were supposed to be obedient and cheerful, no matter what you told them to do. She grumbled to herself and wished she had the energy, not to mention the dexterity, to add some more water to the bath. She heard water running some place close by and even imagined she felt droplets of cold water splashing against her exposed skin. Caribbean rain, that's what it was. Everyone knew it rained a lot in the Caribbean. She tried to will it away, but the droplets flew at her faster and colder, and the whole thing was becoming quite annoying.

And what happened to the sweet smell of flowers? Instead of scented candles, she smelled burnt fabric. She forced her eyes open again. She wasn't focusing very well, but there he was, holding her poor bathrobe under running water. Had she let him in? She couldn't remember, but it was clear somebody had because there he was.

Or then again maybe he wasn't. Why would he be washing a silk bathrobe in her sink? Surely she could think of something more interesting for him to do.

Of course he wasn't really there. Good thing he was the by-product of three glasses of extremely cheap champagne, because otherwise the fact that she was lying there naked in the bathtub while a strange man ruined her favorite robe might actually be something to worry about.

Sam was no detective, but it wasn't hard to figure out what was going on there. The empty bottle of cheap champagne, the drained glass on the rim of the tub, candles burning everywhere, and a tipsy naked woman who was starting to add up the clues.

"My robe . . ." She sounded fuzzy, as if she had a mouthful of cotton candy. "Water ruins silk."

"Yeah?" He tried not to glance her way but he was, after all, a man, and she was naked. "Fire does a better job."

"Fire?"

Talking to someone who'd made short work of a bottle of bubbly was never easy, not even when the someone in question was a woman with a body he'd be seeing in his dreams for the next twenty years. "Not too hard to figure, is it? You have enough candlepower going here to light the way to Bangor." As far as he could tell, the belt on her robe had touched the open flame of a candle and things went from there.

"And you—?"

"You're not going to remember a word of this later, are you?" he asked, wringing out the sopping wet robe over the sink. "For the record, you have Max to thank. He knew something was wrong. I'm just the guy with the prehensile thumbs who did the breaking and entering."

She gave him a loopy, dreamy smile. "Kiss Max for me."

Looking at her was dangerous business. He redirected

his attention to the robe. The left side of the robe was badly scorched. Another two or three minutes and the entire garment would have been in flames, followed by the house. Maybe Max did deserve a kiss.

He held up the robe to show her. "Not much point to saving this."

Her eyelids fluttered open. "I love that robe."

"Not anymore you don't."

She sighed deeply and lifted a bare foot, toes pointed. "New beginnings," she said. "Lots of 'em today." She frowned slightly, as if she were trying to focus in on just one of him. "Goodnight."

"That's it?" He started to laugh. "No 'thanks for saving my life' or 'who the hell are you'?"

"Too sleepy . . . Some other time." She closed her eyes and started to slip beneath the surface of the water.

"C'mon, don't do that—" What choice did he have? He dropped the robe in the sink, then tried to find the least incendiary part of her slippery wet body to grab hold of. There wasn't one. He slid his hands under her arms and pulled her against his chest, trying to pretend she wasn't round and soft and naked. Her head dropped against his shoulder. He could feel her breath against the side of his neck. Hell, he could feel it everywhere. Her long curly hair was wet and smelled of shampoo. He wondered how it would feel spilling across his bare chest while she straddled him.

Dangerous ground. He'd never taken advantage of a woman and he wasn't about to start now, even if his mind was taking him places he hadn't been in a long time.

Somehow he managed to get her to loop an arm around his neck long enough for him to scoop her out of the tub.

She murmured something, then nuzzled closer, and he struggled to hang on to his rapidly shredding sense of all that was right and decent. The connection he had felt when he first saw her leaning over her shopping cart in the parking lot was nothing compared to the powerful desire that was wreaking havoc on him.

"What the hell am I going to do with you?" he said aloud.

He had saved her from fire and drowning. All he had to do now was save her from himself.

The cottage was tiny, and ten steps later he found himself in the doorway to a bedroom that seemed to be all bed and no room. A beautiful sleigh bed, the wood smooth and unstained, rose up from the polished floor like something from a Russian fairy tale. Two black-and-white cats watched from the foot, alert to Max's whimpering from the doorway. All Sam had to do was settle the bundle of woman onto the mattress without enjoying himself any more than necessary.

The bed was piled high with clothes: jeans, sweaters, a velvet dress the color of the midnight sky. Everything but sheets and a blanket.

"Work with me," he said as he tried to sit her up at the edge of the bed. "I have to clear a spot for you."

She bestowed another one of those loopy smiles on him, then proceeded to slide off the bed onto the floor, where Max tried to sniff her hair.

"She has enough trouble," Sam said, as he gave the dog a gentle push toward the living room.

He quickly shoved the clothes to the far side of the mattress, then picked her up one more time. He told her to stay put while he searched out some towels and blankets, but the soft thud as he left the room told him otherwise.

"What the hell am I going to do with you?"

The cats' unblinking stares followed every move he made as he placed her on the mattress, tucked a pillow under her head, and hunted around for towels and a blanket to cover her. He tried to wrap a towel around her wet hair, but she pushed him away. It would be easier to gather mercury in your bare hands than to persuade her to stay put for more than ten seconds. He grabbed an assortment of sweaters and a winter coat from the jumble of garments, then covered her with them. She mumbled something he assumed wasn't "Thank you."

"Don't move," he said, then laughed out loud. As if she had any idea what he was saying.

He stood in the doorway for a minute. Her face was buried against the sleeve of a dark navy wool coat. Her eyes were closed. With a little luck she was sound asleep and would stay that way until morning. He used the opportunity to extinguish the candles in the bathroom, pull the stopper on the tub, and put towels down on the wet floor. Max watched him from the hallway, tail thumping in pure enjoyment.

The front door was a whole other problem. He'd kicked it off its hinges, and it now hung crazily in the frame. He'd need to make a trip to a hardware store in the morning so he could set it right again. He fit the door into the opening, then pushed a suitcase in front of it. The solution wasn't going to win any awards, but it would keep strangers out and Max and the cats in, and right now that was the most he could ask for.

He barely had time to secure the door when he heard another thud from the bedroom. He found her sitting naked on the floor in the hallway—the bed took up the entire room—looking so completely astonished that he couldn't help laughing.

"Here," he said, taking off his shirt and handing it to her. "Put this on."

She had trouble coordinating her movements, so he helped guide her arms into the proper sleeves. Her fingers fumbled at the buttons.

"Wrong side," he said.

She tried again. "I'm really not this stupid," she said, her words slightly slurred.

He knelt down on the floor in front of her. "Here," he said. "I'll do it for you." She smelled sweet, and his body responded fiercely to her nearness. Her fair skin was rosy from the bath. Her curly hair drifted wild and damp across her shoulders. Her breasts were round and full and beautiful, and she was completely at his mercy. The champagne had demolished her defenses. It would be easy to draw one of her tightly budded nipples between his lips and tease the tender flesh with his teeth. She would moan softly in the back of her throat and arch her back, and he would slip his hand between her legs and feel her desire. It would be quick and fierce and primal. She would come first, he would see to that, and then when she was beginning her slow descent from the pinnacle, he would let himself go and she would rise again with him, higher and higher, until they crashed into the stars.

He thought about flat tires, the Yankees' batting order, the mileage between Shelter Rock Cove and every major city in the United States while he quickly buttoned up her shirt, being careful not to touch even a millimeter of her lush and sensual body. When they made love, he wanted her to be there with him, body and soul.

FOUR

"Call her," Susan said as she scrunched down into the pillows with the phone pressed to her ear. "You screwed up. You created an awkward moment. Apologize before it goes any further."

"Apologize for what?" Hall demanded, his voice slightly muffled on the other end of the line. "I didn't do anything wrong."

"You acted like a jerk. You let yourself get all bent out of shape over some guy whose dog trashed her car."

"He skips out after his dog trashes her car, and you're calling *me* a jerk?"

"You're missing the point."

"And you're missing Letterman," her husband grumbled from his side of the bed.

She poked him in the shin with her heel.

"What point?" Hall asked. She could hear the sound of papers rustling in the background. What was it with men and the telephone? They never gave it the full attention it deserved.

"The point is that this guy and his dog aren't the point

at all. Why waste time worrying about some tourist passing through town? Annie's here, and so are you. So what are you going to do about it?"

More paper rustling on the other end of the line.

"Stay out of it, Susie," her husband said in a low voice. "You're asking for trouble."

She ignored him. He hated it when she played matchmaker, but, as she frequently pointed out to anyone who would listen, she was responsible for three happy marriages in Shelter Rock Cove over the last ten years and she was gunning for number four.

"Quit reading your mail while we're talking," she snapped at Hall. "You've waited twenty years for a chance to ask Annie out. I hope you're not planning to wait another twenty before you actually get around to it."

She slammed down the phone. Sometimes a man needed emphatic punctuation before he got the point.

"You're wasting your time," Jack said as she scooted closer to him.

"You don't know what you're talking about." She slipped into the crook of his arm and rested her head on his chest.

"It'll never work out between them."

"Sure it will."

"Annie doesn't see him that way."

"She doesn't see *any* man that way yet, but when she does—"

He held her close and kissed the top of her head. "When she does, it won't be the Good Doctor Talbot."

"You don't know that."

"Yes, I do," he said, "and so do you. When Annie falls in love again, it won't be with anyone from Shelter Rock Cove."

"Crystal balls," she asked dryly, "or is this just your way of telling me to mind my own business?"

He laughed, which was one of the reasons she loved him. "Kevin's shadow is everywhere in this town, Suze, and she knows it. One day some stranger's going to come riding in, and our Annie will take a look at him and *pow!* We'll get a phone call from Vegas from the happy couple."

Susan pretended to shudder. "That's horrible."

"That's the way it's gonna happen, and we both know it."

"Vegas?"

"One of those little chapels on the Strip."

"Not with a total stranger. Annie's not the impulsive type."

"We all are," Jack said, "given the right circumstances."

"Nope," she said with conviction, "not Annie. She's too level-headed for that."

"Our girl's changing—"

"She is not." *Don't lie, Susan Mary Frances Galloway Aldrin. Isn't that exactly what you said to Annie in her kitchen?*

"Take another look, Suze. This isn't the same woman who was Kevin's wife."

Tears filled her eyes. She wasn't the type of woman who gave in to her feelings easily—at least, not when anyone could see her. "I don't want things to change." At least, not in a way that was beyond her control. "Dad's gone, and so is Kevin, and my mother isn't getting any younger . . . Who knows what's around the next corner. I've had enough." She struggled to rein in her emotions. "I've just had enough change to last a lifetime."

"You sound like Claudia."

She laughed despite herself. "That's a terrible thing to say."

"You know I love your mother, but if she had her way, we'd all be watching Lawrence Welk on a black-and-white TV. Can't do it, Suze. Life keeps finding a way."

She understood what he was saying but she wasn't ready to accept it.

"I wish we could stop time . . . just stay the way we are right now." She took his hand and kissed each callused fingertip. "Is that so much to ask?"

"No," said her husband of twenty years. "Not too much at all."

Hall hated it when Susan was right. They had been friends since grade school, and her taste in women was a hell of a lot better than his. Women had been interested in him since his voice changed. That had never been a problem. Picking the right one for the long haul—well, that was something else again.

When he married Margaux straight out of med school, Susan had told him it would never work, but he refused to listen. Six years later when he was getting ready to walk down the aisle with Denise, Susan had waggled her finger under his nose and ordered him to think very carefully about what he was doing, because she absolutely refused to buy him a third wedding present. She had made a joke of it, but they both knew she meant every word. She was kind enough not to mention that fact when he married Yvonne.

Funny thing was, each time he had believed the marriage would work. He wanted a family. He wanted a marriage that would last a lifetime. He had been brought up with those values and he still believed in them. His ex-wives were beautiful, accomplished women whose backgrounds and beliefs matched his down to the ground. He made good money as a doctor, so they could pursue their own careers and other interests without worrying about where the next meal was coming from. There had been no screaming fights during any of his marriages, no wide expanses of disappointment or disinterest. In each case the marriage should have worked and worked well, and when he found himself in the middle of an amicable split, nobody was more surprised than Hall and nobody less surprised than Susan Galloway Aldrin.

"You're never going to be happy as long as you're still carrying that torch for Annie," she had told him during the Memorial Day Haddock Fry on the town green. "You need closure, Dr. Talbot, and until you find it, nothing's going to work out for you."

Three months had passed since that conversation, and he was still wondering how in hell to make the first move. How did you tell the woman you'd loved since high school that you knew the reason why she didn't sleep well at night, why she was so determined to keep her flower shop thriving, why she'd sold the beautiful center hall Colonial and all of the furniture in it and moved to a shack by the water? How did you tell her that her husband had asked you for money a few days before he died and that you'd sent him away empty-handed and told yourself you were doing them both a favor when maybe that wasn't strictly true?

Hall had told Kevin it was for his own good, that he had to come clean and figure a way out of the mess he'd made of his life before it was too late. He offered Kevin the name of a financial counselor who could help him figure a way back from the abyss, but it was like talking to the wind off the ocean. Kevin was always a gentleman, even when his back was to the wall. He listened, he thanked Hall for his time, then he turned and walked out of the office. That was the last time Hall saw him alive.

Two days later, thirty-six-year-old Kevin Galloway was dead of a massive heart attack. Kevin left behind a grieving widow, a heartbroken family, and an old family friend who wondered if he was somehow to blame. He couldn't look at Annie without feeling responsible for the sorrow in her beautiful eyes.

Call her, Susan had said. Pick up the damn phone and call her. Stop being the Family Friend and start acting like a man.

Easier said than done, Susie. He didn't even know her new phone number.

He could hear his pal's snort of derision. What's the matter with you, Talbot? Get in your fancy-schmancy Rover and drive over there. Bring a bottle of wine with you and toast her new address.

He glanced at the heavy watch on his left wrist. Ten minutes to midnight. The Family Friend still knew the boundaries. He leaned back in his chair and closed his eyes. The Noonan cesarean had been rescheduled for tomorrow afternoon. Rounds were midmorning. Maybe he would buy a bag of donuts from DeeDee's first batch of the day and bring them over as a low-key housewarming present. It wasn't a bottle of Pouilly-Fuissé, but even the Family Friend had to start somewhere.

She wouldn't stay put. No matter how hard Sam tried to keep her in the sleigh bed, she kept finding a way to slide out of it. Finally he climbed in next to her and blocked her exit with his body. She'd already nearly set the house on fire and then come close to drowning. He wasn't about to test the theory that bad luck came in threes.

The two cats were still at the far corner of the bed, down by the foot. Max was curled up in the hallway, snoring deeply. Outside the ocean crashed rhythmically against the shore while he spent his first night in Shelter Rock Cove in bed with a beautiful woman. They hadn't made love or kissed or held each other close, and yet he felt as if they had shared all of that and more. He had come up here to be alone for the first time in his life while he tried to figure out his next move. The career that had defined his life for so long was dead, and the future—hell, he couldn't see it through the fog.

And then he saw her leaning over a grocery cart in the parking lot of Yankee Shopper, and everything changed. He had made his living playing the odds, balancing the wise choice against the gamble, and he had always come out a winner. But when it came to life, he took few chances. The lives of his brothers and sisters were in his hands, and he wasn't about to screw that up. There had been women, not many but enough, but no one woman who made him feel as if everything that had come before was only a dress rehearsal. Besides, how many women wanted to throw in their lot with a guy who had five kids to raise at age nineteen?

He had watched as his friends met and married. He toasted a trio of godchildren and bought more baby presents than he could count. The wheel kept turning, and after a while he wondered if maybe he was meant to be the helpful big brother, the terrific best friend, the world's best godfather who even endured the "Uncle Sam" jokes with a smile.

Funny how he had finally reached a place where he understood that not every man had a happily-ever-after ending in his future when fate sent The One into his life.

She murmured something in her sleep and shoved her rump up against his side. Her sweet warmth was more intoxicating to him than the champagne she would regret in the morning. He knew how she looked when she stepped from the tub and that she had a tiny birthmark near her right nipple. He knew that she wore a wedding ring on her left hand even though she was a widow and that the guy with the thinning blond hair had seemed taken with her.

Was she sleeping with him? The thought that another

man might have the right to touch her twisted his gut into a painful knot.

And where was her furniture? She didn't strike him as the minimalist type, not with this enormous sleigh bed. The sleigh bed was the property of a sensualist. No doubt about it. The wood was smooth and curved and lustrous. The mattress, high and firm and welcoming. The abundance of pillows belonged to a woman who understood comfort and went out of her way to find it even if the bed took up the entire room.

There was so much he wanted to know. Who did she love? Was she happy? He wondered if Warren Bancroft knew the answers and, if he did, would he share them with Sam?

But tomorrow was still far away. He turned on his side and fitted his body around hers, drew her warmth into his skin, and let the world fall away.

Tomorrow morning they would introduce themselves and go their separate ways, but until the sun rose up over the ocean, the night belonged to them.

Annie opened her eyes, then quickly closed them. Angry beams of sunlight stabbed her in the retinas, the temples, across her forehead, and around the back of her head. She took a deep breath, then tried again. This time the room tilted at an odd angle while her stomach threatened to slide out from under her. Bad idea. She wasn't about to do that again.

The vague memory of an empty stomach and a bottle of supermarket champagne swam into view. That would explain why she felt as though a herd of elephants were learning to tango across her brain. Since when did George and Gracie snore like 747s on takeoff?

Just take it slowly. No sudden movements. All you have to do is get from here to the shower and you'll be okay.

Eyes tightly closed, she rolled over carefully, one little inch at a time, and was about to swing her legs over the side of the bed when she found herself face-to-face with the man she'd met in the Yankee Shopper parking lot yesterday. He was lying there next to her, bare-chested and in jeans, with his face pressed deep into one of her pillows. She glanced down at herself and realized she was wearing his shirt, half-unbuttoned, over her clearly naked body.

"Oh . . . my . . . God!"

He woke up on the last word, just before she let out a scream loud enough to bring the entire Shelter Rock Cove police department to her door.

"Nothing happened," he said. "You're not in any danger."

She felt like someone was blowing up balloons inside her head. "What in hell are you doing in my bed?"

"I was making sure you didn't hurt yourself."

Hurt herself? Just breathing made her fillings hurt. "Ten seconds," she said. "If you're not out of here by the time I count to ten, I'm calling the police."

He swung his legs from the bed and stood up in the hallway. "You got drunk. You took a bath. Your robe caught fire, and then you almost drowned in the bathtub."

"Please." It was hard to look dignified when you were nursing the mother of all hangovers. "Do you really expect me to believe that?"

He met her eyes. "Yes."

The smell of scorched fabric . . . the dream about him carrying a flaming robe . . . the sight of him plunging that robe into the bathroom sink . . . "I thought I dreamed it."

"The robe's hanging over the shower rod, and I used all of your towels to sop up the water on the floor." A grin tugged at the corners of his mouth. "And don't worry about the front door. I'll take care of it as soon as the hardware store opens up."

She groaned and fell back against the pillows. "What happened to the front door?"

"I didn't have a choice," he said. The grin widened. "Good thing I took kick-boxing."

Another awful thought, one even worse than the kicked-in front door and the ruined robe, occurred to her. "You were in my bathroom last night."

He nodded. "Yep."

"And you—" She couldn't finish the sentence. It was too horrible.

"I tried not to look," he said as the grin turned into a downright smile, "but I'm only human."

She sat up, tugging at the shirt, wishing it covered her from neck to toes. "Then you got what you deserved," she snapped. "I'm ten pounds overweight and I haven't done a sit-up since 1997." Each word reverberated through her cranium like gunshot.

"You're beautiful."

"You're nuts."

He said nothing, just watched as she coiled her tangle of hair into a knot on top of her head. Her fingers felt disconnected from the rest of her aching, queasy body, and she fumbled about, growing clumsier with each second that passed.

"Are you going to stand there blocking the doorway all day?"

"You had a bad night," he said. "I want to make sure you don't have a worse morning."

"I can take care of myself, thank you."

"You weren't too good at it last night."

"Listen," she said with as much dignity as she could muster, "I'm sure you'll understand that making polite conversation with a strange man who saw me drunk and naked in the bathtub is more than I can handle in my current condition. Now, if you'll step out of the way, I'd like to make it into the bathroom before I disgrace myself any further—"

She must have looked as green around the gills as she felt, because he stepped aside immediately, and she made it to the john in the nick of time.

She was deeply embarrassed, visibly angry, and, unless Sam missed his guess, badly hung over. The last face she would want to see when she came out of that bathroom was the man who had seen her at her worst.

She was also deeply vulnerable to kindness. She radiated loneliness the way some people radiated power, and his own lonely heart responded to it.

He was already in over his head, drunk on the smell of her skin, branded by the feel of her body pressed against his in the heart of the night. He had no words for the way he felt, no easy explanation for what he knew in his bones was more than lust. He was hungry for her, for the sound of her voice, her smell, hungry the way a man would be if he had lost her once and then been lucky enough to regain a piece of heaven.

The feeling scared the hell out of him. He had no job, no home, no glittering prospects on the horizon. He had failed the people who had relied on him to protect their future and he had no way to make it up to them. She'd be better off with the man in the Rover, the one who had looked at her as if she had hung the moon.

The thing to do was bail out now before things went too far. He would call Warren from the road and let him know he wouldn't be using the house and then he would drive north until he found a town where he could disappear. He needed solitude, not complications, and that was one thing he would never find here in Shelter Rock Cove. Not now.

He opened the door to his truck and dug out a faded brown sweater stashed in among his things. He slipped it on over his head then snapped his fingers for Max who was lying on the front porch watching him.

"Come on, Max," he called to the dog. "Let's go."

No response at all from Max. He didn't even blink.

Sam snapped his fingers again.

Max refused to budge. The dog rested his head on his forelegs and wagged his tail.

"You, too, huh?"

Max wagged his tail harder. Nothing short of filet mignon was going to move him from that spot. The place felt like home to him, and the dog saw no good reason to leave.

And that was that.

Life's big decisions weren't always made after days of somber deliberation. Sometimes a man just got lucky, and his dog made the decision for him. The woman with the sad blue eyes had cast a spell over both him and Max, and only the dog was smart enough to know they should wait around a while and see how it played out.

Sam climbed into the truck and gunned the engine. He hoped the hardware store opened early.

Once Annie's stomach finally decided to quit doing somersaults, she washed her face, brushed her teeth, and was about to leave the bathroom when she noticed her beautiful green robe hanging over the shower rod. The sight sent a chill up her spine.

Half of the sash was charred black, as was a six-inch swath on the left side of the robe. Annie's fingers trembled as she folded the robe and tossed it into the tiny trash can next to the sink. How many floral arrangements had she sold over the years meant for victims of house fires? The number was well into triple digits. A misplaced cigarette. Faulty wiring. Candles left unattended.

An idiot woman with too much champagne and too little common sense.

He hadn't exaggerated. If anything, he had soft-pedaled the story. The man had saved her life—yes, probably saved it twice if her hangover was any indication of her level of inebriation—and she had railed at him as if he'd committed a crime against humanity. So what if he had seen her naked. The sight of her unclothed body was hardly likely to send him into a fit of wild desire. The man had been too busy keeping her from either going up in flames or under water to waste any time on lust.

At the very least she owed him an apology, not to mention a home-cooked breakfast.

He wasn't in the living room, the bedroom, or the kitchen. The spare room was stacked high with boxes. An engine roared to life in her driveway, and she flew out the back door in time to see him turn the corner and disappear.

Great going, Galloway. The man saves your life, and you send him packing.

She started back inside, shivering in the brisk morning air. It was probably for the best. She had more on her plate these days than she could handle. Besides, he might be married with five kids, just as she'd imagined yesterday in the parking lot. She could just hear the story he would tell his wife. *Yeah, she finally woke up, and can you believe it? She didn't even bother to thank me for saving her life.*

"Idiot," she muttered to herself as she climbed the three stairs that led to the back door. Why was she getting herself all tied up in knots over a stranger? It must be last night's champagne that had her emotions rippling so close to the surface. She wasn't one of those women whose eyes teared up over babies and kittens and sappy love songs. She drew her arm across her eyes, wetting the sleeve of his shirt. It smelled like him, a touch of citrus, a touch of spice, a touch of something indefinable. Her bed probably smelled like him, too. The thought made her go weak in the knees.

So do a load of wash and put yourself out of your misery.

There was nothing like housework to bring a woman back down to earth. A capful of Tide and some hot water, and these ridiculous fantasies would be history. She reached for the doorknob and heard a joyous bark. Max? It couldn't be! She turned in time to see the yellow Lab bounding around the corner of the house, headed straight in her direction. He leaped against her, almost knocking her into the kitchen with the force of his affections. Every excited yip was like nails on a blackboard, but she'd never been happier to feel more miserable in her life.

If Max was still here, that meant Max's owner would be coming back, and she would be able to thank him properly for saving her life. And she wouldn't even be naked.

She settled Max in the living room with half a slice of leftover pizza, cleaned George and Gracie's litterbox, then set out to perform a miracle. It was going to take every trick in her beauty arsenal to erase the effects of the night before, but she was determined to give it her best shot. She hadn't devoured all those issues of *Vogue* and *In Style* magazines for nothing.

Ceil's comments about her well-padded form still stung. She rooted through the pile of clothes on her bed in search of something that would make her round body look long and skinny. George and Gracie watched from their perch on the windowsill as the bed all but disap-

peared beneath a mountain of discards. She finally managed to dig up a flattering pair of black bootleg pants and
her favorite red sweater, the one that hung long enough
to camouflage those treacherous hips and thighs.

She wrote down "full-length mirror" on a notepad and
underlined it twice. Standing on the closed toilet seat to
see her reflection in the bathroom mirror would get old
very fast. She put the finishing touches on her hair. Not
great, she thought, but adequate. Her hair was still long
and it was still curly and it would probably always look
like an untended garden. She pressed her hand on the top
of her head in an attempt to flatten some of the puffy
places, but they sprang back the second she let go. She
had been born with big hair and she would die with big
hair.

Annie popped an Altoid in her mouth then peeked out
the living room window. Maybe he had left Max behind
as a housewarming present.

At eight twenty-two, Annie told herself to get away
from the window and do something useful. A few dozen
cardboard boxes waited in the spare room, clamoring for
her attention. It wouldn't hurt to unpack a few while she
waited. Besides, that would put the whole ridiculous thing
into perspective. *Oh, hi,* she would say when he finally
showed up. *I was so busy that I didn't even realize you
were gone.*

At eight-forty, she refilled George and Gracie's water
dishes, replenished their supplies of cat chow, then gathered up her tote bag, wallet, and extra sweater and headed
for the back door. She might as well go to work. She
didn't have time to do the front door repair herself, but it
would hold until evening.

"How do you feel about flower shops?" she asked Max.
He could be the store mascot as long as he didn't find
blossoms as appetizing as pepperoni pizza.

Max cocked an ear and barked.

Annie winced. "Max, if you knew about hangovers, you wouldn't do that to me."

Max wagged his tail and barked again, three times in quick succession, then ran to the front door as a black Trooper with New York plates came to a stop at the edge of her driveway.

She opened the back door, and Max burst out in a frenzy of barking and what she assumed to be the canine equivalent of high-fives as his owner rounded the corner of the house.

"I'm sorry," she said, meeting him halfway. The words tumbled out of her unchecked. "You really did save my life. I don't know how I can ever thank you for what you did." Not the elegant response she had planned, but at least it was heartfelt.

He stopped a few feet away from her. He held two large white paper bags aloft and out of Max's reach. "How're you feeling?" His manner was a little subdued, but who could blame him. She hadn't exactly been Miss Congeniality so far this morning.

"I'll live, but I doubt I'll be drinking champagne again any time soon."

"You might think twice about the candles, too."

She shivered at the memory of her ruined robe. "I don't know what would have happened if you hadn't been there."

"Max sounded the alarm," he said, neatly sidestepping her gratitude. "He ran up to your front porch and tried to scratch his way through the door." He told her about the red glow behind the bathroom window and the smell of smoke. "So far I've managed to trash the inside of your car and wreck your front door. That's one hell of an introduction to your new neighbor."

The fishing rods in the back of the truck. The New

York license plates. The fact that he even knew Bancroft Road existed. "You're Warren's friend?"

"Guilty."

"I thought you were old and retired."

"I thought you were just old."

"Annie Galloway," she said, extending her right hand over Max's furry yellow head. "I own Annie's Flowers in town."

"Sam Butler." He hesitated just long enough for her to notice. "On sabbatical."

"So you're not retired."

"At thirty-five?" His quick burst of laughter was tinged with something dark. "Nothing that permanent."

Their hands were still clasped tightly. Neither one was willing to be the first to break the contact. An edgy current of warmth seemed to move between them. Since Kevin's death, other men had approached her—good-looking men, kind men, interesting men, men she had known and liked forever—but not one of them had ever made her feel she wanted to bury her face against his chest and breathe deeply.

You did that last night, don't you remember? You slept with your nose pressed against the side of his neck, and he held you and wouldn't let go.

She liked the way his hand felt clasping hers. So solid and warm. His fingers were rough, a little callused. A workman's hands. Hands that would know their way around a woman's body.

Get a grip, Galloway. Just because there was a man in your bed last night doesn't mean there was a Man in your Bed. Save your fantasies for Friday nights and the Romance Channel.

But she met his eyes and something clicked into place and it was as if she had been waiting all her life for that moment. It was the difference between black-and-white and Technicolor, except that it wasn't a movie; it was her life. One second she was living her life in the half-sleep that she'd called living for so long, and the next second her blood was bubbling through her veins and her temperature was rising and the world exploded in colors and sounds and smells she had all but forgotten existed. She knew there was no turning back, not even if she wanted to.

Sam probably would have stood there in the middle of her yard with her hand in his for a week or two if Max hadn't decided enough was enough. The dog made a running leap for one of the two white paper bags Sam had clutched in his left hand, and it took some quick maneuvering to keep the donuts from going the way of last night's pepperoni pizzas.

"Good ol' Max," he said with a shake of his head, and she laughed and reached for one of the bags.

"You went to DeeDee's!" she said, peering inside.

"Me and everyone else in town. They were lined up out the door."

"If you think that's bad, you should see the line on Sunday morning. Father Luedtke threatened to say mass there one day. He thinks he'll triple attendance."

The soft approachable woman he'd first met in the parking lot of Yankee Shopper was back. He thought he'd lost her behind the slicked-back hair and sleek outfit. Her wild mane was brushed back from her face and twisted into a heavy coil. Only a few wispy curls around her forehead and temples had managed to escape. Her lush curves were masked by black pants and a long red sweater with a metal zipper down the front. Her freckles were hidden behind some kind of light makeup, as were the shadows beneath those dark blue eyes. As lovely as she looked right now, she had been infinitely more beautiful last night when she was naked in his arms.

"DeeDee's donuts are legendary around here," she said, ushering him into the postage-stamp-sized kitchen.

"A baker's dozen," he said. "I had to wait for the powdered sugars."

"You're off to a good start. First day here and you homed right in on the best bakery in town."

"Actually it's not my first day in Shelter Rock. I spent a few weeks here when I was seventeen. I probably put away a few hundred of her raspberry jellies."

"You're kidding!" She turned toward him, coffee filter waving between her fingers. "Aren't you?"

"Strange thing to kid about."

"This is such a tiny town. I'm surprised I don't remember you."

"Warren kept our noses to the grindstone. There wasn't much time to mingle with the townies."

"Still, if you hung around DeeDee's, I'm sure we must've crossed paths at least once."

"You probably had so many boyfriends hanging around you wouldn't have noticed the new guy in town."

"Just one," she said, "and I married him."

The poor bastard was dead, and Sam still envied him.

"Nancy told me," he said. "I'm sorry."

Her only acknowledgment was a slight nod of her head. "Stay here long enough and you'll know everything there is to know about everyone in town."

"All she told me was that you were a widow."

She faked a shudder. "I hate that word. I keep waiting for someone to call me the Widow Galloway and then I'll be forced to do something violent."

"I've been called a hell of a lot worse than the Widow Galloway."

She looked at him then burst into laughter. If possible,

he found himself more charmed than before. Her laugh was rich and full and as real as she was.

"Ouch!" She winced and closed her eyes. "Cheap champagne should come with a warning label."

"Other than the head, is everything okay?" *Do you feel it, too, Annie Galloway, or am I the only one?*

He watched, mesmerized, as color flooded her throat and cheeks.

"Mostly I feel embarrassed," she said. *We spent the night together, and I don't have the slightest idea what happened between us.*

"No reason to be."

She lifted a brow. "I got drunk in my bathtub and set fire to my robe. Sounds like two pretty good reasons to me." *I wish I could remember how it felt in your arms.*

"You dodged a bullet. You should be happy." *I can still smell your perfume on my skin.*

"I wouldn't have dodged anything if you hadn't come along."

"I'd like to take the credit, but as I said, Max was the one who sounded the alarm."

"I don't think Max put out the fire." *My hands are shaking. Can you believe that? I'm thirty-eight years old, and my hands are trembling like a girl's.* "You saved my life. I'm not sure I can ever thank you enough for that."

"You just did."

"I wasn't very nice to you this morning."

"You weren't that bad."

"I shouldn't have yelled at you."

"At least you didn't hit me in the head with a lamp."

"I wish you'd stop making me laugh," she said. "My head might fall off."

Your laugh is as real as you are, Annie Galloway. I wish you'd never stop. "Coffee, aspirin, and donuts. World's best hangover remedy."

She glanced down at the filter in her hand. "Coffee! I knew I was forgetting something. Let me get a pot started for us before the donuts get cold."

He popped a piece of donut in his mouth, then broke off another piece.

"Here you go."

She was juggling coffee filter and measuring spoon. "Just a sec," she said. "Let me—"

"Open," he said. "Grab 'em while they're hot."

"I'll just be a—"

He popped the sweet piece of donut into her open mouth and laughed at the way her eyes widened with surprise that was followed quickly by delight. A spot of white sugar clung to her lower lip, and he brushed it away with the tip of his index finger. Her eyes never left his. There was no guile in them, no pretense. Just curiosity and the same touch of wonder he felt growing inside his chest. The atmosphere between them was charged. He swore he could hear the pop and sizzle of neurons dancing in the air.

I want to kiss you, Annie Galloway. Don't turn me away.

He dipped his head toward her. She swayed closer.

Don't ask, she thought. *Don't give me the chance to say no.*

Their lips touched lightly then touched again.

"You taste like sugar," he said.

"You taste like raspberry jam." Were donuts occasions of sin anywhere besides Shelter Rock Cove? She would have to ask Father Luedtke about that.

He reached into the bag and produced another donut. "This one's strawberry."

The temptation to indulge was powerful, but she stayed strong.

"I'd better not. Once I start I might not stop."

He earned full marks for letting the straight line slide by without the easy double entendre, but somehow the temperature in the room still managed to rise another degree.

"You're not one of those lettuce-leaves-and-water types, are you?"

"With these hips? I was issued a weight warning yesterday and I'm thinking Ceil just might be right."

"This Ceil must have a problem with her eyesight." *I know how you look beneath that red sweater, Annie Galloway. I know how you feel.*

"Ceil works register one at Yankee Shopper and she doesn't exactly mince words with her customers. She's right. I have put on a few pounds."

He described Ceil down to the mole under her chin. "That's terrible," she said. "You shouldn't mention things like moles and wattles when you describe a woman."

"Why not?" he asked. "It's not as if she doesn't have both."

"It's rude."

"Rude? That woman knew more about me than the IRS does."

"Ceil does keep a finger on the pulse of Shelter Rock."

"You mean she keeps her eye to the keyhole."

"Ceil is a little nosy."

"I'm surprised she didn't ask who I'm sleeping with."

"Good thing I'm not sleeping with anyone or—" *OHMYGOD, Annie, what have you done?*

"Good thing," he said, not missing a beat, "because I'm not either."

Her entire body registered his words in one giant rush of almost ridiculous pleasure. Their eyes met and held above the bag of DeeDee's donuts. If she didn't know better, she would swear she heard music somewhere in the distance.

"Good thing," she repeated.

A very good thing.

FIVE

Claudia was beside herself by the time Hall walked into Annie's Flowers and asked if Annie was around. He had seen her in various states of emotional anxiety before, but this one was off the chart.

"I haven't seen or heard from her all morning, and it's almost ten o'clock," Claudia said, tugging the leaves off a perfectly good yellow rose. "She should have been here by eight forty-five at the latest."

"She didn't call?" he asked, wondering where Claudia's diastolic pressure was right about now.

"Not a word!" Her voice trembled. "And she probably doesn't even have phone service turned on yet in that ridiculous new house of hers. I told her she should keep the cellular service, but she wouldn't listen to me."

She can't afford it, Claudia. She's lucky she has a roof over her head.

"I don't know what on earth Warren was thinking, selling her that miserable little place. I intend to give him a piece of my mind next time he shows his face around here."

"Warren cut her a terrific deal," Hall said, editing much of what he really wanted to say. It was, after all, none of his business. "She seems happy to me."

"She's made a terrible mistake," Claudia said in a tone heavy with foreboding. "She'll never be happy in that place." She ripped another leaf from the rose. "Never!"

He was well acquainted with Claudia's occasional outbursts. He remembered them from his high school days when she could clear the basement of Susan's friends with one lift of her left eyebrow. Just the hint of an outburst was enough to send everyone running. She didn't unnerve him anymore. Mostly he felt sorry for her. She had lost her identity when John died. Everything she was had been tied up in being a wife and mother. She was at loose ends with half of her job description no longer valid, and that often manifested itself in the close scrutiny of her grown children's behavior. Needless to say, she considered Annie one of her own and watched over her with hawklike intensity that had only increased since Kevin's death.

Hall wasn't much in the mood for hawklike intensity that morning.

"Why don't I drive over and see if everything's all right?" he suggested, eager for an easy exit line. He still had a few free hours before he was due at the hospital, a rare occurrence for him, even on a Saturday.

"Would you?" Claudia's face lit up with gratitude, and he felt like a louse. Ulterior motives could do that to a man. "I would do it myself, but somebody has to watch the store. We're expecting a huge shipment for the Sorenson-Machado wedding tomorrow, and I'd better stay here and make sure everything's there."

"My pleasure," he said, meaning every word. "She probably started unpacking and lost track of time."

"I'm sure that's it," Claudia agreed. "Anne is extremely

punctual." A beat pause. "Most of the time. I'm sure there's a good reason."

He turned to leave, but a hand on his forearm stopped him.

"You went to DeeDee's for us!" Claudia exclaimed, laying claim to the bag of still-warm donuts. "Aren't you the sweetest thing?"

Since Annie didn't have a kitchen table or chairs yet, she and Sam carried their coffee and donuts out to the front porch where they could enjoy the morning sunshine. The ever-vigilant Max began dancing for donuts, and Sam, obviously a pushover, rewarded him with a chunk torn from a glazed whole-wheat.

"That will go well with the pizza I gave him for breakfast," Annie observed. "I don't know how you're going to reintroduce him to plain old dog food."

"I already told him not to get used to pizza and donuts but I don't think he believed me."

She sipped her coffee, savoring the sweet warmth against her tongue. Had there ever been a more perfect morning? Sam Butler was right. All she had needed to vanquish her champagne hangover was caffeine, sugar, and two thousand calories' worth of DeeDee's donuts.

Max finished his whole-wheat, then eyed her strawberry jelly with mournful desire.

"Don't even think about it," she warned him. "You're as bad as George and Gracie."

Sam glanced at her over his mug of black coffee. "George and Gracie?"

"My cats. You must have seen them last night."

He grimaced and gestured toward his right shin. "See them? I still have the scars."

"They scratched you?"

"Nothing serious," he said. "I don't think they appreciated sharing the bed with me."

"They're a tad territorial."

"Territorial." There was that great smile again. "And Max is just high-spirited."

"Let me see."

"It's just a scratch."

"Cat scratches can be nasty. You should put some antiseptic on it."

"Don't worry. I'm fine."

"I have some Neosporin in the medicine cabinet. It'll only take a second."

He put his coffee mug on the railing, then lifted his right pants leg above the ankle. "See? No big deal." Nothing but a faint red line above his snowy white sock.

"I'd still put something on it if I were you." Max sidled up to Annie and settled down with his head in her lap. "For a while there I thought you'd left Max behind as a housewarming present."

"I tried to take him with me, but he refused to leave. I think he's in love with you." *I wanted to grab Max and get the hell out of here before it was too late.*

She scratched the dog behind the ear, and Max's eyes closed in blissful enjoyment. "We've bonded," she said. "I think it was the pizza."

He felt her touch along his nerve endings, same as Max. "Speaking of pizza, if you'll leave me your truck today, I'll take care of the cleanup."

"You don't have to do that."

"I can take care of it this morning after I fix your front door."

"How will I get to work?"

"You have to work today?"

"Saturday's a big day in my business." Weddings,

birthday parties, anniversary celebrations, all of which required mountains of beautiful blooms.

"Take my truck."

"Then you'll be stuck here."

"We'll trade back when I'm finished."

"You're not going to take no for an answer, are you?"

"Not this time."

"My tools are stashed in the shed behind the house. I must have a half-dozen jars of nails and screws back there, too. I was planning on fixing the door when I came home tonight."

"You know your way around a ballpeen hammer?"

She flexed a muscle and laughed. "Good thing, too, because my husband had no talent for home repairs."

"That's how I met Warren Bancroft."

She looked at him over the rim of her coffee mug. "Doing home repairs?"

"Boat repairs," he said. "I was still in high school and working part-time at the marina near the old World's Fair grounds in Queens. I was your typical smartass city kid who thought he knew everything. Warren made it his business to prove me wrong."

"So he took you under his wing, too." She told him about the Bancroft Scholarship that had enabled her to obtain a Bachelor of Fine Arts degree at Bowdoin College down in Brunswick.

"I'm surprised he never had kids," Sam said, polishing off the last donut in the bag.

"He made up for it in wives," Annie said then laughed at the look of surprise on Sam's face. "Don't tell me you didn't know about the wives."

"We never talked about personal stuff."

"Male conversation," she said with a sigh. "Name, rank, and serial number."

"You forgot baseball scores."

"You do know you're living in his sister Ellie's old house, don't you?"

"We managed to cover that."

She gestured over her shoulder. "Did you know he grew up right here?"

"In your house?"

"Four rooms, eight Bancrofts. Boggles the imagination, doesn't it?"

She told him about Warren's parents, first-generation Irish who had moved up from Gloucester to fish the friendlier waters off Shelter Rock Cove. She wove the story of a family deeply rooted in tradition, who didn't understand why their eldest son kept saying that there was a better way.

He loved the sound of her low-pitched voice. She hit her consonants precisely, then elided her vowels like the true Yankee daughter she was. There was a musical rhythm to her speech that seemed to turn his brain into cotton candy. Her face came alive as she spoke of the sea, an odd mixture of love and sorrow. He tried to concentrate on Warren's history, but it was her own that engaged his curiosity.

She was around his age, too young to be a widow. He tried to imagine her as a young bride, a contented wife, a loving mother. Did she have children? He hadn't seen any evidence of them. No bronzed baby shoes or graduation pictures on the mantel over the fireplace. He knew that marriages were like fingerprints; there were no two alike. He wondered if hers had been close and companionable or volatile and sexually charged. Maybe they had been one of those couples who inhabited the same space but not the same lives. Had she been happy? She liked to laugh and did it better than most. He couldn't imagine her in a laughless marriage. He hoped her memories were all good ones.

Annie knew he wasn't listening to her words, but she had no doubt that she had his full attention. When she leaned to her left to pour more coffee into her mug, his eyes followed her. She could feel his gaze on the curve of her breasts, her thighs, the fine lines at the corners of her eyes. The intensity of that gaze enveloped her like an embrace, and after a bit she let her words drift away on the gentle breeze off the ocean. Who needed words when you could sit on the front porch together in the morning sunshine and know there was no other place in the world you'd rather be.

A few minutes later, a donutless Hall made the turn onto Bancroft Road toward Annie's house. What could he have said to Kevin's mother? *Sorry the donuts aren't for you, Claudia, but I'm hoping to use them to seduce your former daughter-in-law.*

Seduce? The word actually made him laugh out loud. Hell, at this point he'd settle for a lobster roll and a movie with Annie Galloway.

Annie's truck was parked down at the curb, and he wondered why she hadn't bothered to pull it into the garage or at least park it in the driveway. He didn't notice the New York plates until he pulled in behind it. Had Sean Galloway driven up from Albany to help his sister-in-law with the move? That made sense. Sean was one of the good guys, the kind who would give up part of his Labor Day weekend to be there for family.

Too bad that wasn't Sean sitting on the front porch with Annie, staring at her over a bag of DeeDee's damn donuts. A code blue alarm went off inside his chest when he realized she was staring right back at the guy, staring and leaning toward him with the kind of body language women used so well when the moment was right. Where had he seen that junker SUV before? That couldn't be the guy whose pizza-eating mutt trashed Annie's Trooper yes-terday. There was something about the guy that seemed vaguely familiar, but Hall couldn't quite place him.

He pasted a fake smile on his face as he walked toward them, but only the dog seemed to register his presence. Hall coughed discreetly.

"Hall!" Annie leaped to her feet. She seemed startled, disoriented, like a woman waking from a dream.

"Sorry to drop by without calling." He used the upbeat, slightly impersonal tone he employed when he made rounds at the hospital with the residents in tow. "I stopped in at the store, and Claudia was—"

"Oh, no!" Annie looked at the man's watch strapped to her left wrist. "The Sorenson flowers are due in, and Clau-dia doesn't have a clue what to look for." She dusted pale flecks of powdered sugar from her sleek red sweater and black pants. She looked better than he had ever seen her before, glowing and radiant. "You don't know Claudia in a crisis."

She gathered up her tote bag and other assorted carry-alls, then turned toward the guy with the New York li-cense plates. "Thanks for the donuts," she said. "I hate to run like this and leave you in the lurch."

"I told you I'd take care of everything," he said. "Don't worry."

The man rose to his feet, and Hall noted that the guy was a good two inches shorter than he was. He wasn't above taking petty satisfaction in that fact.

"Make sure George and Gracie don't escape," she said to Shorty. "You can use one of the white bowls by the sink if Max needs some water."

"Don't worry," Shorty said. "I'll be finished before you get to the store."

The smile she gave him was the one Hall had spent

most of his adult life dreaming of, and the bastard took it as his due.

She turned to Hall and became platonic friendship personified. "Thanks so much for driving over here," she said. "You have single-handedly saved the floral integrity of the Sorenson-Machado nuptials. I owe you one."

"If that's the case, then how about dinner tomorrow night?" The words came out as easily as if they had been rehearsed, and in a way they had. It had taken him almost two years to get up the nerve.

She struggled not to glance over at the boy from New York City. "I really shouldn't—"

"You'll need a break from unpacking by then." He sounded smooth and self-assured, the direct opposite of how he was feeling. "We'll go to Cappy's for the fish fry. I'll get you back here early."

Her hesitation stung like a slap in the face, but it was his own damned fault for putting her on the spot like this in front of her new friend.

"Listen," he said, taking a step back from the happy pair, "bad timing on my part. We can always make it some other—"

"No," she said, looking flustered and embarrassed and lovely all at the same time, "Cappy's is a great idea. I can meet you there around seven."

And there you had it. With one smooth move, she turned a date into something a whole lot less.

One quick look at Shorty, and she was gone.

They both watched as she ran across the damp front yard and climbed into her aging SUV. They both waited until her car disappeared around the curve, then turned to each other.

"Sam Butler." Shorty put out his right hand.

The guy not only looked familiar, he sounded familiar, too. "Have we met before?"

"I don't know," Shorty said, his hand still outstretched. "You tell me."

It wasn't often that a stranger made Hall feel inadequate, but Shorty managed it with six little words. Time to regroup and approach from a different angle.

"Hall Talbot." Hall extended his own right hand. He waited until they clasped hands. "*Doctor* Hall Talbot."

Sometimes a man had to play his best cards early in the game.

It took Sam all of ten seconds to peg the good doctor as the man he had seen with Annie in the parking lot yesterday. The same polished good looks, same regal bearing, same sense of entitlement that made Sam want to knock him down a peg or three. A knee-jerk reaction left over from his teenage years back in Queens when the gulf between the haves and have-nots had seemed impossible to bridge.

"Don't stay on my account," Hall Talbot said with classic lock-jawed Yankee precision. "I'll close up for Annie."

"Sounds great," Sam said. "After you fix the door, lock up and leave the key under the mat."

He watched as the doctor's gaze finally landed on the kicked-in door. "What happened?"

Good going, Columbo. Took you long enough.

"Minor mishap," Sam said. "I told Annie last night that I'd fix it." He added a little extra spin to the words *last night*. He sounded thirty-five going on fifteen.

He had to hand it to the doctor. That fine old Yankee breeding was a wonder to behold. The man didn't betray any curiosity at all.

"Then I'll leave you to it," Dr. Hall Talbot said with a slight nod of his head. "Good morning."

Sam watched as the guy climbed behind the wheel of his $60,000 Land Rover and drove off.

Max nudged him with his nose. He reached down and scratched the dog behind the ear.

"I'm not impressed either, Max. I had a fancy car once, and look where I ended up."

Was that what Annie Galloway's husband had been like? A tony well-dressed WASP who never lost his cool unless he was playing a game of extreme croquet on the back lawn. Maybe he'd even been a doctor like the one who just got away, well-respected in town, the one they all looked up to, the kind of guy all women dreamed of marrying.

He glanced back at the small cottage. Scratch that thesis. A doctor's wife wouldn't end up sharing eight hundred square feet of precious floor space with a giant bed, two cats, and little else.

Then again, people didn't always get what they expected out of this life or even what they deserved. Somewhere along the way her life must have taken a sharp turn off the beaten path and led her to this place, and he couldn't help but wonder how she felt about that.

He knew all about those sharp turns and where they took you. Who would've thought he'd end up halfway through his life with nothing to show for the years?

There had never been time to pursue a wife and family of his own, not while the futures of his brothers and sisters had been his responsibility. He had learned to be the master of the casual relationship. He knew how to end things before they went too far. No angry scenes. No broken hearts. The woman in question was usually as ready to say goodbye as he was. Most women were when they knew there was no future involved.

No regrets. That was the funny thing. It was over once they said goodbye, and he never looked back. One day, when the time was right and he was free from family responsibilities, he would meet the woman he was meant to be with, and everything would fall into place: the engagement, the big wedding, the two point five kids, and the corner house on a big lot with the minivan in the driveway. He would have it all: a great career, a wonderful wife, terrific children, and an extended family of brothers and sisters who couldn't wait to babysit.

He never figured that he would end up as a thirty-five-year-old unemployed, never-married, flat-broke freeloader on the verge of falling in love.

Back out now, he told himself as he set to work on fixing the front door. *Let the good doctor take the home-field advantage.* Sam had always been good at ending things before they went too far. How hard could it be to end them before they began?

It was ten-fifteen when Annie burst into the store.

"We were going to send out a search-and-rescue squad," said Sweeney, the woman who ran the Artisans Co-op, which rented display and work space from Annie. She was hanging stained-glass suncatchers in the main display window. "Claudia has been tearing the heads off the roses."

Annie groaned. "That's what I was afraid of." She glanced around the shop. "Where is she?"

Sweeney gestured toward the back. "Raking the delivery girl from Bangor Blooms over the coals."

"Please don't tell me the Sorenson order was botched."

Sweeney shrugged her caftaned shoulders. "Don't know, dear, but the delivery girl said she was getting a migraine."

Annie tossed her bags behind the counter. "I'd better get back there and see what's happening. Ring the bell if anyone comes in, would you, Sweeney?"

"I'm on top of things," Sweeney said from her perch on the stepstool, then threw back her head and laughed.

Annie, who was used to Sweeney's bad jokes, groaned and then hurried past display cases, various work areas, and the tiny kitchen where Claudia kept the soup pot simmering all winter long. The decision to lease floor space to the Co-op was one of the best ones Annie ever made. Not only did the income help her own bottom line, but also she found she loved the company. Shelter Rock Cove had a thriving artistic community of weavers, potters, watercolorists, sculptors, glassblowers, fiber artists, and everything in between. The ever-changing displays helped make Annie's Flowers a popular stop for both tourists and locals.

She found Claudia on the back steps, clipboard in hand, checking their order against what Bangor Blooms had actually delivered. Her brow was furrowed, and the girl from Bangor, who was still unloading crates of flowers, didn't look too happy.

"Sorry I'm late," Annie said as she joined them. Claudia didn't look up. "Did they remember the anthuriums?"

"The anthuriums are here," Claudia said, ripping the top sheet with the force of her checkmark.

"Good," said Annie, a bit surprised by the vehemence of Claudia's response. "And the ginger blossoms? We ordered—"

"Done."

Claudia was obviously annoyed with Annie for being late and was letting her know it in no uncertain terms. She had seen Claudia in one of her moods many times over the years, and they always passed as swiftly as they came, leaving only tiny bruises behind. Annie left her mother-in-law to her inventory and pitched in to help the delivery girl finish unloading the crates of flowers.

"She scares me," the girl whispered to Annie as they both tugged on a huge box of plumeria.

"She scares everybody," Annie whispered back, and the girl tried not to laugh. "She's all bark and no bite, I promise you."

The girl didn't look convinced, and she continued to give Claudia a wide berth, which, all things considered, was probably a very wise idea.

"I hate to bother you when you're so busy," Sweeney said, poking her head out the door, "but we have a small problem inside with a hospital order."

Claudia looked up from her clipboard. "I'll take it," she said. "Anne seems to have everything in hand out here."

Annie, who wasn't quite sure if she had been complimented or reprimanded, thanked her. "If it's about the McGowan order, let me know," she said to Claudia's retreating back. "They moved her to intensive care and forgot to tell us to hold up on the arrangement until she's in a private room."

Twenty minutes later the girl from Bangor was on her way back to the turnpike, and Annie was tucking her bags into the storage bin under the order desk when Claudia finally came out with it.

"I was worried sick about you today, Anne," she said. "When it got to be nine-thirty and you still hadn't shown up, why I—" Her voice quavered, and she paused to draw in a breath. "The least you could have done was phone."

You know I love you, Claudia. Why are we always at loggerheads these days? "I'm so sorry," Annie began, choosing her words with care, "but—"

"You could have used your cellular."

"I don't have a cellular any longer, remember? I cancelled it last spring."

"I don't know why you'd do such a ridiculous thing. With all the driving you do, you shouldn't be without a phone. It's a dangerous world, Anne, and—"

"—and cell phones cost an arm and a leg, and it was time for me to cut costs. I explained this to you at the time."

"Cut costs? The shop is doing splendidly, and you must have pocketed a pretty penny from the sale of the house. Surely you can afford a phone."

"I don't want to talk about this with you, Claudia. I'm sorry if you were worried about me, but that won't be a problem now that my phone service at home is up and running."

Claudia's stern expression softened, which made Annie feel more like a rebellious sixteen-year-old kid than ever. A mother's guilt was a powerful thing, even when it was your late husband's mother wielding the sword.

"I'm a worrier," Claudia said, patting Annie's forearm. "I always was and I always will be. Now that you're in that little house in the back of beyond, you need to be more careful than ever."

"I met my new neighbor last night," Annie said, wondering about the bag of DeeDee's donuts near the cash register. She could feel the extra fat cells settling themselves around her hips and thighs just thinking about more donuts.

Claudia was measuring out lengths of shimmery white satin ribbon. "Susan told me that a New Yorker was moving into Ellie Bancroft's old place." She reached for the shears. "Is he nice?"

Annie told her about their first meeting in the parking lot of Yankee Shopper.

Claudia looked up from what she was doing. "I hope he's going to pay to have your interior cleaned."

"He said he'd take care of it."

"Good," said Claudia, scissoring her way through the glossy ribbon. "You have to set certain standards with a new neighbor. Let them know where your boundaries are. Otherwise you'll wake up one morning and he'll be sitting on your front porch saying, 'What's for breakfast?' and you'll never get rid of him." Claudia looked at her across the litter of ribbon and wire. "Hall brought over some donuts this morning." She pointed her shears in the general direction of the kitchen. "I put them next to the coffeemaker."

Donuts as metaphor. Hall was a local. He knew that DeeDee's donuts were serious business around Shelter Rock Cove, at least among townies their age. The thought gave her a sinking feeling in the pit of her stomach. And now she had a dinner date with him for tomorrow night, all because she was so flustered with Sam Butler's eyes on them that she said yes just to put an end to the discussion. If Hall got the wrong idea, she had nobody to blame but herself.

"Is something wrong?" Claudia asked.

"No," she said. "Nothing at all."

They worked in silence for a while until Sweeney drifted back into the front of the store. Sweeney didn't believe in silence. She was always talking or singing or humming along to the radio she kept hidden somewhere in that enormous caftan of hers. Today she was whistling selections from *The Sound of Music,* and Annie was reasonably sure she would be reaching for the earplugs before Sweeney launched into "Edelweiss."

At a few minutes before one, Annie put down her shears and stretched. "I don't know about you two ladies, but it's my lunchtime. Why don't I go in the back and heat up some soup for us?"

The words were no sooner out of her mouth when the bell over the front door jingled and Sam Butler walked in and the petals hit the fan.

SIX

As soon as he walked through the door, Claudia knew the man would be trouble. She didn't often take an instant dislike to someone, but this time she made an exception. He looked dangerous, as if he knew exactly where they kept the cash box. Just looking at him made her want to hide her jewelry in her shoe.

"Whoa," said Sweeney from her perch on the stepladder. "Wouldn't I like a piece of that."

Claudia glared at the woman. She prayed the man hadn't heard her. What on earth was the matter with the younger generation? Sweeney sounded like one of those tramps on *Sex and the City*. A fifty-year-old tramp.

Annie was halfway to the kitchen, so Claudia stepped forward.

"Can I help you?" she asked him in her most professional tone.

He smiled, and to her dismay, Claudia noted that it was a most extraordinary smile. It seemed to light up his ordinary face in a way that made him almost handsome. Claudia waited for him to say something, but he kept on smiling, and she realized he was looking right past her and straight at Annie, who was standing a few feet behind her with the most ridiculous look on her face.

How long had it been since Annie had looked that young or that pretty? Claudia couldn't remember, and she hated this stranger for having that kind of power over her.

"I brought your house keys," he said. He spoke directly to Annie. Claudia didn't know if he even realized there was anyone else in the shop.

Annie glided forward as if drawn to him by some unseen force. "You didn't have to do that." She sounded so happy, happier than Claudia could remember her sounding in years. "I told you that you could leave them under the mat."

"I'm from New York, remember?" His voice was deep, a little rough. Not at all like Kevin's golden baritone. "I couldn't do it."

A New Yorker? He couldn't possibly be the neighbor Annie had been talking about, could he?

"Helllooooo!" Sweeney called out, waving her staple gun in an attempt to catch their attention. "Isn't anyone going to introduce us? New talent is hard to come by around here, and I'm all for building up the home team."

To his credit, the man looked slightly discomfited, but that was nothing compared to the look of embarrassment on Annie's bright pink face. *Oh, Anne,* she thought sadly. *You always did wear your heart on your sleeve.* Was it really so long ago when a ten-year-old Annie used to follow Kevin around town, just so she could be near him? The memory was etched on Claudia's heart.

"This is Sam Butler," Annie said. "He's renting Ellie Bancroft's place on the water." She placed a hand on Claudia's shoulder. "This is my mother-in-law, Claudia Galloway."

"Beautiful shop you have here," Sam Butler said as he shook her hand.

"It's Annie's shop. She deserves all the credit." She smiled when she said it, although the effort to be gracious cost her dearly. She wanted to bar the door and build a moat around Annie's heart, and the fierceness of her emotions startled her.

Poor Annie had eyes for no one but this Sam Butler as she continued her introductions. "And that vision in paisley is Mary Sweeney. She made the stained-glass inset on our front door and every other beautiful glass piece you see around here."

Sweeney leaned down and pumped his hand. "Just call me Sweeney," she said with one of her trademark lusty laughs. "And I do mean call me." Her dark eyes flickered from Annie to Sam to Annie again, and the last of Claudia's hopes shattered. Sweeney saw it, too.

Annie laughed, and after a moment so did this Butler person. Claudia could manage only the tightest smile. She was grateful when the phone in the work room rang, and she excused herself to answer it.

"I'm sorry," she said to the person on the other end of the line. "Of course I'm listening to you . . . Yes, yes . . . a dozen red . . . long-stemmed . . . no card . . . absolutely . . . I understand . . . We'll have them ready by five o'clock."

She hung up the phone, and her eye was caught by a small photo of Kevin and John tacked to the corkboard over the phone table. Annie had pinned it up there the day the store opened, and there it had stayed for almost twelve years. Sometimes you couldn't see it for the blizzard of notes and orders, but if you looked hard enough you would always find it. The photo had been taken at the end of Kevin's first year in Little League—oh, how that uniform had swamped his skinny body. John called him The Shrimp, and Kevin had despaired ever growing as big and brawny as his father. The years, however, took care of that, and by the time Kevin and Annie married, he looked like a younger version of John with the same towering height, wide shoulders, and ready smile.

They had been alike in other ways, too. They had both loved their family above all, both believed in a world filled with poetry and laughter, and to Claudia's eternal regret, they both died much too soon.

"Oh, John," she whispered, touching the edge of the photo with the tip of her finger. "Why does everything have to change?"

Sam gave Annie her house keys, made a minimum of small talk with a cool Claudia and a very warm Sweeney, then said he'd better get moving.

"I looped Max's leash around the bicycle rack outside," he said. "Knowing Max, that isn't going to hold him for long."

Claudia sniffed loudly, and Annie wished she could stick a planter over her mother-in-law's well-coiffed head. Sweeney watched them quietly with a Cheshire-cat smile on her face. All of this because a man returned the keys to her house.

Annie walked Sam outside. "I don't know what's the matter with them," she said by way of apology. "That was outrageous, even for Sweeney." She shook her head in dismay. "And I won't even try to explain Claudia. She's really a very nice woman, although you'd never know it by the way she acted."

"I didn't stop by to see them," he said. "I came to see you."

"And I really appreciate it. I guess leaving the keys under the mat really wasn't the greatest idea. I—"

"What's the story between you and the doctor?"

"What?" His question left her flat-footed.

"You and the doctor. Is there a story?"

"You don't waste time on small talk, do you?"

"Is there something between the two of you?"

"He's an old friend."

"You're going out with him tomorrow."

"He took me by surprise. I didn't know what to say."

"He thinks it's a date."

"He's wrong."

"Are you sure?"

"I don't think that's any of your business."

"I think it will be."

I'm melting, she thought as she looked deep into his eyes. *Right here in front of the store with Claudia and Sweeney watching.* She was melting just like one of those women in the books Claudia kept hidden under the *TV Guide.* All she needed was the pirate ship and the beautiful dress.

"No," she said at last. "It isn't a date."

"I'm glad."

"So am I." Could you have an out-of-body experience right there on Main Street with everybody watching? Their gazes held for what seemed like forever. She thought he was going to take her hand or maybe even pull her into his arms and kiss her, but he did none of those things. He just looked at her, longer and more deeply than anyone had ever looked at her before, then he unravelled Max's leash from the bike rack and started off down the street, leaving Annie feeling thoroughly kissed just the same.

He walked the way they walked in the city, quickly and with purpose. She had the sense that he knew his relative position to everyone else on the street, and she wondered what had happened in his life to bring him to Warren's house by the water. Men like that had high-powered careers and lovers who wore little black dresses and a single strand of pearls. They didn't show up in Shelter Rock Cove in a beat-up truck with a wild yellow Lab and turn a woman's heart inside out over a bag of donuts and a cup of coffee.

Somebody tapped on the window behind her. She could feel Claudia's and Sweeney's eyes burning holes in the back of her sweater, but she couldn't go back inside. Not until she managed to push all of her unruly emotions back inside her chest where they belonged.

As it was, it took all of her self-control to keep from touching her fingertip to her lips to capture a kiss that never was.

She stood there on the sidewalk until Sam and Max turned the corner from Main to Mariner, and then when the memory of his walk turned the corner after him, she went back inside.

"So where have you been hiding him?" Sweeney demanded the second she stepped into the shop. "He's sure not homegrown."

She tried for cool nonchalance. The way she felt inside was new to her, and she wasn't about to share it with anybody. "He moved into Ellie Bancroft's place yesterday." She reclaimed her wire cutters and took her place behind the counter. "His dog had a run-in with my truck yesterday, and he was making amends." She carefully edited out the champagne, the nudity, and the night he spent in bed with her.

"Can I borrow the beasts for a week or two?" Sweeney asked. "Sounds better than spending another Friday night over a pint at the Yardarm Inn."

"Oh, please," Claudia snapped, tearing the head off a perfectly innocent white lily. "You two sound like teenagers."

Annie moved the basket of blooms out of her mother-in-law's reach. At the rate Claudia was going, they would need to double their orders. Claudia's reaction struck Annie as every bit as over the top as Sweeney's, and she refused to rise to the bait. Instead, she centered herself and gave them more information.

"My front door wouldn't close properly, and Sam offered to fix it for me. I told him to leave the keys under the mat but, as you heard, he wasn't comfortable with that." Clear, concise, factually accurate. They seemed happy with her explanation. Clearly full disclosure was highly overrated.

"No wonder my stomach's growling," Sweeney said, with a glance at the time piece dangling between her breasts from a velvet cord. "What about that soup you mentioned?"

Annie brushed her hands along the sides of her black pants. "I think we have some crackers back there, too."

"And Tabasco sauce?" asked Sweeney.

"Do you think I could live without Tabasco?" She turned toward Claudia. "Do you want your soup with or without hot sauce?"

Claudia reached behind the counter and extracted her purse. "If you don't mind, I think I'll go to Bernie's for a half turkey and brie on rye. I won't be long."

"Don't let her get to you," Sweeney said as soon as the door closed behind Claudia. "If you want him, go for it. She'll come around."

"You know, Sweeney, if you were half as good at marketing your stained glass as you are at managing people's lives, you'd be the next Tiffany."

"I know," said Sweeney with a good-natured laugh. "It's a gift, isn't it?"

A few minutes later they sat down to eat. The sight of the creamy red soup sloshing around the bowl made Annie queasy. Lifting her spoon to her mouth required major effort.

"Migraine or hangover?" Sweeney asked. "My bet is on the latter."

"Cheap champagne on an empty stomach," Annie said, massaging her temples with cautious fingers. "Now I know why I'm not much of a drinker."

"Moderation, honey, in all things but love and chocolate. That's my motto." She rummaged deep into a pocket and withdrew a small bottle. "Industrial-strength Advil and lots of caffeine. That'll set you right."

Of course it wasn't just the hangover that was making Annie's head pound like a steel drum in the Bahamas; it was the shock of seeing Sam Butler walk through the door of Annie's Flowers and onto Claudia's radar screen. Not that you could keep a newcomer secret in Shelter Rock Cove. Annie knew that was downright impossible. Still there was something very unnerving about introducing the man in whose arms you'd slept the night before to your mother-in-law. It wasn't something most sane women would care to repeat.

Sweeney, who had been watching Annie carefully, pushed her bowl aside and leaned across the counter. "So how long have we known each other?"

"I can't remember ever not knowing you." Sweeney's colorful dress and language had been part of the landscape since Annie was a little girl dreaming of a career in the arts herself.

"Then you know I only want the best for you."

"Uh-oh." Annie dusted crumbs from her fingertips then reached for the slender bottle of Tabasco. "That sounds ominous."

"I went down this road myself after number two died, and I know how hard it is to start over again."

"The house will work itself out. I don't know what Claudia's been telling you about it, but—"

"Annie." Sweeney's tone brooked no argument. "We both know I'm not talking about your new house."

Annie pushed her own soup bowl aside and fiddled with her paper napkin. "I think you're jumping the gun."

"Maybe I am," Sweeney conceded, "but I know what I saw, and you can't deny it."

"Really, Sweeney, a relationship is the last thing I'm interested in right now."

"Is it?"

"Of course it is. Between the store and the new house, when would I have time for anything like that?"

"You might be able to fool yourself but you don't fool me. I've seen you tap dance away from Dr. Talbot and the other men who've come calling around here. You didn't do that today, Annie."

"Claudia noticed, too, didn't she?"

"You bet your patootie she did and she's out there right now, trying to figure out what to do about it."

"Claudia is strong-minded, but I don't think she's manipulative."

"Neither do I, sweetie, but I do know she's scared and she's lonely and she's not about to lose you if she can help it."

"Lose me? She's not going to lose me."

"You know what I'm saying. More so than any of her own children, you're her link to her son. She wanted you to turn your big house into a shrine to him the same way she did for John."

Sweeney was right. Selling the house had cut Claudia to the quick. She could only imagine how Claudia would feel if she knew the real reason for the sale.

"I'm not looking to replace Kevin and certainly not with a man I just met yesterday."

"Maybe not, but one fine morning you're going to open your eyes and find out that, like it or not, you're in love. Don't postpone the rest of your life just because you don't want to hurt Claudia."

Annie rested her forehead on the cool wooden countertop. "Can you tell me why life has to be so damn complicated?"

Sweeney threw back her head and laughed. "Honey, if I could tell you that, I'd rule the world."

Annie finished assembling the three bridesmaids' bouquets for the Sorensen-Machado wedding a little before three o'clock and began the bride's bouquet. Sweeney and Claudia were working on the altar flowers, and Annie was pleased to see they were all right on schedule despite the holiday weekend and her move. Her part-timers had done a wonderful job manning the shop yesterday while she was settling into her new house. She owed Tracy and Joan a weekend off with pay for stepping into the breach.

She was grateful Sweeney was working with them today. Sweeney never met a silence she couldn't conquer with another story from her colorful life. If Claudia had hoped for the chance to grill Annie about her new neighbor, she never had the opportunity.

Eileen's daughter Jennifer and her friends burst through the front door a few minutes later, smelling of suntan lotion and high spirits.

"Hi, Aunt Annie, Grandma." She kissed them both, then plucked a chocolate candy from the bowl Claudia kept at her right elbow. "Hey, Sweeney! Can we turn on the radio? Do you have any soda in the back? You don't think I look fat in this top, do you?"

"Fat?" Sweeney exclaimed as the girls disappeared into the back. "My left thigh is bigger than she is."

"She's beautiful," Annie said wistfully, "and she doesn't have the slightest idea."

"Neither did you two when you were her age." Claudia twisted some wire ribbon around the stem of an unarmed alstromeria. "If I had a penny for every diet you girls embarked on, I'd be a wealthy woman."

"I wouldn't want to be sixteen again," Sweeney said as she reached for a creamy white rose. "You think the world's spinning on your axis. I didn't realize I wasn't the center of the universe until I was thirty-three."

"I'd go back to sixteen," Claudia said wistfully. "All of that wonderful energy and enthusiasm." She paused for effect. "Not to mention knees that don't click when you walk up the stairs."

"And no cellulite," Annie said, trying not to think about how she must have looked when Sam found her asleep in the tub. "I can't remember my thighs without cellulite."

"Honey," said Sweeney, "I can't remember when my thighs didn't rub together like two sticks at a Boy Scout campfire."

Claudia snipped off a length of ivory satin ribbon with a pair of shears. "Dim lighting and a peignoir set have saved more marriages than separate bathrooms." She looked across the table at Annie and Sweeney, who burst into laughter. "Go ahead and laugh," Claudia said, joining in, "but believe it or not, you won't be young forever. One day you'll be grateful for kind lighting and a floor-length robe."

Oh Claudia, thought Annie as she got up to find more baby's breath. *What would you say if I told you it was kind lighting and a floor-length robe that got me into this mess?*

The girls finished the boutonnieres around five o'clock and left in a flurry of giggles and broken blossoms. Sweeney and Claudia completed the last of the centerpieces, then stowed them in the huge refrigerator along with the bridesmaids' bouquets.

"Sorry to bail out on you, ladies, but I have myself a hot date tonight and I need a little time to change my sheets and shave my legs."

"Good Lord!" Claudia sounded appalled, but there was no denying the twinkle in her eyes. "Is there a man in this town you haven't . . . dated?"

Sweeney threw back her head and roared with laughter. "Honey, I'm importing them from New Hampshire these days." She gathered up her huge tote bags and rummaged around for the keys to her old VW bus. "I'll be here at noon to help decorate the church."

"You don't have to do that," Annie said, meaning it. "You've helped me enough already."

"And you'll help me when the Autumn Art Fair rolls around," Sweeney said with another laugh. "You know I'm not shy."

Sweeney went out the front door as Amelia Wright and her sister Terri Cohen came in through the back, carting a huge box filled with their latest soft sculptures. They specialized in whimsical creatures like griffins and unicorns and delighted in setting them in unlikely spots around the shop. When they saw what Annie was up to, they quickly rolled up their sleeves and pitched right in.

"I still haven't closed the books for August," Claudia said, extending her fingers then shaking her hands in front of her. "Maybe I should see to that while Amy and Terri are here."

"Sounds fine," Annie said, aware of Claudia's troubles with arthritis. She felt vaguely guilty for not relieving the woman much sooner. But then, what didn't she feel guilty about these days? She felt guilty for selling the old house, buying the new one, auctioning off her furniture, you name it, and she was certain she'd felt guilty over it at one time or another over the last two years.

Claudia closed the books at six-thirty and came forward to collect her purse and sweater. "Eileen and the children are stopping by for breakfast tomorrow morning after church. You know you're welcome to join us before we set up for the wedding."

Annie stretched and managed to stifle an end-of-the-day yawn. "Thanks, but I think I'd better tackle some of those boxes waiting to be unpacked. If I don't do it now, I'll still be staring at them come Christmas."

"I'd be happy to come over and lend a hand."

"I know you would," Annie said, feeling like a rat for thinking unpleasant thoughts about her mother-in-law, "but you do enough for me already. If I do a little each day, I'll be finished in no time."

Claudia slipped into her pale ivory sweater and tucked her purse under her arm. "You work too hard, Anne. You've looked so tired lately. I worry about you."

"I'm strong as an ox." She flexed a muscle. "At least Ceil seems to think I look like one."

"That woman's tongue could curdle cream. She told me about her cousin's eye-lift, then gave me one of those knowing nods of hers."

Annie laughed. It was the first natural moment they'd shared all day. "Did she offer you the doctor's business card?"

"No," said Claudia with a shake of her head, "but that pudgy hand was dipping into her apron pocket for one as sure as I'm standing here." She cupped Annie's face, and Annie saw a world of caring and love in her soft blue eyes. "You get some rest tonight, do you hear me? You've been pushing yourself way too hard."

Annie's eyes closed briefly against a rush of emotion that was as comforting as it was complicated. "I love you,

Claude," she said softly. "Don't ever forget that."

Claudia patted her cheek briskly. "As if I could."

Claudia always stopped at Yankee Shopper on Saturday evening to do her marketing. Ceil rarely worked on Saturday, and Claudia considered it a small victory for personal privacy when she managed to purchase her pair of veal chops and Idaho potatoes without enduring the woman's shameless scrutiny. Thomas in produce waved hello to her from across the aisle, and she nodded back in greeting. Thomas had been one of Kevin's high school friends, a likable young man who hadn't quite managed to live up to his potential. Not that Claudia was being judgmental. Far from it. It was just a terrible shame when a smart young man allowed himself to be content stacking tomatoes in a small-town supermarket.

Thomas was nearing forty now, and it was beginning to show in the lines around his dark brown eyes and the slight paunch billowing under his Yankee Shopper apron. Kevin had been built on a grand scale, same as his father. She liked to think he would have retained his impressive proportions well into old age without running to fat.

She had bumped into Thomas's mother Audrey last week at the Breast Cancer Bridge Marathon at the hospital. Audrey was beside herself with grandmotherly pride as she spread a fistful of photos on the felt-covered table. "Thomas and Mary Ann just had number four," she said, beaming with delight over the little red-faced bundle in the photographs. "That makes six for me and one more on the way."

Claudia, who was no slouch in the grandmother sweepstakes, whipped out the thick packet of photos she kept always at the ready and treated the girls to a rundown of ages, weights, and accomplishments that would have sent her spinning into a coma if she'd been on the receiving end.

"Good Lord in heaven," Audrey exclaimed, same as she did every time. "They're certainly a fertile bunch!"

Eleven grandsons and granddaughters and two on the way. Claudia loved each and every one of them, but not even the richness of her blessings was enough to make up for the fact that there would never be a baby for Kevin and Annie. When Kevin died, he took the future with him, and the empty spot he'd left inside his mother's heart would never be filled. The sorrow she had known when her husband died had almost destroyed her, but even that, terrible as it was, paled beside the towering grief she experienced when she buried her son. A mother shouldn't bury her son. It was against the laws of both nature and humanity. Some sorrows cut too deep for healing.

She and Annie had clung to each other during those early days, one supporting the other when their grief threatened to overcome them. How grateful Claudia had been that Kevin had been fortunate enough to marry a girl like Annie Lacy. Annie had loved him the way a wife should love a husband, and Claudia had loved her all the more for that fact. Sometimes she had wondered if there were problems in the marriage, but if there were, Annie kept her own counsel, and Claudia respected that. Husbands were imperfect creatures, and a smart wife learned how to work around the flaws.

Had she told Annie lately how dear she was, how the family would not be the same without her vibrant presence at its heart? She couldn't remember. The truth was she thought of Annie as one of her own, and that was the problem. To Claudia's mind, Annie was just like Eileen or Susan or any of her other children, and she expected her to know that she was loved and valued.

But Annie wasn't blood. She had come to Claudia just

before her sixteenth birthday, as scared and needy a young girl as Claudia had ever seen, and Claudia had done what any other mother in her circumstances would have done: she opened up her heart and home to the girl.

When did you stop trying to keep a child out of harm's way? Did the caring stop when your son turned twenty-one? Did it end when your daughter turned thirty? How did you steel your mother's heart against the dangers that waited for the ones you loved more than life itself? Oh, how young and lovely Annie had looked this afternoon when that man stepped into the flower shop. Her dark blue eyes twinkled, her skin grew luminous—she even walked with a graceful sway that Claudia had never noticed before. She wasn't so old that she had forgotten the way it all began and she wished with all her heart that she could protect Annie from the pain that was certain to follow.

How much safer it was to wrap yourself in the memory of love . . .

"No coupons today, Claudia?" Midge Heckel began running her purchases over the scanner. "There's a cents-off coupon in *Pennysaver* this week for sweet butter."

Claudia sighed. "No butter for me, Midge. My cholesterol is giving me fits."

Midge launched into a litany of her medical woes, which Claudia matched, ailment for ailment. The woman laughed as she bagged Claudia's purchases. "The wonder is we're still alive and kicking."

"I guess God isn't quite finished with us yet," Claudia said as she removed two twenty-dollar bills from her wallet.

"Well, He'd better hurry up," Midge said, "because it seems to me we're running out of time."

"We land in Bangor in fifteen minutes, Mr. B."

Warren Bancroft looked up at the young man in the

dark blue uniform and nodded his head. "Right on time, Jason," he said with a glance at his watch. "That's ten in a row. I'm impressed."

The young man grinned. "Captain Yardley said you would be."

Warren managed to withhold a grin of his own. "You tell Captain Yardley—" He stopped in mid-sentence. "On second thought, I'll tell her myself once we're on the ground." He liked to deliver bonus checks personally.

Jason gathered up Warren's empty juice glass, a discarded copy of *The Wall Street Journal*, and a deck of playing cards with loons on the back, then disappeared into the galley while Warren folded his reading glasses and put them away in his breast pocket.

Sonia Yardley was turning out to be one of his greatest successes. He had met her ten years ago when she was flying kids for a nickel a pound out of a little air strip near Wiscasset and using the proceeds to help pay for her college degree. He did a little discreet checking and discovered she had a 4.0 GPA and damn little else. He never once regretted seeing that a Bancroft Scholarship went her way. Now Sonia had a handsome pilot husband, a beautiful baby girl, and a future that could take her as far as she wanted to go.

Warren felt sorry for rich old men and women who sheltered their money in ice-cold tax havens and never knew the joy of seeing that money turn a young person's life around.

Of course it didn't always work out the way he intended it to. Sometimes not even a man's best intentions could coax good fortune out of hiding for the ones he cared for most of all. That was how it had been with Annie and Sam. Annie's blossoming art career had been put aside before house payments and her husband's problems. When was the last time she had set up her easel and taken out her paints? Five years. Maybe ten. What about the carvings and sculptures she'd wanted to make? She'd laughed when he asked her to consider creating something for the museum and said she wouldn't remember how. He was saving the place of honor for her just the same. She used her gifts to create exquisite floral arrangements, and that was all well and good, but it wasn't what she was born to do, and anything less was a crying shame.

And look at Sam. He had carved out a brilliant career that had given him nothing in return except money, and now not even that. He had sacrificed everything for his brothers and sisters, and they hadn't a clue that he was in the fight of his life.

Warren understood the boy straight through to his marrow. There was no greater sorrow in life than letting love slip through your fingers because you couldn't find it in your heart to say the two little words she needed to hear.

Don't go.

But that was his story, and he had made his peace with it a long time ago. He had moved on to other loves, but none had ever burned as brightly in his heart as the first.

He wanted Sam and Annie to have the one gift he had never had: the singular joy of loving and being loved for a lifetime. For all of their bright promise, they were both still alone, and he was determined to change that before his Maker called him home.

Matchmaking wasn't half as easy as bestowing scholarships and jobs on deserving candidates. There was no Wharton School for love, no Harvard Business for romance. The most you could do was put a man and a woman on the path toward each other and hope for the best.

When Sam had called earlier that afternoon with his request, it was all Warren could do to keep from offering unsolicited advice. *She's a fiercely proud woman, boy,* he'd wanted to say as he listened to the younger man's idea. *If it smells like charity, she'll throw it back in your face like a week-old cod.*

But Sam was high on the idea, and in the end Warren acquiesced. He wouldn't be at all surprised if Sam found his offerings in the street before the night was over.

It was nearly seven by the time Annie closed up the shop and climbed behind the wheel of her truck. She waved at George, one of the local cops, who was ticketing young Vic DeLuca for a parking violation. George and his wife Sunny had lived next door to Annie and Kevin for seven years before they moved to a small farmhouse a few miles outside of town. If George had ever wondered about some of those late-night visitors who occasionally found their way to Annie and Kevin's front door, he never gave any indication. There were times she had almost prayed somebody would see a strange car idling in her driveway or wonder aloud why so many of the Galloways' checks bounced each month, but it never happened. Not once in all those years.

People saw only what they wanted to see, and what they had wanted to see was Annie-and-Kevin, everyone's favorite couple, the high school sweethearts who had almost managed the happy ending everyone dreams about.

How did you tell the people who loved you that there was no Annie-and-Kevin anymore? How did you make them hear you when you said you were suffocating under the weight of the past? She'd seen Claudia's eyes when Sam Butler walked into the shop this afternoon. If looks could kill, Sam would have been knocking on the Pearly Gates before he said hello.

You have nothing to worry about, Claudia, she thought as she pulled into her driveway. *Now that he's fixed the front door and cleaned out the truck, there won't be any*

*reason for him to stop by unless he's hoping to catch me
butt naked in the tub again.*

Fat chance of that. He was probably installing blackout
curtains on his front windows so he wouldn't run the risk
of seeing her without her clothes on. The poor man was
probably still reeling from the sight. He probably thought
she was some needy, pathetic widow who couldn't add
two plus two without a man to help her. Cheap champagne. Candles around the tub. A silk robe nobody but
the cats had ever seen her wear. She wouldn't be surprised
if he'd called Warren and told him the whole story, right
down to her hangover.

If that thought wasn't enough to snap her back to reality, nothing was.

In less than twenty-four hours, her new neighbor had
seen her disheveled, exhausted, exasperated, dead drunk,
butt naked, unconscious, without makeup, hung over, and
stuffing her face with DeeDee's donuts. So what if there
had been some inexplicable pull of attraction between
them? They were human, weren't they? A man and a
woman caught in an intimate situation couldn't help striking a few sparks. Of course their hormones would dust
themselves off and take a quick spin around the block. It
couldn't be helped. Blame human nature.

Better still, blame the champagne.

She was a serious, thoughtful woman, not the tipsy
birdbrain he'd pulled out of the bathtub. She was the one
people turned to when they had a problem. She was the
one you could trust, the one who knew how to hold your
secrets close to her heart.

Of course, he had no way of knowing that about her.
All he knew was that she liked to sip champagne and set
fire to her bathrobe. And how could she forget that he
also knew that she had cellulite, two tiny stretch marks,

and a birthmark only her husband and gynecologist had ever seen?

So if he's not interested, why did he ask if you were seeing Hall?

Because he was nosy, that's why. Sam was new in town, and he was trying to figure out the connections between the various players. Hall showed up—acting quite proprietary, come to think of it—and two seconds later Annie was saying yes to dinner at Cappy's. He was just more direct in his curiosity than most people she knew.

That still doesn't explain the way you almost melted into the sidewalk this afternoon, does it?

"I'm an idiot, that's why," she said as she pulled into her driveway. She knew as much about men as sixteen-year-old Jennifer and her giggly girlfriends. She'd heard them talking about boyfriends this afternoon while they worked on the flowers. Jen was less than half Annie's age, and she already had twice the experience. Annie had fallen in love with her first and only boyfriend and married him three years later. She was already part of his family; loving the favorite son just made the whole thing that much sweeter.

When it came to men, she was stuck somewhere back in the 1980s with big hair and shoulder pads. She'd learned everything she would ever know about dating and courtship by the time she was sixteen, which left her thirty-eight-year-old self pretty well in the dark when it came to being single.

So what if she and Sam Butler had shared a few donuts on her front porch. People did that all the time. So what if they'd shared a chaste and sugary kiss. How else would you thank someone for saving your life? And it wasn't as though he had kissed her back. Their lips met, and then it was over. Case closed. There was a rational, logical reason for every single thing they did and said, and not one of those reasons came embroidered with red hearts and pink flowers.

And then she opened her front door and found out just how wrong she was.

Where there had been empty space, there now was furniture.

Lots of it.

A reading lamp on a dark pine end table. An upholstered rocker big enough to get lost in. A small maple table with two chairs that exactly fit the tiny space allotted for a dining area. A pitcher of wild-picked daisies graced the center of the tabletop. George and Gracie had already claimed the upholstered cat condo by the living room window. She'd always wanted to buy one of those silly things but could never rationalize the cost.

Who on earth would do such a thing for her? Warren, of course, but he would have furnished the entire house and he knew that would make her very angry. Claudia certainly didn't have the money. Neither did Susan or any of the others. Besides, they were all way too practical to risk such an expensive surprise.

She ran her hand across the weathered surface of the maple table, relishing each bump and gouge. She remembered sitting at a table just like this once upon a time, writing up a list for Santa Claus on a lined tablet with a big fat No. 2 pencil. Warren's sister Ellie was baby-sitting for her parents and—

She was out the door in a flash.

Sam heard Annie's truck long before he saw it. The crunch of tires on the sandy road, the marbles-in-a-bowl sound of her engine that matched his own—funny how quickly a sound could become part of your personal landscape.

"No turning back now, Max," he said, scratching the

dog behind the left ear. "It's up to her now."

He and Max were sitting on the back step of Ellie Ban-croft's old cottage, watching a trio of seagulls scavenging for a last tasty morsel before the sun went down. The idea that had seemed inspired this afternoon when he was fu-eled on donuts and coffee and the way her hair looked in the sunshine seemed dubious now at best. He had planned to tell her when he brought her house keys to the flower shop, but when he saw the other two women there he decided against it. Public humiliation had never been his thing.

So he just did it.

He'd never been one for grand gestures. He thought before he acted, considered every option and their con-sequences. You had to when you were nineteen years old and responsible for five younger brothers and sisters. This was the first time he had ever acted out of romantic im-pulse, and it felt great.

Terrifying as hell, but great.

The engine noise cut out. He heard a car door slam shut. The squeak of a front door opening then closing. Silence. At least she hadn't screamed. That was a good sign. He drummed his fingers on the top step. He tapped his foot.

He looked down at Max.

Max looked up at him.

"You're right," Sam said. "I should go over there and explain."

He put the dog inside the house and made it halfway down the driveway when he saw Annie Galloway walking up the road toward him. She was still wearing the sleek black pants and red sweater he'd seen her in that after-noon. The pants clung to her womanly hips like a hug while the sweater glided over her breasts, just snug enough to tantalize. She was backlit by the setting sun;

its red glow made her wild mane of curls shimmer like living fire. She looked a little tired, a lot curious, real and earthy and beautiful enough to bring him to his knees.

In other words, nothing had changed.

She stopped a few feet away from him.

Their eyes met.

"You shouldn't have, Sam."

"I wanted to."

"You could have asked."

"Then it wouldn't have been a surprise."

"You know I can't accept it."

"Why not?"

"I barely know you."

"It's just furniture, not a truckload of Victoria's Secret."

"Strangers usually don't buy each other living room furniture."

"I didn't buy it."

"Okay, then, they usually don't steal living room furniture for each other either."

"I have a houseful of the stuff. It's either give Max more to wreck or find a safe haven."

"You can't just give away Warren's furniture."

"He said you could help yourself."

She jammed her hands in the pockets of her sleek black pants. Her belly was slightly rounded, womanly and inviting. His entire body remembered how she had felt naked in his arms.

"I don't know what to say, Sam."

"I'm so happy . . . Wow, what a great idea . . . How about a wide-screen TV while you're at it . . . Did you get those massive muscles moving furniture . . . Any one of those would be okay."

Again that laugh, that wonderful laugh. Did she have any idea what that laugh did to him?

"Would you settle for a thank-you?"

"No," he said. "Not good enough."

A gust of wind blew a lock of hair across her right cheek. She didn't seem to notice it. "What would be good enough?"

He looked at her mouth and grinned.

Honeyed warmth spread outward from the center of her chest.

"I'm not going to ask you," he said.

She nodded.

"I'm just going to do it."

"Good idea," she whispered.

They were in each other's arms before they drew their next breaths.

"Annie . . ." Did he say her name, or was it already a part of his soul?

"Shhh . . ." No words. No sound. All she wanted was the feel of his lips burning hers, the cool sweet taste of his mouth, the smell of his skin. She was on fire from within. She couldn't think. She didn't want to think. If she thought about what she was doing she would turn and run, and that was the last thing she wanted to do.

She melted against him, molding her body to his in a way that brought him halfway to the brink in a heartbeat. Her hunger matched his. She was a thousand dreams in the middle of a cold dark night brought to warm and vibrant life in his arms. Her fingers touched his throat, his jaw, his ears, the bridge of his nose, his temples. They tangled in his hair, then slid over his back and shoulders as if she were trying to memorize his body with fingertips and palms.

He cupped her buttocks and drew her closer to him, and she gasped into his mouth when he moved against her. If they didn't stop now, they would be making love right there in his driveway.

Still kissing, still touching, they stumbled up the driveway and into his house, where they fell together onto the big soft sofa near the fireplace. She sank deep into the cushions, and he covered her with his body. He tugged at the zipper on her sweater and pulled it down. Her bra was made of soft beige cotton. Her hard nipples were clearly visible through the worn fabric. Black lace couldn't have had a more powerful effect on him.

She fumbled with the buttons on his shirt. Her fingers felt clumsy and awkward in her eagerness to bare his skin to her lips. A button popped off and danced crazily across the braided rug then rolled to a stop.

"I'll fix it," she said as she pressed her mouth to his chest. "I'm great with a needle and thread."

He ripped off his shirt and threw it across the room.

She laughed softly, her breath hot and moist against his skin. She smelled like flowers dipped in honey. He wanted to drench himself in her.

There was nothing yielding about him, nothing soft or comforting. He was all hard muscle and sharp angles, her opposite in every way. They both knew her welcoming softness made him possible, made everything possible.

She hungered for his hands on her bare skin and cried out when he undid the clasp on her bra and cupped her breasts in his palms. It had been so long, more years than she wanted to think about, and she had been so deeply, achingly lonely for someone who saw her through the prism of desire. She loved the way he touched her. He didn't ask. He didn't hesitate. His hands claimed her body with a lover's sure and gentle touch. Each place he touched—her breasts, her rib cage, the base of her throat—burned beneath his fingertips, his palms, his tongue.

It was all so sweetly familiar, so terrifyingly strange. Only one other man had ever touched her this way. Her body knew only one man's rhythm, one lover's dance.

She felt clumsy at times, amazingly sensual at others. Each kiss, each touch, led her down a different pathway until she was wonderfully lost. He kissed his way along her collarbone, lingering at the hollow at the base of her throat, then found her mouth. Oh God, his mouth . . . so sweet, so hot, so demanding. The explosion of sensations made her dizzy, and she allowed herself to sink even more deeply into the cushions, shielded from reality by the delicious weight of his body poised over hers.

His kisses stole her breath. She wanted to lose herself in them, lose the Annie Galloway everyone thought they knew and find out who she wanted to be.

Holding her was like holding quicksilver. Even with her body melting against his, Sam had the sense that the real Annie Galloway had somehow slipped his grasp. She was warm and willing in his arms. Her kisses scorched him from the inside out, but he wasn't sure she was really there.

He wanted to kiss her until her brain clicked off and there was nothing left but desire. He wanted to bury himself in her, anchor her in the here and now until there was no room for anything but each other.

She moved her hand down his chest, over his flat belly, then stopped. Her open palm hovered over his obvious erection.

The only sound in the room was the wild pounding of their hearts, the quick pace of their breathing . . . and Max's shotgun sneezes.

Annie's eyes flew open, and so did Sam's.

He cupped her face and was about to kiss her again when Max sneezed three more times, ran one lap around the living room, then threw himself down on Sam's discarded shirt and went happily to sleep.

Max snored.

Later on Annie would say that Sam was the first one

to laugh, but he knew better. Her creamy shoulders began to shake, her lower lip quivered, and then before he had the chance to process what was happening, her full rich laugh filled the room. His own laughter wasn't far behind.

They laughed so hard that Max woke up, shot them an indignant look, then stalked from the room. That, of course, only made them laugh harder. They clung to each other, gasping for air, as their laughter ricocheted off the walls. Half naked, wrapped in each other's arms, they laughed until their sides ached and their throats hurt and tears ran down Annie's cheeks.

After a bit their laughter stilled, but the sense of connectedness between them grew deeper and more intense.

"This is crazy," she whispered, her mouth soft against his bare chest.

"You talk too much," he said then kissed her quiet.

She liked that he didn't ask, didn't tiptoe around her, didn't treat her like St. Annie the Virgin Widow. He treated her like a flesh-and-blood woman, and her response was as natural as breathing. Her lips parted at his gentle pressure, and she sighed deeply as his tongue slid across the swell of her lower lip before claiming her mouth. It was all so strangely familiar, the sensual duel where both won the battle. She drank him in as if she had been parched for the taste of him, as if her soul required his essence. He would run if he knew how long it had been for her, years and years since she had been kissed this way, as if he wanted to steal her breath and make it his own.

The rough hair on his chest scraped pleasurably against the delicate skin of her breasts, causing ripples of sweet sensation to shoot straight to her core. She stiffened as he eased the flat of his hand beneath the waistband of her pants and rested his palm against the softness of her belly.

"I should do sit-ups," she said, as a wave of self-consciousness overcame her. "I bought one of those tapes and—"

He leaned over and kissed her belly, dipped his hot tongue into the well of her navel, then laughed low at her sound of surprised pleasure.

Oh, God. His fingers moved down and down until they tangled in the thick curls between her legs. He caressed her gently, easily, pressing lightly here and then there, until she was almost mindless with pleasure. How easy it was to let go, to give in to the moment, to open her thighs for his touch. She'd dreamed this last night as she slept in the circle of his arms, dreamed of the moment when her bones melted and everything else fell away. She was hungry for him, starved for the feel of his body. For once in her life, desire was more powerful than her sense of caution, and she reached for the button on the waistband of his jeans.

Moments later they were naked on the floor next to the sofa. He flipped onto his back, cushioned by the pile of discarded clothes, and pulled her on top of him. She straddled his hips, and his slick erection pressed against her cleft. She stroked him with her hand, velvet on steel, how long had it been too long, too long. . . .

Her breasts were full and beautiful, her nipples deep rose set against the alabaster of her skin. Her wild mane of hair brushed his chest as she leaned forward to kiss the flat plane of his belly. His erection leaped to life between them, and she laughed softly but did nothing more. He wanted her to ride him, to pull him deep inside her body and ride him hard. He wanted to see her face when she came, see the look of wonder in her dark blue eyes, hear the sounds she made deep in her throat when it happened. She was wet. He could feel her dampness against his belly and thighs. His hands clasped her hips, and he rocked with her rhythm, his own desire growing hotter and more urgent by the second when he realized, with devastating clarity, that he was totally unprepared.

Her body was supple, moving above him with heart-stopping grace. He wanted her more than he wanted his next breath, but some things were nonnegotiable.

"Annie." Her name seemed to hover in the charged air between them.

She struggled to bring him into focus. She felt drugged, heavy with longing.

"I didn't plan this," he said.

Of course he hadn't planned this. Neither had she. How could you plan spontaneous combustion?

"Protection," he said. "You need to be protected." Another pause. "You're not on the pill, are you?"

Reality and magic didn't mix. Annie felt as if someone had poured a bucket of ice water over her head. "No," she said, feeling naked for the first time. "I'm not." She wanted to tell him that it really didn't matter, because in almost twenty years of marriage she had never once been pregnant, but the words wouldn't come. That was part of her old life, and she wanted it to stay there.

The silence between them was deep and profound. She wanted to gather up her clothes and run back to her cats and her cottage and fit herself back into her old life, but it was too late. His grasp on her hips tightened, and he inched her forward, sliding her up his chest in a way that made her feel as if she were about to burst into flame. She could feel his moist hot breath between her legs.

"Sam?" She sounded hesitant, a little fearful. The truth was, she was both of those things and more.

"Let yourself go, Annie." He didn't sound hesitant and he didn't sound fearful. He sounded like a man whose hunger matched her own. "There's more than one way to love a woman."

His lips brushed her inner thighs. A thousand reasons

why this shouldn't be happening battled with the powerful lure of desire. She didn't do things like this . . . she wasn't a very sensual woman . . . oh God what he was doing with his tongue . . . or maybe she was . . . she'd never had the chance to find out . . . his hair felt like silk against her inner thighs . . . nobody not even the man she had loved had ever made her want to slip away from reality and vanish into a world where the senses ruled . . . wasn't it supposed to be about love . . . that's what she had been taught . . . but you couldn't love someone you'd just met . . . not even if he looked at you as if you were someone to be cherished . . . not even if he had saved your life . . . it wasn't about love . . . it couldn't be . . . she was getting confused . . . don't stop . . . there . . . yes yes . . . love was just what people called it when their bones were melting and they were about to burst into flame . . .

Giving her pleasure was the most selfish thing Sam had ever done. Her smell, her sounds, the long muscles of her thighs as she shuddered against him when she came—all of those things brought him a deeper pleasure than he had ever known before. Her deeply sensual, overwhelmingly female response to his lovemaking carried him to a place he hadn't known existed, and he knew that was only the beginning. She made him feel anything was possible.

So why then was she crying softly against his shoulder as if her heart would break?

He didn't know what to say. A second ago he had been invincible; now he was reduced to stroking her hair and murmuring nonsense in her ear in an attempt to soothe her. His desire vanished in the face of something much more complicated.

Faint red marks blossomed along her inner thighs, and he was filled with remorse. Had he hurt her? She was so soft and beautifully made, and his passion had been veering out of control. How in hell had something so right suddenly turned into something so damn wrong?

"I'm sorry, Annie," he said, wishing they could start all over again. "I didn't mean to hurt you."

She brushed the tears from her eyes with two quick gestures, and he could feel her gathering her strength around her like a shield. Those two gestures captured what little was left of his heart. He was hers for the asking, and, dammit, she hadn't a clue.

Annie berated herself for letting things go too far . . . and for not letting herself go far enough. She'd had too much time to think, that was the problem. Too much time to remember who she was in the eyes of everyone in town. *Annie Galloway. Kevin's wife. Claudia's daughter-in-law. Kevin's widow.* Everything but Sam Butler's lover. Oh God, how she wanted to touch him, to hold him, to run her lips over every inch of his body, but she couldn't move. His body ached for her. The evidence was both plain and powerful, and she knew he deserved that and so much more from a woman with far less baggage.

She wasn't a wife any longer but she wasn't sure she was ready to be a lover. She felt greedy, selfish, and altogether a failure.

"Guess you're having a few second thoughts right about now," she said, trying to ease a laugh around her words. He had given her more pleasure than she had ever known and she repaid him by bursting into tears like a wronged virgin. "I promise you that the rest of the women of Shelter Rock Cove don't start sobbing after a man makes love to them." Only the one who'd buried her husband but still hadn't quite buried her guilt.

"I don't give a damn about the rest of the women. Did I hurt you?" He sounded worried. If he was angry or disappointed, he hid it well. His touch spoke only of tenderness and concern.

She was hungry for both of those things and so much

more. For comfort and a warm body next to hers and the crashing pleasures of touch and the wonder of someone who knew you right down to the marrow of your being and loved you anyway. The depth of her need terrified her. It was deeper than her loneliness, wider than the dreams she had put aside all those years ago when she realized they would never come true.

"Did I hurt you, Annie?" he repeated.

"No, no!" Why did deep emotion always bring her to tears? "It's just—I mean, it was all so—" She was stumbling over her words, suddenly more comfortable with the imperfections of her body than the longing inside her heart. She glanced down at the gold band on her left hand and felt a dizzying combination of anger and shame. "Until today there had never been anyone else."

"Not even before you married him?"

"There was no 'before.' " Kevin Galloway had always been part of her emotional landscape, from as far back as she could remember. "I suppose you think it's laughable, marrying the first boy you ever dated, but there was never any question that we were meant to be together."

"I don't think it's laughable," Sam said. "I think he was lucky."

The look she gave him was equal parts sorrow and anger and gratitude, and he wondered where one emotion ended and the other began. Marriage was a secret society with only two members, a society he'd never had time to join. The rest of the world was on the outside looking in, trying to figure out what was innately without logic or reason.

"Claudia thinks I should have stayed in the old house, but I couldn't, not any longer. Two years is long enough. Once I finally—" She caught herself, horrified that the secrets she had kept locked away for so long had almost come spilling out. "I'm not really like this," she said, shaking her head in dismay. "I'm the one people go to when they have problems."

He stroked her hair with those large and beautiful hands. "And who do you go to when you have a problem, Annie Galloway?"

"Haven't you heard?" she said. "I don't have problems. I'm the one who solves them." And she knew how to solve his problem, too.

He started to say something, but the phone rang. They listened to it ring once, twice, four times, and he finally went in search of the cellular. The room was bathed in shadows. A cool breeze ruffled the curtains and from the kitchen Max made mournful sounds for his supper. Scraps of conversation floated toward her on the night air as he talked to one of his sisters.

". . . not a good time, Marie . . . why don't we talk later . . . yeah, yeah . . . you pay the super . . . he'll call . . . it's not an emergency, is it . . . ask Jimmy . . . no, it's nothing to worry about . . ."

She slipped back into her black trousers and red sweater.

". . . I'm kind of busy right now, Marie . . ."

She tucked her stockings and bra into her pocket.

". . . none of your business . . . I don't ask you questions about . . ."

She retrieved her shoes from under the sofa.

". . . I'll call you back . . . I don't know when, Marie . . . Jesus, why don't you . . ."

She slipped out the front door and didn't look back.

SEVEN

Claudia's doorbell rang at eight o'clock on the dot, same as it had almost every Saturday night for the last fifteen years.

"I have a bone to pick with you, Warren Bancroft," she said as she ushered the man into her living room.

"Keep it to yourself, old woman." He gave her a hug that she endured with little grace. "You're watching your blood pressure like you should?"

"My pressure wouldn't be a problem if you would keep your meddling nose out of my family's business."

"Not that again!" He reached for the tumbler of scotch she always had waiting for him on the side table. "So I undersold the market to give Annie a break on the house. How is that meddling in your family's business?"

Oh, there were a million things she could say to him about that! Over the years he had developed the annoying habit of always being there when she needed him, a cigar-smoking guardian angel who watched over her family as if he actually had the right.

"I'm talking about that man you installed in Ellie's old house."

"Watch that viper tongue of yours, Claudia. You almost drew blood that time."

She ignored him. "I hope you're not trying to push the two of them together, because if you are—"

"Speak English!" he roared. "If you're going to wrap up your words in riddles, I'll finish my scotch and head for home."

She drew herself up to her full height—which wasn't quite as impressive as it used to be in her glory days—and snapped at him. "Keep a civil tongue in your head, Warren Bancroft, and tell me you're not up to your old tricks again."

He took a long slow sip of scotch, and she all but flew across the room and pulled an answer out of his throat with her bare hands. "Sam is an old friend of mine," he said at last. "He needed a place to stop for a while, and that's what I've given him."

"Why didn't you ask him to stay at the big house on the Point?"

He took another sip of scotch, savoring it in the way he knew irritated her almost senseless. "You know I like my space, Claudia."

"Make an exception. It isn't like your help has much to do."

He pulled one of those dreadful cigars from his breast pocket and patted himself down in search of his lighter. She refused to offer him a match.

"Next thing you'll be telling me how to run my businesses."

"Business has never been a problem for you, Warren."

He retrieved his lighter from a back pocket with a flourish. "And speaking your mind has never been a problem for you."

The nerve of him, lighting up without even asking if she minded. "Leave Annie alone," she said in a fiercely protective tone of voice. "Bad enough you encouraged her to sell her house. Don't go playing matchmaker."

He touched the flame to the tip of his cigar. His cheeks sank in as he drew the rich smoke into his lungs. The old fool.

"Not everyone turns widowhood into a career. Annie's too young to take the veil."

His words hurt as they were meant to. Even after all these years, their history still loomed between them, but the days of crying in front of Warren Bancroft were a thing of the past.

"Anne is a grown woman," she said. "She'll make her own decisions without any help from either one of us."

"Remember those words," Warren said, "because one day they'll come back to haunt you."

You don't know her the way I do, Warren. I know what's best for her. "Do you want your supper or are you just here to make my life difficult?"

"I never should have let you go, Claudia," he said as he followed her into the kitchen at the back of the house. "If I had my way, I'd marry you all over again."

In his senior year of high school, Warren Bancroft was voted by unanimous proclamation the most popular boy in the class of 1950. He was also named the boy least likely to succeed without a dissenting vote as well. Warren agreed with both assessments. He was the kind-hearted, fun-loving son of a lobsterman who was also the son of a lobsterman, and it never occurred to anyone, including Warren, that he would spend his life doing anything beyond setting lobster traps and grousing about the weather.

Weather was important to the residents of Shelter Rock

Cove. Weather determined if you could head out to sea in the morning. Weather determined what kind of catch you came back with. When you came down to it, weather determined if you came back at all.

On his third trip out after graduation, Warren Bancroft found himself in the middle of a nor'easter the likes of which even the old salts had never seen before. When they limped back to port four days later, Warren kissed the scarred wood of the dock and swore there had to be a better way to make a living. And then he set off to find it.

At the ten-year reunion of the class of 1950, Warren came home to Shelter Rock Cove filled with talk of computers like the Univac on Art Linkletter's television show or Spencer Tracy's beloved Emerac in the movie *Desk Set.* Because he still looked and sounded like the Warren they had grown up with, they all just listened politely, then forgot all about his crazy notions until their twenty-year reunion rolled around and he drove up from Boston in a big black Lincoln Continental with a chauffeur behind the wheel.

It seemed that Warren Bancroft, the boy least likely to succeed, had struck it rich, and he didn't mind sharing what he had with the town where he grew up. But what the good people of Shelter Rock Cove didn't know was that for six short months in 1951 he and Claudia Perrine had been husband and wife. It wasn't that he was ashamed of the fact. Hell, he wanted to shout it from the rooftops. It was Claudia who was determined to keep her brief marriage a secret from one and all.

"The marriage was annulled," she told him the day they said goodbye, "and that means it never happened."

And because he loved her, he kept their secret.

Claudia had wanted a husband who came home every night at five-thirty and read the paper in his easy chair while she finished preparing dinner. She had wanted a family, a brood of children who would grow up to be healthy and happy and have children of their own. She didn't understand adventure. She didn't believe in taking risks. She couldn't imagine a life that didn't include all of the things her mother and grandmother had enjoyed over the years.

Too bad Warren hadn't wanted any of those things. He wasn't even twenty yet and he wanted to see the world. Make his mark on it. There would be time enough for picket fences and babies, but not now. Not yet.

He could still see the tears in her eyes the night she told him she wanted an anullment. "I spoke to the priest at the parish house," she had said, her voice trembling slightly. "I told him that you refused to have children with me."

"Someday I will," he said, knowing that the battle he fought was already lost. "Just not now."

"He said that was grounds enough for us to end the marriage swiftly."

She went on to marry John Galloway and raise a half dozen children plus Annie Lacy while he watched from a distance and wished they were his.

Because Warren had a kind heart and kind hearts required an outlet, his name had become synonymous in Shelter Rock Cove with quiet generosity. He paid off the mortgages for everyone in his family. He made sure his friends' medical bills were taken care of. If the town needed a new police car or funds to shore up the sagging pier, Warren Bancroft was the first in line with his checkbook. He established a scholarship for the children of fishermen lost at sea, donated a wing to the local hospital, and generally kept a sharp eye on who might be in need, even if the one in need wasn't from Shelter Rock Cove.

It seemed somehow to him the least he could do for all he had been given.

But there had been two among the many who stood out. Two who had claimed the part of his heart that ached for children of his own.

Annie Lacy and Sam Butler.

Sam was fifteen years old when he met Warren. Sam was working at the marina near the World's Fair in Flushing, Queens, doing whatever small repairs the boat builders threw his way. He was smart, a hard worker who was good with his hands. He loved being around boats, and his enthusiasm made him a favorite on the docks. That year Warren was sailing his favorite yacht up from the Bahamas to Shelter Rock Cove, trying to finish the trip before hurricane season broke for real. He ran into some trouble near the Battery and somehow managed to bring the boat into the marina for repairs. It was a hot July evening. Nobody was around except for a wiry kid with a thick shock of dark hair and enough energy to power the city across the river. By the time Sam had the yacht up and running, he and Warren Bancroft were fast friends.

They saw each other each year at the beginning of the summer when Warren sailed up the coast to Maine and again at the end of the season when he made the return trip to winter the yacht in the Bahamas. The summer before his mother, Rosemary, died, sixteen-year-old Sam and a group of inner-city kids crewed for Warren, then spent a few weeks learning about the fisherman's life at the hands of the men who knew it best. It was Sam's last great summer.

Two years later they buried Sam's father Patrick next to Rosemary.

That was the summer Warren didn't make it back to Maine. He was living in Japan at the time, overseeing a huge project with one of the giant electronics firms that would translate one day into a lot of jobs back home. Warren's first wife had left him many years ago for a man whose greatest ambition was to get home from the office in time to see the evening news. Warren told himself it was a good thing that he and Claudia hadn't stayed married long enough to have children—a split was never easy on children—but in his heart he knew he was lying. He envied his ex-wife her big noisy family and he often thought that was why he took so many youngsters under his wing.

When he saw Sam again, he barely recognized the boy. Sam's natural enthusiasm had been replaced by an intensity Warren rarely saw in even the most driven businessman. Sam didn't tell him about his father's passing. Warren had to learn that from Bill, the owner of the marina.

"The kid's working himself to death trying to take care of that brood," Bill told him. "I've given him as many hours as I can, but it's not enough." Sam was juggling his job there with selling sporting equipment at Macy's and working nights as a maintenance man at one of the office buildings along Queens Boulevard. He had dropped out of St. John's last semester, and unless a miracle occurred, he wouldn't be going back any time soon.

Warren wanted to provide the miracle, but he knew the boy's pride wouldn't allow it. Sam was quick and smart and good with people. He had a natural affinity with facts and figures that would put most other young men his age to sleep. It was the beginning of the roaring, good-time 1980s when the stockbroker was king, and how better to help Sam than to make him a young prince of the realm?

Sam was honest, and the business disturbed him, but he had to put aside his own discomfort in favor of his siblings and their future. There was no other way—at least, none that was legal—for a college dropout to make the kind of money Sam needed to keep his family safe and secure.

And now it was over. The kids were grown; the job was history. He was free to do anything he wanted to do, go anywhere, maybe even go back to school and get that degree he used to talk about.

You would think the boy would be happy. Hell, just being thirty-five again would be enough to put a smile on Warren's face.

But the feeling that he could have done more, been more, still lingered with Sam, and no matter how much it grieved Warren Bancroft, only Sam Butler could make it all come out right.

The man wasn't listening to a word Claudia said to him. He sat there, flat-eyed as a squid, shoveling in her world-class meatloaf and thinking about whatever it was rich old men thought about.

She took a dainty sip of decaf from one of her favorite porcelain cups—the ones with the damask roses hand-painted on them—and sighed loudly.

"Oh, put a sock in it," he grumbled goodnaturedly. "I heard every word you said, old woman."

"Hearing and comprehending are not the same thing, Warren."

"Eileen thinks she's pregnant again, Sean's opening another store, three of the grands left last week for college, and you're bellyaching about Annie and Sam."

Claudia shivered. "Anne and Sam! Don't say it that way. They're not a couple and—" She stopped and looked toward the window.

"You might as well come out with it, old woman, because I know just what you're going to say."

She wanted very much to empty the contents of the coffeepot over his head, but good breeding won out over her baser instincts. "And they never will be," she finished with a show of defiance. "If Annie is looking to date again," she said, barely suppressing the *God forbid,* "there are plenty of fine available men right here in Shelter Rock Cove." Oh, how she wished she still smoked, but her doctors absolutely forbade it. Nothing punctuated a woman's anger better than a gesture made with a lighted cigarette.

Warren snorted his derision. "Men who still see her as Kevin's wife." He pushed his empty plate aside and looked straight at her. "Same as you do."

"She *is* Kevin's wife."

"She's Kevin's widow." He patted her hand. "Now don't go getting all weepy on me, Claudia. Life goes on. You don't have to like it, but it goes on just the same."

She pulled her hand away from him. "I don't like it," she snapped. "I don't like it one bit. Not every widow is looking for a replacement husband, you fool. Anne is like me. Kevin was the love of her life. You can't replace the love of your life."

"I know," said Warren Bancroft softly. "I've been trying for almost fifty years."

EIGHT

Sam was fetching a stick for Max the next morning during low tide when he heard Annie's truck rattle off down the road toward town. He fought the urge to scramble up the rocks and try to catch a glimpse of her.

Slow down, he warned himself as he flung the stick for a reluctant Max. *Let her set the pace.* She was the one who had been married before. She had made the commitment to love a man forever, and even now, two years after her husband's death, that commitment still had weight and meaning.

At first he'd blamed Marie's's ill-timed phone call for everything, but in his gut he knew that wasn't true. Annie had been looking for an opportunity to sprint for the exit, and his sister's call had been just what she needed.

"Don't go ripping my head off because you're in a foul mood!" Marie had snapped at him. "I don't know what's going on up there but I think I liked you better when you were a New Yorker."

How did a man compete with a ghost? He knew how to compete with living, breathing men like the doctor who had come calling yesterday morning, but how the hell did you shadowbox with a dead man? She still wore his wedding ring. Her in-laws were part of her daily life. The entire fabric of her existence was woven with threads created during her marriage, threads that grew stronger with time.

What did he have to offer that could come close to that? The real world didn't stand a chance. He had no job and no prospects. Hell, if it weren't for Max's hyperactive bladder, he wouldn't have a reason to get up in the morning. Sooner or later he was going to have to figure out what came next, but right now he wouldn't even hazard a guess.

Marie's call had been filled with questions about his apartment. She and Paul and the kids wanted to stay there while they waited to close on their house in Massapequa. Why didn't the super return calls? Where was the fuse box? Did he ever consider ripping up the carpets and going with bare wood? "The place is empty, Marie," he'd told her. "You'll be sleeping on the floor."

Tucked in the middle of her domestic concerns was a quick observation that, no doubt, was the real reason for her call. "The rumors are flying down on the Street about the trouble at Mason, Marx, and Daniel. Did you hear the SEC might be called in?" She'd paused to give him time to comment, but he said nothing. "Your timing was pretty good, big brother. I wouldn't want to be around when the shit hits the fan either."

Marie was a reporter for *Newsday*. She had been on the financial beat for a few years but had recently downshifted into softer news. She was married now and had a family, she had explained to him when she made the decision. She had to put her husband and children first. She said it almost apologetically, as if she didn't believe he would understand.

He had come this close to laughing. He had been putting family first since he was nineteen years old, ahead of his dreams, his future, and his ethics.

He was glad she was no longer on the Wall Street beat. Marie was a good reporter and a smart woman. It wouldn't take her long to put two and two together and come up with a story that involved her brother. She still retained a strong curiosity about activities on the Street but she didn't have the time to pursue them. He could have told her about information he had hidden away in the safe-deposit box in Queens: the screen shots, the contemporaneous notes, the names and dates and numbers that didn't quite add up. The names of the people whose lives had been turned inside out. He could have told her about the suits who came to call; the mailing address in Arlington, Virginia; the cell phone that did double duty as his electronic leash. He could have told her that unless something happened and soon, her brother would be taking the fall.

"What happens to the clients?" Marie had asked him in full reportorial mode, her instinct for news guiding her uncomfortably close to the real story. "We both know the big guys will land on their feet, but what about the people who trusted them?"

He had no answers for her. Hell, he had no answers for himself. You did what you had to do when you needed to do it and then hoped you'd be able to live with the results.

He didn't know if he had a week there in Shelter Rock Cove or a month or maybe a year. For all he knew the phone could ring tomorrow morning, and he'd be on his way down to New York to face the music.

For the last sixteen years, every move he'd made, every decision, every dollar spent, had been evaluated with his siblings' welfare in mind. He had made compromises in almost every area of his life—working at a job he hated just so he wouldn't have to ask them to do the same. Friends and neighbors had called him a hero, applauded the fact that he hadn't taken off and left the kids for the state to worry about. "Nobody keeps promises anymore," Mrs. Ruggiero had said. Jesus, how he'd wanted to run. The dreams he had about hitching a ride to JFK and boarding a plane for anywhere, leaving the lot of them behind. A few times he'd thought of asking Warren Bancroft for help, swallowing his pride like bad medicine and asking for the money that would make his life easier, but each time he caught himself before he took that final step. No, he wasn't a hero. Heroes didn't rail against fate or look for escape hatches. Heroes did what had to be done and found a way to like it. He loved his brothers and sisters but he'd never wanted to be their parent, and the fact that he was had changed his outlook on life forever.

No wonder he'd never married. He'd been in his share of relationships, but, almost instinctively, he had found himself drawn toward women whose attitudes toward him were casual and temporary.

Until now.

There was nothing casual or temporary about Annie or his feelings toward her. She was lovely and grave and serious and she carried with her every bit as much baggage as he did. She had lived an entire life before he'd come into the picture, and those experiences had made her the woman she was. A kitchen table and four chairs might not put him in the romance hall of fame, but you wouldn't have known it by the glow on her face when she thanked him. And what about the sofa and end tables? It wasn't a dozen roses, but hell, the woman owned a flower shop. Bringing Annie roses was like lugging coals to Newcastle or lobster to Maine. The gesture was well-meant but essentially meaningless. A woman without furniture couldn't ignore a sofa. A sofa said a man meant business.

Better think again, hotshot, because she walked out on you last night.

He could still hear the sound of the front door closing behind her. He'd hung up on his sister and walked back into the living room to find her gone. His clothes were neatly folded on the sofa, and the air still smelled faintly of her perfume, but other than that, it was as if the whole thing had never happened. In her heart she was still married to a man named Kevin Galloway, and Sam had no remedy for that.

He took Max on a forced march along the shoreline, then headed back to the house. The tide was rolling in, and it wouldn't be long before it was lapping up against the base of the rocky cliff that divided Mother Nature's property from humanity's. Max was glad to call it a morning. The dog sprawled in the middle of the kitchen floor and panted while Sam filled his bowl with chow.

"You're a lazy one," Sam observed as Max began to eat from a supine position. He bent down and scratched the dog behind the right ear. "Good thing I remember you when you were young and fearless."

He used to see Max and Max's first owner heading off on weekend camping trips up in the Adirondacks. He'd only known Phil to say hello to on the elevator and he'd been shocked the day the guy asked him if he knew anyone who wanted an aging yellow Lab with bad breath and a penchant for destruction.

"I'm getting married in September," Phil had said, "and she hates dogs. It's find a home for him or have him put down."

Out with the old. In with the new.

Before he knew what he was doing, Sam said, "I'll take

him," and Phil was handing over the leash, the water bowl, and half a box of Milk-Bones.

What the hell ever happened to sticking it out for the long haul? Dogs. Girlfriends. Jobs. Families. It was all the same. First rough patch to come along, and they bailed out faster than the first-class passengers on the *Titanic*. Annie had said she would have been married twenty years this year. Nothing lasted twenty years anymore, sure as hell not most marriages, and he found himself wondering again about the man she'd married and the life she had led. It must have been a good life, or she wouldn't be holding it so close to her heart.

He still didn't know if she had kids. He hadn't asked, and she hadn't volunteered the information. It was hard to imagine being married almost twenty years and not having children. He found himself hoping she had a daughter away at college somewhere, a young woman with her smile. Or maybe a strapping son with a football scholarship, a lovable kid who wanted the best for her.

The thought that she might be alone struck him as too unfair to even consider. Some women were meant to be surrounded by kids and cats and dogs and lots of loving commotion, and Annie Galloway was one of them.

Get real, Butler. You don't know a damn thing about her. You're making this up as you go along.

He couldn't argue that, but a man had to start somewhere. He wanted to know everything there was to know about her, the good and the bad and the painful. He wanted to see the empty places in her life where she could make room for him.

Forty-eight hours ago he hadn't known Annie Galloway existed. Now he couldn't imagine his world without her in it.

She thought he was a hero. All he did was put out that fire before it had a chance to do any real damage, and now he could do no wrong. He had seen it in her eyes when she looked at him, something he had never seen before in a woman's eyes, and he didn't deserve it. Max was more of a hero than he was. Ask any of the clients he'd left behind, the ones whose futures were no longer quite so secure. They could tell her a thing or two about the heroic Sam Butler.

Maybe it wasn't such a bad thing that she'd put some space between them.

He was reaching for a box of cornflakes when the phone rang somewhere in the house. Damn cordless phones. He finally found it wedged between the sofa cushions.

"Took you long enough," Warren Bancroft said. "Seven rings. I was about to hang up."

"Are you back in town or still down in New York?"

"I got back last night. I have to go back to New York tomorrow afternoon, but it's good to be home."

"Tell Nancy the pie was first rate."

"Tell her yourself," Warren said. "She's making her famous blueberry waffles, and there's enough to feed an army."

Fifteen minutes later, Sam and Max entered the kitchen where Nancy was ladling thick batter onto the waffle iron.

"Just in time," she said, acknowledging Sam's kiss on her cheek. "He's digging in right now."

Max stayed behind, just in case Nancy needed help with the bacon or a runaway waffle.

Warren was in the sunroom that overlooked the harbor. The water was a little choppy, and the frothy whitecaps made a wonderful contrast with the deep steel blue of the ocean. He leaped to his feet the second he saw Sam and clasped his hand warmly.

"You're too skinny," he said by way of hello. "Nancy!"

he bellowed. "Double up on the order. We need to put some meat on his bones."

"I'm one step ahead of you!" Nancy bellowed back.

"What is it with you people?" Sam asked as he took the seat opposite Warren. "You're always trying to fatten me up."

"Wait until you've been through a Maine winter," Warren said, reaching for the heated pitcher of real maple syrup. "Then you'll know."

They ate in companionable silence for a while, making short work of two batches of blueberry waffles.

Finally Warren pushed his chair back from the table and loosened his belt. "So how did Annie like the furniture?"

"She loved it," Sam said as he bit into a piece of perfectly fried bacon. "Once she heard it was Ellie's, she seemed pretty happy with it."

Warren lit up a cigarette, took one drag, then stubbed it out in a small ashtray next to his plate. "Bet she made you sign a receipt of some kind."

"Right down to the embroidered pillow on the sofa. What's with that anyway?"

"That's our Annie. Scrupulously honest, right down to the penny." He watched Sam with open interest. "Anything else to tell me?"

Sam directed his attention to his cup of coffee. "Nope."

"Good," said Warren. "None of my business anyway."

Annie delivered the bridal flowers to a calm Karen Sorenson at nine A.M. and the boutonnieres to a slightly frantic Frankie Machado at nine-thirty. The day promised to be a long one, and in a way she was glad. She needed some distance from the surprising events of the night before and maybe a little distance from Sam as well.

Last night she'd met a woman she'd never known existed. A passionate woman ready to throw caution to the four winds, a woman half crazed with desire. The insides of her thighs were still faintly red from the stubble on his cheeks and chin, and the memory of how the marks had come to be there was almost enough to send her flying back into his arms.

Not that she imagined he would have her. Last night he had been everything a lover should be. He had protected her when she needed protection. He had made love to her with his hands and mouth in ways that shattered her very core, made her climax again and again until she thought she had fallen off the edge of the earth, and she had responded by sneaking out of his house while he was on the telephone and running back home like the coward she was.

She was half surprised he hadn't egged her house and let the air out of her tires.

She had wanted to make love to him. She had burned to memorize every muscle of his lean, hard body with her tongue. Her sexual experiences might be limited to one man, but she wasn't an innocent. She knew how to give pleasure as well as how to take.

If only she hadn't noticed the way her hand looked as it rested against his tanned chest.

If only she hadn't noticed her wedding band.

Memory after memory of Kevin pushed in on her: their first kiss behind the marina, the senior prom when he gave her the failing gardenia, the day he proposed to her on the steps of the library at Bowdoin, their wedding day when it rained so hard they gave up on the umbrellas and just let it fall on them because how could a little rain hurt you when you held a world of happiness in your arms? And then there were the memories of sleepless nights waiting for him to come home, the strangers knocking on the door, the phone calls from men with deep voices who left messages she didn't want to understand, the night when it all ended in the middle of their brass bed as Annie kept whispering no no no no . . .

For two years she had struggled to make peace with his death, but it wasn't until last night in the arms of another man that she finally realized that she was alive, fully and completely alive, and that she was free to build a new life on the foundation of the old. She had been marking time for too long, measuring her days by bills paid and disasters averted.

She liked the Annie Galloway she had discovered last night: the passionate woman who wasn't looking over her shoulder all the time, wondering when life would deliver the next right hook. Sam Butler seemed to like her, too; or at least he had before she gathered up her clothes and slipped out the door on him without so much as a "Thank you, it's been swell." Of course, maybe she was making too much of the whole interlude. What had been a turning point of Olympic proportions to Annie might have been an hour's pleasurable pursuit to Sam and nothing more. Her face reddened as she remembered her deep satisfaction and what she assumed was his own deep discomfort at being left unfulfilled. Just how pleasurable the pursuit had been for him might be open for debate.

Assuming she ever saw him again.

Oh, yes, she was definitely glad she had a wedding to work today, a big demanding job with lots of details guaranteed to trip her up when she least expected it. She thrived on the pressure of time schedules and the never-ending surprises most weddings provided.

Today she was the Annie everyone knew and depended upon. The one with the lists and the schedules and the stopwatch embedded in her brain. That was how you built a business: by delivering everything you promised when you promised it . . . and just a little bit more. It made for some long days, but the fact that she would soon be able to go to her mailbox without being afraid of the bills she might find lurking inside was worth a little sleep deprivation.

She left Frankie's house, then rushed back to the shop and began loading the church flowers into the back of her truck, taking care to keep the delicate blooms cool and their stems in water. She threw wire cutters, three heavy spools of satin ribbon, and a huge box of ferns, misty, and baby's breath in with it, then raced for the church. The last mass of the day ended at eleven, and by eleven-ten Annie and Claudia were hard at work turning the somber old church into a wedding bower of blooms.

"I'm not sure Frankie's going to make it through the ceremony," she told Claudia as they placed the lush and fragrant arrangements of plumeria, ginger blossoms, hibiscus on the altar. "He looked scared out of his own skin."

"They always look that way," Claudia said with a fond laugh. "God knows my three boys did."

Annie turned to her ex-mother-in-law in surprise. "Not Kevin!"

"Oh, yes, Kevin," the woman said as she straightened the heavy satin ribbons draped over the altar cloth. "He was so nervous John finally had to sit him down and make him drink a shot of whiskey."

"I don't believe it."

"I'm not saying he didn't love you more than life itself, because he did, but when it comes to taking that walk down the aisle, I think most of them feel it's the last mile."

Annie thought back over the hundreds of weddings she had been to, either as a guest or as the florist, and a pattern began to emerge through the haze of orange blossoms. The brides had invariably been regal and steadfast in their resolve as they glided down the aisle, while the grooms wiped beads of sweat from their temples and tugged at shirt collars grown suddenly too tight.

"You're right," she said as she layered baby's breath and lacy ferns around the bigger arrangements. "Why didn't I ever notice that before?"

"We're the practical ones," Claudia said, gently shaping a flurry of plumeria with the pads of her fingers. "Once we make up our mind about a man, it's all over."

"Is that how it was for you and John?" They had been one of the happiest couples Annie had ever seen, as perfectly matched in every way as a husband and wife could wish for.

"Eventually," Claudia said.

They chatted quietly about the upcoming nuptials as they decorated the front pews. Claudia took the bride's side, Annie the groom's, and they were finished in short order.

As they were sweeping up fallen blossoms and scattered greenery, Claudia peered at Annie, then stepped closer.

"What's this?" She placed a gentle finger against Annie's left cheek. "Did one of those cats scratch you again?"

"No," Annie said, busy picking up tiny bits of feathery green leaves from the pristine white bridal carpet. "Why do you ask?"

"Your cheek is all red, honey. A little network of scratches."

"I can't imagine how I—" She stopped midsentence and willed herself not to dissolve in a crimson blush. Sam's stubble, which had felt delicious against her skin, had apparently left a calling card behind. She hated to lie but she wasn't up for the truth. "You know how it is with cats," she said, vowing to give the maligned George and

Gracie extra treats to make up for what she was doing to their reputation. "After a while you don't even notice the scratches."

"But you said—"

"I wasn't paying attention, Claude. I'm sorry, I was thinking about the reception and all I have to do there." She glanced at her watch. "In fact, I'm meeting Jen, Becky, and Sweeney at the Overlook in ten minutes."

"Ten minutes! Good Lord, honey, we'd better hurry."

Another crisis averted.

"Thanks for the help, Claudia," Annie said as they stepped out into the brilliant September sunshine. "We should have everything ready by the time they say 'I do.' "

Claudia retrieved her sunglasses from the bottom of her navy blue purse, then slipped them on. "You know I would be there with you if I didn't have my seminar this afternoon."

Annie slipped on her own sunglasses and rummaged through her tote bag for her car keys. "What is it this time: tai chi or low-fat cooking?"

"You're as bad as Susan," Claudia said with a shake of her well-coiffed head. "For your information, it's called Investing in Your Future, Part Two. This one is aimed at seniors on fixed incomes."

Annie couldn't help groaning. "Please tell me this isn't that terrible financial analyst with the radio show out of Boston."

"His name is Adam Winters, and his show is the number one financial program in all of New England."

"He's a huckster, Claudia. He's selling snake oil."

"He happens to be highly respected in his field."

"If his field happens to be scamming people."

Claudia lowered her sunglasses and stared closely at Annie. "I've never heard you sound so cynical before."

Back off, Annie, before you reveal a few family secrets. "Remember that financial analyst out of Bangor, the one who was brought up on charges? Some people actually lost their homes because they got involved with him."

"I'm insulted," Claudia said. "I'm hardly a fool, Anne. I'm not about to turn over my life savings to a stranger."

"I know you're not," Annie said, "but those guys make their money by being charming and convincing."

Claudia slid her sunglasses back into position. "I'll be sure to tell Roberta you think we're two old fools soon to be parted with our money."

"Claudia!" Annie didn't know whether to laugh or cry. "I didn't say that. I just said you should be careful."

But it was too late. Claudia marched down the church steps toward the parking lot in high dudgeon. Unless Annie missed her guess, Roberta would be in high dudgeon, too, before the day was over.

She didn't envy Adam Winters one single bit.

Sam ate enough blueberry waffles to make both Warren and Nancy happy for at least a year, then put away an extra one for himself.

Nancy sighed loudly as she gathered up the dirty plates to whisk them back into the kitchen. "Men eat, women gain weight. Wicked unfair, I say, and you can quote me."

Warren waited for Sam to polish off the rest of the coffee, then invited him out back to check out the boat.

"Nancy gave me the guided tour," Sam said as they walked across the backyard toward the converted barn, where Max was waiting for them. "You didn't get much done this spring."

"That's the trouble with being rich," Warren said. "You have the money to do what you want but you don't have the time." He looked over at Sam. "In case you haven't figured it out, that's where you come in."

The inside of the barn was dim and cool. It smelled of cedar shavings, dried hay, and salt air. Sam greedily filled his lungs with the pungent aromas.

"You already know I'm looking to open up the museum this time next year," he told Sam, "but we've fallen behind on the exhibits." The building he had purchased, formerly an old Catholic church at the foot of Small Crab Harbor, had been completely renovated right down to the wiring and floor joists. Local artwork had been commissioned for the museum, including murals, sculptures, folk art, and a wide range of photographs, both antique and current. The Ladies' Auxiliary and the VFW had managed to gather up a healthy collection of family albums, letters, and diaries that portrayed the day-to-day lives of fishermen and their families in a vividly moving fashion. A company in Bath was restoring a mailing boat from the 1920s and a nineteenth-century whaler. Both vessels would be berthed at the marina in Shelter Rock Cove and run three short cruises a day when weather permitted.

"Have you ever been to the Air and Space Museum at the Smithsonian?" Warren asked.

Sam shrugged. "Maybe when I was a kid."

"I'm looking to follow their lead and hang some of the exhibits from the ceiling using very thin wires. Your new neighbor, Annie Galloway, has been helping out with the lighting and the interior landscaping, and we think the effect will be pretty damn striking if I do say so." The church's vaulted ceiling made it a natural for the technique. Warren envisioned a range of handmade canoes, dating from seventeenth-century Penobscot to nineteenth-century Passamaquoddy to twenty-first-century third-generation Irish-American, swinging out over the main display area. "Kieran O'Connor was set to make us three canoes, but he busted both arms and a leg in a car wreck in Montreal and he's out of business for a while." He waited a good long moment then exploded, "You're too smart to be this dumb. Do I have to spell it out for you? I need you to make the canoes for the museum."

"That's a whole different craft," Sam said. "I'm better at repairs and restorations."

"How difficult can it be?" Warren pressed. He hadn't gotten where he was by throwing in the towel at the first sign of resistance. "You get some wood, a few hand tools, none of that fancy stuff, and you make a canoe."

"I'd rather work on finishing the restoration on your old man's fishing boat."

"Nope," said Warren, laying a fond hand on the still-battered hull of the *Sally B*. "This is mine. I'll be seeing her through."

"We'll need two kinds of wood for the canoe," Sam said, "another steamer so I can bend the hull, that old one doesn't—" He caught himself. "You old SOB. You knew I wouldn't be able to say no."

"That's what I was hoping."

"Why not farm it out to one of those canoemakers near Boothbay? They do great work."

"They're not local."

"Neither are the restorers down in Bath."

"Jake and Eli were born and bred in Shelter Rock Cove. I don't hold the move against them."

"I'm not a Mainer," Sam pointed out. "All I have to do is open my mouth, and everyone knows where I'm from. If you're looking for authenticity—"

"You're third-generation Irish, right?"

"Yeah, but—"

"And you put in some time here when you were a boy."

"That still doesn't make me—"

"And you're living here now."

"Only until I figure out my next step."

"Who knows," said Warren as he pulled the plans for the canoe from the back pocket of his trousers. "Maybe you're looking at it."

NINE

～∽◎∽～

Annie broke a few speed limits between the church and the Overlook, but luck was with her, and the Shelter Rock Cove police force of two officers and one chief were apparently busy elsewhere. The Overlook was situated atop one of the cliffs that, appropriately enough, overlooked the cove itself. It had been built some eighty years ago by a wealthy shipbuilder who intended to use it as his summer mansion. The Great Depression, however, put an end to that dream, and over the ensuing years the beautiful structure had served as an orphanage, a spa, a hotel, and now most recently as a reception hall for weddings, conventions, and other large and noisy gatherings.

Sweeney's old VW bus was angled crazily into the spot nearest the service door, and she was busy unloading centerpieces onto the pair of rolling carts Annie had found at a going-out-of-business auction over in Bangor a few months ago.

"You're awfully punctual for a woman who refuses to wear a watch," Annie said when Sweeney turned around to see who was approaching.

"All those years on the commune taught me how to—" Sweeney threw back her head and laughed with delight. "As I live and breathe! Whisker burns on Annie Galloway's cheeks!"

This time Annie was prepared. "Blame George and Gracie," she said as she reached into the bus for one of the centerpieces. "Cat owners deserve hazard pay."

"Oh, no," said Sweeney with a shake of her head, "those aren't cat scratches. I live with six of the little beasties, and those aren't cat scratches, honey, those are manmade."

"You've been reading too many romance novels."

"And you haven't been reading enough of them," Sweeney countered. "I think it's great, honey." She grabbed for a centerpiece herself. "In fact, if the whisker burns are from the man I think they're from, I think it's downright fantastic."

Annie couldn't help herself. She started to laugh. "You don't know the first thing about him, Sweeney. He could be married and have six kids."

"Is he?"

Annie hesitated. "I—uh, I don't think so." *Of course he isn't, Annie. Didn't he say he wasn't sleeping with anyone?*

"You don't sound terribly sure."

"We didn't exchange résumés, Sweeney."

"I did a reading on him last night," Sweeney said as they started trundling the dozen centerpieces into the building, "and I saw lots of family but no wife or children."

"Not those tarot cards again."

"I know, I know," said Sweeney. "You're much too practical to believe in the cards, but the second I saw the two of you standing together outside, I had this funny feeling—"

Annie made a face and resumed pushing her cart toward the entrance. "It's probably that bag of Oreos you carry around with you."

"Believe me, honey, if I thought I had a chance with the man I wouldn't be here right now talking with you. I'd be doing the Dance of the Seven Veils on his front porch. I threw those cards three times, and each time the answer was the same: Your futures are intertwined."

Annie tried to make a joke out of Sweeney's prediction. *You knew it all the time, Annie, from the first second you saw him in the parking lot.*

Damn Sweeney anyway for putting these ridiculous thoughts in her head. If their futures were intertwined, why did she run for the exit last night as though her life depended on it?

You know the answer to that one, too. You had a glimpse of the future, and it scared the hell out of you.

"Oh, shut up," Annie muttered as she navigated the cart of flowers through the doorway.

"Shut up?" Sweeney sounded much aggrieved.

"Not you," Annie said. "I'm talking to myself."

"You, too?" Sweeney held the interior door open with her behind and motioned for Annie to precede her. "That's why I have cats," she said as she pushed her own cart into the main ballroom. "When someone catches me talking to myself, I just say I'm talking to the cats. Sounds weird, but it's surprisingly effective."

"I did that last week when the Flemings did the walk-through on the house. They're dog people, but I think they understood."

Whisker burns, bouts of talking to herself. Before long Annie would be blaming George and Gracie for her bad taste in window treatments and the proliferation of nuclear weapons.

The idea tickled her fancy and, more than that, kept her

mind away from the thornier problem of Sam Butler and her feelings for him for at least six minutes. She considered that a genuine triumph. It seemed to Annie that he had been dominating her every waking thought since she first laid eyes on him in the Yankee Shopper parking lot. One moment she was the Annie Lacy Galloway everyone knew and depended on, and the next she was some hot-blooded stranger, ripping the clothes off a man she barely knew and loving every second of it. How could you live thirty-eight years on this planet and know so little about yourself?

She doubted if even Sweeney's tarot cards had an answer for that one.

Susan looked at Hall over the top of her reading glasses. The entire contents of all the major New England Sunday newspapers were spread across the picnic table, along with crumbs from a peanut-butter-and-jelly sandwich and chocolate-chip cookies.

"Let me see if I got this right," Susan said, obviously trying to torture him. "You forgot your kids were coming to spend the night."

"Completely," said Hall, resting one foot on the bench across from his friend. "I was in the shower when they started pounding on the front door."

"The big ones or the little ones?"

"Little ones," he said.

Susan groaned. "Yvonne must've loved that."

"She put a good face on it," Hall said, "but she looked pretty disappointed."

"I'll bet." She glanced around her backyard. "Where are they?"

"Waiting by the car."

"Go get them. They can hang out with Jeannie by the

pool." She laughed at the look on his face. "Don't worry. Jack's playing lifeguard. They'll be fine."

Five minutes later Hall was back in position, one foot on the picnic bench, his gaze riveted to his oldest friend, butterflies flapping around inside his abdominal cavity.

"Since when can't you entertain your own children for the afternoon?" Susan asked him, cutting to the chase as usual. "Unless you're trying to wangle dinner invitations for the lot of you."

"Just two."

Susan's eyebrows lifted. "You have other plans?"

Disappointment welled up inside him, giving the butterflies a run for their money. "She didn't tell you."

Susan was smart. She knew without being told that "she" meant Annie. "I haven't spoken to her since she moved into the new house. Tell me what?"

"Cappy's," he said, trying not to hang too many hopes on one word. "Seven o'clock."

She leaned over to look at his watch. "And it's—"

"Five forty-two."

"I suppose you want to go home and shower."

"Something like that."

"And it's easier without having the kids hanging around, asking all sorts of embarrassing questions."

"Definitely."

"So go," she said, giving him an affectionate swat on the arm with the Arts and Leisure section of the *New York Times*. "And tell her to call me. I want the scoop from both of you."

"I owe you for this, Susie," he said, pressing an affectionate kiss to the top of her head.

"Darn right you do," she called out as he dashed for the car. He was older and a tiny bit grayer but he was the same Hall she remembered from high school, single-minded focus hidden behind a casual, easygoing exterior that never failed to charm.

She managed to wait until his car was halfway down the driveway before she hurried around to the pool where Jack was supervising the kids in a game of water volleyball.

She sat down next to him and dangled her feet in the water. "I have big news," she said.

He shot her one of those husbandly looks that sometimes made her want to hit him. "Don't tell me you're pregnant."

"Wash your mouth out," she said, then lowered her voice. "Hall and Annie are going out tonight."

"Jeez, Susan, I told you to—"

"I had nothing to do with it. Apparently he drove over to Annie's house yesterday morning at Claudia's request, one thing led to another, and they have a date tonight."

"You don't really think anything's going to come of this, do you?"

"Hall can be terribly charming," she said then paused a beat. "And he's a doctor. That doesn't exactly hurt."

"And she's known him all her life. If something was going to develop between them, you'd think you might've seen a hint somewhere along the way."

"There was always Kevin," she said softly as thoughts of her brother tugged at her heart. "He's a tough act to follow."

"You know what I'm talking about," Jack said. "Like you and Tony Dee at the real estate office."

"Jack!" She sounded both outraged and deeply flattered. "Tony Dee!?"

"I've seen the two of you at those office get-togethers," her husband said in his matter-of-fact way. "Your flirting generates a hell of a lot of heat."

"Oh, don't be silly. We just—"

"I'm not criticizing you, Suze. Just stating a fact. You've never seen anything like that between Hall and Annie, have you."

"Well, no, but—"

"Case closed."

"Now wait a minute. Annie's a very serious person. She never even flirted with Kevin."

"The hell she didn't."

"Not so you'd notice."

"But it was there," her suddenly observant husband confirmed. "It either is or it isn't, Suze, and I'm telling you it's not there for Annie and Hall."

Susan watched her youngest daughter throw a volleyball at her little brother's head. He didn't scream, and there was no blood, so she dismissed the action as business as usual.

Things changed as the years passed. The dreams you dreamed when you were twenty-five and thirty might not seem quite so compelling when you were knocking on forty's door. Nobody doubted that Kevin had been the love of Annie's life, her soulmate. All you'd had to do was watch them together and instantly you knew that all those two needed to be happy was each other. They guarded their time alone together and were loath to squander a precious weekday evening or weekend with friends or family when they could be spending it alone together.

She barely managed to suppress a sigh. Kevin had adored Annie. Right up until the very end, he was still writing poems for her and sending her flowers just because. She'd never admitted to anyone how much she had envied Annie. Oh, it wasn't that Jack didn't love her. He did. She was as sure about that as she was sure about tomorrow's sunrise. Jack's love for her was a cozy comforter on a cold winter's night, but Kevin's love for Annie had been starlight and moonbeams and the sound of violins, and sometimes a woman longed for a little night music.

It was silly, and she knew it, envying a widow the marriage she no longer had, but there you had it. No wonder Annie wasn't striking sparks with anyone. Who could ever compete with what she'd had with Kevin? Maybe Hall hadn't been Annie's knight in shining armor back when they were young, but who could say he wasn't just right for her today? She'd had her once-in-a-lifetime love. Now she needed someone mature and responsible, someone who would fit right in with the family, someone who had grown up in the same town and knew the same people, to share her life with, and as far as Susan was concerned, Hall fit the bill to a T.

How much fun it would be to go to the movies with Annie and Hall, stop for a bite to eat at Cappy's, maybe even—

"Hey, you two!" Jack bellowed next to her as their daughter attempted to decaptitate their son while Hall's two well-behaved children looked on in horror. "One more stunt like that and you're both out of the pool."

Susan shook her head in dismay. "Why is it always our children who act up?"

"Genetics," her husband said, draping an arm around her shoulders and holding her tight. "Our poor kids don't stand a chance."

Annie took Sweeney and the girls out for some ice cream after they finished at the Overlook, and by the time they'd all finished eating and laughing and gossiping about the latest doings in town, it was nearly six o'clock. The girls hurried for home, and Sweeney headed off to meet another one of her many boyfriends at an outdoor concert two towns over.

"Why don't you come, too," Sweeney said as they

walked to their cars. "Fred and I have pretty much run our course. I could use a buffer, to be honest."

Annie shuddered. "I've met Fred," she said. "You could use a moat and a drawbridge."

"The pickings get wicked slim when you're my age, honey. They're not all Harrison Ford."

Annie was still laughing when she pulled into her driveway. The small house was dim and cool. George and Gracie were sound asleep on adjacent platforms of the cat condo and paid Annie little attention. The only sound was the ever-present drumming of the waves against the shore, punctuated by the occasional cry of a hungry seagull. Sam's truck wasn't parked in his driveway, and she wondered where he'd gone.

Not that it was any of her business. She was, after all, the one who had slipped out his front door without so much as a goodbye, all because moving forward had proved to be every bit as frightening as standing in place.

You know what to do, Annie. You're a grown woman. Fix yourself up, then march over to his house with a bottle of wine and some leftover pizza and apologize for running out on him.

There was a small window of opportunity to make amends. She glanced at her watch. And an even smaller window of opportunity to do something about her hair.

Susan tried her best to stay away from the telephone, but at six-thirty she lost the battle. She left her brood—plus two—gathered around the barbecue grill and slipped into their home office, where she pressed number three on the speed dial and listened to Annie's phone ring.

"I can't believe you didn't tell me," she said by way of hello. "I waited as long as I could but I can't take it anymore. What are you wearing? Those white pants I hope and maybe that red sweater ... It's cool enough for the sweater tonight . . . Maybe you could—"

"Who is this?" Annie demanded.

"Who is this?" Susan repeated, stung to the quick. "It's Susan, and I want to know why you didn't tell me." Silence. A long, protracted silence. "Annie?" She tapped the mouthpiece with a fingernail. "Did you hang up on me?"

"No." Another silence, then: "How did you know?"

"How did I know? How do you *think?* He told me, that's how."

"He told you? I didn't even think he knew you."

"Did I wake you up?" Susan asked. "You don't sound like yourself. He came over to ask me to watch his kids tonight and he told me."

"Ohmygod . . ."

"Annie, you really don't sound like yourself. Are you okay? Is something going on? Do you want me to come over and—"

"I completely forgot about Hall," Annie said through what sounded like hysterical laughter. "Gotta go . . . I'll call you tomorrow."

Click.

"She hung up on me," Susan said to the empty room. Annie Galloway, the most polite woman on earth, hung up on her and laughed when she did it.

Something was rotten in Shelter Rock Cove, and Susan was going to find out what it was.

Sam and Warren spent the day down at a maritime museum not far from Camden. Warren was friends with the curator, who shared some insights on interactive displays and the feasibility of adding cruises to the mix. There were safety considerations to take into account, insurance costs, Maine's changeable weather. Warren, who was underwriting the entire venture, absorbed the information without taking a single note, something that never failed to astonish Sam.

While Warren talked business, Sam wandered the shipyard. It had been a long time since he'd breathed in that particular blend of wood, varnish, fuel, and fish. He filled his lungs with it and grinned at nothing in particular. It smelled like home to him, like the marina back in Queens where he'd worked as a teenager. Had any job ever made him as happy as that one? Closing deals for a million and more never once gave him the rush of happiness he'd found when he was up to his elbows in marine grease and loving every minute of it.

Maybe that's how he'd end up, fixing boats at some broken-down marina, his fingernails stained permanently black, his skin smelling of sea spray, his bank balance hovering around zero. There were worse ways for a man to spend his life, especially if he had the right woman to share his days and nights with.

But what the hell did he have to offer a woman these days? Six months ago he could have made a case for himself: great car, great apartment, great prospects. Now he had even less than Annie Galloway. Annie owned her house and her business. He was owned by an aging yellow Lab.

"You look like you've got the weight of the world on your shoulders," Warren observed as they headed back to Shelter Rock Cove. "Anything I should know about?"

"I think you need transmission fluid," Sam said as he switched lanes. "This old Jeep needs more babying than you give it." He slowed down behind a sluggish Audi. "Think it might be time to spring for something built in the last decade?"

"Wiseass," Warren said amiably. "So are you going to tell me what's really going on, or will you make me beat it out of you?"

Sam laughed out loud. "You don't think I'm dumb enough to take you up on the latter, do you?" Warren had been an amateur boxer at one point in his youth, and he still maintained an impressive set of biceps.

"You'll figure it out," Warren said, "whatever it is."

"Yeah?" He shot Warren a look. "Think I'll manage it before I'm your age?"

"Not if the problem is a woman."

There was no arguing that.

"How about we stop along the way for a steak and baked potato?" Warren suggested.

Sam glanced at the clock on the dashboard. Six thirty-five P.M. Annie was supposed to meet the Town Doctor at seven for dinner.

He was maybe thirty minutes away from Shelter Rock Cove.

It was fate.

"I'm thinking lobster," he said, knowing Warren would understand. "I heard about some place called Cappy's . . ."

"Now that was a wonderful seminar," Roberta said as she and Claudia strolled across the parking lot of the Bangor Holiday Inn. "That boy must have kissed the Blarney Stone somewhere along the way."

"He's young enough to be our grandson," Claudia said with a shake of her head. "So smart! Do they make them smarter these days, Bobbi, or does it just seem that way?"

"It's all those Flintstone vitamins," Roberta said, adjusting the strap on her purse so it angled just so across her pillowy breasts. "Imagine how smart we would've been if we'd had half of the advantages our children had."

Oh, there was truth enough to that statement, Claudia thought as Roberta drove them back toward Shelter Rock Cove. Today's young people had no idea what it was like to scrimp and save for every penny. They expected to step out of school and into some fancy, high-paying job, and that was usually exactly what happened. Back in her day, you considered yourself lucky to find a position and you clung to it until the day you retired. It was a whole different world that Adam Winters painted for them during the four-hour seminar. "Don't think it's too late to influence the future," he had said to them as he strode the aisles, aiming his snowy-white smile right at Claudia and Roberta and other women just like them. "Americans are living longer than ever before, and their standard of living is growing right along with them. Why shouldn't you be part of the golden age of seniors and grab a piece of the American pie for yourself?"

Why, indeed. Everything the young man had said made perfect sense to Claudia. She and John had worked very hard for their money, and she had watched over it carefully since his death. The house was paid for—that was a blessing—and she owned her own car. Her health insurance was adequate, but it would take only one serious illness to put a dent in what remained of her nest egg. She was comfortable but she wasn't secure, and Adam Winters said she had the right to be both or know the reason why.

Susan would be downright horrified if she knew that Claudia had written out a check for $2,000 as tuition for Adam Winters's week-long seminar to be held next month. "Have you lost your mind, Ma?" she would bellow. "Why don't you give the guy the key to your safe-deposit box, too, while you're at it?"

It was truly a wonderful deal, a once-in-a-lifetime opportunity. If she decided to let Adam Winters Associates manage her funds, $1,500 of the tuition monies would be plowed right back into her account. Even Susan would have to admit that was more than generous.

Her children thought they had the right to rule her life.

They had opinions on everything from the house she lived in to the food she cooked and the company she kept, and she resented it deeply. She tried very hard to keep her nose out of their business and she expected the same consideration in return. This was her money, hers and her beloved John's, and if she wanted to use it as a stepping stone toward building her investment, then that was exactly what she would do.

"I'm not telling Jessica and Peter," Roberta said as they neared the outskirts of town. "One more lecture about how it might be time for me to hand over my power of attorney and I'll leave everything to Sparky." Sparky was her Airedale.

Claudia nodded. "I'm not telling any of mine." She had thought she might confide in Annie, but now that was out as well.

"They'll thank us one day," Roberta said.

"Absolutely," Claudia concurred. "When we've tripled their inheritances, they'll sing a different tune."

Roberta made a left turn onto Willow Road. "Steak at Brubaker's or the fish fry at Cappy's?"

"Cappy's," said Claudia. "I'm in the mood for french fries."

"Damn the cholesterol," said Roberta as she gunned the engine of her Buick Riviera. "Full speed ahead!"

TEN

Cappy's-on-the-Cove was a former lobster shack with delusions of grandeur. What had begun as a modest establishment with window service only had grown by bits and pieces over the years until it could now seat forty with just minor discomfort. The floors were uneven. The ceilings varied in height. The tables near the kitchen were a good ten degrees hotter than anywhere else in the place. But when it came to mouth-watering lobster and world-class blueberry pie, it didn't get much better than Cappy's.

"Been too long, Doc," said Gloria, the original owner's daughter-in-law. "We haven't seen you since the Fourth of July."

"Lots of babies born this summer, Glo," he said as he followed her to a table near the window. "How's the chowder tonight?"

"First-rate," she said, plopping down a menu in front of him. "Should I start you off with an iced tea?"

Awkward moment number one.

"Hold off on the iced tea," he said, striving to sound casual and unconcerned. "I'm meeting someone here."

"Yeah?" said Gloria, leaning over the table. "Who?"

"A friend."

"Anyone I know?"

"You know everybody in town," he said, feeling like a sixteen-year-old being grilled by a girlfriend's parents.

"Unless she's wearing a disguise, I'll figure it out soon enough," Gloria said with a laugh. "Two iced teas coming right up."

Why even bother to order, Hall wondered, when Gloria was going to bring him exactly what she wanted to bring him. That was one of the best and worst parts of spending your life in the same little town where you grew up: You lost the capacity to surprise people around the time you went into puberty. The librarians knew your taste in books. The clerks in the record store knew your taste in music. The guy behind the counter at the coffee shop knew you liked it black with three sugars, while Gloria here at Cappy's could recite your favorite menu even if you hadn't been in to visit since summer began. And because everybody in town knew everybody else, all of the information ended up in one gigantic database meant to ensure that you had no privacy at all. Maine's version of the Akashic record, he thought, and wished he had someone with whom to share the observation.

Gloria returned with the iced teas. "She's late, whoever she is."

"Not very." Eleven minutes and thirty seconds.

Not that he was counting or anything.

The cowbell over the front door jingled. "Hi, Annie!" Gloria called out. "Pick a seat. I'll be there in a second."

Annie walked over to the table and claimed the seat opposite him. "I hope one of those iced teas is for me."

Gloria just barely managed to keep her jaw from hitting the tabletop. "You bet. And two lobster specials," she said, "coming right up."

"How does she do that?" Annie said, shaking her head as Gloria walked away. "She knows what I want before I do."

"Practice," he said, glancing down at the advertisements printed on his paper placemat. *Teeth getting you down? Visit The Tooth Factory for 21st Century Solutions.* Real romantic. Why hadn't he suggested they go to Renaldi's in town, someplace with a tablecloth and ventilation that didn't reek of dead fish?

If she noticed, she didn't let on. She told him a funny story about the Sorenson-Machado wedding, and he laughed when he was supposed to laugh, but her words never got through. Something was different about her. Her hair was still the same wild mass of unruly curls. Her blue eyes were still framed by spiky lashes and the faintest beginnings of crow's feet. She still had the same off-center smile. He couldn't point to any one thing that had changed, but somehow everything had, and he had the sense of being left behind.

She pointed toward the window that looked out over the dock. "Isn't that Susan leaning against the railing?"

You're dead, Susie, he thought as he saw a familiar face trying to pretend she had a reason to be there. What the hell was wrong with her anyway?

"We should ask her to join us," Annie said.

"She's probably with the kids."

"That's not a problem," Annie said. "We're godparents to a few of them, right?"

He was about to say something incredibly witty when he saw two more familiar faces pressed against the front window of Cappy's. Four fists rapped on the glass.

"It's Daddy!" Willa cried out. Who knew her voice was that piercing?

"Daddy!" Mariah, the older of the two, hooked her pinkies in either side of her mouth and crossed her eyes.

The gesture was particularly effective coupled with the fact that her nose was squashed flat against the window.

Annie waved at the girls. "I didn't know you had your kids with you this weekend."

"Neither did I," he muttered.

"We might as well ask them to join us," Annie said. "It's either that or pretend they're not out there."

"Great idea," he said, summoning up that old bedside manner once more. "The more the merrier."

"Pull over some chairs," she said to the newcomers as they approached, "and join us."

Hall's smile never wavered. It was part of his training. "I'm sure our Susie has something better to do than watch us eat dinner."

Susan looked guilty as sin.

"Hall's right," she said, leaning a hand on Annie's shoulder as she reached over and plucked a tomato off her sister-in-law's salad. "We're out of here. We came out for pizza and got a little sidetracked."

Is that what they call it these days, Susie?

"You know," said Jack, the only innocent in the room, "I haven't had a lobster roll in a while. Why don't we just pull up another table and those chairs Annie was talking about and join them?"

"Look at this!" Gloria exclaimed as she deposited more menus. "The whole family's here."

It was like trying to stop lava from rolling downhill. Jack shoved two tables together. Susan gathered up some chairs. The kids turned a quiet evening into a free-for-all. Not that his kids were loud all the time. They didn't have to be. They accomplished their goals with a few well-chosen words.

"Are you going to marry my daddy?" Willa asked Annie. "Aunt Susan said—"

"Willa!" Susan looked as if she wanted to crawl under the table, but Annie remained unruffled.

"No, I'm not," Annie said calmly. "I'm not marrying your daddy or anybody else for that matter." She laughed and looked over at Hall, expecting to find him laughing, too, at the crazy question. Only thing was, Hall wasn't laughing. He was sending Susan looks that would send a sane woman heading into the witness protection program.

"Daddy likes getting married," Mariah confided as she nibbled the edges of a heavily sugared lemon wedge. "Mommy says that's why he does it so much."

"And I'm going to keep doing it until I get it right," Hall said.

Everyone laughed, and the tension at the table fell away. They all knew that kids said the damndest things, and if you took any of their gossipy pronouncements seriously, you'd string them up by the umbilical cord. Better to laugh and change the subject and hope that wiser heads than yours didn't know exactly what was going on.

"Awfully crowded for a Sunday night," Roberta observed as she carefully eased her way into a parking spot in Cappy's lot.

"It's Labor Day weekend," Claudia pointed out, rooting through her purse for her lipstick. "This is the last hurrah, so to speak."

She found her tube of clear red and applied it swiftly without using a mirror. That was one of the few benefits of being as old as she was: there were certain beauty rituals a woman could perform in her sleep. Roberta flipped open her silver compact and painstakingly applied her pink lipstick, then carefully brought down the shine on her aquiline nose. She shut the compact with a loud click, then laughed.

"And who are we doing this for?" Roberta asked as

they climbed from the car. "Men don't notice you once you reach our age."

"Men stop noticing you once you reach forty," Claudia said. "That doesn't mean you stop caring about how you look."

"Are we really this vain, Claudia?" Roberta smoothed her coif with the flat of her hand.

"Yes," she said, opening the door to Cappy's for her dearest friend. "We really are."

Time was having its way with her each and every day, wrinkling what once was smooth, lowering what used to sit high, playing tricks on her digestive tract she wouldn't wish on her worst enemy. Was it so wrong to want to fight back just a little?

Gloria waved to them from behind the counter. "Should've known you weren't far behind, Claudia. C'mon in and join the family."

"Over there," Roberta said, nudging her in the side. "Susie's here with her brood, and isn't that Dr. Hall and Annie? Well, well, well."

Something inside Claudia's chest began to burn, and it had nothing to do with the buttered roll she'd treated herself to during the break at the seminar. Hall and Anne? How ridiculous.

"Grandma!" Susan's youngest tackled her before she was halfway to the table. "Tell her we can so have dessert first."

Claudia chuckled. On her darkest days, her grandchildren could call out the sun just for her. "Your mother makes the rules, sweetie," she said, ruffling his hair. "Same as I did when she was your age."

It was clear from the look on the boy's face that he didn't believe his mother had ever been his age. One day she would blink her eyes, and he would be walking down the aisle like Frankie Machado this afternoon.

Hall, ever the gentleman, leaped to his feet when he saw Claudia and Roberta approaching.

"Ladies," he greeted them, as casually as if he'd never once held an icy speculum to their nether regions, "you'll join us, won't you?"

Roberta almost giggled as she took a seat at one of the tables. The woman had herself a small crush on the middle-aged doctor, an affliction shared by half of the women in their crowd. Their foolishness appalled Claudia. To her, he was still the same gangly high school student who ran with Susan and her crowd. Oh, there had been a time when Claudia had entertained the hope that maybe he and Susan would one day get together (there was nothing wrong with wanting a doctor in the family), but her Susan had a mind of her own. She looked over at Jack, who was chatting amiably with one of Hall's impeccably well-groomed little girls. Jack was a good husband and father, and, on a purely selfish level, it was grand to have a first-class auto mechanic in the family. Her four-year-old Oldsmobile still ran like a dream, and she had her son-in-law to thank.

"I didn't know you were all meeting here for dinner," she said, trying very hard not to single out Annie and Hall when she said it. "What a nice surprise."

"We'd just placed our order when we saw Susan out there on the dock," Annie said. She turned to Hall's youngest and stroked her silky blond hair. "This is more fun than pizza, right?"

Claudia's internal alarm system began to buzz softly. Did Annie say, *"We'd just placed our order,"* or had she imagined it?

Susan leaned over and pressed her lips close to Claudia's ear. "Say one word and so help me, Ma, you'll never babysit again."

She pretended to peruse the laminated sheet of paper

that served as Cappy's dinner menu. If there were sparks
flying between Annie and Hall Talbot, they were invisible
to her. They seemed friendly, very comfortable with each
other, and as devoid of chemistry as two people of the
opposite sex could be. Annie chatted easily with him, the
same way she did with everyone else, although Claudia
did notice that Hall's eyes kept drifting back toward Annie in a way that seemed a tad more than platonic. That
didn't worry her. Hall was free to pursue Annie in as
ardent a fashion as he might like, just so long as Annie
didn't return his ardor in kind.

Now that man who'd showed up at the flower shop the
other morning—well, he worried her. The atmosphere between him and Annie had veritably crackled with something Claudia didn't like one single bit. She had given
Warren a good talking-to last night about keeping his nose
out of her daughter-in-law's business. Annie was fine,
even if she had made a terrible mistake when she chose
to sell the house she and Kevin had lived in for most of
their marriage. If she ever—and it was something Claudia
could scarcely bear thinking about—found herself in love
with another man, it would be someone from Shelter Rock
Cove, someone who shared her history, someone who understood what was important in life. Not some surly-
looking stranger from New York.

Besides, when it came to love and romance, men were
just along for the ride. Women were the ones behind the
wheel. They decided where the romance went and how
fast and when it was time to slam on the brakes or put
pedal to the metal, as the kids liked to say. She glanced
over at ardent Hall and cool Annie and smiled to herself.
As far as Claudia could tell, they were still in separate
cars.

●   ●   ●

Claudia, you're looking a little bit too self-satisfied for my taste, Annie thought as she nibbled her side of cole slaw.

She had seen her mother-in-law's blue eyes zeroing in on both her and Hall as she tried to assess the situation for potential landmines. Apparently she had decided that Hall presented no threat to the status quo and was settling down to enjoy her meal in peace and harmony.

I love you, Claude, but this is really none of your business.

She glanced toward Susan, who looked edgy, guilty, and very disappointed.

Serves you right, Suze. This is what you get for being so nosy.

She smiled at Hall, who was busy cracking a lobster claw for Willa.

It's easier this way, Hall. I'll never know if you were really interested, and you'll never know that I'm really not.

"So, Roberta," she said, "how was the seminar?" She would have asked Claudia but she wasn't sure her mother-in-law was speaking to her.

Roberta cast a furtive glance at Claudia. "Long," she said. "More information than you can absorb in such a short time."

Hall looked up from Willa's lobster claws. "Another seminar, ladies?" Roberta's and Claudia's penchant for seminars and workshops was well-known. "What was it this time?"

The two older women exchanged glances. How peculiar, thought Annie. It wasn't like it was a secret or anything.

"Informational," Claudia said. "The history of American finance, that sort of thing."

Hall frowned. "Not that Adam Winters I saw on television."

Claudia laughed, but nobody believed her. "Now don't you start casting aspersions, young man. My own children do enough of that to last me a lifetime, thank you very much. Roberta and I look at these seminars as performance art."

"You do not," Susan said. "You—ouch!" She turned and glared at Jack. "She's my mother, Jack. I can say whatever I want to say to her."

"Oh, no, you can't," Claudia retorted. "What I do with my time is my business, young lady. I don't tell you how to live your life—"

"Hah!"

"—and you don't tell me how to live mine. That way we'll get on quite well together."

"Say something, Hall!" Susan commanded. "You're the only one here who isn't related to her. Tell her those so-called financial experts are bad news."

Hall seemed deep in thought.

"Don't tell me you're secretly addicted to those seminars, too," Annie said with a laugh.

"No," he said. His brow was deeply furrowed. "Damn it. This little piece of memory has been circling around all day, and I almost grabbed it when you mentioned that seminar."

"Run through the alphabet," Roberta suggested. "That always jogs my memory."

"It probably wasn't important," Jack said. "If it was, you'd remember it."

"There's a brilliant statement," Susan said, rolling her eyes. "Like *you've* never forgotten a birthday or anniversary."

That kicked off a mildly amusing round of marital banter that served to forestall further discussion of Adam Winters and his financial wizardry.

Annie decided she would finish her lobster, have a little ice cream, then say goodnight before Hall made a move or Claudia said something incendiary or Susan threw herself on her sword.

She had never been one to push her luck and she wasn't about to start now.

"The place is crowded," Warren observed as Sam whipped into a parking spot at the far end of the lot. "Bet there's plenty of room at that new steak-and-ribs joint."

"We're here," Sam said, turning off the engine. "Might as well give it a try."

"Nothing like a big juicy slab of prime rib with a baked potato piled high with sour cream." Warren sounded downright wistful.

"Heart attack on a plate," Sam said. "You're better off eating fish."

"Lots of cholesterol in shellfish, too," Warren pointed out, but Sam ignored him.

He was exactly where he wanted to be. Hell, where he needed to be. Annie was in there. He'd spotted her Trooper before he even turned into the driveway and right away he felt like a teenager getting ready for his first date—the gaping hole in the pit of his stomach, the sweaty palms, the fear he might walk in there and say something they would both regret. Something irrational and downright crazy like, "I love you." You couldn't love somebody you didn't know. Love at first sight was a construct of romantic fantasy. It didn't exist in a brick-and-mortar world.

But try telling that to his heart. He felt expectant, hopeful, terrified, elated, determined, uncertain, every combination of emotion possible. He'd never done anything like this in his life. She was in there with another guy, on something that came pretty damn close to being a date, and he was about to crash their party.

"I've had a wonderful time," Annie said as she reached for her purse, "but it's been a long day, and I'm just about out on my feet."

"You're not going already," Hall said in a voice meant for her alone.

"I'm afraid so." Had he always looked at her with so much longing, or was she just seeing him for the very first time? "There was the Sorenson wedding today, and tomorrow's the Labor Day picnic." She forced a light-hearted chuckle as the cowbell announced another new arrival. "I'm not getting any younger, you know. Long days and late nights can do a woman in."

"Why don't you—"

He stopped speaking midsentence. Annie followed his gaze. Her heart slammed hard against her rib cage. Sam and Warren were standing by the cash register. Warren was chatting happily with Gloria. Sam looked edgy, solitary, strange and familiar both. She'd slept in his arms. He'd made love to her and asked nothing in return. She knew everything about him and nothing at all.

His dark eyes met hers.

You shouldn't have done this, Sam. He'd heard her make plans with Hall that first morning. He knew exactly where she would be and when, and the fact that he was standing there was the loudest declaration of intent she had ever heard.

A thrill of unabashed delight raced through her, and she couldn't help herself. She started to laugh.

The silence at the table was deafening. They looked at her as if she'd lost her mind, and maybe she had. Maybe this was how it felt to be crazy out of your head in love with a man you just met. Maybe this was how it felt to be happy for the first time in way too long.

She pushed back her chair and stood up.

Nobody said a word.

She slung her shoulder bag back across her body.

Nobody breathed.

She put a ten-dollar bill on the table, then started the long slow walk across the room to where Sam stood by the cash register.

Nobody moved.

"I'm sorry," she said to Sam, quietly so only he could hear. "I shouldn't have run out that way last night."

He said nothing.

She waited.

They watched.

She felt herself shapeshifting right there in Cappy's, turning into someone she no longer recognized. A woman who needed more than the sound of her own heartbeat for company and who was no longer afraid to take the first step.

Say something, she pleaded silently. *If you don't say something right now, I'll go crazy.*

"Come on," he said, reaching for her hand. "Let's get out of here."

ELEVEN

If a hydrogen bomb had landed on Cappy's, the result couldn't have been any more dramatic than the sight of Annie Lacy Galloway walking out the door hand-in-hand with Sam Butler. Warren had seen many a fine exit in his day, but that was one of the all-time best.

"She knows him?" Roberta asked, breaking the stunned silence.

"No," said Jack.

"I don't know," said Susan.

"Yes," said Hall and Claudia in unison.

Warren claimed Annie's seat. "That's Sam Butler," he said easily, as if hell hadn't just frozen over. "He'll be living in Ellie's old place for a while."

"As if that explains anything," Claudia muttered, rapping her knuckles against the tabletop.

"I've known him since he was a teenager," Warren went on, ignoring her vexation. "A better man you won't find anywhere."

"Oh, my God!" Susan grabbed her husband's arm. "That's the guy with the pizza-eating dog."

Jack gave her one of those looks all men understood. "What the hell are you talking about, Susie?"

She told him the story that Annie had told her, about a man and his dog and a stack of ruined pizzas.

"That's so romantic," Roberta said, oblivious to the glares coming her way from Hall, Susan, and Claudia. "A cute meet, like something from an old Rock Hudson–Doris Day movie."

"You've been watching too much AMC," Claudia snapped. "Life was not created in Hollywood, Roberta."

"I bumped into Annie in the parking lot that night," Hall piped up. All eyes turned toward him. "He took off without bothering to clean up the mess."

"That's the same story I heard," Claudia said, pleased to have a tidbit to add to the mix. She neglected to mention the fact that he did end up cleaning the truck for Annie. She was in no mood to be kind. "I must say he took quite a proprietary air when he brought back the keys to her place."

The gasp at the table brought Gloria running to see what was wrong.

"Annie?!" Susan could barely get the word out of her mouth.

"No way," said Jack.

"Mmmm!" Roberta's eyes twinkled with envious delight.

Mariah and Willa giggled. The boys made gagging noises.

Hall's cheeks were bright pink, but his voice was steady, his demeanor cool. "There was something wrong with her front door that first morning. He was there to fix it."

The girls' giggles grew louder, and Hall shot them a stern look.

"She's earned the right," said Roberta defiantly. "She's

been alone a long time. She's a young woman. Why shouldn't she take a lover?"

"You talk like an old fool." Claudia was rhythmically shredding the paper placemats at the table. "If you can't see he isn't of her class, then perhaps it's time you had your bifocals adjusted, Roberta Morgan."

Roberta glowered at her friend. "And I suppose you never tucked *Lady Chatterley's Lover* under your mattress."

"And I suppose most of you fine folk went to church this morning," Warren said, lighting up a cigar. "Wonder how Father Luedtke feels about this kind of talk."

"The truth is the truth," Claudia shot back. "There's nothing uncharitable about it."

"Sounds to me like the lot of you need to find yourselves a hobby. There are better ways to spend your time than speculating about a man you just met." His disappointment was painfully clear. "Now I could sit here and tell you everything you need to know about that boy, and you would feel damn sorry you ever sat judgment on him the way you just did, but that wouldn't be fair to him. His story is his to share, and I'm not about to break his trust."

Hall Talbot pushed back his chair. It was clear he'd had enough. "It's late," he said, reaching for the check in the middle of the table. "I'd better take the girls home. Tomorrow's going to be a busy day." The town's Labor Day picnic began on the Green at noon, and no parent worth his or her salt dared forget it.

Willa and Mariah leaped to their feet. "Can we play video games before we go to sleep?" Mariah asked.

"Sure," said Hall with a nod to the group assembled there. "Whatever you want."

The doctor had barely reached the cash register before Susan leaned across the table to grill Warren.

"So where do you know this Sam Butler from?" she asked.

Claudia glared at her daughter. "Don't be rude, Susan. You heard Warren. It's none of our business."

"You saw the way they looked at each other," Susan said. "I'd say it's going to be everybody's business by tomorrow morning."

So that's the way the wind blows, thought Warren as he surveyed the scene.

For a small town, things could sure get complicated in a hurry.

He hoped Sam and Annie were smart enough to turn off the phones.

They kissed at stoplights, at street signs, and once they even pulled over to the side of the road and kissed until they couldn't breathe anymore.

"Damn stick shift," Sam muttered as they tried to find a viable position.

Annie gasped as his hand slid under her skirt. "The seat reclines."

They struggled with the lever and got nowhere.

"My place," she said, hands trembling as she clutched the wheel.

"Fast," Sam said. He sounded desperate. She never knew how much she liked that quality in a man.

He plucked the lacy edge of her panties with his big hands, and she nearly drove off the road.

"I can't drive when you do that." Or think. Or breathe.

"You're wet," he said, his voice low and urgent.

They were twenty feet away from her driveway, but it might as well have been twenty miles. She hit the brakes hard. He braced an arm against the dashboard to keep from shooting through the windshield. She shut off the engine and turned to him with the hunger burning in her eyes, and he said, "Jesus," and reached for her, and suddenly the stick shift wasn't a problem or the seat that refused to recline.

She told him what she wanted and how and then she told him that this time there would be no sudden stops, no turning back.

She straddled him and unzipped his pants.

He pulled off her panties and crushed the damp fabric in his hand then brought them to his face.

She stroked him fast and hard, letting him fill her hand.

He grabbed her by the waist and lifted her, and she slowly slowly opened for him engulfed him drew him deep inside her body and she cried out first with the newness of it and then with something else, something she had forgotten existed.

She shuddered when she climaxed, and the rhythmic contractions of her body pushed him over the edge.

And still it wasn't enough. They left the car where it was. Still kissing and touching, still hungry for each other, they stumbled up the driveway. They reached the porch steps, and he swept her up into his arms and carried her up the three steps to the front door.

"The front door's always open in the movies," he said, while she leaned over to fit the key into the lock.

"You should've kicked it in," she said, kissing his chin, his throat, his chest. "Very macho."

"Too soon to repeat myself." He carried her through the dimly lit hallway to the tiny bedroom with the huge sleigh bed and the open window and the moonlight.

And then the magic took over. Clothes slid off the way they did in the movies. The bed sighed sweetly beneath the weight of their bodies. She opened herself to him in heart, soul, and body. He filled the empty spaces inside her heart and in so doing filled the empty spaces inside his own heart as well.

Somewhere out there was the world they knew and the people they loved, but right now none of it mattered. This bed was world enough for both of them.

"You folks have been a lot of fun," Gloria said, "but we're closing up now. Hate to break up a good time, but you know how it is."

"Good Lord," said Roberta, glancing at her narrow gold watch. "It's almost ten o'clock!" She flashed her best smile at Warren. "Time flies when you're having fun."

Warren always did have an eye for the women, and he flashed her a damn good smile right back. "Kind of you to put up with an old man's stories, Bobbi."

Roberta laughed, one of those throaty chuckles that made Claudia want to hit her in the head with a skillet. "We go way back," she said, practically batting her eyelashes at the old fool. "You know what they say: Old friends are the best."

Susan and Jack corraled their kids, and the lot of them stepped out into the crisp night air.

"Goodnight, Ma." Susan hugged her briefly. "We'll pick you up at noon for the picnic."

Claudia sniffed and refused to hug her back. That innocent act simply wouldn't wash. Her daughter had had a hand in this debacle. It was clear as the nose on her face.

Jack beeped the horn.

"Gotta run," Susan said. She waved to Warren and Roberta and was gone.

Claudia turned and started toward Roberta's car. Warren fell into step with her.

"Hang on too tight and you'll lose her," he said quietly. "Don't make that mistake, Claudia."

"If I want your opinion, Warren Bancroft, I'll ask for it. Until then, keep those bromides to yourself."

Roberta coughed delicately behind them, and Claudia reined in her emotions.

"It's late," Warren said. "I'll follow you two ladies home, if you'd like."

Roberta thought it was a charming idea. Claudia was deeply insulted, but she kept her opinion to herself. The headlights of Warren's ridiculous old Jeep followed them over the bridge, up Main Street, around the curve, right into the driveway of the house Claudia had shared with her beloved husband.

"Don't forget to bring the deviled eggs tomorrow," Roberta said as Claudia climbed from the car. "And Peggy wants her Tupperware serving bowl back."

Labor Day was a major holiday for the various tradespeople and volunteer workers of Shelter Rock Cove. Shops on Main Street threw open their doors and sponsored contests and giveaways and generally said thanks to the town for supporting them all year long. The various volunteer groups—DAR, Lions Club, fire department, and the like—sponsored a giant picnic/barbecue on the town green that started at noon and ended after the fireworks display many hours later.

Claudia said goodnight and didn't so much as glance over her shoulder at Warren. Back straight, head held high, she walked up the curving driveway and let herself into her house. She closed the door behind her, turned the locks, then set the alarm. The children had insisted on the alarm system, even though it seemed foolish to Claudia. *We worry,* they had said to her. *A woman living alone should have an alarm system.*

They were always telling her something. Get an alarm system. Get a dog. Move to a condo . . . a retirement complex . . . a nursing home. That's the way it went. Once you gave in to the first request, your independence began to fall like a line of dominoes.

She leaned against the door for a moment and closed her eyes. She saw Annie and Kevin on their wedding day, so young and filled with hope. She saw them the day they moved into their first house, short on money but long on happiness and plans for the future. She saw them together year after year, and something began to take shape, a darkness she'd never allowed to enter the picture before. The pinched look around Annie's mouth. The exhaustion in Kevin's eyes. The silences between them that spoke louder than words.

"I wish you were here with me, Johnny," she said aloud.

But, as usual, he didn't answer.

Hall poured himself a tumbler of scotch and took it out onto the deck. He sat down on one of the three Adirondack chairs he'd had specially made and rested his feet on the railing. The scotch was old and mellow, and it burned its way smoothly down his throat.

Too bad it couldn't burn away the memory of Annie's face as she walked out of Cappy's hand-in-hand with the Boy from New York City.

He raised his glass high in a salute to bad timing.

He'd waited out her marriage and her widowhood. For two years he bided his time, sensitive to her feelings, aware of her family's expectations, waiting for the right moment to finally make his move, only to come in a day late. Hell, not even a day. Twelve hours. That was all. Twelve goddamn hours too late and all because some guy comes riding into town with the stink of newness all over him, and that's all she wrote.

He'd never seen her look that way, not even on the day she married Kevin. She'd looked nervous on her wedding day, painfully young, alarmingly innocent. It was clear to everyone standing there that she was marrying the family as well as the man.

But the girl was long gone. She knew life didn't always play fair and that happy endings were found in books, not real life. She knew all of those things and more and yet she looked at that raggedy son-of-a-bitch like he'd hung the moon.

He took another gulp of scotch and waited for the fire to build in his gut.

That nagging memory still tugged at him. A sense of familiarity he couldn't define. He knew this Sam Butler from somewhere but he couldn't seem to place him. The guy looked like he worked the docks, but there was no denying the fierce intelligence burning in his eyes. There was something about the man that made you want to take a step backward to put some space between you.

It hadn't been that way with Kevin Galloway. Kevin had greeted the world with open arms, even as he shielded his obsession from the eyes of the town. This new guy had none of Kevin's heft and presence. None of his poetry. Kevin was as flawed as they come, but it had never been hard to understand what Annie saw in him.

Sam Butler was from New York. You could hear it in his voice. That odd little glottal stop that pegged some New Yorkers as incontrovertibly as a strand of DNA. But it was more than that. Was it possible he'd met Butler somewhere along the way, at a party maybe or some other social gathering? He couldn't imagine the circumstances where their worlds would intersect, but he'd long ago learned that anything was possible. After all, it had already happened.

"Don't say it," Susan warned as she and Jack got ready for bed. "If you value our marriage, you won't say one single word."

Jack tossed the damp towel into the hamper and grinned at his wife. "Told you so."

She glanced around for something moderately lethal to heave in his direction, but everything in the tiny bathroom was either bolted down or too grungy to consider. "We don't really know anything," she said, slipping her cotton nightgown over her head. "So what if she left with him? All she was doing was trying to slip away before Hall asked her out again." She padded into their bedroom with her husband close behind. "You can't blame her for taking the first escape route that presented itself."

Jack pulled off the comforter and tossed it on the slipper chair near the window. "You don't really believe that crap, do you?"

She sank down onto the bed. "No," she said miserably. "I don't."

The mattress dipped as he sat down next to her. "What's the real problem here, Susie? It isn't Annie at all, is it?"

"You're a grease monkey," she said, sniffling back her tears. "You're not supposed to be so perceptive."

"So what is it?" he persisted. "You jealous?"

"I don't get it," she said. "You couldn't find your socks if they stood up and saluted at you in the morning, but you always know exactly what's wrong with me."

"I don't love my socks."

She couldn't withhold a smile. "You old sweet talker. You always could charm me with poetry."

He whispered something in her ear that did more than charm her.

"Maybe," she said. "I'll think about it."

"Might be fun."

"Might be." She leaned against him and rested her head on his shoulder. "She looked so happy," she whispered. "They looked so much in love."

"We're in love."

"Not like that."

"No," he said, "not like that. We were like that twenty years ago. Now we're like this."

"I miss the way we used to be."

"So do I."

She looked up at him. "You do?"

"With work and the kids and everything else—" He shook his head. "Sometimes I feel like I'm losing you in the crowd."

"Yes! That's it, that's exactly the way I feel, like I'm calling your name in a crowd and you just don't seem to hear me."

"I hear you now, Susie. I'm right here next to you and I hear you."

"What if he hurts her?" she whispered as they lay down on the bed they'd shared for so long. "She doesn't have any idea what it's like out there."

"Was it so good with Kevin?"

Susan froze. "What did you say?"

"I loved him, Suze, but your brother wasn't perfect."

"Meaning what?"

Jack sighed. "Forget I said anything."

"No," she said, suddenly angry. "I won't forget. Tell me what you're talking about."

"His gambling."

She made a face. "That was never a real problem."

"Open your eyes, Suze. Take a look at Annie. She didn't sell the big house because she was tired of the view. She sold it because he left her with nothing."

"You don't know that."

"I know what I see."

"She wanted to start fresh," Susan said, trying to ignore the hollow ringing of her words. "She was rattling around in that big old barn all by herself."

The expression on Jack's face was so sad—and so knowing—that it brought her up short.

"I think you're wrong," she said as the fight drained out of her. "Kevin was a wonderful husband. They were the happiest couple I've ever seen. Nobody will ever make her as happy as Kevin made her."

But how happy was that really? No matter how hard she tried, she couldn't come up with examples to prove her thesis, not unless she went back fifteen years or more. Annie had thrown herself into making the flower shop a success, and the hours she worked became a source of debate within the family. Of course everyone knew teachers didn't make huge salaries, even if Kevin was the most gifted English teacher the town had ever seen. He worked long hours, too, meeting with parents and children after the school day ended, giving workshops, and taking classes on the weekends. The wonder was that he and Annie ever saw each other at all. How many family gatherings had they had to decline because Kevin was out of town or Annie was too swamped with work to break away? After a while everyone had lost count. Invitations to the big old Victorian house dwindled until they became once- or twice-yearly occasions.

Was that happiness? She had no answer to that question.

"We can't stop her," he said, stroking her hair. "Annie deserves some happiness, and she won't find it if she doesn't take a few chances."

He was right. She knew he was right. But the thought of Annie out there somewhere with a man who wasn't family sent a chill of foreboding through Susan, and not even Jack's warm kisses could make it go away.

Warren sat in his library with a glass of brandy in his hand and poor old Max asleep at his feet. It was a few minutes after midnight, and unless he missed his guess, Max would be spending the night.

"You can sleep at the foot of the bed," he told the dog, "and Nancy will make you bacon and eggs for breakfast."

The yellow Lab looked up at him with mournful eyes.

"Don't worry," Warren said, reaching down to pet the old guy on the scruff of his neck. "He hasn't abandoned you." That was one thing Sam Butler never did, even if the boy didn't quite believe it himself yet.

He heard himself and started to laugh. Now did that beat all? There he was, the man who was on the cover of last month's *Forbes* magazine, trying to explain love to a dog who drank water from the toilet bowl. Hell, he had himself a nerve trying to explain love to anybody since he knew so damn little about it. He knew that love complicated matters. He knew that when it went wrong it made a man's life a living hell.

And he also knew that without it, nothing much else mattered.

Were Sam and Annie in love? He wasn't sure. They'd barely known each other three days, but stranger things had happened in a lot less time. His own parents had met on Sunday and married on Monday and spent the next thirty years telling the tale.

He hoped they were happy. He hoped they would be kind to each other. He hoped that if it didn't work out, they would both be left with hearts that were better off for the experience.

Patience wasn't his long suit, but he would do his best. He had brought them together. There was nothing more he could do. Nobody yet had found a way to make love happen when it wasn't meant to.

Or to deny it either. He thought of the scared look in Claudia's eyes, the bristling anger that didn't quite hide her fear that their beloved Annie just might slip away with a man who wasn't Kevin. They still saw her as the vulnerable young girl whose parents had been lost the year she turned sixteen. The entire Galloway clan had opened their hearts to her and welcomed her into their fold, and she had gone gratefully, eager to be one of the crowd, to be so indispensable she would never have to worry about being alone again.

That was how they still saw her. Needy. Vulnerable. Unsure of herself and her place in the world. They hadn't a clue. Not a one of them had an inkling of all she had done to protect the reputation of the sainted Kevin. She was the one who had held it all together and never once asked for help from anyone.

Warren had never told Annie that he knew about Kevin's gambling. He wondered how many other people in town had kept Annie's secret and never let on. Sometimes he thought he should sit Claudia down and tell her the whole story, tell her how her daughter-in-law worked around the clock to keep a roof over their heads and food on the table while Kevin fell deeper into despair.

That conversation at the dinner table still rankled. They had all teed off on Sam as if he had come to town with the express purpose of ruining their happy family. Where the hell did they all get off, passing judgment on a man they'd never met? And who did they think they were, trying to run Annie's life for her as though she were still sixteen years old and scared to death? She was a grown woman now. If the gods had been kinder, she could have had kids in college who came home on weekends so Mom could do their laundry. She could have had a husband who—

Well, no sense going there. Some things couldn't be changed.

Sam Butler was the best thing that could happen to her,

and if those narrow-minded morons were too blind to see that, then to hell with them.

They would learn soon enough.

And maybe so would Sam.

TWELVE

~~~

Sam and Annie were in her kitchen making scrambled eggs and toast.

"This is crazy," Annie said as she pulled the carton of eggs from the refrigerator. "We should be asleep." She wore nothing but his denim shirt and a loopy smile.

"You're tired?" Sam, clad in nothing but a towel, popped two English muffins into the toaster and depressed the lever. "Can't imagine why."

Maybe having a postage-stamp-sized kitchen wasn't such a bad thing after all. She leaned over and pressed a kiss to his shoulder. "Liar," she said.

He took the carton of eggs from her and placed them on the counter. "Come here," he said then gathered her into his arms.

"This is a kitchen," she said as she wrapped her arms around his neck. "We don't do things like this in the kitchen."

"Why not?"

She thought for a second. "Tradition?"

"Turkey for Thanksgiving is a tradition."

"You really shouldn't make me laugh when you're trying to be romantic."

He loved her laugh. He loved everything about her. "You laughed before," he said. "A lesser man might've worried."

"I'm happy," she said, knowing he couldn't understand—not yet—all that those words meant to her. "You make me happy."

They stood there for a long time, bodies pressed together, and maybe they would have stayed like that until dawn if George and Gracie hadn't chosen that moment to tear through the kitchen as if the hounds of hell were after them, then skid to a stop in the door.

"They're not too crazy about me," Sam said, eyeing them over the top of Annie's head.

"You're new," she said. "They'll get used to you."

"How about you? Think you'll get used to me?"

"No," she said, raining kisses along his throat and jaw. "I hope I never get used to you."

Sam was no stranger to the kitchen. It didn't take Annie more than a few seconds to see that he knew his way around colanders and chopping blocks.

"You're awfully good at this," she said as he buttered the English muffins and slathered on the blueberry jam. "Did you ever work as a short-order cook?"

"Only at home," he said. "I come from a big family."

"So did my husband." She felt surprisingly comfortable mentioning Kevin, as if it were the most natural thing on earth to do. "How big is big?"

"Three boys, three girls."

"Including you?"

"Including me."

"And you're the oldest."

"How did you know?"

"You like to take charge."

"You mean, I'm aggressive."

"No, I mean you know how to get things done."

The look she gave him was pure heat, and he laughed.

"You have a way about you, Annie Galloway," he said and popped a piece of muffin into her mouth. He took a good look at her. "Only child of older parents. You were spoiled rotten."

The look of sorrow in her eyes almost brought him to his knees.

"Only child." She cracked a large white egg against the side of a stainless-steel bowl, then tossed the empty shell into the trash pail under the counter. She reached for another egg. "My parents married right out of high school. I came along six months later." She chuckled and tossed more shells into the trash pail. "You can imagine the whispering that went on around here, can't you?"

"Makes you glad times have changed."

"Don't get me wrong. They loved each other and they were planning to marry anyway, but I don't think they were planning on doing it quite so soon—or starting off with an instant family."

He had the sense that he was treading into uncertain territory but he took the next step just the same. "Are they still together?"

She rested her hands on the counter, and it was a moment before she answered him. "I hope so," she said then met his eyes. "They died just before I turned sixteen." She told him in plain, unadorned language about the nor'easter that capsized the small fishing boat and took the lives of Eve and Ron Lacy. "The Galloways took me in. Can you imagine that? I was nobody but Kevin's girlfriend, and they opened up their hearts to me and made me one of the family. When I think of what might have happened—"

"I was seventeen."

She stared at him. "What?"

"I was seventeen when my mother died. My father died two years later."

"Oh, Sam—"

"Courtney was four when the old man died. She was the youngest."

"So you know," she whispered. "You know what it was like."

"Yeah," he said quietly. "I know."

Their eyes met, and once again they both experienced a sense of inevitability that ran deep and true.

"You're lucky you have a big family," she said. "There was somebody to take you in." *I was so young, Sam, just a girl really, and the world seemed so big and cold. Claudia made a home for me . . . a real home . . . Marrying Kevin only made it that much better.*

He shook his head. "Afraid not. My mother was an only child, and my father's family thought we should be broken up and parceled out to foster homes. There was no way in hell I was going to let that happen." *They weren't much more than babies . . . The whole lot of us were scared shitless . . . The only thing we had was each other . . . What else could I do?*

"You mean, you took care of the rest of the kids?"

"Not much choice," he said matter-of-factly. "Nobody else stepped up to the plate."

"But you did," she said. "Somebody else might have turned and run away." *You were only a kid yourself. Who would have blamed you for handing it all over to somebody else?*

"I thought about it. Hell, there were days I wondered why I bothered." *The night Tony broke his leg . . . the weekend Courtney ran off with that guy . . . Nothing prepares you for any of it.*

"But you didn't," she persisted. "You were there for

them when they needed you." *Claudia used to sit by my bed until I fell asleep those first few months . . . She would hold my hand and tell me I was safe . . . If only you'd had that, too.*

"Warren helped me find my first serious job," he said as she poured the beaten eggs into the sizzling pan, then moved them around with a narrow spatula. "There wasn't much available for a college dropout with five dependents, but he knew I was quick and hardworking and had the gift of gab, and next thing I knew I was cold-calling down on Wall Street."

The mid-1980s had been rife with financial opportunities in the world of stocks and bonds. Sure, the Ivy League graduates with the MBAs had their pick of jobs, but there was still plenty of room for a street-smart kid driven by need rather than ambition.

"Warren put me through college," she said as they sat down at the kitchen table that had once belonged to Ellie Bancroft. "I was the first winner of the Warren Bancroft Scholarship. You had to be a fisherman's kid to qualify."

"A smart fisherman's kid."

"Good thing I was, otherwise somebody might've thought the whole thing was rigged."

"A slam dunk?"

"Afraid so. If Warren can't help you directly, he'll find a way to help you indirectly and he won't take no for an answer."

"He told me about the work you're doing for the museum," he said. "It sounded pretty ambitious."

She tapped her forehead with her index finger. "I have all sorts of knowledge tucked away up there but no place to use it. Did he show you the mock-up of how the whole thing will look when it's finished?" She had an idea for a sculpture of a fisherman's family, but it had been so long since she'd even attempted anything that ambitious that she couldn't bring herself to broach the topic with Warren, even though he had been encouraging her to tackle something for the museum.

"No, but he did end up recruiting me to build the canoes."

She made no attempt to disguise her pleasure. "Then it looks like we'll be working together." She explained how some of the lighting techniques she hoped to use needed to be built into the structure of the boats they suspended from the ceiling.

"Sounds like we'll be working closely together," he said, and they smiled at each other like two lovestruck teenagers.

George and Gracie strolled into the room and surveyed the scene. Gracie indulged in a few delicate sips of water from their bowl while George fixed Sam with one of those patented stares cats are known for.

"He hates me," Sam said.

"George hates everyone but Gracie. Don't pay any attention to him."

Gracie stepped away from the water bowl and strolled out of the room, tail at full mast, with George close behind.

"There's a metaphor here somewhere," Sam said.

"Or a punchline." She gestured toward his plate. "Eat your eggs before they get cold. There's nothing worse than icy, rubbery scrambled eggs."

He made short work of his food, then reached over and grabbed a bite of her muffin.

"Hey!" she protested, then remembered that she had swept him out of Cappy's before he had a chance to grab a meal. She pushed her plate toward him. "Here," she said. "Eat."

He said something to her, something earthy and blunt and so sexual she almost melted right there on the spot.

Kevin's praise had been couched in metaphor and allusion. It had vanished in the face of reality. Sam's praise was—oh, God, it was flesh and blood and pure heat and she felt it in every part of her body. It anchored her in the world yet somehow gave her wings.

A second later they were in each other's arms again. He backed her up against the refrigerator. She wrapped her legs around his hips and lowered herself onto his amazing erection, taking him deeper than she thought possible. He groaned as she tightened her muscles around him, and she grew stronger with every movement of her body, every sound of pleasure she drew from him. This was a kind of lovemaking she'd never known. There was nothing gentle about their coming together. Their union was fierce and urgent, as if they had waited all their lives for that moment, and for all they knew, maybe they had.

"Start the waffles, Nancy," Warren called out. "They're pulling into the driveway."

Max was beside himself with excitement. He leaped against Warren and placed his big hairy paws on his chest and barked at full volume.

"I told you he'd be here," he said to the big yellow dog and threw open the front door. "Go say hello."

Max tore down the steps and galloped across the lawn at full speed, barking at the top of his canine lungs. He skidded to a stop inches away from Sam and Annie, then threw himself at his master in a frenzy of pure pleasure.

"My second and third wives never gave me a greeting like that," Warren said as he walked down the driveway to meet them.

"Dog biscuits," said Annie, waving a large Milk-Bone. "Wins their hearts every time."

He slipped an arm through Annie's while Sam and Max bonded.

"You look happy," he observed as they strolled back to the house.

"I am," she said.

"He looks happy, too."

She glanced over her shoulder. "He does, doesn't he?"

"I'm glad you two are getting along," he said, "because Sam will be working on the museum with you."

Her eyes danced with amusement. "I'm sure that was worrying you."

It was one of those days that made an old man glad to be alive. These two young people—they would always be young to him—had changed before his very eyes. Annie glowed with pure happiness. Her loveliness had always been shadowed with worry, and since Kevin's death sorrow had taken its toll. This morning, with her thick curly hair pulled back in a ponytail and her face scrubbed clean of makeup, she was the girl he'd watched grow up before the sadness came to stay.

As for Sam—hell, he hardly recognized the boy. His laughter was loud and easy, and his eyes never left Annie. The expression in them warmed Warren's heart. It was everything he'd hoped for when the notion first presented itself. Not that he could take any credit for the laughter that rang out as they shared blueberry waffles and stories at his breakfast table on that sunny Labor Day morning. All he did was sell a house to Annie and give Sam a place to stay while he sorted out his problems. Love was a funny business. Just because you thought two people were right for each other, it didn't mean spit if the magic wasn't there.

And all you had to do was look at Sam and Annie to know the magic was present and accounted for.

You could keep your fancy offices and jet planes and the deals that made page one of the *Wall Street Journal*. This was what was real, he thought as he watched the two children of his heart as they whispered over their coffee. This was what made everything else worthwhile. Pray God it was the real thing.

Hall and Ellen met up with each other in the doctors' lounge a little after ten A.M.

Ellen, still in scrubs, ran a hand through her thick red hair and barely managed to stifle a yawn. "So now I know why it's called Labor Day," she said as Hall poured them each a cup of coffee. "Who thought Perrin and Bradsher would pop the same day?"

"It's the full moon," Hall said, handing her a cup.

Ellen rolled her eyes. "Oh, great. That doesn't bode well for the doings on the Green, does it?"

They found an empty table near the door and sank wearily into their chairs. "Small-town life beginning to pinch, Dr. Markowitz?" he asked.

"I'm not sure," she said with her characteristic honesty. "The social aspects can be a little overwhelming for the newbie. The most I ever did on Labor Day was readjust my beach towel."

"Welcome to New England," he said, wishing he had a bagel and cream cheese to go with the coffee, "where idle hands are the devil's workshop."

Ellen grinned at him. "Or something like that."

"It won't be so bad, Markowitz," he said. "It's not like we're being put in stocks or anything. Just a small booth near the barbecue pit where we hand out coupons for free health services."

"Burgers and mammograms to go," she said, shaking her head in amusement. "I have a lot to learn."

"You're doing fine," he said, noticing briefly the dark circles under her light gray eyes. "Everyone likes you"— he paused for effect—"even though you're a New Yorker."

She tossed a sugar packet in his direction. "Just wait," she said, laughing. "Next time we're down there for a seminar, I'm going to take you back to the old neighborhood and show you what real bagels taste like."

His eyes widened. "How did you know I was thinking about a bagel?"

She leaned forward, elbows on the cheap Formica tabletop, and fixed him with a kind but serious look. "So what's wrong?" she said, lowering her voice so only he could hear her. "You look like hell today."

He thought about the way Annie Galloway had looked when she walked out of Cappy's hand-in-hand with Sam Butler. "I forgot Willa and Mariah were spending the night," he said, dodging the real truth.

"Where are they now?"

"Stevens from Pediatrics said they could color in the sunroom while I met up with the Perrins."

"And that's it?"

"That's all I'm going to tell you."

"She's a fool," Ellen said, "and you can quote me on that."

"You're a good friend, Markowitz," he said, "but you don't know what you're talking about."

Ellen smiled and said nothing at all.

Claudia didn't sleep a wink all night. Every time she closed her eyes, she saw Annie and that man, and her stomach started to churn and she found herself reaching for the antacid tablets she kept on her nightstand. Finally she gave up and went downstairs to the kitchen and made the deviled eggs for the Labor Day picnic. If she remembered, Annie would oversee the goings-on at Annie's Flowers while Claudia and Roberta and the rest of the Golden Age Volunteers hustled for donations for the new senior citizens center the hospital planned to build.

She arranged the two dozen deviled eggs on the round glass platters with the egg-shaped depressions made specially for the cholesterol-laden treats. The platters had belonged to her mother and to her mother's mother before her. Her granddaughters found it hard to believe there had ever been a time when such deadly fare had not only been consumed in quantity, but had merited its own service pieces as well.

She dearly wanted to sample one of those buttery-yellow, eggy treats but she didn't dare. She had lost a husband and son to the cruelty of heart disease and she wasn't ready to offer herself up on that particular altar just for the sake of egg yolk and mayonnaise.

By six A.M. she had made the deviled eggs; three dozen pinwheels of ham, cream cheese, and scallions; and a medley of lightly steamed veggies and a virtuously low-fat dip to enjoy with them. Everything had been carefully wrapped and stowed in her refrigerator until it was time to load them into Susan's minivan for the trip into town.

She took a bath, attended to her morning needs, then made herself eat a breakfast of bran cereal, skim milk, and decaf. All of that only took her up until seven-thirty, which meant another four and a half hours until it was time to leave. She considered tidying up the front rooms, but they were already immaculate. Since John's death, she had found herself taking great comfort from routine chores. She did the wash on Mondays, the floors on Tuesdays, the bathrooms on Wednesdays. Thursday nights were reserved for supermarket shopping. Once you added in her work schedule at Annie's Flowers and the hours she put in as a Golden Age volunteer, you had something that looked like a full life. It helped to know there was a reason to get up in the morning, some place where she was expected to be.

What was it the young people called it? Anal-retentive,

or was it obsessive-compulsive? Either way, she was afraid the term fit. "You're getting too set in your ways, Ma," Sean had said the last time he came home for a visit. "Loosen up. You'll live longer."

Well, Sean, she thought as she settled down with the new John Grisham, *when you get to be my age, that may not sound quite so inviting.*

As usual, Susan was running late. She had to fix breakfast, clean up, make sure Jack knew where everything was and what he was supposed to bring to the picnic later, then put herself together in a reasonable facsimile of a successful real estate broker at a town picnic. She hated business casual dressing. How much easier things had been in the 1980s when all you needed were shoulder pads and a silk dress. She opted in the end for a nice pair of walking shorts, her best sandals, and a camp shirt. She wouldn't win any fashion awards, but it would do.

She pulled up in front of the house where she'd grown up at about a quarter after the hour. She'd expected to find Claudia standing at the foot of the driveway, tapping her foot and glancing pointedly at her watch, but to her surprise there was no sign of her mother anywhere.

"Oh, great," she muttered as she pulled into the driveway and shifted into park. Claudia was probably inside on the telephone, reading poor Jack the riot act because her daughter was a few measly minutes late. If only her mother would learn to cut them some slack, but that was like asking the earth to stop spinning. Claudia was the way she was, and only an act of God could change her.

Okay, Ma, you made your point. You can come out now.

She drummed her fingers on the steering wheel, stared at the clock on the dashboard then over at the quiet house. *She's your mother, Susan, even if she does drive you*

*crazy. Get your butt out of the car and go see what's
going on.*

The back door was open. She wasn't sure if that was a
good sign or a bad one. "Sorry I'm late, Ma," she called
out, "but you know how it is with kids."

No response.

Her heartbeat quickened.

The kitchen was neat as a pin. No surprise there. Your
average hospital operating room harbored more germs
than her mother's trash bin.

"Ma?"

Still no response. Oh, God. Terrible things happened to
old people every day of the week. Wicked falls down the
basement staircase. Slips in the bathtub. How many times
had they told her the house was too big and too dangerous
for a woman alone? Susan had even gathered up all the
brochures from the new retirement village on the outskirts
of town, the one with the staff on call twenty-four hours
a day in case of emergency.

She burst into the living room and was halfway up the
stairs to the second floor when she realized Claudia was
curled up in the wing chair with a book open on her lap.
For a second a river of fear flooded her body until she
saw the gentle up-and-down motion of her mother's chest,
and relief almost knocked her flat. She placed a hand on
her mother's forearm. How small her mother seemed.
How vulnerable.

"Ma," she said softly. "Ma, wake up."

Claudia inhaled deeply, frowned, then opened her eyes.
"You're late," she said.

"Since when do you take a nap in the morning?"

"I didn't sleep last night," Claudia said. "Not that it's
any of your business."

"Is something wrong?" Her mother managed a variety

of medical problems, any one of which could cause the occasional bad night.

"You were there," Claudia said. "You saw them."

"I know," Susan said, amazed to find herself on the same side of an issue as her mother. "I can't believe it either."

"I gave Warren a piece of my mind," Claudia said as they headed for the kitchen to pack up the foods.

"What did Warren do?" She opened the refrigerator door and pulled out the covered platters of deviled eggs.

"He's responsible."

"All he did was let the guy stay in Ellie's old house."

"That's what he says, but I know him. He has ulterior motives."

"Now you sound like one of those conspiracy theorists Sean and Eileen idolize."

They looked at each other, and Claudia was the first one to laugh. "Was I always this bad, or is it that I'm getting old and set in my ways?"

Susan gave her a hug. "You were pretty much always this bad."

How fragile her mother felt, how painfully human.

"Did you see the way she looked at that man last night?" Claudia sounded wistful.

"I think we all did, Ma."

They fell silent for what seemed like a very long time.

"That's how I felt about your father," Claudia said at last. "That's just how it was between us."

Susan exhaled on a sigh. She and Jack loved each other very much, but she wasn't sure they had ever looked at each other that way. "You don't think she'll bring him to the picnic, do you?"

"After the way she behaved last night, nothing would surprise me."

"Ma, really! It's not like she jumped his bones right

there in Cappy's. They held hands. There isn't a law against it."

From the look on Claudia's face, it was clear her mother thought there should be.

And, if Susan were honest with herself, she just might agree.

THIRTEEN

Sweeney was the first one to notice.

They were setting up the sidewalk displays when Annie reached for one of the suncatchers, and Sweeney grabbed her left hand.

"Your ring," she said, looking at Annie with a question in her eyes.

Annie's fingers automatically curled into a soft fist. "It was time," she said.

Curiosity won. "Does this have anything to do with the guy who showed up here the other day with your keys?"

She considered dodging the question but decided there was little point. After last night at Cappy's, she was bound to be at the top of the Shelter Rock Cove gossip hit parade.

"Yes," she said much to Sweeney's delight, "but the less we talk about it around Claudia, the happier we'll all be."

"She might not notice."

Annie arched a brow. "You don't believe that any more than I do, Sweeney."

"Is he coming to the picnic?"

"He's here already," she said. "I think he's over by the fire truck."

Warren would be there later, too. He'd told them that he was manning the grill for the museum barbecue. Claudia and Roberta were busy setting up the huge tables of picnic food under the maple trees near the bandstand, while Susan, who was in charge of the real estate office's spot not twenty feet away from Annie, seemed to be giving her the cold shoulder.

"What's with your sister-in-law?" Sweeney asked as they draped ropes of greenery along the edge of their display table. "Why is she ignoring you?"

"She is, isn't she?" Annie said. "I was wondering if it was my imagination."

"Then your imagination just gave me frostbite." Sweeney feigned a shiver. "Don't tell me she's upset about what's-his-name."

"His name is Sam," Annie said, laughing, "and I can't believe she'd be upset about something like this." It seemed so unlike Susan, who always did her level best to keep Claudia from trying to run Annie's life.

"You know what happens when you drop a pebble into a pond, don't you?"

"Ripples," Annie said. Concentric rings of them expanding outward until they ran out of water. "What does that have to do with anything?"

"That's easy," Sweeney said. "The Galloway clan is the pond, and your Sam—well, he's a hundred-pound boulder."

The Shelter Rock Cove Volunteer Fire Department consisted of seven members, one of whom was eight months pregnant and relegated to phone duty for the duration. They ranged in age from late teens to early sixties. They were probably the most unlikely-looking firefighters Sam had ever seen, but this strange mix of dentist, hair stylist, hardware store owner, short-order cook, daycare operator, and two lobster fishermen were as tightly bound to each other as any flesh-and-blood family could ever be.

"Now that Becky's not going out with us anymore, we could really use a new face around the fire house," said Ethan Venable, the retirement-age dentist. "You look like a prime candidate to me, son."

Sam couldn't deny the pull of the shiny red truck and the sense of community and friendship among the small crew of volunteers. "I'm staying in Ellie Bancroft's old place for a while, but it's only temporary." He mentioned something about being between jobs, and Ethan nodded politely.

"Too bad," the man said, shaking Sam's hand. "You look like you'd fit in up here just fine."

If you'd said that to Sam two weeks ago, he would have suggested some serious couch time. He was a New Yorker, born and bred. He lived and breathed the crowds, the noise, the way life moved faster than the speed of light. But there he was, wandering along a village green, sampling Sarah's Famous Blueberry Pie and Amanda's World-Class Potato Salad and enjoying every minute of it. Annie had lived her entire life in this small town. Except for her years in college, her views on life had been shaped right here among these people. He wanted to ask the woman at the photo booth if she had known Annie as a little girl. *Tell me about her,* he thought as he absorbed the sights and people around him. *Was she quiet? Was she popular? Did everyone love her, or didn't you even know she existed?* He wanted to know about the night her parents died and her life changed forever. *Did Kevin Galloway hold her in his arms and make it all better? Had he tried to kiss away her pain? Did she really love him or did she just love being part of a family?*

He'd seen a picture of Galloway at Warren's place that morning. Max had disappeared somewhere in the house, and he'd left Warren and Annie chatting in the breakfast room while he tried to track down the errant yellow Lab. Max being Max, he wasn't hard to find, and Sam called to him from the door to the private study adjacent to Warren's bedroom. Max, however, was having none of it. He was curled up on a luminous Oriental carpet and ready to indulge in his favorite pastime of power napping.

"C'mon, old pal," he said in what he hoped was a no-nonsense tone of voice. "You're going to wear out your welcome around here."

Max busied himself finding exactly the right scratching spot behind his left ear.

Nothing short of a seven-point-one on the Richter scale was going to move Max until Max was good and ready. Sam had turned to leave the room when his attention was caught by a display of framed photographs on the long table by the window. Unless he was crazy, there was one of him right in the front row. He crossed the room and plucked the photo from the pile and started to laugh. There he was in all his fifteen-year-old glory, looking up at the camera from the pier at the old marina near the World's Fair site. He was smiling one of those goofy, blissfully unself-conscious smiles that life usually knocks out of you by the time you're old enough to vote, and looking pretty much as if he had the world by the tail.

And maybe he had. His parents were still alive back then. He didn't have to worry about keeping a roof over his head and food in his brothers' and sisters' bellies. He skimmed the surface at school then dove headfirst into learning everything he could about the dirty, messy business of repairing boats. There was nothing glamorous about the work. You wouldn't get rich doing it. But no job before or since had ever made him happier than he was in those early days when life was an open road by the sea and the speed limit hadn't been invented yet.

He glanced at some of the other photos but didn't recognize anyone. He was about to turn away when a candid shot of a painfully young bride and groom caught his eye. The guy couldn't have been more than nineteen, if that. He was tall and rangy with broad shoulders and a wide smile, good-looking in an open, all-American way that was foreign to Sam. He looked like the kind of guy you met on an airplane and spilled your guts to between Cincinnati and Houston just because he was so damn easy to talk to. He had a thick head of curly dark hair and movie-star good looks and the best luck in the world because Annie Lacy was his bride.

Jesus, how young she looked in her long white dress and veil, like a little girl playing dress-up. Her long curly hair spilled over her shoulders, wild despite the obvious attempts to tame it. There were no dark circles under her beautiful blue eyes, no worry lines. She leaned into her husband as if he were her very foundation. The sight of the dead man's big hand on her delicate shoulder awakened some complicated feelings inside Sam, envy and sorrow and anger at a world that refused to allow happiness to last forever.

Hell, maybe it would have lasted forever. If Kevin Galloway hadn't died, Sam had no doubt she would still be at his side, still leaning against his breadth the way she had on their wedding day. The dark circles and worry lines would be way out there in the distant future; time enough when she was old and gray for things like that. She would have had the life he'd envisioned for her when they met in the parking lot of Yankee Shopper, a life that included kids and a dog and a big house and all the things the rest of the world took for granted because they seemed so easy and inevitable to everyone but people like Annie and Sam.

"You look wonderful, Annie! Did you lose weight?" Grace Lowell asked, eyeing Annie's hips.

"Wow, you're looking terrific." Bob Haskell's eyes actually twinkled as he looked at her. "Been on vacation?"

Sarah Wentworth leaned close to Annie's ear and dropped her voice to a whisper. "I promise I won't tell a soul: Who's your surgeon?"

Annie waited until Sarah was out of range before she turned to Sweeney. "What on earth is going on around here? That's the tenth person who commented on how great I look today."

"It's called love, honey," Sweeney said with a big smile. "L-U-V, and it shows."

Annie felt the blood rush to her cheeks. "I'd rather they thought it was a facelift."

"Sorry," Sweeney said. "Nobody will believe it, not with the way you two have been looking at each other."

Annie did her best not to cast a quick glance in Sam's direction, but Sweeney caught her.

"See? And he's been doing the same thing."

They had tried very hard not to make a spectacle of themselves. She had work to do promoting Annie's Flowers to anyone who stopped to smell the roses, while he had done an admirable job pretending he was interested in Phyllis Riley's beadwork and the big display of corncob art that was courtesy of Marge Rhodenbarr's third-grade class at Shelter Rock Elementary. Warren showed up around two o'clock. He motioned Sam over to where he stood by the display table and engaged the two of them in an animated conversation about the museum that focused even more of the town's attention on the new couple.

Claudia stopped by to use the bathroom in Annie's Flowers. She managed a hello for Annie but breezed by Warren and Sam as if they weren't there at all.

"She'll get over it," Warren said. "Tomorrow it'll be Eileen's new haircut or the way Susan is bringing up her kids. The woman isn't happy unless she has something to complain about."

Warren was right, but only up to a point. Annie knew that the reasons ran much deeper, and so did the hurt. Because that's what it was. Claudia wasn't angry. She was hurting, and Annie knew why.

"I'll be back in a second," she said, then darted into the shop as Claudia was ready to leave.

"You look lovely today," Claudia said stiffly as Annie blocked the doorway. "That sweater flatters you."

"I've been hearing that all day," she said with a self-conscious laugh. "These compliments have made me wonder how bad I've been looking lately."

A long, awkward silence rose up between them.

"I should get back to the booth," Claudia said, shifting her purse from under her right arm to under her left. "Roberta couldn't make change if her life depended on it."

Annie placed a hand on the woman's forearm. "Claudia, about last night—"

"You don't owe me any explanations, Anne. You're a grown woman. You can make your own decisions."

"I should have said something," Annie said, fumbling for the right words. "At the very least, I could have introduced you."

"Perhaps you had other things on your mind."

Annie took a deep breath. The easy social lie was on the tip of her tongue, but maybe this was the time to go a little deeper. "You're right," she said. "I did have other things on my mind. I'm sorry if I hurt you. That wasn't my intention."

Claudia held her gaze for a moment, then looked out toward the village green. Annie covered her ringless left hand with her right. Sounds of laughter and music drifted through the open door along with the delectable smells of hamburgers and hot dogs sizzling on the grill.

Please, Claudia, say something . . . anything. Tell me you were angry. Tell me he's not good enough for me. If we can talk about this, we're halfway there.

They had been through so many tough times together. She hated to think that her happiness could ever drive them apart.

"What took you so long?" Roberta demanded when Claudia returned to the booth. "I've been doing turnaway business."

Claudia looked at her friend of almost sixty years. "Am I a bitch?" she asked.

Roberta's round face froze. "What did you say?"

"Oh, don't act like you never heard the word before, Roberta Morgan, because I know you have. I've even heard you use it once or twice."

"That may be, but I've certainly never heard *you* use it. Not once in all these years."

"Well, you're hearing it now." She glanced around to make sure nobody was within earshot. "Do you think I'm a bitch?"

"Good heavens, Claudia, what kind of thing is that to ask?"

"It's a perfectly reasonable question. I've been doing some thinking today and I haven't liked some of the conclusions I've come up with."

"Were you watching *The View* again?"

"None of your business. Now, are you going to answer me or not?"

Roberta looked as if she would rather be any place on

earth but there. "That's a terrible question. You've put me in an impossible spot."

Poor Roberta. She dithered on, never quite realizing she had answered Claudia's question.

Yes, you're a bitch, Claudia Galloway. It's official. Are you happy now?

The thought had first occurred to her when Susan told her she had always been a difficult woman to be around. It wasn't at all the way Claudia viewed herself. John, bless his heart, had always told her she was the sunshine in his life, the one person he could count on to be in his corner no matter what. They had been through their share of tough times, things she wouldn't tell a living soul about, but their love for each other had never wavered. He had thought of her as an even-tempered woman, good-natured and easygoing. Everything her children thought she wasn't. Susan would have driven right off the road laughing if Claudia had ever told her any of that, and she had no doubt the rest of her children would do the same.

Like just now at the store with Annie.

Would it have hurt you to bend just a little? She was reaching out to you, and you wouldn't give an inch.

It wasn't that she wanted Annie to be unhappy. What kind of woman would she be if she wished unhappiness on the girl she'd raised as one of her own? A bitch, that's what, the worst kind of bitch. Heartless and unyielding. But oh God, how it hurt to think of her with a man who wasn't Kevin. In a way it was like losing him all over again.

She had never wanted another man after John's death. Oh, she had had plenty of offers from some of the kindly gentlemen of Shelter Rock Cove, but she had spurned all of their advances. John was the love of her life, her only true love, and there wasn't a man on earth who could compare. She had always believed it was like that between

Annie and Kevin. Kevin had worshipped Annie. The family used to tease him about the poetry and the flowers. His brothers and sisters were practical, down-to-earth types who wouldn't be caught dead knowing the difference between a couplet and a sonnet. But Kevin not only knew the difference, he wanted to tell you all about it and he did so in a way that made his words a permanent part of your heart.

Annie had glowed in those early years. The whole town had basked in that glow. KevinandAnnie. AnnieandKevin. You couldn't tell where one ended and the other began. Even today you couldn't look at Annie and not see Kevin, so tall and handsome, right there by her side.

Tears welled up, and she reached into her purse and retrieved her sunglasses and slipped them on. Last night, seeing Annie hand in hand with someone who wasn't Kevin—well, there was no explaining how that had felt.

Had she really been in denial all this time? It didn't seem possible, but what other explanation could there be for that feeling of utter shock? Up until that moment she had been able to pretend that Kevin was in the next room, or maybe on the next block, beyond her reach but not gone. Never that. But nothing could explain away the sight of Annie, luminous and filled with joy, as she looked up at that wiry, edgy man who had walked into Cappy's with Warren.

Get a grip on yourself, Claudia, or else everyone in town will be talking about the way you fell apart during the Labor Day festivities.

That would give the town years of good gossip, and she wasn't about to make that mistake.

Next to her, Roberta was chatting away like a magpie, telling Adele Roscoe and Jean Gillooley all about the Adam Winters seminar they had taken and how they were thinking of becoming investors, and Claudia all but leaped for her best friend's crepey throat.

"Now what did you go and blab to Adele and Jean for?" she demanded the second the women wandered off. "Why don't you call our children, too, while you're at it?"

"They saw the brochure sticking out of my tote bag," Roberta said with a mutinous look in her beady little eyes. "What was I supposed to do, lie to them?"

"Yes," Claudia snapped. "You could have told them about the seminar without blabbing our business all over town."

"Remember that question you asked me a few minutes ago? I think I can answer it now."

"Oh, hush up," Claudia said. "Why don't you just—"

Well, of all the nerve! Annie's new friend—what was his name, Sam something-or-other—was heading toward their display as if he had an urgent need to win a mammogram.

Roberta squinted in his direction. "Isn't that—"

"Yes," Claudia hissed, "and if you—"

"Mrs. Galloway?" He stopped right there in front of them and stuck out his right hand. "We didn't have the chance to meet last night, but Warren and Annie told me a lot about you."

She knew his name was Sam Butler and she had no choice but to shake his hand. His grip was strong but not too familiar. She was glad he knew his place.

Roberta gave her a poke in her ribs.

"This is my friend Roberta Morgan," she said, although why Bobbi couldn't introduce herself was beyond her.

Roberta eagerly shook his hand. "Pleased to meet you. I saw you last night with our Annie." She actually batted her eyelashes at the man. "I must say you make an adorable couple."

He thanked Roberta, but it was clear her comment had embarrassed him.

"I heard you talking to the other two ladies about a financial seminar."

Claudia arched a brow. "You were eavesdropping?"

"Yep," he said with an easy smile. "Afraid so."

Roberta, ever oblivious to nuance, plunged right in. "I have an extra brochure if you'd like it."

He flashed a big toothpaste-commercial smile at her foolish friend, who all but swooned. "I wouldn't mind taking a look at it."

Roberta whipped out the brochure and handed it to him. "You can keep it if you like."

He wasn't listening. He flipped through the pages, eyes scanning the columns of text as though it were the most fascinating thing he'd ever seen. She and Roberta exchanged looks.

So handsome! Roberta's look said. *And so interested in finance.*

He's just looking at the pictures, Claudia's own look retorted. There was something scruffy about him, even though his clothes were clean and relatively stylish. But then, didn't they all wear jeans and sweaters these days, as if someone somewhere had decreed everyone under fifty must wear the uniform or be drummed out of their generation? Just a touch of carelessness that some women found very attractive. From the foolish look on Roberta's face, it was clear that she was one of them, but not Claudia. She had always loved the way her John had looked in a suit and tie, so proper and distinguished and above reproach. Kevin hadn't been quite so formal, but he had always been perfectly turned out in tweed sportcoats and fine cords that befitted his position as a teacher.

". . . we went to his seminar the other day," Roberta was saying. "In fact, we're—"

"Bobbi," Claudia interrupted her friend, "we need some more of the sign-up sheets. Would you see if you can find Dr. Markowitz and ask her if she has any she could spare?"

"In a minute," Roberta said, glaring at Claudia. She turned back to Sam Butler. "He offers a—"

"Roberta." Claudia employed the same tone of voice she used to use when her teenagers came home after curfew. "We need them now."

Roberta smiled at Annie's friend. "Why don't you keep one of those brochures," she said amiably. "I never knew money could be so much fun until I started listening to Adam Winters on the radio!"

From the look on this Sam Butler's face, Claudia knew she had to say something. After the unpleasant response from Susan and Annie the other night, she intended to keep her further workshop plans to herself.

"Roberta is very enthusiastic," she offered, a bit discomfited by the look of curiosity in his eyes. "We took a class in Japanese flower arranging, and by the time it was over she was ready to become a Zen master."

He laughed, which was exactly what she had hoped he would do. His rough edges weren't quite as rough as she'd first thought.

"One of my sisters is the same way," he said in what was really a very friendly tone of voice for a New Yorker. "She took three classes in oil painting and was ready to move to Paris and live in a garret."

She smiled despite herself. "I have two shelves filled with my experiments in pottery. I tried to bribe my children, but even they won't touch them."

It was clear to Claudia that he was sizing her up in much the same way she was sizing him up, and she wondered what family stories Annie might have shared with this stranger, stories that maybe Claudia herself knew nothing about.

You may not last, she thought as she smiled at him. *You might be nothing more than a fling.*

But there was something in the way he looked across the Green at Annie that told her she was dead wrong.

FOURTEEN

"You're right," Ellen said to Hall as another wave of visitors drifted away from their booth. "He does look familiar."

"I know," he said as they watched Sam Butler attempt to charm Claudia Galloway. "Maybe he did some repairs on one of my boats."

Ellen groaned and hit him in the arm with a rolled-up mammogram fact sheet. "And since I've never set foot on one of your boats, how would that make him look familiar to me?"

He blinked at her in surprise. "You've been on the sloop."

"Afraid not, Cap'n."

"The small sailboat."

"Nope."

"The kayak I keep up at the cabin."

"Not even close."

He looked at her. "We're going to have to remedy that, Markowitz."

She ignored him. "Do you really think he worked on one of your boats?"

"No," Hall said, "but it's the best I can come up with. The guy's from New York, and I'm down there once every two years if I'm lucky. It doesn't seem likely our paths would've crossed, does it?"

Her eyes widened. "He's from New York?"

"His accent's worse than yours," he said, ducking a paper clip tossed in his direction.

"Did you know I can peg a New Yorker to within two blocks of his last apartment?" She pushed her unruly mop of red hair off her face. "I can almost tell you what floor you lived on."

"Ten bucks says you can't even name the borough."

She threw back her head and laughed. "You're on, Doctor. Easiest ten bucks I'll make this year."

Adam Winters had put together a first-rate, four-color, glossy pile of bullshit designed to romance the bucks out of retirement plans up and down the East Coast. He plastered his boyish face on the cover—big guileless smile, shock of hair flopping over his unlined forehead—in an attempt to charm his sixty-something, female audience into believing he was no more threatening than one of their own children. He was the son who came to dinner every Sunday, the one who brought flowers and a box of candy and telephoned every morning to see how you were.

The dream son who did all that and tripled your investment before the first year was out.

Sam knew the technique. He'd seen the way it worked a thousand times during his years on the Street. He'd employed a few of the tricks himself on more than one occasion. There was nothing innovative about anything he'd read in the text, no guarantees that you would end up with more money than you'd started with. Winters fished familiar waters. *Listen to me and you won't end up in one of those nursing homes that stink of urine and decay. I'll show you how you can protect yourself.*

They were all scared. You couldn't grow old in this country and not be. You wanted to make sure your time ran out before your money did, and many a fortune had been made by capitalizing on those fears.

He could tell Claudia some of these things, but she wouldn't believe him. *Didn't you earn your living the same way?* she would ask. *Why is this so different?*

And he wouldn't be able to answer because he was every bit as guilty as Adam Winters and all the other half-baked scam artists who had come along in the last hundred years.

It wasn't a legacy he was proud of.

A tall skinny woman with a curly mop of red hair appeared at Sam's right elbow.

"Dr. Markowitz," Claudia said with a friendly smile. "How are you enjoying your first Labor Day picnic in Shelter Rock Cove?"

"Please call me Ellen," she said with a smile for both of them. "We can save the 'Dr. Markowitz' for the lady with the stethoscope."

"Sam Butler," he said, extending his hand. No point to waiting for Claudia to introduce them.

"Queens," she said, tilting her head to the right. "Somewhere around Bayside."

He nodded. "Not bad. Bayside it is."

She smiled at him, but there was nothing flirtatious about it. "It was either Queens or western Suffolk County."

"Manhattan," he guessed. "Upper West Side near Columbus Circle."

"Guilty as charged. What gave me away?"

"Nothing," he said. "It was the first place I could think of."

She laughed, and even Claudia joined in.

"I was just saying to Hall that you look familiar," she said. "Have we met before?"

He shook his head. "I didn't spend too much time around Columbus Circle."

"You must have one of those faces," she said. "I'll bet you hear that all the time."

He didn't, but he let it pass. Ellen Markowitz seemed like a nice enough woman even if she did have an ulterior motive. Sam had noticed her talking earnestly with the good Dr. Talbot, and Annie had told him they were partners in an OB-GYN practice. Talbot had probably sent her over here on some sort of half-baked reconnaissance mission.

"This is your first Labor Day picnic in Shelter Rock Cove, isn't it, dear?" Claudia asked.

"It is," Ellen said, "and I'm amazed by it. Our booth has been so busy, there hasn't been time to wander around and sample some of those delicious foods I see everyone enjoying."

"Have a deviled egg," Claudia offered, reaching into the ice chest for the platter. "You, too," she said to Sam.

Ellen reached for an egg, then caught sight of the brochure in Sam's hand. "Oh, what's this!" She bent down and peered at the cover then chuckled. "Don't tell me you're one of his devotees."

Claudia yanked the glossy folder away from Sam. "Roberta and I take workshops," she said with a visible straightening of her Yankee spine. "Mr. Winters is quite a showman."

"My aunt got involved with one of those radio financial wizards," Ellen said, shaking her head. "She ended up losing everything but her house. Stay away from guys like this, Claudia. They have radar when it comes to women and money."

"Good heavens," said Claudia with a little laugh. "You take these things much too seriously. For us it's investments one week and tai chi the next." She looked calm and completely in control, not at all the type of woman who handed over the keys to the kingdom without a full background check.

They were usually the first to fall.

"You tell her," Ellen said, turning to Sam.

"Why me?" A ripple of alarm moved along his spine.

"You seemed pretty absorbed in that brochure when I barged in. I just assumed—" Something in his eyes must have registered on her because she stopped abruptly. "Delicious deviled eggs," she said, wiping the corner of her mouth with a paper napkin. "Good to see you, Claudia. Great to meet you, Sam. I'd better get back to the booth before Hall sends out a search party."

"Well," said Claudia as the doctor dashed off across the Green, "that was certainly rude."

Sam, who wasn't about to stick a toe in the waters of Shelter Rock Cove politics, kept quiet and thanked his lucky stars.

He brought her icy cold lemonade; a platter piled high with fried clams, fresh lobster meat, and french fries; and a slice of juicy blueberry pie fit for the gods.

"Sam, this is too much!" Annie said, laughing, as he placed the bounty down on the table in front of her. "You have to share it with me."

"I was hoping you'd say that." He reached for a crisp, golden curl of clam, then popped it into her mouth.

"I've missed you," she said, popping a fry into his

mouth in return. "I hope this hasn't been too deadly dull for you."

"I hung out with the fire department for a while," he said. "The dentist tried to recruit me, but I told him I was just passing through."

Some of the day's brightness dimmed. "*Are* you just passing through?"

"I can't freeload off Warren forever."

"Sure you could," she said lightly. "Warren loves you. He'd be thrilled if you decided to make Shelter Rock Cove your home."

He didn't say anything, and who could blame him? She had backed him into a spot like one of those terrible women on the afternoon talk shows, the ones who ended up stalking some poor guy and soaping his car windows when he took another woman to dinner.

Well, now you've done it, Galloway. Why don't you just sew your heart to the sleeve of your sweater while you're at it?

"Forget I said that." She picked at the lobster with a plastic fork. "It's the lemonade speaking."

"I didn't know I'd find you here," he said quietly. "I wasn't expecting this."

"Really," she said, wishing she could crawl under the bandstand and stay there until New Year's Eve, "you don't have to say anything. This is what happens when your last date was during the Reagan administration."

She was embarrassed and upset. He could see it in her eyes, hear it in her voice, and the fact that there was nothing he could say to make it all better tore at his heart. He wanted to tell her that this was forever, that nothing in the world could tear him away from her, but that would be unfair to her. He had no right to ask her to hand over her heart into his keeping, when hovering out there just out of sight was the real world and all that went with it.

One day soon it would come calling for him, and he would have no choice but to answer.

The less Annie knew, the better. He didn't want to see her dragged into a mess she had nothing to do with, all because he was too selfish to keep his own troubles to himself.

How could you promise a woman forever when you couldn't see around the next corner to tomorrow?

He took her hand and as he raised it to his lips he saw the narrow white strip that marked where her wedding ring had been. The band of paler skin spoke volumes.

"It was time," she said. "I was always catching the ring on the florist's wires at the shop—"

"This is real," he said as he kissed the place where her wedding ring had been. "Whatever happens, I want you to remember that."

"I know that," she said. "I knew it the first moment I saw you."

But she didn't understand, not really, and in a way he was glad. She thought he was talking about the uncertainties of life and death, and in a way he wished he were. It would be easier to explain the hand of fate than the series of decisions and compromises that had brought him into her life.

All they had, all anyone had, was the moment, and although it wasn't close to being enough, for now it was the best he could do.

Teddy Webb had been working for the *Shelter Rock Cove Weekly News and Shopper* for more years than he cared to remember. He had covered the last twenty Labor Day picnics on the Green and had run out of adjectives to describe hamburgers, hot dogs, and Ceil's award-winning apple strudel. Once you got past *delicious, mouth-watering,* and *delectable* the next step was *scrumptious,* and the day his gnarled old fingers typed a word like *scrumptious* was the day he handed in his press pass and retired for good.

Teddy had filled a small reporter's notebook with details, and once he got back home he would take a shot of Pepto Bismol, type it all up on his computer, and zap it over to the office before they put the issue to bed.

But he still needed a photo to go with it. Oh, he'd snapped a few of apple pies bursting with fruit and one of Eileen Galloway's sons with a faceful of watermelon, but nothing that really rang his chimes. Hell, he could just recycle last year's sack race and be done with it. Nobody would ever know the difference. He was debating the viability of that idea when his gaze happened to land on a sight that did his grizzled old heart good. Annie Lacy Galloway was gazing into the eyes of some guy he had never seen before, and you could just about see Cupid aiming his arrows straight at their hearts. Everyone in town loved Annie, and they were bound to love seeing her looking so happy again.

Grinning to himself, Teddy aimed the camera, and two clicks later he had his page one photo.

Susan was extolling the virtues of a central vacuum cleaning system when she saw the kiss. She had been about to tell George and Lily Williams about the glories to be found in not dragging around a ten-pound canister when Sam Butler lifted Annie's hand to his lips and kissed it.

"Susan?" asked Lily, who operated the daycare center near the town hall. "Is something wrong?"

"Sorry," she said, trying to snap herself back to attention. "What was I saying?"

"About the vacuum cleaning system," George prompted her. "We were wondering about filtration capabilities."

Was that English they were speaking or some foreign

tongue Susan had never heard before? She couldn't make sense of any of it, not when Annie was looking into Sam's eyes that way, as if she had been waiting her entire life for that moment.

A deep yearning awoke inside her chest, and its power almost knocked her flat. The last time she had felt anything close to this depth of emotion was when her children were born. When she heard her babies' first cries she had been filled with a rush of love so intense she thought she would die from it. That was how she felt as she looked at Annie and Sam, radiant with new love, as untouchable as the stars.

Hall was brushing grass off the back of Willa's white shorts when Mariah pointed across the Green. "Eee-yewww," she said, making a face. "That man's kissing Annie."

"Yuk," said Willa, without even looking. "Gross."

He knew he shouldn't look. What was the point to seeing everything he had dreaded come to life in front of his eyes? He couldn't change it. He couldn't make it go away. More to the point, he couldn't make Sam Butler go away. Butler had come to town without history or baggage. He didn't give a damn that Annie was Kevin's widow. He didn't know squat about the gambling, the babies that weren't meant to be, all the things that had kept Hall trapped in place. No, the guy just drove into town, took a look around, then swept Annie off her feet and into his arms while Hall sat on his deck, nursing a scotch and wondering where to begin.

"It might not last," Ellen said, joining him as the girls ran off to play. "I don't think Shelter Rock Cove is his kind of place."

Hall shook his head. "It doesn't matter," he said. "Do you see the way she's looking at him?"

Ellen's only answer was a sigh.

• • •

"Will you look at that!" Roberta nudged Claudia. "If that's not the most romantic thing I've ever seen, I don't know what is."

Roberta was too late. Claudia had watched the whole scene unfold from behind her sunglasses. She had seen Annie's smile disappear. She had watched as he fumbled for words. Her breath caught when he took Annie's hand and looked at it as if reading her palm, and when he lifted her hand to his mouth, she thought her heart would break.

She wasn't one for crying. Tears had never changed a thing in this world. They certainly didn't pay your bills or fix the roof on your house, and they could never bring back the ones you had loved and lost. But those damn tears slid down her cheeks, and there seemed to be nothing she could do to stop them.

"I'll be right back," she said to Roberta. She started out across the Green toward Annie's Flowers where she could compose herself, but wouldn't you know that old coot Warren fell in step with her before she was halfway there.

Warren didn't say anything, and neither did she. They met each other's eyes, and a lifetime of memories passed between them. He reached for her hand as they approached the hill, and this time, just this once, she didn't pull away.

FIFTEEN

Their lovemaking that night was fierce and deeply thrilling, as if they were trying to forge a bond that nothing, neither time nor circumstance, could ever undo. That they both believed such a thing was possible forged a deeper bond than either realized. After a while Sam slept, but Annie was too filled with energy to close her eyes. It had been years since she had been all one piece, her body and soul and mind working together as one seamless entity. She was more than an intellect, more than a body, and it was their lovemaking that had restored her soul and brought all the disparate parts of herself together again, the way it should be. The way it used to be before disappointment and sorrow became her constant companions. She could feel the energy flowing from her heart to her mind and shooting out from her fingers and toes in a rainbow of color and form.

Nothing lasts forever, but this is real . . . This is real.

Was it? You couldn't see or touch the bond between them, the sense of destiny, but she knew it was there just the same. He had an idea what it was like to lose your parents before you were old enough to vote. There was nothing in the world that could prepare you for that, no club you could join to help you through it. They both knew that life could be both cruel and capricious, and there was nothing you could do to sway the outcome. That knowledge had kept her paralyzed for so long, but suddenly she didn't feel stuck in place any longer.

She wanted to capture it all, gather up the stars and the moon and splash them on a canvas, run her hands along a satiny block of wood until she found the form hiding within.

Quietly she rose from the bed and slipped one of Sam's T-shirts over her head. Stepping over Max's sleeping body, she let herself out of the bedroom and padded down the short hallway to the room where she'd stashed the boxes left to unpack. Way in the back, tucked behind the boxes marked "Music, Books, Misc" was an old picnic basket that had belonged to her mother. It was an enormous wicker contraption with foldout trays and neat little compartments for cutlery and dishes and food that made a perfect storage box for her pens and inks and painting supplies. She pulled out a vine of charcoal, sharpened it against the sandpaper block, then dug out a nice toothy sketch pad that still had a fair amount of empty pages left.

She could see the six figures deep inside her head, and now she called on them to materialize on the page before her so they could get acquainted. Her hand moved automatically across the paper, leaving shape and shadow behind. The man was young, twenty at most, wiry and strong and fearless, and the five children radiated out from him like spokes in a wheel. Each stood separate and apart but were somehow linked to the man in the center by invisible threads. Sorrow was in their eyes and hope, too, because that was the gift he gave them. Hope and love, a home of their own where no harm could find them. It was all there, waiting for Annie, flowing from heart to hand as if by magic. She filled page after page with sketches of those people. Long shots, portraits, individual and group. She played with proportion and angle, tried various groupings. In every sketch, the man looked like Sam.

She saw it as it would look when it was released from a shroud of maple: six figures forming one perfect unit as they gazed out over Shelter Rock Cove, waiting for the sailors who would never come home.

Sam watched her from the doorway. She worked with intensity, her hand inscribing graceful arcs and angles on page after page of drawing paper. He couldn't see what she was working on, but watching her in motion was more than enough. She sat there in that tiny room, lost in the middle of a pile of boxes, and created beauty just by the act of being. She wore his T-shirt and nothing else, her lush curves barely hidden from view. George and Gracie slept happily atop her bare feet while Max looked up at her with open adoration.

Me, too, Max, he thought as he caught a yawn with the back of his hand. She looked rosy and sated as she sat perched atop a cardboard box filled with books and pursued some private vision of her own. He could spend a lifetime watching her smile. Was that love? He didn't know. He had never felt this way before about anyone; just the fact that she existed in this world was enough to make him happy. His siblings had told him that he would know it when the right one came along. Some secret door to his heart would swing open, and she would step inside and fill all the empty places.

It had sounded like a lot of romantic crap to him, and he had said so on more than one occasion. Now he was beginning to think they might have been right.

"You'll see," Marie had said to him a few years ago

over pizza and a bottle of Bolla. "When you least expect it, she'll show up and you'll be a goner."

Marie had the head of a reporter and the heart of a romance novelist. She believed in love at first sight and happy endings, and while her own marriage was filled with the stuff of daily life—diapers and deadlines and bills to pay—there was no denying she was happy.

He felt like his best self around Annie. When she looked at him, he wanted to try harder, do more, be the man she believed him to be, and the only way he could do that was to push her away.

"Are you going to stand there all night," Annie asked "or do you want to see what I'm doing?"

"How'd you know I was here?"

She threw him a glance over her left shoulder. "Max's tail started thumping, so I figured you were close by."

He picked his way through the stacks of boxes to where she sat by the window. "What're you working on?"

"I'm not sure," she said. "Maybe something for the museum." She laughed nervously. "Or maybe something for the circular file."

He held out his hand. "Show me."

"I don't think this is such a good idea after all," she said, then handed over the sketch pad.

What he saw took his breath away. His younger self looked up at him from the page. He saw loneliness in his eyes and fear and a strength of character he wasn't sure he had ever possessed. His brothers and sisters surrounded him, and somehow, through what magic he couldn't say, Annie had managed to capture bits and pieces of each one of them.

"They're just preliminary sketches," she said. "I'm trying to block out positions . . ." She saw the figures carved from maple that would grow rough and weathered with time.

"Warren was right," he said when he could find his voice again. "You're gifted."

"You're partial."

"Not in this. You've never met my brothers and sisters, but here they are on the page."

She blushed deep pink with pleasure. "You told me about them, and I improvised the rest."

"This is what you should be doing, not arranging flowers."

"Believe me, every bit of my training comes into play at the flower shop."

"You know what I'm saying."

"Pretty pictures don't keep a roof over your head," she said simply. "I had to find a way to make a living."

"Warren said your husband was a teacher. Didn't he—"

She shook her head. "Big house, big mortgage. We were your typical two-income family, overextended to the max."

Now it was beginning to make sense to him. The move to the tiny house by the water. The empty rooms. The beat-up truck. She was digging out from under the same American dream he had sold to others at Mason, Marx, and Daniel.

If anyone had missed seeing Sam kiss Annie's hand at the Labor Day picnic, the front-page color photo in the weekly newspaper brought them up to speed.

Annie turned bright red on Friday morning when Sweeney dropped a copy of the paper on the sales counter and said, "Way to go, girl!" Claudia peered over Annie's shoulder to see what the commotion was all about, and when she saw the very romantic photo, her smile grew tight, and then she turned away.

As the days and weeks progressed, Annie found herself thinking of the Labor Day picnic as the dividing line between her old life and her new one with Sam. Suddenly her life was filled to the brim with passion and joy and a renewal of creativity that had lain dormant for far too long. She felt truly herself in all the ways that mattered. Each night in Sam's arms she rediscovered another long-buried part of the woman she used to be: the sensual, curious, happy woman she had come close to losing.

There was no denying that they were a couple now. Claudia remained pleasant but distant, as if Annie's feelings for Sam somehow diminished her love for the woman who had opened her heart to her all those years ago. Nothing could have been further from the truth, but each time Annie tried to broach the topic, Claudia found another chore that needed doing or suddenly remembered a meeting she had to attend. Annie was more than a daughter-in-law but not quite a daughter by blood, and the thought that loving Sam might mean she had lost the woman who had mothered her for over twenty-two years made her terribly sad.

"Pay no attention to her," Warren had said when she dropped off the latest batch of typed manuscript for him. "She's worked herself into a snit. She'll work herself out of it sooner or later."

Annie wasn't so sure about that. Claudia seemed to spend most of her free time poring over piles of documents connected to her Adam Winters seminars, and when she wasn't reading, she was entering numbers into the computer, then saving them to a floppy disk that went everywhere with her. Under normal circumstances, Annie wouldn't have hesitated to ask her what was going on, but these days they were walking on eggshells around each other, and Annie wasn't about to make the situation between them any more uncomfortable than it already was.

Even Susan's attitude toward Annie had changed. Oh,

she still was the master of lighthearted banter, but there was an awkwardness between them that had never been there before.

"You're so busy all the time," Susan said to her one afternoon in early October. She had stopped in at the shop to pick up an arrangement for a client's housewarming. "The kids keep asking when they're going to see their Aunt Annie."

"Aunt Annie's right here," she said as she draped moss over the wire frame of a harvest cornucopia. "Tell them they can drop in anytime."

"You know what I'm talking about."

"No," said Annie as she reached for some broad and glossy ivy leaves, "I don't. I'm here, Susie, every single day of the week and when I'm not here I'm over at Warren's working on a project."

"Or you're with Sam."

"So that's what this is about."

"Yes—I mean, no—oh, hell, I don't know what I mean."

Annie wiped her hands along the sides of her jeans. "Why don't I brew some tea?" she suggested, glancing at the clock. "Claudia's off at her seminar today, and the crew from the co-op are at Bar Harbor setting up for a sidewalk show this weekend."

"I really shouldn't," Susan said. "I'm at the front desk this afternoon."

"Ten minutes," Annie urged. "It's been too long, Susie." She flipped the sign on the door to read *Closed*. "Now, how can you refuse me?"

They fell together into the old rhythms of friendship. Annie took down the red teapot she had found years ago at a yard sale and broke out the loose tea.

"Fancy-shmancy," Susan remarked as she ferreted out

a box of Oreos in the narrow cupboard off the workroom. "Will you read my tea leaves?"

"I don't have to," Annie said as she poured the boiling water into the pot. "I know we're all in for clear sailing."

"Speak for yourself," Susan said as she separated the two layers of cookie and exposed the filling. "I think I see a few storm clouds on the horizon."

"Anything you want to tell me about?"

"I don't know . . . I mean, it's all—damn it, Annie, I'm jealous as hell."

Annie started to laugh. "You're kidding, aren't you? You have everything I ever wanted." A husband, kids, a beautiful house, a job, a big family all of whom loved her unconditionally.

To her astonishment, Susan's dark brown eyes filled with tears. "You're so happy these days. Everyone's noticed it. The two of you actually light up a room when you walk in. If I could feel that way again for just ten seconds I—" She caught herself. "Don't mind me. I'm premenopausal."

"You're jealous of Sam and me?" She couldn't believe she was even saying those words.

"Yes," Susan said as the tears spilled down her cheeks, "and if you want to hear something really sick, I was jealous of you and Kevin, too."

"I don't know what to say."

Susan laughed raggedly and dabbed at her eyes with the edge of a paper towel. "You and Kevin were the most romantic couple I'd ever known. We were all wildly jealous of you two in high school, and then when you got married—hell, it was better than the romance novels we were reading under the covers at night. Do you know what we called you two?"

Annie shook her head. She was beginning to think she knew very little at all.

"The Orphan and the Penniless Poet."

Annie started to laugh.

"I know, I know, it sounds funny now, but back then we thought it was the most thrilling and romantic thing in the world."

"Even when Kevin and I were working double shifts at McDonald's to make ends meet?"

"What's more romantic than poverty when you're young?"

Oh, Susan, if you only knew . . .

Annie poured tea for both of them, then settled back down opposite her friend. "I know you and Jack are happy," she said. "Knowing you, I can't believe you'd still be with him if you weren't."

"We're happy," Susan admitted, "but sometimes I find myself wondering what else might be out there." She fiddled with her spoon. "I'm forty-two, Annie, and I can't believe this is as good as it's going to get."

"Isn't that what Sweeney said when she left husband number six?"

"I'm not saying I want six husbands," Susan said with a mock groan, "but sometimes I see a man, and next thing you know I'm having him stripped and brought to my tent." She laughed at the look on Annie's face. "Figuratively speaking, of course."

"I thought I was the only one who did that."

It was Susan's turn to look shocked. "You? You're kidding!"

"All the time," Annie said. "You wouldn't believe what I did with the new attendant at the gas station last spring."

Susan started to laugh, and then before you knew it, Annie was laughing, too, huge loud belly laughs that left no room for jealousy or anger.

"When I was pregnant with my last one, I actually

started fantasizing about Hall in the delivery room," Susan admitted.

"Did you know Roberta Morgan spritzes herself with Shalimar before every visit?"

The two of them convulsed in laughter again, falling across the table in helpless mirth.

"Now where did you hear something like that?" Susan demanded when she could finally speak again.

"I heard it right here," Annie said. "She and Claudia were talking about gyno visits, and Roberta piped up with that revelation."

"I would've given anything to see my mother's face when she heard that."

Annie poured them some more tea and broke into a new bag of cookies.

"You know I was disappointed that it didn't work out for you and Hall," Susan said.

"I figured as much." Annie sipped her tea. "He's a good man," she said, "but there's just no chemistry there."

"Maybe there could be if you gave him a chance."

Annie shook her head. "You can't force chemistry, Susie. It's either there or it isn't."

"Now you sound like Jack."

"Your husband's a smart man."

"I know," said Susan.

"And he loves you."

"I know that, too."

"That's more than most of us get in one lifetime."

Susan broke apart another Oreo. "Did you love Kevin?" she asked suddenly.

"What kind of question is that?" Annie bristled. "Of course I loved him."

"Were you happy?"

Why didn't she ask how many angels could dance on the head of a pin?

"I think you've had too much orange pekoe."

"No, no," Susan said. "Don't push me away with a joke, Annie. I want to know if you and my brother were happy together."

"Is this a test?" Annie asked lightly. "Miss one question and I'm drummed out of the Galloway clan."

It was Susan's turn to bristle. "You looked happy. You sounded happy. But lately I've found myself wondering what happiness is all about."

"You're married," Annie said, choosing her words with great care. "You know it isn't always a matter of being happy or unhappy."

"He adored you."

Annie couldn't deny it. "He wasn't the most practical of men."

"He was a poet," Susan said. "A poet dropped in the middle of a bunch of bean counters. Mother was the only one who really understood him."

"It isn't always easy living with a poet." *We almost lost the house, Susie. Strange men used to show up at our door in the middle of the night. Our poet had a terrible problem . . .*

"Is Sam a poet?"

Annie shook her head. "Only when he's working on one of Warren's boats. He seems to understand them from the inside out."

"Is that what he does for a living, repair boats?"

She couldn't help smiling. "Would you believe he's some kind of bean counter?"

"You're happy, aren't you?"

"Very."

"And you're being careful. It's a different world out there from when we were young and dating. The rules have all changed."

"He's a good man." *Remember how I fell apart when*

my parents died, Susie? Sam lost his parents, too, when he was about the same age, but he didn't fall apart. He did what he had to do to keep his family together. I would never have been able to do that. "I've never known anyone like him."

"He'd better be good," Susan said fiercely, "or he'll have to answer to me."

"He saved my life."

"Very funny."

"I'm not joking, Susie. He saved my life the night I moved into the new house." She told her the whole story, from the bottle of cheap bubbly on an empty stomach to setting fire to her beautiful green robe to waking up in bed with him the next morning.

"Ohmygod," Susan whispered, wide-eyed. "Ohmygod!"

"And as if that's not enough," Annie said, "he brought over a bag of DeeDee's donuts."

Susan pretended to fall across the table in a swoon. "You're trying to kill me, aren't you? First you tell me the guy is a bona fide hero, then you tell me he wooed you with DeeDee's donuts."

"Afraid so," Annie said. "I didn't stand a chance. He's as close to perfect as a man can get."

"The donuts alone would have done it for me," Susan admitted.

They talked about other things, too, touching on subjects near and dear to their hearts in a way they hadn't for far too long. Family and friends and the latest gossip making the rounds about town. "You're the number one topic these days," Susan said as Annie washed the cups and teapot.

Annie handed Susan a wet cup and a dry dishtowel. "What are they saying?"

"Mostly that you never looked so good. Ceil at Yankee Shopper thinks you're doing tae-bo."

Annie burst out laughing. She wanted to tell her friend how wonderful it felt to have a secure roof over her head, to no longer worry about strangers on her doorstep or late-night phone calls. She might not have much but what she had belonged to her free and clear, and the sense of freedom and independence that gave her was exhilarating. And then to have someone like Sam walk into her life at that very moment—well, it was enough to make a woman believe she just might have been born under a lucky star after all.

SIXTEEN

Hall looked up from his computer to find Ellen standing in the doorway to his office. She was holding a newspaper clipping in her right hand.

"I found this in the fax machine," she said. "Nice picture of Annie Galloway and Sam Butler, isn't it?"

"Thanks," he said. "I was wondering what happened to it."

"You have to check the machine now and again, Hall." She walked over and dropped the clipping on his keyboard. "One day you might leave something incriminating behind."

He leaned back in his chair and looked up at her. "If you have something to say, why don't you just say it."

"I am saying it." She leaned against the edge of his desk and crossed her arms over her chest. "I'm just not sure you're listening."

"I faxed a copy of a newspaper story to a friend. Is that a crime?"

"That picture goes back to Labor Day. How long are you going to hang onto it?"

"It's not what you think."

"Yeah," she said. "Sure it isn't."

"Annie's in love with the guy. I know that." There were times when he even believed it.

"So what are you doing hanging onto this stupid picture?"

"A hunch," he said. "A reminder." He shoved away from his desk and stood up. "Hell, Markowitz, I don't know why but I'm glad I did."

She looked weary and more than a little bit irritable. "You still think he looks familiar, don't you?"

"More than ever. What can it hurt to check him out with a few sources?"

"You mean, apart from the fact that it's none of your business?"

"I've known Annie since we were kids," he said, not quite sure why he wanted her to understand. "She's been through a lot in her life. I don't want to see her go through anything else."

"Never knew you were such a Boy Scout."

"You're not acting like yourself today, Markowitz. What's going on?"

"Forget it," she said. "If you can't figure it out for yourself, it's hopeless."

She slammed the door behind her so hard the certificates on his wall rattled. No matter what Ellen thought, he hadn't been trying to duck her question. Right from the beginning he'd had the feeling he knew Sam. There was something familiar about him, something he couldn't quite put his finger on, and it was driving him crazy.

The sense that Sam Butler was hiding something was too strong to ignore. So was the certainty that Annie was going to be hurt. He knew there wasn't any hope for him, but he'd be damned if he stood still while some other guy broke her heart. If he couldn't have her, the least he could do was make sure a better man did. And there was no way in hell that Sam Butler was the better man.

What could it hurt to fax the clipping to some of his friends and colleagues down in New York and see what, if anything, he could uncover? Susan had said the guy was some kind of bean counter on Wall Street. That was a good place to start. He had failed Annie once with his silence. He didn't want to make that mistake a second time.

Sam spent his days at work in Warren's barn and his nights in Annie's bed, moving easily between heaven and paradise. The first of the canoes was almost finished. All that remained was the time-consuming job of stretching the canvas over the frame and securing it at one-inch intervals. Most people would have found the work tedious and repetitive, but not Sam. He loved everything about the process. The sharp-sweet smell of freshly cut wood. The graceful curve of the shell. The symmetry of the bench seats. The taut crispness of canvas stretched to its limit.

Canoes were wonders of maritime construction, elegant and efficient, the perfect example of the "less is more" philosophy. They glided silently through the waters same as they had two centuries ago when the Penobscot still outnumbered the white man. Canoes were rich with the history of the place, and Sam found himself drawn more deeply into the process with every day and, by association, more deeply drawn into the lure of the region and its people.

Both Annie and Warren were of this place. The rugged shoreline and fertile waters had helped shape them. They were both strong and honorable and fiercely loyal to the people and things they loved, old-fashioned virtues he understood even if he fell far short in applying them to real life.

Warren and some of his old friends were up in Canada on their annual mid-October fishing expedition, which coincided with Pete and Nancy's week in Rhode Island with their daughter and new grandbaby. Sam said he would take in the mail and keep a casual eye on the house, but except for an occasional FedEx delivery, nobody ever drove past the mailbox at the foot of the driveway. Solitude of this richness and magnitude was new to Sam, and he was surprised to discover how much he liked it. He was able to sink deeply into his work to the point where the rest of the world fell away. Annie was that way, too. He had noticed the way she blocked out everything but the project at hand when she worked, sailing away deep into some interior world that was hers alone. Further proof, as if he needed any, that they were meant to be.

Warren had been elated when she told him that she'd nailed a concept for the front of the museum, and he had faxed her list of materials to a friend who promised to fulfill the order within the next two weeks. Annie alternated between excitement and terror, convinced one minute that she was about to make her mark and equally convinced the next that she was doomed to failure.

She fascinated him, delighted him, made him feel anything was possible. She understood the deep loneliness that never quite went away because she felt it too. Losing both parents was like being cast adrift in hostile waters without a compass. It marked you, changed you forever in the most primal way possible. Life would never again seem safe or easy. He was glad she'd had the Galloway family to draw her into their circle and make her one of their own. He wished his own brothers and sisters had been half that lucky.

He began to close up shop around six o'clock. Max,

who had been sleeping peacefully in a quiet corner of the barn-turned-workroom, barked twice and took off through the open door.

"Max!" Sam bellowed. "Get back here now!"

Warren's house was situated deep in the woods, and neither he nor Max had a good sense of direction. He could be out there half the night looking for the yellow Lab if he didn't grab him right now.

Night came early these days. The side lawn was bathed in shadow, and he caught a glimpse of Max's form as the dog raced around the corner of the house. Sam picked up speed. Max was headed for the driveway, which meant it wouldn't be long before he was down on the main road.

Except there he was, barking his brains out at a strange car parked right behind Sam's Trooper. The car's lights were on, but the engine was off.

"It's okay, boy," Sam said, scratching Max behind his ear. "I'll take it from here."

The dog did one of those fast-footed dog dances that no human on earth could imitate, then, still barking, he ran toward the front door of the house.

Sam did a quick check of the front and back seats. A woman's purse lay open on the passenger seat. Papers spilled from purse to seat to floor. Checkbook, pen, some stapled pages filled with typing, one of those Adam Winters brochures. The keys dangled from the ignition. The perfume was rich and a little too strong for his taste. Definitely not Annie's.

He heard Max's hysterical barking from the front of the house and a woman's high-pitched call. To hell with the car. Moments later he bounded up the front steps and found himself face-to-face with Annie's former mother-in-law, who was in what seemed to be a state of near hysteria.

"Where is he?" she demanded. Her face was streaked

with tears. "I need to speak to Warren right now."

"He's down in Boston," Sam said. "Can I help you with anything?"

"That old fool is never here when I need him." Her voice was ragged, and she brushed tears off her face. "What am I going to do?"

"You'd better sit down," Sam said. "You're swaying on your feet."

He put a hand on her arm, and she pulled away.

"I'm not senile yet," she snapped. "I can stand on my own two feet."

"Sorry." He backed away, palms held outward. "Why don't you come in and sit down." *Lady, you're acting like it's a Prozac moment.*

He pushed open the door and ushered her into the front hall. He gestured toward the living room. "Sit down," he said, risking another outburst. "I'll get you some water."

She ignored him and headed toward the back of the house. "I know this place like the back of my hand," she said over her shoulder. "I'll get my own water."

"Whatever," he muttered, as he and Max followed close behind. It was clear she didn't like him, and at the moment the feeling was mutual.

She fumbled in the cabinet over the stove, looking for a water glass. "Wineglasses on the bottom shelf. What is Nancy thinking of?" Her hands shook as she reached for a chunky little glass on the second shelf.

Sam reached over her head and took down the glass. "Here," he said. "This is what you were looking for, right?"

"Thank you."

"You're welcome." Who knew polite could sound so angry?

She filled the glass from the tap then took two noisy gulps. She sounded like Max at his bowl. He had the feeling it was the first time in her life that Claudia Galloway fell short of perfection.

"I'm great with cars," he said. "If you need a tire changed or anything—"

"My son-in-law is a master mechanic," she said through a fresh fall of tears.

"You left your lights on," he said. "I turned them off for you."

"That wasn't necessary."

"It will be when you try to start your engine."

She waved a hand in the air. "I don't care."

He thought about the mess on the front seat of her car. The spilled contents of her purse. The checkbook. The papers that looked a hell of a lot like signed contracts. Adam Winters's glossy four-color face staring up at him from the front of a brochure. Her desperate need to see Warren. *I'll give it one more shot, Mrs. G, then I'm outta here.*

She was seated at the kitchen table, her slim body curled over the stubby glass of water. She looked the way his mother used to look when they were going to be late again with the rent. She looked the way his clients must have looked when they realized they were bleeding money.

"You signed a contract with Adam Winters, didn't you?"

She looked up at him, her face a study in despair. "How did you know?"

"Lucky guess," he said. "How bad is it?"

"Bad," she said, burying her face in her hands. "Terribly bad."

He could let it drop right here. It was Claudia's problem, not his. Why risk his own butt in an attempt to save hers?

If he backed away now, she would never know the difference.

He asked for a number, and the one she told him rocked him back on his heels. One year ago the amount wouldn't have made him blink.

"You're right," he said. "That's pretty damn bad."

"You tell anyone, and I'll have your head," she said angrily. "I don't know why on earth I told you."

"You didn't," he pointed out. "I guessed."

"Well, now you can just forget all about it," she ordered him. "This is none of your business."

Let it drop, Butler. You don't need this. Lie low just a little while longer.

"You're right," he said, "it isn't any of my business, but what would you say if I told you I might be able to help?"

"You?" She looked as if she'd be surprised to find out he could count without using his fingers and toes.

He repeated the dollar figure she'd quoted and waited a moment for its magnitude to sink in. "You're already in about as deep as it gets. Will it hurt to listen to what I have to say?"

Sam Butler insisted on driving behind Claudia all the way home. She pulled into her driveway and gave him her best Queen Elizabeth wave, then let herself into the house. He didn't leave until she switched on her lights, and even then he waited a minute or two just to be sure. If one of her sons had shown such good manners, she would have been insufferably proud, but this was the man who was trying to take Kevin's place, and she was not about to grant him any quarter.

He didn't have to help you, Claudia. He could have left you to figure your own way out of this mess.

"What nonsense," she muttered as she hung up her

jacket in the hall closet, then slipped out of her shoes. So what if he wrote down some names and phone numbers for her. That was hardly putting himself out, was it?

You're turning into a bitter old woman. He isn't the one who signed away your life savings.

No, she did that herself. Even now, with the evidence spread across the kitchen table, she couldn't quite believe she had done such a thing. Roberta was usually the one who leaped before she looked. Claudia couldn't count the number of crazy schemes her friend had been involved in, but this time Roberta had folded up her certified check and slipped it back into her purse before Adam had finished his presentation.

But not Claudia. Roberta's prudence had seemed more like cowardice to her at the time. Adam Winters's speech had been rousing and prophetic. He had promised them freedom from HMOs and greedy children. Who wouldn't want to be independently wealthy, able to call their own shots without worrying about co-payments or becoming a burden later in life? Adam understood their needs without being told. It was hard to believe he was only thirty years old; he was as mature as a man twice his age. He had seemed so interested in her. He had answered her questions, almost anticipating them—or so it had seemed. He had opened her eyes to the precarious nature of her financial existence. Best of all, he had provided answers, a sensible way to invest her money and double it within the first two years.

"Of course, the larger the investment, the more spectacular the payoff," he had said. "Why put a limit on your dreams?"

Claudia couldn't answer that. The thought of being dependent upon her children for the basic necessities of life terrified her. She couldn't imagine relying on Susan for groceries or Eileen to pay the property taxes. And what if she lost the car and was reduced to asking Annie for a lift to the flower shop every day? She had read once about old people in Greenland or some other cold and lonely place. When a man or woman was too old to be of value any longer, the old person would crawl onto an ice floe and just drift away. The first time she'd heard that story she had been horrified, grateful to be living in the modern world with its enlightened views on growing older. But with every year that passed, and there had been many of them, she found herself understanding the ice floe mentality just a little bit better.

Adam Winters had a chart for everything. He diagrammed the Dow and NASDAQ over the last five years. He pinpointed the growth areas of communications and pharmaceuticals. He projected earnings off a sum of money close to what Claudia had ultimately signed over, and the totals were awe-inspiring. How could she resist?

You fool, she thought bitterly. *You know that's what this is all about. He paid attention to you. He remembered your name. He touched you on the shoulder each time he walked by. He looked at you, really looked at you, when he talked.*

Now she was getting down to the real story. She was a fool. A lonely old woman whose head had been turned by a man who was almost young enough to be her grandson. It was pathetic, that's what it was. Downright pathetic. Even Roberta, who made a hobby of having her head turned, had been smart enough to put her checkbook away when it was time to sign on the dotted line.

But not Claudia. The old demons had reared their ugly heads, whispering for her to go ahead and take a chance. Spin the wheel. Throw the dice. This wasn't really gambling, was it? Not when such a nice and educated young man told her it was the right thing to do. After all, what did she have to lose but everything she owned?

Sam Butler told her to stop payment on the check first thing in the morning. As if she needed him to suggest the obvious. Would she be so upset if she could do that? Adam Winters had wanted certified checks only, bank checks that guaranteed payment. "Then call my friends," he said, wasting no time on recriminations. He would let them know they'd be hearing from her. She didn't have to worry about cold-calling.

"Why should I call one of your friends?" she had asked.

"Because they're the best in the business," he said. One of the men was a Wall Street lawyer. The other was a consumer affairs specialist.

"And how would you happen to know them?" After all, he wasn't the kind of man who went to work in a suit and tie the way her John and Kevin had. He was working class. All he had to do was open his mouth, and you knew that for a fact.

She would never forget the look in his eyes when he said, "Because they used to work for me."

She had laughed out loud. She couldn't help it. The thought of that scruffy man telling a lawyer or analyst what to do was absurd. But Sam Butler didn't laugh with her. He launched into a rapid-fire barrage of growth funds, low-risk/high-yield ventures, the pros and cons of banking your monies or investing them, why you should never hand over the financial reins to anyone any time for any reason short of physical and mental incompetence. He told her she had every right to her money and that she should make that clear to everyone from Adam Winters on down.

If he had started spouting Shakespearean sonnets, she couldn't have been more surprised, and it didn't take long for her to realize there was much more to Sam Butler than met the eye. How he must be laughing now at the foolish old woman who had been swayed by a nice young man's smile.

She would rather be on that ice floe.

SEVENTEEN

Sam wasn't at all convinced he'd managed to get through to Claudia Galloway. She'd folded the piece of paper with Arnold Gillingham's and William Fenestra's phone numbers on it and slipped it into the pocket of her jacket. He doubted she would use it. She was too deep into despair and self-pity right now to recognize a lifeline when she saw it, and he didn't dare spell it out any more plainly. He had already said more than he should have, but there was no way he could stand there and watch the woman lose everything to a shark like Winters.

Too bad the guy was already halfway to his next gig in Arizona, or Sam would have been tempted to show up at the hotel and demand Claudia's money back.

It had all hit too close to home this time. How many of his former clients were in Claudia's position now, scared shitless and wondering how to salvage a once-bright retirement? He wondered how many cursed him each night before they went to sleep. That was why he'd pulled off the road halfway between Claudia's house and his borrowed cottage and phoned Arnold Gillingham. It was a small-potatoes deal, the kind Arnold had left behind when he went national, but Sam called in a longstanding marker, and Arnold was honorbound to act on it. Besides, the reason Arnold had gone into consumer affairs was because he genuinely hated seeing people taken advantage of by scam artists and con men.

Sam had been living in a dream world these last few weeks with Annie. He'd allowed himself to forget the shadows that loomed large on the horizon, shadows that could change his life forever. The sight of the formidable Claudia huddled in despair at Warren's kitchen table had affected him deeply. In some ways he was no better than that scum Adam Winters, who preyed on fears of loneliness and old age. The only difference was that he had had the full weight of Mason, Marx, and Daniel behind him, lending him the high gloss of credibility.

He wanted to go home and tell Annie everything, spill his guts to her and let hers be the only judgment that mattered, but he couldn't. Telling Annie would be tantamount to dragging her into the middle of the mess. If she didn't know, they couldn't touch her. The moment he let her into the truth of his life, she would be open to public and judicial scrutiny of the harshest kind. What he felt for her was too deep, too important to sacrifice on the altar of his own loneliness. If he did nothing else right in his life, he would keep her safe from harm.

Annie heard Sam's truck crunch its way toward home around seven o'clock. Although they spent every night in each other's arms, they had no set expectations of each other when it came to things like taking meals together. She cooked sometimes, and so did he, and every now and then they splurged and drove over to Cappy's for lobster rolls or the Friday fish fry. The last time they were there, an overbearing Yankee matron had unwittingly entertained the other patrons with a series of cell phone conversations, each of which ended with a Down East "ciao" that almost put Sam and Annie under the table with laughter.

Tonight she had been inspired by the cool early-autumn weather and had whipped up a pot of homemade minestrone to go with the crispy loaf of French bread she'd picked up earlier at Yankee Shopper. More and more they were falling into an easy domesticity that seemed to have *future* written all over it.

Not that they talked about the future. Or the past, for that matter. They were anchored firmly in the here and now, draining every ounce of joy from the moment because they both knew how quickly it could disappear.

But the future was out there waiting, and Annie knew it wouldn't be long before they talked about sharing it together. Everything was so easy with Sam, so right. Because they shared a similar background, they understood each other's soul in a way few others ever could. She didn't have to tell him how much she valued family. He didn't have to tell her that he would put his life on the line to protect those he loved. To find Sam now that she had finally reassembled the wreckage of her life with Kevin was like discovering the pot of gold at the end of the rainbow.

A late bloomer, that's what she was. One of those women who didn't come into their own until they were in their thirties or forties, and then watch out. Even her body seemed different to her lately, more womanly and responsive. Her breasts were fuller, no doubt about it, definitely more sensitive to every whisper of attention. She no longer came alive at only Sam's touch. No, it seemed as though somebody had flipped a switch, sending an erotic current flowing through her body morning, noon, and night, and that current sent shock waves through every part of her life.

The flower shop was flourishing. Her work on the pieces for the museum engaged her heart and soul. And being with Sam, whether it was making love or making breakfast, felt like coming home. Each part of her existence fed the whole in a deep and meaningful way, and she felt blessed to be given this gift at a time when she least expected it.

Next week she was giving a seminar called "Expanding Your Horizons" at the annual meeting of the Maine Floral Professionals down in York Harbor. Sam was going with her, and they planned to spend the night at the inn overlooking the harbor itself. She couldn't wait to see the surprised looks on the faces of her colleagues when she showed up with Sam by her side.

If there was a dark cloud on her sunny horizon, it was the annoying fatigue she'd been experiencing the last few weeks. She knew she was burning the candle at both ends and in the middle, too, but there was no way around it. She was alive with ideas and excitement and joy; sleeping seemed like a waste of glorious time. Sweeney had suggested she try taking a catnap in the middle of the workday, but Annie had just laughed. The thought of trying to explain a siesta to Claudia would be tougher than explaining Sam.

She glanced at the clock. Any minute she'd hear Sam's footsteps on the path.

She smoothed her hair, checking her reflection in the side of the toaster. Five minutes went by, ten minutes, fifteen. She peered out the kitchen window and saw the answering glow of lamplight in his living room window. Usually Max would be waiting impatiently on her front porch by now, eager to see what special something she had for him today.

After twenty minutes she decided something must be wrong. She turned the flame off under the soup, then headed up the road to his house. Max gave one of his who's-out-there barks when she knocked on the front door.

"It's Annie," she called out and was greatly relieved when Sam, cell phone pressed to his ear, swung open the door and motioned her inside.

Max stood up on his hind legs and placed his big paws against her chest as he yipped a greeting. Max's owner, however, looked distracted and more than a little worried.

"Annie from across the road," he said into the receiver. "None of your business . . . Just call the locksmith, Marie . . . Yeah, I'll be here . . . Tell Geo the Jets are going to trash the Raiders on Sunday . . . You, too . . . Talk to you later." He tossed the phone onto the sofa, then turned to Annie. "I missed you today."

"I missed you, too." She moved into his embrace. "Is something wrong?"

"That was my sister Marie. She said my place in Manhattan was broken into."

Annie shuddered. "Thank God you weren't there. Did they take much?"

"There wasn't much to take. Marie said they trashed what was there then left."

That had happened once to her and Kevin early in their marriage. They had come home from work one day to find their place turned inside out. Bookcases overturned. Mattresses tossed. Dishes smashed on the floor. A subtle warning from a man who was tired of waiting for his money. Only thing was, Annie didn't know anyone was waiting for money, especially not for their money. She had wanted to call the police, but Kevin had been dead set against it. She couldn't understand why he refused to report a break-in and entry, and she had argued her point loudly. She'd never forget the look in Kevin's eyes when he said, "There's something I have to tell you, Annie Rose." Words she hoped she'd never hear again.

She tried to shake off the feeling of unease. Manhattan apartments were broken into every day of the week. It was as common as a head cold down there. Not like Shelter Rock Cove, where the police department had nothing to do but keep the two squad cars well-polished and gassed up.

She rested her head against his chest and closed her eyes. "Do you have to go back down there to file a report?"

"My sister took care of everything," he said. "Nothing to worry about."

He still sounded worried. That made them even, because she still felt uneasy.

"I made soup," she said. "You and Max are invited."

"Great." He kissed her, and the world began to right itself one more time. "I'll be there in five with a bottle of wine."

The phone rang again less than a minute after Annie and Max left.

"She'll get her money back," Arnie Gillingham said by way of hello. "No problem."

Arnie was consumer affairs reporter for a national cable station, and he knew where the bodies were buried. Adam Winters was just this side of being legal, and he wanted to stay that way. In order to do that, he needed happy investors, and Mrs. Claudia Galloway of Shelter Rock Cove, Maine, didn't qualify. Her monies, including the two-thousand-dollar seminar fee, would be returned to her by courier within twenty-four hours.

"I owe you one," Sam said as the image of a distraught

Claudia—so like his mother years ago—began to lose some of its power.

"So you're up in Maine," Arnie said. "I would've figured Aruba or maybe the Costa del Sol."

"Can't tell much from a cell phone number," he said with what he hoped was a who-gives-a-damn tone of voice.

"Don't sweat it," Arnie said. "I'd lie low these days, too, what with all that shit coming down at Mason, Marx." Arnie laughed. "You always did have the best timing in town. Leave it to Butler to grab his golden parachute and get out while the getting was still good."

Sam closed the connection a few minutes later with the sense that jackbooted thugs were goosestepping inside his gut. What the hell had he been thinking when he called Arnie from the car? What difference would another day or week have made in the scheme of things? But the sight of Claudia's despair had somehow become linked with his mother at the kitchen table back in Queens, wondering how they were going to pay the bills, and with Mrs. Ruggiero's steadfast belief that Rosemary's son Sam would never steer her wrong. That vision had morphed into himself at nineteen and at twenty-three, faced with an even higher mountain of bills, sitting at the same kitchen table and wishing he had the guts to run away. It had taken him years to understand that sometimes it took more guts to stick around.

He had this fantasy about grabbing Annie by the hand and driving off with her. In his dreams they'd load Max and the two cats into the back of the Trooper and just go, but somehow he couldn't push past fantasy to reality when he was awake. Some people ran when the going got tough. Some people dug in their heels and stayed. He knew which type they were.

Leave it to Butler to grab his golden parachute and get out while the getting was still good.

He had let Arnie's statement slide by without remark, but there was no denying the fact that things were in motion down in New York. He didn't say as much to Marie, but he would bet his Trooper that the break-in at his New York apartment wasn't random. They were looking for something and they knew he was the one man who could blow them out of the water.

It also occurred to him that they probably knew he was living in Shelter Rock Cove. A photo in a small-town newspaper could have the half-life of uranium these days and cause just as much damage. His contact had ripped him a new butt when he found out. "What the hell are you trying to do, Butler, undermine every goddamn thing we've been doing down here?" The point to his exile in Shelter Rock Cove had been to fade into the scenery while they set the machinery into motion that might bring down Mason, Marx, and Daniel and, not incidentally, keep Sam out of prison.

His contact's wrath over the newspaper photo would be nothing compared to the hell that would break loose when they found out he had been in contact with Arnie Gillingham about Claudia's contract with Adam Winters. He had left behind a paper trail a blind man could follow.

But it was too late now. The machinery was in motion, and there was nothing he could do to stop it.

His nights in Annie's arms were numbered.

Warren showed up on Claudia's doorstep precisely at eight o'clock on Saturday night, same as usual.

The greeting he received wasn't usual at all.

"He told you, didn't he?"

Warren doffed his hat and flung it on the hall table.

"Who told me what?" He slipped out of his coat and hung it from the coat tree near the door.

"That friend of yours from New York told you what I did."

"Are you talking about Sam?"

"Yes, I'm talking about Sam. He told you what happened, and you made them give my money back."

"You been hitting the scotch?"

Her gaze was as fierce as it had been when she was a beautiful young wife of nineteen. "No, I haven't been hitting the scotch. Don't tell me you don't know what I'm talking about, Warren Bancroft, because you do."

"I don't understand one word, old woman. Now slow down and start over again."

She talked and he listened while he poured himself a stiff shot of single malt he kept in her kitchen cupboard.

"Nope," he said. "I had nothing to do with it."

She dished up some spaghetti and meatballs and set it down in front of him. "Don't lie to me, you old coot. Who else could have made it happen?"

"Sam," he said as he reached for the green container of shaking cheese. "That's who you should be thanking."

Claudia had been afraid of that. When the courier showed up at her house three mornings after Annie's whatever-he-was had found her sniveling on Warren's doorstep, she had suspected Sam Butler was at the bottom of it. God knew, it was the last thing she had wanted, to be in that man's debt. Bad enough that he knew her for the weak-willed, lonely woman she was. Now she would have to thank him for cleaning up the mess she had made.

She waited until Monday morning when she was sure Warren was on his way to Portland on business and Annie was at the shop. She knew that Sam spent his days in the workshop behind Warren's house, working on some project for the museum.

The lawn sparkled with early-morning frost as she pulled into the driveway behind the house. Autumn was invariably kind to their part of Maine, and this autumn was no exception. Beauty and commerce met and married in September and October, and the honeymoon, if they were lucky, might extend until Christmas. The last two weeks had brought a flood of leaf-peepers to Shelter Rock Cove, and Annie's Flowers had done land-office business. Sweeney, too, had been crowing about the record sales enjoyed by the Artisans Co-op. Everyone, it seemed, was pleased with her lot in life but Claudia.

Sam Butler's disreputable truck was parked a few yards ahead of her sedan. He still had his New York license plates, and she wondered if that meant he planned to go home one day. Annie never said a word about their plans. Surely they must have talked about the future. The only thing lovers enjoyed more than recounting their own intimate history was making plans for the future, but if Annie and Sam had such plans, they weren't talking.

Are you going to sit out here all day, Claudia, or are you going to get it over with?

She checked her lipstick in the rearview mirror, patted her hair, then stepped out of the car. What was the name of that movie with that nice Tom Hanks, the one about death row? *The Green Mile,* that was it, with the long walk the convicted man took to the electric chair. That was how she felt as she approached the huge garage, as if she were walking her last mile and Sam Butler had his hand on the switch.

His noisy dog announced her arrival, which she supposed was a good thing. If the yellow Lab hadn't started barking, she might have been tempted to sneak back to her car and zip away.

"Knock it off, Max." Sam Butler's voice rumbled from somewhere in the barn. "I hear you."

She approached the door, trying to pretend that huge animal wasn't dancing around her knees. Maybe she could write him a note or, better yet, send him a bouquet of something fresh-smelling and masculine as a thank-you.

Coward.

She lifted her hand and knocked twice. The door opened a crack, and a surprised Sam Butler looked down at her.

"Warren's in Portland," he said. "He'll be back later this afternoon."

"I'm not here to see Warren." She willed herself not to look away from him even though she found his gaze unnervingly intense. "I'm here to thank you for what you did."

The door swung open wide. The guarded expression in his eyes was replaced by what Claudia could only describe as flat-out joy. "Arnie came through!"

"Friday morning," she said stiffly. "A courier showed up at my house with a cashier's check."

He motioned her into the barn, and the dog followed right behind her. "They should have provided you with a notarized document stating that your agreement with Adam Winters, Inc. was null and void."

"They did," she said. "It's in my safe-deposit box at the bank."

How handsome he was when he smiled. It wasn't something Claudia wanted to notice, but his happiness was impossible to ignore. You would think there was something in this for him.

What a fool she was. Of course there was something in it for him. What did he care about the future of an aging widow from Shelter Rock Cove, Maine? Claudia was just another old lady to him. Her future was of no consequence. He was looking to charm Annie, and how better than to bail her foolish mother-in-law out of trouble? He would probably make sure this sorry story hit the front page of the weekly paper, same as that picture of him kissing Annie had last month.

"I suppose you've told Anne." She phrased it as a statement of fact, not a question.

"No," he said. "I didn't. Who you tell or don't tell is your business."

Another surge of gratitude washed over her. What nerve he had being understanding and thoughtful. How could she hate him when he was going out of his way to treat her with kindness and respect?

"I don't believe in sharing my financial information with family."

"I understand," he said, and his tone made her believe he really did. "Most people will show you their diaries before they'll show you their bank statements. Money is the last taboo in this country."

She laughed, and he looked almost as surprised as she was by the sound. There was something very appealing about him when he let down his guard, a bracing kind of sharp-edged charm she found most agreeable. The fact that there was an equally sharp-edged intellect beneath the work shirt wasn't lost on her either.

"I would like to repay you somehow for what you've done for me," she said. "Maybe you would like to take Anne out to Bar Harbor for a weekend. I would be glad to—"

"No." His smile softened the word. "But thanks. Just think twice next time before you sign on the dotted line."

He wouldn't take anything from her. Even her thanks seemed to make him uncomfortable. No preening, no angling for an imaginary spotlight. He was straightforward, direct, and kind. He hadn't helped her so that he could

shine more brightly in Annie's eyes. He hadn't helped her
to score points with Warren. He had helped her because
she needed help and because he had help to give.

There was so little kindness in the world that its ab-
sence was taken for granted. Nobody noticed the daily
slights, the snubs, the raised voices and harsh words. They
were all part of the landscape, as invisible as hello and
goodbye. But when kindness suddenly appeared in the
guise of a man like Sam Butler, a woman couldn't help
but sit up and take notice.

EIGHTEEN

Annie had developed the habit of lingering in bed until Sam headed out for his morning run with Max. She waited until she heard the sound of the front door swinging shut behind them, then leaped from bed and made a mad dash for the bathroom.

It was hard to believe an empty stomach could cause so much trouble, but for the last fourteen mornings, Annie had embraced the john and prayed for a bolt of lightning to put her out of her misery. Twenty minutes of utter misery were followed by ten minutes of queasy discomfort that were finally eased into submission by a cup of spearmint tea with sugar and a handful of oyster crackers. By the time Sam and Max came back, sweaty and exhilarated from running along the beach, she looked as if she had done nothing more exciting than brush her teeth and drink some orange juice.

She had been fine this morning when she left for work, but something shifted inside her stomach when she rounded the curve on Shore Drive and she had to pull off to the side of the road and humiliate herself. Thank God nobody was around, because the news that Annie Galloway was upchucking her breakfast on a public street would go from one end of town to the other before lunchtime.

"You look terrible," Sweeney said when Annie finally got to work.

"I feel—" She bolted for the small bathroom behind the giant refrigerator.

"Here," said Sweeney, handing her a cup of hot tea. "Peppermint, for your stomach."

"I've been drinking spearmint," she said, wrapping her hands around the warm cup.

"Peppermint," said Sweeney wisely. "The first trimester's a bitch. You need the heavy artillery."

Sweeney's words sent a shudder of shock through Annie's body. Hot tea sloshed over the side of the cup and dotted her forest-green sweater. "First trimester!" She dabbed at the droplets with a square of paper towel. "I think you're jumping the gun."

"I've been through it three times, honey. Believe me, I know the signs."

"I know what it looks like," Annie said, "but it's impossible."

Sweeney arched a brow. "Impossible?"

"Okay, okay. Theoretically possible but not very likely." She took a sip of the sweet mint tea. It tasted like melted candy canes. "I'm thirty-eight. It's probably early menopause."

"Menopause doesn't give you morning sickness."

"Shh!" Annie glanced quickly around the store. "I'm not looking to make a public announcement, Sweeney." Not that there was anything to announce.

"Claudia's not here yet. She called to say she'd be a little late."

"Well, she picked the right day for it," Annie said as she ran for the bathroom again.

Afterward, she washed her face and was drying it carefully when she caught sight of herself in the mirror. She looked every single one of her thirty-eight years and maybe a few more for good measure. She also looked terrified. Of course she'd wondered if maybe, just maybe, she might be pregnant, but each time she considered the possibility, it seemed downright laughable. She had been married for almost twenty years to a man with a healthy sperm count, and not once in those twenty years had she ever become pregnant. She had dreamed about it, prayed for it, until she finally mourned the children she would never have. Ultimately she had made her peace with her situation, but the sense of loss was never far from the surface.

Loving Sam was nothing short of a miracle. Only a greedy woman would ask the gods for one more chance at heaven.

"You should buy yourself one of those home pregnancy tests," Sweeney suggested once Annie was back behind the counter.

"Can you see me trying to slip one of those things by Ceil at Yankee Shopper?" Annie had to laugh. "She would know the results before I did."

"So would her next-door neighbor," Sweeney admitted. "I'll buy one for you."

Annie shook her head. "You don't have to. I have an appointment with Ellen this afternoon."

"Have you told Sam yet?"

"There's nothing to tell."

"There will be," said Sweeney. "Honey, this time I think you've hit the jackpot."

• • •

Annie told Claudia she was going for her annual Pap smear and exam, and Claudia feigned a ladylike shudder.

"One day they'll learn how to warm up their instruments," Claudia said, "although probably not in my lifetime."

"Ellen's pretty good about that," Annie said as she slipped on her jacket and grabbed her purse from the hook. "I think she's been on the receiving end of cold metal a few times herself."

"You take your time, dear," Claudia said. "I'll watch the shop. In fact, it's been slow today. Why don't you take the afternoon off? You must have a lot to do for your seminar."

Annie looked almost embarrassingly relieved. She kissed Claudia on the cheek, grabbed her jacket from the hook behind the door, then flew from the store with wings on her heels.

"Bless you, Annie," Claudia whispered as the door swung shut behind her daughter-in-law. "Bless you and your baby."

The waiting room was empty when Annie arrived. She hung up her jacket, then let Janna, the receptionist, know she was there.

"Good timing," said Janna, grabbing Annie's chart. "We had a cancellation. Dr. Markowitz can see you right now. Leave us a specimen, and we'll get started."

Annie followed her down the pale blue hallway to room two. Janna stuck the file folder in the plastic holder and gestured toward the screen.

"Change, put on the robe, you know the drill. The doctor will be with you before you get out of your pantyhose." Janna winked and hurried back to her desk.

How many times had she gathered up all of her hopes and dreams and brought them into this cold impersonal room to be inspected? She could see herself as a bride of eighteen, a wife of twenty-three, an exhausted and scared woman of thirty, sitting there on the edge of the paper-covered table with her feet dangling and her hands folded in her lap, waiting for the doctor to tell her what she already knew. *I'm sorry, Annie, but you're not pregnant.*

She had no reason to believe this time would be any different.

"Good to see you, Annie." Ellen Markowitz knocked twice as she opened the door. "How're you doing?"

"Pretty well," Annie said, noticing the goosebumps racing up and down her bare legs. "New hairstyle?"

Ellen wrinkled her nose. "Hope springs eternal. Saranne at Hair Today swears she understands curly hair, but I'm not convinced. I think I look like the love child of Bernadette Peters and Don King."

Annie laughed out loud. "I think it looks terrific," she said. "I should pay Saranne a visit myself."

Ellen slipped her glasses on and scanned Annie's chart. "So you're here for your annual Pap and checkup." She scribbled a note. "When was your last period?"

Annie scrambled for a date. Her periods, her finances, her life—everything had been screwed up since Kevin died. "I don't know exactly," she said. "Late August, maybe."

Ellen looked up. "You're sure."

"Fairly so."

Ellen flipped some pages. "Your cycle ranges anywhere from 26 days to 45, so we're still in the ballpark."

See, Galloway? You're late. You've been late before. You'll be late again.

"Any symptoms I should know about?"

Annie hesitated. "I've been tired a great deal during the day, then I have a burst of energy at night."

"I hear you're working on some statuary for Warren's museum. That must keep you pretty busy."

"It does," she said. "I'll admit to being more than a little obsessed with the project."

"Well, that could certainly explain the fatigue." She met Annie's eyes. "Anything else I should know about?"

Annie took a deep breath. "Morning sickness." She forced a laugh. "Or maybe I should say sickness in the morning."

Ellen nodded and scribbled another note. "One second." She lifted the wall phone and pushed two buttons. "Janna, did you run the Galloway specimen yet . . . Okay . . . Great . . . Add a number three, please . . . Thanks."

This isn't really happening. I'm almost forty years old . . . I've just managed to pull my life back together . . . I've found a wonderful man who has never once said a word about kids . . .

"Lie back and relax," said Ellen as she went over to the sink to wash her hands, "and we'll see what's happening."

The paper crinkled loudly as Annie settled herself in position. Men hadn't a clue how awkward the whole thing was. Did any of them realize the way women obsessed about proper footwear in the stirrups? Bare feet? Socks? Shoes? Silly thoughts designed to take her mind off why she was lying there on that table with her heart even more exposed than her body.

Ellen positioned herself at the foot of the table. "Scoot down a little more . . . Good . . . Let's see . . . There are some cervical changes in keeping with early first trimester . . . Tender here?"

"Yes."

"Here, too?"

"Ouch! Yes."

"Your uterus is slightly enlarged, which may or may

not mean anything." She pulled off her surgical gloves and tossed them in the receptacle. "You can sit up, Annie."

Easy for you to say, Ellen. "So what do you think?" she asked, wishing her voice didn't sound so vulnerable. "Am I—?" She couldn't say the word. It held way too much power.

The intercom buzzed before Ellen could answer. The doctor lifted up the receiver, listened, asked a question, then hung up. "Congratulations," she said to Annie. "You're going to have a baby."

Ellen Markowitz had seen many reactions to a positive pregnancy test during her six years as an OB-GYN. Some women cried with joy. Some cried from sorrow. Some women cursed their husbands or boyfriends or birth control method of choice. Some women had no reaction at all beyond a stolid acceptance of the will of God. She had seen young couples embrace each other with such abandon that she wondered if they were trying to conceive a second child on the spot. She had seen older couples start fighting over a perimenopausal surprise.

But she had never seen the look of almost holy wonder that she had seen in Annie Galloway's eyes.

Annie's joy was so deeply felt, so deeply private, that Ellen's eyes teared up, and she turned away and pretended to scribble some notes on her chart. It wasn't often that she envied one of her patients, but that afternoon she envied Annie Galloway from the bottom of her heart.

Hall had just parked his Rover in the reserved spot near the door to the Medical Arts building when he saw Annie dash down the steps. Her hair was loose, a long tangle of waves and curls that glinted gold and red in the fierce autumn sunshine. The look on her face—Jesus, he could live to be two hundred and never forget the look on her face as she darted past him. She glowed from within. There was no other way to say it. She had always been beautiful to him but now she was radiant. Her hair, her skin, the ripe lushness of her body. But now there was something else added to the mix, a sense of wonder and magic that could only mean one thing.

"Annie!" He stepped out of the Rover and waved to her.

If she saw him, she gave no indication. She floated past him and drifted across the parking lot in the direction of Main Street and Annie's Flowers.

He grabbed the sheaf of papers on the passenger seat, then locked the car. His source in New York had come through with more information than he had anticipated, none of which cast Sam Butler in a good light. If any of the allegations mentioned in the notes were true, there was a good chance Butler would be serving some serious jail time very soon.

"Afternoon, Dr. Talbot." Janna favored him with a friendly smile. "Your three-fifteen called. She'll be a few minutes late."

He nodded and headed back toward his office, the image of a radiantly glowing Annie Galloway still in the forefront of his mind. He couldn't ask Ellen. There was nothing professional about his concern, and they both knew it. Nobody would stop him if he plucked Annie's chart from the mix and browsed through it, but he wasn't sure he would like the man who did such a thing. Then again, he had done a lot of things these last few weeks that he wasn't sure he liked. Digging into Sam Butler's background, for one.

He flipped the lights on in his office and was shrugging out of his jacket when Ellen popped out of her office across the hall.

"You're late," she said with mock disapproval. "Forget to set the alarm?"

"Twins," he said, tossing his packet of papers down on his desk.

"Newborn or age of consent?"

He couldn't help but laugh. "The Pelletiers delivered early."

"Healthy?"

He rapped his knuckles on the side of his credenza. "So far, so good. They'll need a little hospital time until they build up their weight, but it all seems routine."

"Great." The furrow between her brows seemed to deepen despite the good news. "After all they went through trying to conceive those babies, they deserve a happy ending."

"Don't we all," he said, settling down at his desk. "I saw Annie Galloway on her way out."

Was he crazy or was Markowitz glowing now, too?

"Did she say anything?"

"No," he said, "I don't think she even knew I was there."

Ellen nodded but said nothing.

"Is she okay?"

"She's fine," Ellen said as a smile broke across her narrow face. "She's just fine."

And that was how he learned that the woman he had loved and lost was going to have a baby by a man who most likely would be welcoming in the New Year behind bars.

Annie hurried past the window of Annie's Flowers, past the bookshop and DeeDee's Donuts, and ran straight for her truck. She turned the key and slammed it into reverse without giving it even a second to warm up. She would make it up to the Trooper one day, but the need to be with Sam was too strong to deny.

A baby . . . I'm going to have a baby!

She repeated the words out loud and she still couldn't quite believe they were true. Seven months from now, on a warm day in June according to Ellen, she would give birth to a baby whose ribbon of DNA would link her and Sam together forever. A baby whose very existence was proof of their love.

"Any questions?" Ellen had asked her before Annie left the office.

"Yes," said Annie. "How on earth did this happen?"

Ellen, bless her heart, bypassed the easy joke for an honest answer. "I don't know," she said. "All I know is that there couldn't be a luckier baby in the world."

A baby . . . a tiny, helpless, demanding infant whose needs and desires would take precedence over everything for a long time to come . . .

"A miracle," she whispered. A one-in-a-million kind of miracle sent to two people who had believed their chance at real happiness had passed them by.

That's how you feel, Galloway, but are you so sure it's how Sam feels?

They had talked about children only once, when Annie told him she couldn't get pregnant. He had looked at her with deep understanding and never broached the topic again. She had interpreted his reaction as one of compassion and acceptance, but now she wondered if she had only seen what she wanted to see. He had spent part of his teens and his entire adult life raising his brothers and sisters. He had more hands-on parenting experience than most parents his age. Maybe what she had been looking at was sheer relief. Been there, done that, and he was glad he wouldn't be doing it again with her.

But babies weren't just by invitation only. Sometimes

they appeared on the wings of a miracle and left it to you to figure out how to fit your lives around them.

How romantic, Galloway. What if the thought of a baby just makes him feel trapped? Your miracle could send him looking for the exit.

Well, it was too late to worry about that now. It had been too late from the moment sperm met egg two months ago. The sooner she told Sam, the better. That was the one thing she knew for certain. Oh, there were probably better ways to handle a situation like this. Sweeney would no doubt have a dozen strategies all designed to break it to a man gently. But Annie had never been one for strategies when it came to love. If she had been, she never would have stayed with Kevin right up until the bitter end. All she knew, all she cared about, was getting to Sam and telling him that she was pregnant with his child.

Would he be happy about it? *Please, God, please . . .* Would he feel burdened with more responsibility? *Not Sam . . . he'll understand.* Would he swing her up into his arms and kiss her senseless, or would he tell her that she was on her own? She couldn't imagine such a thing. He was as honorable a man as she had ever known, the kind of man a smart woman dreamed about.

He would be shocked, of course. So was she. In truth, the reality still hadn't sunk in, only the need to share the news with the one man on earth who would care as much as she did. They had never discussed a family, not in so many words. What they had together felt like forever, but neither one of them ever talked about tomorrow.

You never discussed the future? Not even once? Doesn't that seem a little strange, Galloway?

How would *she* know what was strange? She had married the first boy she ever dated and she had stayed married to him for almost twenty years. She was still stuck back in the land of senior proms and going steady while the rest of the world had long since moved on.

Maybe you didn't do things like talk about a future together once you were past the first flutter of youthful longing. Maybe you were meant to be sophisticated and mature enough to just let the future take care of itself— or not, as the case may be—and not worry and wonder like a teenager in love for the first time.

Unfortunately Annie felt like that teenager when she was with Sam. Once upon a time her capacity for joy had been boundless, but time and circumstance had taken that gift away from her. But now she could feel herself growing more lighthearted, more joyful with every day she spent in his company, more like the woman she used to be, the one she had all but forgotten. He delighted her, thrilled her, made her believe that the second time around could be even more wonderful than the first—maybe because this time she knew how precious and fragile it all was.

And she would tell him all of that and more right now, this very afternoon.

It was almost three o'clock. He was probably still in the old barn behind Warren's house, working on one of the canoes, but just in case he'd come home early, she decided to drive up their road and see if his truck was in the driveway.

She slowed as she approached the top of Bancroft Road, and a flicker of alarm began in the pit of her belly. A pair of dark cars were angled across her driveway. She gripped the wheel more tightly to stop her hands from trembling. This couldn't be happening, not now, not when she finally thought she had broken free from the death grip of Kevin's gambling debts. Not now when she was on the verge of a new and wonderful life. She peered farther up the road and saw another pair of dark cars angled across the foot of Sam's driveway, and bile rose up into her throat and it took every ounce of self-control at her command to keep the contents of her stomach where they belonged.

She had believed that every sleazy bookie and loan shark in New England had found his way to her door in the weeks following Kevin's death, all of them demanding payment. She had known Kevin was in trouble, but the scope of it was worse than she had imagined.

And now it looked as if Kevin's mistakes were going to put Sam in jeopardy, too. It was bad enough that she had paid for her late husband's sins. She couldn't allow Sam to pay for them as well.

She had to get to him before anyone else did, warn him while there was still time. She would tell him everything, the whole ugly story from beginning to end, sparing no one this time around. The gambling, the racketeers, the threats, the long climb back from the abyss, the sickening realization that it wasn't over, might never be over no matter what she did or how hard she tried. If they knew how much Sam mattered to her, they would use him against her in ways that would haunt her the rest of her life. The father of her child deserved better than that.

She had to love him enough to let him go.

The long red cedar planks had to be steamed until they were pliable enough for Sam to urge them into the curved line of the canoe's hull. It took patience and a lot of pressure to ease a straight piece of wood into the unnatural shape, and once he managed to persuade the planks to conform to the basic design, he had to nail them down before they changed their minds.

He was in the process of hammering down the third plank on the second of four canoes when he heard a familiar vehicle crunching its way up the driveway. Max heard it, too, and he leaped up from his spot in the sunlight and started running circles by the door. Sometimes Sam felt the same way when he saw Annie, like doing handsprings and cartwheels and writing her name in the sky with shooting stars.

Did she know he loved her? He hadn't told her in words. He hadn't the right, not before he knew what his future held. There were no guarantees that things would work out according to plan. What he felt for her ran too deep. He would rather cut her loose than watch her live a life in the shadows, waiting for him. He'd put through a call this morning to his contact in Washington. He needed answers, a time frame, something he could hang his future on. They reminded him that his future hung on getting it right; the success of the sting operation against Mason, Marx, and Daniel would determine whether he remained a free man.

Last night he had dreamed their future. Five years from now, ten years—the two of them together in a house filled with sunlight and dreams and more joy than he would have imagined possible this side of heaven. He had dreamed a family for them, too, big healthy babies born of their love. There wouldn't be babies for them. Annie had told him about the years of trying for a miracle. He told her that she was miracle enough for him. She was his home, his family, his soft place to fall when the world was too much with him. Now that he had found her, he couldn't imagine living a life without her there at the center of it.

"Sam!" She burst into the barn like a beautiful tornado. Her hair whipped around her face in a froth of curls and she looked slightly manic, slightly wild, juicy and sexy. The woman he loved.

Max was practically doing backflips for her attention, but she didn't seem to notice.

He tossed down his hammer and wiped his hands on

the sides of his jeans. "Don't tell me," he said. "You're ditching the flower shop, and we're heading for Tahiti."

He meant it as a joke, something to make her smile at the absurdity of the statement, but the look she gave him was filled with so much pain and downright misery that he couldn't pull air into his lungs.

"There's something you don't know," she said, ducking away from his outstretched arms.

"There's probably a lot I don't know," he said, trying to will himself into something approaching calm. "We've both lived a full life before we met."

She dismissed his words with a wave of her hand. "You don't understand. Nobody knows what I need to tell you, not Susan or Claudia or Warren. Nobody in this entire town, Sam, only me."

He felt a sharp pain in the center of his gut. She stood not three feet away from him but she was suddenly beyond his reach. "And you want to tell me."

"No," she said with almost brutal honesty, "I don't want to tell you at all but I have to. They're back and they know about you and—" She lowered her head and turned away so he wouldn't see her tears fall.

So proud, he thought. Strong and tough and honorable, yet it was her loneliness that had reached out and touched his heart.

"Who's back?" he prodded. "More Galloways on a mission from God?"

The afternoon was so quiet. Not even birdsong cut into the silence. Then in the distance he heard the sound of a car moving closer, and in that moment he realized she was trembling.

"You don't know what they're like," she said as he began to wonder if she was talking about little green men in spacesuits. "You can't hide from them. They'll find you no matter where you go and they'll keep finding you until they get what they want."

He grabbed her by the arms. "You're scaring the shit out of me," he said, hoping to shock her back into coherence. "Who's after you, Annie? What the hell is going on?" She couldn't know about him. There was no way she could have found out.

A car turned into the driveway. A second car followed right behind.

"Take Max and go," she said, trying to push him away. "It's me they want. I did everything I could after Kevin died . . . I sold the house and the car . . . I worked three jobs . . . I paid off everything, every single dime, but you can't break free of them . . ."

A car door slammed shut, then another, then two more.

"Oh, Jesus!" It was almost a keening cry. "Please go, Sam. This is my problem, not yours. You don't deserve to—"

Four men in dark suits stepped from bright sunlight into the shadowy barn. Annie broke free of him and stepped forward. She was Amazonian in her defense of him, and he had never loved her more than he did in that moment.

"Let him go," she said in a voice far stronger than he had ever heard before. "He's nothing to you. I'm the one you're looking for."

The four men exchanged puzzled glances, and that was when Sam knew it was all over. His idyll in Shelter Rock Cove had come to an end. He took her gently by the shoulders and moved her back into the shadows.

"I'm the one you want," he said, wishing with all his heart there had been a way to make this easy for her.

"Sam Butler?" One of the men stepped forward from the pack.

"I thought you'd call first," he said. "That's what I was told." First a phone call, then an agent would arrive to bring him back to New York under protective custody. That was the way it had been explained.

"Check your cell phone," the man said. "We tried, but you never picked up. Your phone must be dead."

A warning bell went off deep inside his gut.

He pulled his phone from the back pocket of his jeans and pressed the power switch, then cupped his hand over the display so they wouldn't see the glowing green numbers. He quickly touched the button again to shut it off.

"Dead as a doornail," he said.

"See?" asked the man. "Couldn't get through."

What the hell was going on? He'd had enough dealings with the feds over the last year to know when something didn't feel right. This wasn't the way they operated. Only one explanation made any sense: Mason, Marx, and Daniel had gotten wind of the sting and Sam's place in it. They weren't big enough to stop the government, but they sure as hell were big enough to stop Sam Butler.

Annie's eyes were wide with fear. He wanted to take her in his arms and tell her everything, walk her through his days and his decisions, shoulder the guilt that belonged to him and even some that didn't, if only it could take them back to where they had been just an hour ago before the real world came calling.

But the less she knew, the better. All that mattered to him now was keeping her safe from harm.

He tossed the phone onto the work bench. "So where do we go from here?"

"Sam Butler, we have a warrant for your arrest on charges of embezzlement. You have the right to remain silent . . ."

Annie cried out, and for a moment Sam wanted to pull her into his arms and lie to her. But he couldn't do it. He couldn't do one goddamn thing but hold out his arms for the cuffs and let the silence between them say everything and nothing at all.

Max growled as the men approached his master. Sam met Annie's eyes, and the look of anguish in them almost dropped him to the ground. *This is what you did to her, Butler. This is how she'll remember you. Can you live with it?*

He wanted to fight the bastards. He wanted to slam his fist into their smug faces, then grab Annie and run as far away as they could. He'd never been one to give up in the face of trouble, but this time there was no choice, not if he loved her.

Annie wrapped her arms around Max's neck and held him by the collar. Poor old Max whimpered a little, but she couldn't help the tears that streamed down her cheeks and darkened the dog's yellow ruff. The men weren't there for her. They had nothing to do with Kevin's gambling debts. For the first time in years, she wasn't the one running scared from strangers who showed up on her doorstep and turned her life inside out.

The funny thing was, Sam hadn't seemed surprised. Startled, maybe, but not surprised. All of that talk about phone calls—it was almost as if he had been expecting this.

Good going, Galloway. You really know how to pick them. Bad enough the first one was a compulsive gambler, now you've snagged yourself a criminal.

She refused to believe that. Sam was a good man. She knew it deep inside her soul.

Kevin was a good man, too, but that didn't stop him from almost ruining your life.

Apples and oranges. You couldn't compare the two of them. Kevin operated from weakness, while Sam operated from strength. You only had to look at him to know he was the kind of man who took charge of situations. The kind of man who would be there for you, no matter what.

Wishful thinking, Galloway. Don't listen to all of those nesting hormones, because they'll lead you astray.

Sam was the finest person she had ever known. He had taken on the responsibility of his five brothers and sisters at an age when most guys were looking to get drunk and party. Because of Sam, his siblings were well-educated, productive men and women instead of the statistics they might have become if Sam hadn't been willing to step up to the plate.

Besides, she owed him her life. If he hadn't broken down her door that night, she wouldn't be there right now with a miracle child growing inside her belly and more happiness inside her heart than she had ever believed possible. Could she be that wrong about a man who had revealed so much of his own heart to her?

Warren had said that Sam was like a son to him. *They don't come any better than Sam,* he told her one day when Sam was out of earshot. *I'd trust him with my life.*

So would I, Annie thought as she rested a hand on her belly. *I'd trust him with two lives.*

Maybe it was crazy. Maybe she was heading down the same disastrous road she'd walked with Kevin, but she was willing to take that chance. What was the point of loving someone if you weren't willing to put yourself on the line when the going got rough?

Her gaze swept the barn. She saw the canoes swaying from the ceiling, the one in progress on his workbench. The elegant curves of wood. The mountain of nails. Shavings of red cedar spiraled on the floor. The cell phone resting on the bench of the canoe in progress. Her heart beat so hard that it hurt. The phone, that was it! What was it he had said—*dead as a doornail.* But it wasn't. She had seen the faint green glow seeping between his fingers as he cupped his hand over the display as if to hide the light from their visitors.

They had lied to him, and he knew it, and now she knew it, too. But what on earth was she supposed to do with the information?

"Ready?" one of the suits asked Sam.

"Now's as good a time as any," he said. He looked toward Annie. "You'll take care of Max?"

"Of course I will."

"Don't worry," he said with a jaunty smile. "I'll be back before sunset."

She favored him with a big smile. "Ciao," she said. She held her smile until he turned away. She refused to let any of those bastards see her cry.

She held onto Max by the collar, and they watched as the suits helped Sam into one of the cars and then drove away. The pain inside her heart was almost more than she could bear. But she didn't have time for pain or disappointment or questions. She counted to ten after the last car disappeared, then grabbed for the cell phone on the work bench.

She had to figure out the phone's importance and fast. She pressed the power key, then watched as green light filled the display. There was nothing special about the phone, at least not as far as she could see. No fancy gadgets or Internet capabilities. The one thing that caught her eye, however, was the red 6 key. How odd. What could be so compelling about the 6 key that you would make it the centerpiece of the keypad?

She did what any normal person would do under the circumstances: she pressed it.

Nothing.

She pressed it again and then hit the Send key.

Still nothing.

She pressed AUTO, then the 6 key, and instantly a no-nonsense voice crackled in her ear.

"Code number, please."

"I don't have a code number."

"Use of this phone requires a specific code number. Please speak it into the mouthpiece."

"I can't," Annie said. "I don't know what it is."

"Please identify yourself by slowly speaking your name, first and last, with correct spelling, followed by street address, ZIP code, phone number, and Social Security number."

"I have no idea who you are. Why should I give you my Social Security number?"

"Ma'am, you are using a phone restricted for use by the United States government. Any other use is a violation of the law."

"You don't understand. The owner has been arrested, and I don't know what to do. I found his phone and—"

"Hold on, please, ma'am. An agent will be with you momentarily."

"Max," she said to the yellow dog by her side, "I think we're in big trouble."

NINETEEN

They were smarter than Sam had figured. Two of the four cars peeled off when they hit the highway, which made them look more like independent travelers and less like a flotilla.

Smarter wasn't good. He had been hoping for a lot less in the way of gray cells and a lot more in the way of conversation. So far the chatter in the car had been limited to gas mileage and that weird knocking sound under the hood. He'd been tempted to strike up a conversation with them and maybe ask them outright what the hell was going on, but an attack of common sense stopped him.

He tried hard not to think of Annie. They wouldn't send anyone back there for her. If they'd wanted to grab her, they would have done it when they found them together. She was safe. He repeated it over and over again, a mantra. She was safe, and he would be back in her arms before the night was over.

When she said "Ciao" instead of goodbye, he had wanted to send up a cheer. They had ended every phone conversation with that word since the night at Cappy's when they'd listened to the Yankee matron trill "Ciao" into the mouthpiece after each call. Annie knew about the phone. She had listened and watched and added up the clues. Now all Annie had to do was punch in a few keys and headquarters would be swarming all over Shelter Rock Cove in the blink of an eye.

He wouldn't be at all surprised if they had a little welcome party waiting for them at the airport.

He glanced out the window. They were almost at the airport. His heart raced so quickly he had trouble breathing. The cops had to be there. Maybe the feds, too. They would swarm the car before the driver shifted into Park, and Sam would be free.

It's not going to be that easy, Butler. These guys kidnapped you. That's a federal offense. They're not going to go down without a fight.

Which meant guns. Sweet Jesus, what the hell was happening? He sank down lower in his seat. If the airport was teeming with law enforcement types, it was bound to get ugly. He had the feeling neither side would think twice about opening fire, and guess who was the only one around for miles without a weapon? But then, it wouldn't have mattered if he had one because his wrists were cuffed. A real good news/bad news situation.

The driver made a sharp left, and they proceeded through the gates and out onto a runway that hadn't seen a repair crew—or anybody else—in a long time. A small jet waited some hundred yards away while a man in a pilot's uniform walked around it. He did everything but kick the tires.

No cops. No feds.

He was on his own.

I love you, Annie, he thought as they opened the car door and he stepped out into the afternoon sun. *Whatever happens, I'll always love you.*

He let it all out, all of his rage and frustration and love, every bit of it, in a series of kicks meant to kill. His first kick took the taller agent by surprise, and the guy dropped like a sack of rocks. The agent clutched his midsection and rolled on the tarmac in agony. His second kick clipped the shorter agent's shoulder but didn't slow him down. He kept coming at Sam, aiming blows to Sam's head that Sam couldn't ward off with his hands in cuffs.

Sam's balance was off. He was dizzy. His head felt like it was spinning. He dug in and tried to center himself for another kick but he couldn't position himself in time and space. He heard the sounds of car engines close by, voices, people running toward them.

You're running out of options, Butler . . . better make it work . . . better get it right . . . I love you, Annie . . . love you. . . .

He spun into his third kick, but it was too little and way too late. Out of the corner of his eye he saw one of the agents moving toward him, and that was the last thing he saw before everything faded to black.

Warren's home and barn were swarming with more agents, cops, and detectives than Shelter Rock Cove had taxpayers. Sam hadn't been arrested; he had been kidnapped, and the question now was by whom. Annie was being grilled by a man named Briscoe who acted as if she had singlehandedly tried to overthrow the government. He made innocence feel like it should come with jail time. He even held out the theory that Sam's kidnapping might actually be a set-up.

"I don't know who they were or what they wanted with Sam," Annie said for the third or fourth time. "They're the ones who kidnapped him, not me." She had trouble even saying the word. The thought that Sam was some-

where out there being held captive by God knows who terrified her even more than the thought of an arrest.

"Nothing about the situation seemed strange to you."

"I didn't know there was a situation until they showed up. All I can tell you is that Sam asked why they hadn't called first, and they claimed his phone wasn't working. I remembered seeing the green light flash when he tried it and—I've told you this over and over for the last hour and a half. Why are you wasting time asking me all these questions when Sam's out there in danger?" With that she did what she'd been trying not to do for the last hour: She burst into tears.

"You need a shot of whiskey," Briscoe said. "Any around here?"

"C-can't drink whiskey," she said. "I'm pregnant." Then she cried even harder.

Tough-as-nails Briscoe turned instantly to mush, and Annie wondered why she had wasted so much of her adult life being stalwart and independent when it was clear a woman's best weapon was still a well-placed tear. Briscoe ordered his colleagues to make her a cup of tea and bring it to them in the living room right away. He offered her a pillow, a blanket, an aspirin. She shook her head and kept on crying. She couldn't have stopped crying if she had wanted to. Fear, joy, wonderment, love, disappointment, all of the emotions she had felt in the last few hours washed out of her in a torrent of tears. She was pregnant. She, Annie Galloway, was actually going to have a baby, and the man she loved, the father of her child, had vanished without a trace.

Oh, Sam, I drove out here to tell you right away. I don't know how you're going to feel about it . . . We never talked about children . . . I didn't think it could happen . . . A baby, Sam, our baby . . .

"Here," said Briscoe, handing her milky tea in a thick mug. "This'll help."

She thanked him. Max, who had been by her side every second since Sam was taken away, looked up at the agent and growled low.

"What's with that dog?" Briscoe took a step back. "Is he always that protective?"

"Yes," she said, giving Max a kiss on his yellow head. "He's a great boy, aren't you, Max?"

She took a huge gulp of tea. It was hot, sweet, and bracing, exactly what she needed. "Please go look for Sam. I'm afraid he's in danger."

"We're working on it, Ms. Galloway. Believe me, we want to find Mr. Butler as much as you do."

I doubt that, she thought as she took another gulp of tea. *You're not carrying his baby.*

"This is my house, goddammit!" a familiar voice rang out from the foyer. "Now let me in, or I'm going to have your asses in a sling before you know what hit you!"

"Jesus H. Christ," muttered Briscoe. "What now?"

Warren strode into the room with all guns blazing. He was a good thirty years older than anyone in the room, but he dominated the place through sheer force of will. He walked right toward Annie and bent down to look at her.

"You're okay?"

She nodded. "It's Sam. He's been kidnapped."

"I heard." He stood up and went toe-to-toe with Briscoe. "You better have one damn fine explanation for all of this."

Briscoe repeated the same company line he'd spun for Annie. They were there in response to Annie's phone call, not to disseminate information.

"What made you call the feds?" Warren asked her quietly.

"I used Sam's cell phone," she said. "Press the big red six and it's hello Washington."

Warren whistled low. "Any idea who kidnapped him?"

"I haven't a clue," she said, "and I'm not convinced they do either. Can you believe they suggested the whole thing might be a set-up?"

Warren pulled his own cell phone from his shirt pocket and made a call to a highly placed Washington official. "They're tracking the progress of a private jet that flew out of the strip north of here about two hours ago. It's registered to the wife of one of the big chiefs at Mason, Marx, and Daniel where Sam worked."

Annie's spirits plummeted. That would only fuel Briscoe's set-up theory. Warren handed the phone to Briscoe, who listened, said little, then hung up.

"We may need to speak with you again tomorrow," Briscoe said to Annie. "Where can I find you?"

She gave him the address and phone number for Annie's Flowers.

"We'll be in touch," said Briscoe. "Remember: the public story will be that Mr. Butler was arrested. It's in his best interest and yours that you stick with that."

The news of Sam's arrest spread from one end of Shelter Rock Cove to the other at the speed of light. By the time she got home, everyone in town knew that Annie Galloway's boyfriend had been seen being taken away in handcuffs. Nobody knew where he had been taken, or by whom for that matter, but that didn't stop the gossip. Ceil from Yankee Shopper said her brother-in-law Stan had seen them boarding a private plane at the landing strip north of town, but everyone knew Stan had a deeply personal relationship with Jack Daniel's and couldn't be counted on for accurate reportage.

Still, the bare bones of the story stayed the same no

matter who did the telling. Poor Annie had picked herself a real loser. Oh, the sex was probably great—did you *see* the way they looked at each other and in public no less— but what good was great sex if the guy was behind bars? Maybe next time she would use her head and not her hormones and pick a man like that nice Hall Talbot. Everyone in town knew he'd been carrying a torch for her since high school. Wouldn't it be grand to see her with someone who had grown up in town same as she had?

Warren, who was a world-class worrier, drove home behind her to make sure she was okay. She invited him in for a cup of coffee and so he could satisfy himself that no bad guys were hiding in her closet or under the sleigh bed.

She played back her phone messages then deleted most of them. Sweeney sounded genuinely concerned. Susan sounded shocked. Hall sounded almost guilty. "I'm sorry about this. It's all my fault," he said. "Call me." Too ridiculous to even think about.

She poured Warren a cup of coffee, and they sat down at the kitchen table to compare notes.

"You've known Sam a long time," Annie said. There was no point to beating around the bush. "Is there something you're not telling me? Some deep dark secret, maybe, that—"

"He's not like Kevin, honey."

Her head snapped back in surprise.

"Didn't mean to throw you a curveball, but we don't have time to mince words."

"You knew about Kevin and his . . ." She couldn't get the word out. She had spent too many years keeping his secrets from the people who knew and loved him so they could go on loving him.

"Gambling," Warren said. "He asked me for money not long before he died."

"And you gave it to him?"

"No." Warren looked sadder than she had ever seen him, and his sadness served as a balm to her aching heart. "I tried to help him work his way out of it. I volunteered to go with him to Gamblers Anonymous." He dragged a gnarled hand through his still-thick white hair. "I was afraid to give him the money. I figured he'd gamble it away before the ink was dry on the check."

"You're right," she said. "That's exactly what would have happened."

"I didn't want to embarrass you," he said. "I know the way you guarded your privacy. You protected Kevin's reputation with your own."

"I was wrong," she said. "I should have shouted it from the rooftops and forced him to get help."

"You did what your heart told you to do. Can't ask more than that of a person."

"You knew why I had to sell the house."

"Ay-up," said Warren. "I knew."

"And you lowered the price on this one to help me out."

He scowled, but the twinkle in his eyes gave him away. "This dump? I was lucky anyone wanted it."

"I love this place," she said, then reached for his hand. "Almost as much as I love you."

They went over the afternoon's events again from beginning to end but still came up empty-handed. Warren whipped out his cell phone and made a few calls to his attorneys and a private investigator who kept track of comings and goings in the area. "I want every scrap you can dig up on who these guys were and where they were headed," he ordered, "and I want it yesterday."

"Yesterday?" Annie arched a brow. "You've been watching too much TV, Warren."

"If you don't tell them yesterday, you'll get it a week from tomorrow," Warren said as he ended the call. "Now let's start again from the beginning."

Annie had just begun to run through the sequence of events when they heard Claudia's footsteps coming up the walk.

Warren shook his head. "I don't know how such a little woman can make so much noise."

Annie glanced around the room as if she were looking for an escape hatch. "I'm not up for this," she said. "I can't face a round of I-told-you-sos from Claudia."

"I'll keep her in line," Warren said. "Any nonsense from her, and I'll boot her narrow butt out the door."

Claudia knocked politely, waited a half second, then said, "I know you're in there. I'll camp out here all night if I have to."

Warren rolled his eyes as Annie got up to open the door for her mother-in-law.

"How are you?" Claudia cupped Annie's face in her hands and inspected her for signs of wear. "You look exhausted."

"I'm okay," Annie said, "all things considered." She motioned for Claudia to join them at the tiny kitchen table.

"I should've known I'd find you here." Claudia fixed Warren with a stern look. "Sticking your nose where you don't belong."

"Put a sock in it, old woman," he said. "If you don't have anything helpful to say, don't say anything."

"I'm here for Anne." Claudia claimed the rocking chair Annie had pulled over to the table. "And I'll thank you to keep a civil tongue in your head."

"If you two don't—" The room started to spin, and Annie grabbed the back of the rocker for support.

"Good God Almighty!" Warren was on his feet in an instant. He put an arm around her waist and sat her down in his chair. "The girl's about to faint."

Claudia leaped to her feet and pushed Warren out of the way. She bent down and peered into Annie's eyes. "When did you last eat?"

"I—I don't know."

"Make yourself useful," Claudia snapped at Warren, "and get her some crackers and a glass of milk." She waited until Warren hurried away then looked again into Annie's eyes. "Your doctor visit this afternoon," she said in a much softer tone. "It went well?"

Their history together filled the room. Playing in the Galloways' big backyard when she was a little girl. Helping Claudia carry out the giant pitchers of cold lemonade. Learning how to make blueberry jam from her new mother-in-law. Sharing her grief with the one person who loved Kevin as much as she had. Working side by side with the strongest woman she had ever known. It was all there in the room with them, every year, every minute of it.

Annie nodded her head. "It went well," she whispered. "Very well."

It only hurt for a moment. One exquisite, blinding moment of pain so intense that Claudia thought she might die from it. All those years of trying, the monthly heartbreak that Annie and Kevin had tried to hide, and now this miracle. Annie, her beloved Annie, was going to finally have her baby, and the last link remaining between them would be broken.

Life went on, no matter how hard you tried to stop it in its tracks. Love bloomed where you least expected it, and that was part of what made life such a wonder to behold. Claudia didn't have to understand Annie's need

to build a new life of her own; all she had to do was find
it in her heart to send her on her way.

It was the hardest thing she had ever been asked to do
and in some ways the easiest.

Claudia took Annie's hands in hers and squeezed them
tightly. "A baby," she whispered, her voice cracking ever
so slightly. "God's finest miracle."

Annie managed a small laugh. "Definitely a miracle.
I'm thirty-eight, Claude. I'm looking at fertility's last out-
post."

She looked into Annie's lovely blue eyes and wished
she could erase the years of fear and loneliness. How
blind she had been to the younger woman's pain. How
devoted to polishing Kevin's tarnished halo in the eyes of
a town that knew better. It all seemed such a tragic waste
in the face of the new life inside Annie's belly.

"I was going to tell Sam this afternoon," Annie said. "I
know you don't like him but—"

"I was wrong." The words hurt less than she would
have imagined. She should have said them a long time
ago. She should have said so many things. "Your Sam
went out of his way to help with a problem, and I'm afraid
his generosity may be what triggered this whole mess."
She inhaled deeply. *In for a penny, in for a pound.* "I saw
him only as Kevin's replacement, and that wasn't fair to
any of us. Sam has a good heart, Anne, a generous heart,
and he loves you."

"You can't possibly know that."

"Honey, everyone in this blessed town knows how Sam
Butler feels about you."

"Do they know how I feel about him?"

"I can't speak for the town, but I'm pretty certain I
know." *You love him, Annie Lacy Galloway. You always
did wear your heart on your sleeve.*

She looked so young, like the girl she had been just the

day before yesterday. "One day I just might ask for your blessing."

Claudia's eyes filled with tears. "As if you needed such a thing! You were a good wife to my son, Annie. I know it wasn't always easy. Maybe if the rest of us hadn't always looked the other way—" She sighed deeply. "But that's the way it was handled in our family." She pushed Annie slightly away and met her eyes. "That's the way we handled it when I was the one with the problem."

"You?" She looked the way Claudia's youngest had looked when she found out there was no Santa Claus. "I can't believe this."

"I'm not proud of what I did," Claudia said, "but I am proud that I managed to beat it. I had hoped Kevin would be able to follow my example, but it wasn't meant to be." Kevin had been the dearest son a mother could have asked for, the gold standard by which she had judged her other children and found them wanting. If they hadn't all loved him just as much, she would be a very lonely woman today.

"I tried, Claude," Annie said through her own tears. "I did everything I could think of. I even told him I would leave if he didn't get help."

"Shh," Claudia said, stroking her hair. "My John threatened to leave me many times, but it wasn't until I was ready to change that the changes began to happen. We all loved Kevin and we all helped keep his secrets. This whole town helped. No wife could have done more than you did. Your mother would have been very proud of the woman you've become." She hesitated a moment, praying she still had the right. "The same way that I'm so very proud of you."

Annie could feel both women's blessings raining down on her, surrounding her with love. If love could keep you safe from harm, she had it made.

• • •

The sleigh bed seemed empty without Sam there with her. George and Gracie were curled up together near the foot of the bed, which left plenty of room for Max to join them, but not even his solid presence was enough to fool Annie into forgetting Sam was gone.

She could hear Claudia and Warren chatting softly while they played cards at her kitchen table. She had told them it wasn't necessary for them to stay, but they had insisted, and, to be honest, she was grateful for their company. It felt good knowing they were out there bickering and laughing together. It helped her believe that everything was going to work out the way it should.

Keeping the truth from Claudia had been impossible, and the three of them had spent a long time trying to figure out why someone would want to kidnap Sam. They had all come up empty.

"He's unemployed," Warren said, "which means he has no power."

"And he has no money," Claudia added.

"But maybe he has something more important," Annie had said "Maybe he has information."

She had never thought much about what he had done for a living before he showed up in Shelter Rock Cove. He had told her that he had worked for a big Wall Street firm, but he might as well have told her that he cracked coconuts for fun and profit for all that it meant to her. The man she knew and loved was the man who owned a big yellow Lab and drove around in a beat-up Trooper just like her own. He lived in a borrowed house and he made canoes for Warren's museum when he wasn't making love to her.

She couldn't imagine why anyone would want to kidnap that man, but the one who had worked on Wall Street just might be another story.

• • •

"Your boyfriend sure knows how to grab the headlines," Sweeney said when Annie walked through the door of Annie's Flowers the next morning. Claudia stayed behind at the cottage in case Sam called. "This is some story, kiddo."

"I'm afraid to look," Annie said, taking a quick glance at the county daily, which was probably a risky thing to do with her stomach threatening to secede from her body every morning. It was worse than she'd feared. There was the photo of Annie and Sam from the Labor Day picnic and above it the headline *Local Shopkeeper's Friend Arrested at Gunpoint.*

They flipped on CNN Headline News just in time to hear "Wall Street sting goes bust as former executive disappears." The newsreader launched into a brief synopsis of a developing story that included fraud at Mason, Marx, and Daniel, the company where Sam had worked. Thousands of investors had been bilked out of millions of dollars at the hands of top-level executives. A photo of Sam looking almost unrecognizable in a sleek and pricey suit flashed on the screen just long enough to push Annie into a bout of tears that sent Sweeney scurrying for some hot peppermint tea with lots of sugar.

"They said he disappeared," Sweeney said as she sugared her own cup of peppermint tea. "I thought you said he was arrested."

"That's what it looked like," Annie said. "What would you think if some guy whipped out a pair of handcuffs?"

"Honey, you don't want to know what I'd think."

Annie tried to call Agent Briscoe, but reached his voice mail instead. She phoned Warren, who had been trying all morning to glean information from various sources, but he kept butting his head against a brick wall of silence.

"Nothing new to report," Warren said. "Considering the

plane was registered to Marcella Dixon, my guess is somebody from his old company saw that photo of Sam from the Labor Day picnic and tracked him down."

"Tracked him down to do what?" Annie asked. "You're scaring me, Warren."

"Don't mean to, but they might try to buy his silence with a ticket to Switzerland or some little Caribbean island without a ZIP code."

"The news reports make it sound like he's taken them up on it." Five minutes of CNN or MSNBC would convince anyone that Sam was a high-flying financial type who would sell out his mother to shore up his own bottom line. The idea that the whole kidnapping had been a set-up, staged to whisk Sam out of the government's reach, was getting more airplay than Annie could cope with.

"Don't give up on him," Warren said. "This will all work out."

But the question of which side Sam was on wouldn't go away. Had he been one of the executives accused of stealing monies from clients or had he been working with the government from the start to nab them? Was it possible to straddle both sides of the fence and escape unscathed? She didn't want to touch the ethics involved in that one.

A man who would take responsibility for five brothers and sisters couldn't possibly be the kind of man who took money from innocent people. Or could he? The financial pressures on him must have been unbearable at times. Who could say what a young man might do to get by when the futures of five innocent kids rested on his shoulders and he was barely old enough to vote. The world wasn't the black-and-white place of her childhood, and she knew the truth was often buried deep in shades of gray. It was true of her own life and it was probably equally true of Sam's.

Everyone she had ever known or gone to school with or even bumped into at Yankee Shopper found a reason to drop into her flower shop that morning. Some of them at least had the decency to buy a single rose or a half-dozen daisies, but the majority didn't bother to sugarcoat the reason they were there. They wanted gossip, some juicy tidbit of information that they could pass around as firsthand information. The Virgin Widow's fall from grace was the hot topic of the day in every home in town.

"Go home and watch CNN," she snapped at poor Mrs. McDougal from the library. "Then you'll know as much as I do."

"The woman's eighty-five," Sweeney said, eyes wide with shock. "You might've gone a little easier on the old girl."

"I hate them all," Annie muttered as she flipped the *Open* sign to *Closed.*

"Since when do we close for lunch?" Sweeney asked.

"Since right now."

"That's not good for business, honey."

"Neither is assault and battery, and that's what I might do to the next person who asks me for the real story."

"You need more peppermint tea and something to eat," Sweeney said.

Annie made a face. "What I need is a martini, but I'll settle for the tea."

"Now's not the time to stop eating."

"Sweeney, for God's sake, don't start acting like you're my mother. I'll eat when I want to eat, and that's the end of that."

Wonderful. Now she sounded like a pregnant perimenopausal four-year-old.

She was about to make herself that cup of hot tea when somebody rapped on the door. "Can't you read?" she mumbled. "Closed means closed."

"It's Hall," Sweeney said, peering over the top of her newspaper. "Gee, I wonder what he wants."

Annie unlocked the door and ushered Hall in. "If you're here to gloat or gossip, you might as well leave."

His aristocratic cheeks reddened just enough for her to notice. "I'm here to apologize."

"What for?"

"For being a bastard."

She stared at him in surprise. "*Bastard* takes in a lot of territory."

He inclined his head in Sweeney's direction. "Is there someplace we can talk privately?"

Sweeney looked up. "You can talk right here," she said as she pushed back her chair. "I'll just ask Annie for the details later."

"I didn't mean to insult her," Hall said as Sweeney swept past him and out the back door.

"You can apologize to her, too, if you like."

"You don't sound like yourself today, Annie."

"Well, maybe that's because I've never had a day like today before." She found it difficult to disguise her impatience. "So why do you think you have to apologize to me?"

"Because I think I'm the one who caused this whole mess."

Take a number, she thought. "And how did you do that?" First Claudia had tried to take the blame for Sam's troubles, and then old Teddy Webb from the *Weekly* had stopped by to apologize for the Labor Day photo of Annie and Sam kissing. "Never meant to blow his cover," Teddy said, sounding like a character from an old spy movie. Now here was Hall claiming full responsibility.

Annie didn't know whether to laugh or cry.

"I was worried about you, Annie. There was something familiar about Sam. Ellen and I both noticed it. I couldn't shake the feeling that I knew him from somewhere, so when that photo of the two of you ran right after the picnic, I faxed a copy of it to a few friends in New York, and one of them came back with some information about him."

She hated him in that moment, a fierce burst of emotion that almost buckled her knees. That one selfish decision might have lost her the man she loved.

He told her that Sam had been a financial analyst with a huge clientele and lots of publicity. His track record and gift of gab landed him on a Manhattan cable station, which was how both Ellen and Hall were familiar with him. They had watched his show while they were attending a conference in the city. "They fired him this summer, Annie. Rumor has it he was stealing money from his clients and putting it into his own account."

"Embezzlement?" It hurt to think of Sam being anything less than the man she had believed him to be.

"Looks like it."

"People don't get fired for embezzlement, Hall. They go to prison." *And they don't end up flat broke in Shelter Rock Cove.*

Hall looked at her with an expression of such deep sadness that she wanted to haul off and smack him. "That might happen yet."

"And you felt I really needed to know this."

"I didn't want you to get hurt. I felt I owed it to you."

"You owed it to me to investigate Sam behind my back?"

"I owed it to you as a friend to give you the information and allow you to make your own choices." He paused, and she could see he was struggling with what to say but she refused to feel any compassion for him whatsoever. "It's what I should have done the first time around."

"Now you've lost me."

Their eyes met, and suddenly she knew.

"Kevin?" she asked, and he nodded.

"He came to me for money a few days before he died, and I refused him. It wasn't the first time, Annie. Maybe if I'd told you—"

All of the anger and fight went out of her. "It wouldn't have made a difference, Hall. You did what you thought was right, same as I did and Warren did and Claudia and everyone else in town."

"I'm a doctor. I know what stress can do to a man with a bad heart. Maybe if I'd helped him out with a few bucks, his stress level would've gone down, and he might have survived the heart attack."

"And maybe I shouldn't have threatened to leave him an hour before he died."

"Ah, Jesus, Annie—"

"We're all guilty and innocent and every shade of gray in between. I've spent twenty years of my life trying to make sense of this, and that's still the best I can do."

"I didn't want to see you get hurt again. That's the only reason I looked into Sam's background."

"No other motive?"

"A month earlier there might have been," he admitted, "but even I catch on eventually. You two are right for each other. I hope it works out."

She offered him a cup of tea, which he refused. He said he had patients due within a half hour, and she didn't press him. Too much had passed between them today. How sad that one gifted man's weakness could still cause so much sadness and dissension even now, two years after his death.

And yet in a strange way, this was exactly what she needed. She had learned more about her own life and marriage in the last twenty-four hours than in the thirty-eight years that had come before it, and the things she had learned helped ease the guilt she had carried around like a shield. She had loved Kevin and stood by him, but it was time to move on. Kevin had been her first love, but it was Sam who would be her last.

Annie remained glued to the small television set in the workroom behind the display area while Claudia and Sweeney handled the chores up front. She was hungry for every bit of information she could glean about Sam. Warren had been unable to reach Agent Briscoe, and his other sources were suddenly dry as a bone. She noticed a dark blue car that seemed to be following her around and recognized the driver as one of the agents who had answered to Briscoe. Even she was under a cloud of suspicion.

At three o'clock the all-day cable news networks reported that government agents had closed down the firm of Mason, Marx, and Daniel and made numerous arrests. She waited and prayed, but there was no news about Sam until the phone rang a little after five o'clock.

"They found him!" Warren's voice was triumphant. "They found him in some shack on St. John's. He's in protective custody."

"Protective custody?" Annie said. "That means they think he's innocent, doesn't it? You don't put a criminal in protective custody."

"Quick!" Claudia called from the front of the store. "Channel 49—they're talking about Sam."

Annie zapped the channels in time to hear: ". . . found the former top-rated executive in an abandoned building near the piers. He was badly bruised but otherwise unhurt. Local law enforcement took Butler into custody, pending arrival of U.S. officials who will be looking into the apparent kidnapping."

Claudia, who had joined Annie in the workroom, gathered her into her arms. "It's going to be okay, honey," she said, smoothing Annie's hair. "It's all over. He'll be home before you know it."

But as the days passed, Annie began to wonder if Sam was coming home at all. She followed the events as they unfolded around the Mason, Marx, and Daniel sting and committed every sentence about Sam to memory. Thank God, the one thing about which there was no longer any doubt was that he had been in league with the Justice Department against his former company. Talk of a set-up or double sting had been abandoned for the juicier story of an in-house informant. Depending upon who was doing the talking, Sam was either a hero or the worst kind of rat. Popular opinion leaned heavily toward the latter.

By day three well-meaning visits to Annie's Flowers had dwindled to almost nothing. By day four even Claudia was finding it difficult to meet her eyes.

"Isn't this taking an awfully long time?" she asked Warren, who seemed to know about such things.

"It takes as long as it takes," said Warren, which was really no help at all. "Let it unfold the way it needs to, Annie. He'll be here before you know it."

"You old coot," said Claudia who had happened into the back room and overheard some of the conversation. "She's in love with the man. Has it been so long that you can't remember how that felt?"

The two of them launched into one of their patented sparring contests that Annie knew were a display of affection between them. Thank God for those two wonderful, generous people. She couldn't imagine how she would have made it through the last few days without their rock-solid love and support. They were parents to her in every way that mattered except blood, and she knew her son or daughter would be blessed to have two such wonderful grandparents.

Because that was what Claudia and Warren would be. Maybe it was unorthodox, maybe it would raise an eyebrow or two, but Annie felt the rightness of it deep inside her soul, and she knew Sam would feel it, too, once he came home to her.

If he came home to her.

The street sign read "Welcome to Shelter Rock Cove," but to Sam it seemed to say "Welcome home."

He leaned forward and tapped the driver on the shoulder. "You can let me out here."

"You were promised door-to-door service," the driver said. "It's on the government. You won't be hearing that again any time soon."

"Here is good."

"Bet it's good to be home," the driver said, and Sam laughed.

"Better than you can imagine."

The driver wished him well and left him at the corner of Main Street and the docks. He stood there in the late-afternoon sun and breathed in the briny salt air that had always powered his dreams. There was Cappy's about two hundred yards to his left and Rich's Bait and Tackle Shop near the stop sign. If he angled his head just a little bit more, he could make out the church steeple where Warren's museum was taking shape.

And, if he followed his heart straight up Main Street, it would lead him home to Annie Galloway.

Home.

He tried the word on for size and found it a perfect fit. This tiny dot on the map called Shelter Rock Cove was home because Annie Galloway was there. For four days his every waking thought had revolved around the woman he loved and his need to be with her again, and now that he was a three-minute walk away from her arms he found himself scared into immobility.

Would she want him now? He hadn't a clue. He'd been shown some of the news coverage of the downfall of Mason, Marx, and Daniel, and it hadn't been pretty. He had been portrayed in an unfavorable light in most of it, and, the world being what it was, it wasn't very likely that his redemption would be mentioned at all. Annie had cast him early on as a hero. How would she feel about him as a man who had made mistakes a better man would have had the strength to avoid?

He had no answers for any of it. All he knew, all he cared about, was seeing her again.

Much of the last few days was a blur for him. He'd regained consciousness when they landed for refueling somewhere near Miami, where he conned one of his captors into uncuffing him so he could use the john. He had managed to pry open the window over the toilet and was about to shove himself through the opening when the son-of-a-bitch came in to see what was taking him so long.

They would both be carrying around a shitload of bruises after that encounter.

The plan had been to deliver him to a designated safe house in the Bahamas where some of Mason, Marx, and Daniel's best and brightest would try to convince him that his life would be much happier if he took them up on their generous offer of money for silence. He never did get to hear the details—or the chance to tell them to shove it—because by the time they reached the safe house, it was clear that the bottom had dropped out of their scheme. The Justice Department was closing in on associates in New York, Chicago, Fort Lauderdale, and London.

They tied Sam to a chair in the middle of the safe house and took off, and that was where local cops finally found him. They turned him over to the feds, who ferried him to a small hospital where he remained overnight for observation, then spirited him back to Miami where he was subjected to intense questioning by a series of interrogators, each of whom seemed determined to prove him guilty.

He had a lot to tell Annie, but there would be time enough for all of the stories. A lifetime, if they were lucky. One day he wanted her to meet Mrs. Ruggiero; he owed the old woman a debt of gratitude even if Mrs. R didn't know it. The same act of compassion that had cost him his job had turned out to be the key to setting him free. The trail he had inadvertently created when he tried to bail out Mrs. R, Lila, and Mr. Ashkenazy ran counter to the one the company had hung his name on, and only his trail stood up under questioning. His own sense of guilt ran deep, but in the eyes of the law he was innocent. He would be deposed at a later date and eventually called upon to testify in court, but all charges against him had been officially dropped, and he was a free man.

But not for long. Life was too short, and he loved Annie too much to wait any longer. He liked the man he was when he was with her. He liked the way she made him laugh and think and dream. He knew that in the eyes of the world he was a loser, a thirty-five-year-old man who could fit everything he owned in the back seat of his Trooper, but when Annie Galloway smiled at him, he felt like a king.

He was going to tell her that he loved her, that she was the home he had always longed for, that without her the future was nothing but a string of days and nights without meaning. He was going to tell her what he had never told a woman before. He was going to say, "I love you."

And then he was going to pray she loved him back.

• • •

"We're not taking no for an answer." Susan said as she, Claudia, and Sweeney surrounded Annie. "You're coming out for supper with us, or we'll know the reason why."

Annie, who was seated on her stool behind her work bench in the back of the shop, mustered up a smile. "That's a nice idea, really it is, but I think I'd better get some more work done on the Selkirk-Holder wedding preparations."

Susan groaned loud enough to be heard at Cappy's. "You need a break, Annie. You can't spend every moment staring at CNN and waiting for the phone to ring. You need to get out for a while."

"What if Sam—"

"He'll find you," Sweeney said, laughing. "This is a small town, and he's the number one topic of conversation. If he shows up, I guarantee the entire population of Shelter Rock Cove will escort him to Cappy's for the reunion."

"There's a good reason to work late," Annie muttered.

Claudia placed a gentle hand on Annie's shoulder. "You need to keep up your strength," she said softly. "The baby deserves that much."

Claudia was right. They were all right. And they would keep on hammering away at her until she agreed. "Okay," she said. "I give up. You've worn me down." She slid off the stool and stood up. "Give me two minutes to wash my face and try to do something with this hair, and I'll be ready."

The three of them exchanged glances. Annie could just imagine what those glances meant. They were worried about her. They thought she was spending too much time brooding over Sam, who just might not decide to come back to Shelter Rock Cove after all. He had a life down there in New York City. He had an apartment down there and brothers and sisters and nieces and nephews, all of whom loved and needed him. Why would he want to leave all of that to live in some little town in Maine where it snowed too much in the winter and rained too much in the summer and couldn't make up its mind the rest of the year?

Because he loves you.

That would be a wonderful reason if it were true, but was it? How could she possibly know for sure when they had never said those words to each other, those magical words that unlocked the heart and soul? They had danced all around them, but never once had either one of them stepped out to the edge of that cliff and said, "I love you."

She wished she could do it all over again. She would tell him she loved him, tell him about the baby, tell him that in a lifetime spent searching for a home of her own, she had finally found it in his arms.

She would tell him all of that and more if only he would come back to Shelter Rock Cove.

The door to Annie's Flowers swung open, and Sweeney leaned out and grabbed Sam by the sleeve. "Hurry!" she said, dragging him inside. "Get in here!"

"That's what I tried to do five minutes ago when you shoved me out the door."

"Shh!" she said, holding a paint-stained finger to her lips. "We want this to be a surprise, don't we?"

It occurred to Sam that it couldn't be anything but a surprise to Annie, but he had three sisters. He knew there was no dealing with a woman on a mission.

Claudia Galloway and her daughter Susan were leaning against the counter. They sported matching cat-that-ate-a-cageful-of-canaries smiles.

"Congratulations," said Susan. "I think you'll learn to—

ouch!" She turned to glare at her mother who had administered an elbow to her ribs. "What was that for?"

"My daughter is only forty-two," Claudia said with a wicked twinkle in her eye. "Sometimes she forgets her manners."

Sam grinned back at her. He could learn to like the woman. He glanced around the store. "Where's Annie?"

"Will you keep your voice down!" Sweeney ordered. "She's in the bathroom fixing her hair. She thinks we're going to Cappy's."

They heard footsteps moving down the hallway.

"Quick," Sweeney said. "Hide behind that display."

He felt like a damn fool but he let himself be pushed behind one of those froufrou displays of flowers and little breakables that no sane person would have in the house.

"So who's driving?" Annie sounded exhausted. That had to mean she loved him, didn't it? "We can all go in my Trooper if you want."

"There's someone to see you," Sweeney said.

"Oh, no," Annie groaned. "Who is it this time?"

Sweeney poked her head behind the display. "Now, you dope!"

He rounded the display, and there she was. Tired, a little rumpled, the most beautiful woman he had ever known.

"This wasn't my idea," he said, but his words were lost as they ran into each other's arms.

"You're home," she said against his mouth. "You're home!"

His heart soared. She was laughing and crying, and so was everyone around them, but he only had eyes for Annie. He drank in the sight of her, those beautiful blue eyes with the dusky shadows beneath them, the laugh lines, the smile that told him that he could open his heart to her and she would understand.

He heard a lot of sniffling all around him and then the sound of footsteps heading for the door.

"I thought they'd never leave," he said.

"Just as long as *you* never leave me again." The look in her eyes was so filled with love and longing that he wondered how he had ever walked through his days without her. "You're hurt," she said, gently tracing his battered face. "Oh, Sam—"

"You should've seen the other guy." He gathered up the last of his courage. "I have a lot to tell you, Annie. I'm not too proud of some of it."

"I've followed the news," she said, "and I know the kind of man you are. When you're ready to talk, I want to listen."

"For a long time I looked the other way when I should have been doing something to help. I hurt innocent people."

Her eyes welled with tears. "I know all about looking the other way, Sam. I did that for most of my marriage to Kevin."

Her words were balm to his soul, the first step in his journey to regain his self-respect.

"I love you," he said. "I've never said that to a woman before." The power of those words and all they represented—you built families on their foundation. You built generations.

"You're my soulmate," she said softly. "I've never said that to a man before." Her voice broke on the last word. "I never will again."

"I'm not rich," he said, "and my prospects these days are lousy." It would take time for his reputation to be restored and by then, that world would have long since passed him by.

"I'm one step up from being flat broke," she said, "but I'd say my prospects are terrific."

"I might end up building canoes for a living."

"Sounds good to me."

"If you'd met me this time last year, you would've gotten a hell of a better deal." He'd had a career, a new car, money in the bank. Now all he had was his heart on his sleeve.

"I'll be the judge of that. I fell in love with the guy in the ratty old Trooper, didn't I?"

"The one with the pizza-eating dog."

"Yep," she said, "that's the one. He stole my heart, and I don't want it back."

"There are a whole lot of Butlers out there for you to meet."

She took a deep breath. "Actually there's one more Butler even you haven't met yet."

He looked at her intently. "You want to say that again?"

"One more Butler," she said, taking his hand and placing it against her soft belly, "due to join us in June. That's what I was coming to tell you that afternoon."

"But I thought you couldn't—"

"So did I," she said, "but I guess when we found each other more than one miracle happened." New life where there had been none before. Laughter where there had been only silence. Joy where sorrow had lived for too long. "I know we never talked about this—I mean, you may not even want children. You've spent your whole life raising kids, and now here I am telling you that you're going to be starting all over."

She looked radiant and joyful and so uncertain that his heart ached with love for her and the future she carried deep within her beautiful body.

"Tell me again." He bent down and pressed his lips to the roundness of her belly. "Tell me this is really happening for us."

"It's really happening for us," she said as her tears fell

softly onto his forehead. He could feel her relief flowing into his bones. "Just one miracle after another from the moment we met."

He told her of the dream he had dreamed of children with her eyes and her smile, children who would carry their love into the future the way it was meant to be.

"And your heart," she said as he took her in his arms and held her close. "I couldn't ask for more for our child."

Everything he was, everything he had ever done or dreamed of doing, came together in that moment when she smiled at him and he saw their future in her eyes. He loved Annie Galloway and she loved him and they were going to have a baby.

Sam Butler had finally come home.

THE WAY IT ALL
ENDED UP

~⚬~

Late June

"Push, Annie!" Ellen Markowitz urged. "One good push, and you'll have your baby."

"I . . . don't . . . want . . . to push!" Annie yelped in the voice everyone in the birthing room had come to know. "I want to get out of here." What was the matter with these people? Didn't they know she had been in labor for the last eighteen hours? Weren't they paying *attention*?

Sam, who was sweating almost as much as his wife, leaned over and brushed her lips with an ice cube. "One more push, Annie. You can do it." Ellen had said he could be the one to receive the baby—if Annie would only push.

Her eyes locked with his. "I can't, Sam, I can't—"

"You can and you will. She's almost here, Annie. All you have to do is push."

Next to her, Claudia squeezed her left hand. "All these years, and nobody's come up with a better way to get the job done. You can do it, Annie. I promise you, you can do it."

"Oh, look!" Ellen cried. "We're almost there, Annie . . . just one more push."

"Come on, Annie," Sam urged. "It's time we met our little girl."

Annie took a deep breath and reached down deep to a place she didn't know existed but all women somehow found, a place where the power of love could perform miracles, and she pushed their daughter out into Sam's waiting arms.

"Sarah Joy Butler," her husband said through his tears, "welcome to the world."

A second later a small cry filled the room, and a new life had officially begun.

Annie and Sam had their miracle.

It hurt to look at them. Ellen had helped deliver hundreds of babies, but she had never been as deeply moved by the experience as she was today. Sam kept kissing Annie and telling her how much he loved her, how much love and joy she had brought into his life, while Annie—oh, God, the look of wonder and joy on her face was so profound that Ellen turned away. She talked Sam through cutting the cord, then went back to the work of delivering the afterbirth and making sure the baby's vital statistics had been duly recorded.

Then came the moment she always waited for, that magical moment when a couple became a family. Sam laid the baby down on Annie's chest. Sarah Joy was slick with blood and birth fluids, a squalling little bundle of humanity whose nursing instinct guided her right to her target. Annie's tears fell onto the baby's fuzzy head while Sam tried to wipe away his own tears with the back of his sleeve. There were no celestial fireworks, no host of angels sent down from on high, but the sense of almost heavenly wonder couldn't be denied.

Ellen waited a moment while Claudia drank in the sight of the newborn family, and then the two of them stepped out into the waiting room where forty-two assorted Butlers, Galloways, and their friends all jumped up at once and gathered around them.

Warren Bancroft, who looked as if he'd been in hard labor himself, met Claudia's eyes. Claudia, who was laughing and crying simultaneously, nodded her head, and Warren shouted with joy.

"You old coot," Claudia said. "Now don't go taking all the credit for yourself. This was God's doing, not yours, and don't you forget it."

Warren winked at Ellen over the top of Claudia's head, and she knew he wasn't about to share credit for Sam and Annie's happiness with anyone, not even the Almighty.

Ellen cleared her throat. "I am very happy to report that Sarah Joy Butler joined us at one twenty-eight P.M. She weighs seven pounds, two ounces, and measures nineteen inches long. She has her mother's curly hair and her father's nose, and right now I think it's safe to say she also has everyone's heart in the palm of her little hand."

"She's healthy?" Warren asked in a suspiciously husky voice.

"Very," Ellen said.

"And Annie," Susan said, "she's okay?"

"She did great."

Two of Sam's sisters looked at each other and grinned. "He fainted, didn't he?" the one named Marie asked. "Sam never did like the sight of blood."

Ellen laughed. "I'm sorry to disappoint you, but your brother maintained consciousness throughout the delivery."

Laughter and high fives and lots of happy tears filled the room as the two families celebrated the new addition. They didn't even notice when Ellen slipped out the door, which was, of course, as it should be. She had done her job, helping Annie bring little Sarah Joy into the world, but now the rest of it was up to them. She leaned against the wall and let her emotions seek their level once again. You would think she would be used to it by now, but each time she saw a tiny head crowning, each time she heard a newborn baby greet the world, she was filled once again with a sense of wonder that carried her through until the next delivery.

But sometimes, like today with Annie and Sam, it was even more wondrous. To see them with their baby girl, to be privileged to witness the happiness on their faces and on the faces of the people who loved them—

"Are you crying again, Markowitz?"

She looked up through teary eyes as Hall approached. He was fresh from the delivery room himself, wearing the look of wonder she knew all too well.

"Boy or girl?" she asked him. "I know Aileen was looking for a boy."

"Aileen got her wish," he said, leaning against the wall next to her. He smelled faintly of Betadine and that made her smile. "Nine pounds, six ounces, with lungs like his mother." She heard him draw in a breath. "Annie?" he asked.

"A beautiful little girl," Ellen said as those damn tears flooded down her cheeks and splashed onto her scrubs. "Sarah Joy Butler." She provided the vital statistics and tried very hard not to notice that his own eyes filled with tears. "I have never seen so many people in a waiting room in my life."

"The Galloways stick together," Hall said.

"Looks like the Butlers do, too." *Lucky Annie*, she thought. *Lucky Sam.*

Lucky, lucky Sarah.

They were quiet for a while, then Ellen stifled a yawn.

"I think I'm going to call it a day," she said.

He looked at her, and for the first time she didn't see Annie Butler reflected in his eyes. She didn't know if it meant anything at all, but she was open to the possibility. "How about we grab some lunch at Cappy's?"

"I'd like that," she said, then smiled at him. "I'd like it a lot."

They watched for a moment as Sarah Joy Butler took her place in the nursery next to Baby Boy Whitcomb. They held the hopes and fears and dreams of their parents tight in those little fists. A smile from either one of them could make a grown man cry.

She didn't know what Hall was thinking, but she could guess. "Another day, another miracle," she said, pretending to dust off her hands. "All in a day's work around General Hospital."

He laughed and turned away from the window of sleeping dreams. "Ain't it the truth, Doc," he said. "Ain't it the truth."

"Cappy's in fifteen minutes?"

"Sounds great," said Hall. "I'll meet you in the parking lot."

Ellen was smiling as she hurried back to her office to change into street clothes. It wasn't a miracle, but it would do for now.